The Kremlin Armoury

The Kremlin Armoury

Matthew Hunter

Walker and Company
New York

First published in the United States of America in 1992
by Walker Publishing Company, Inc.

Published simultaneously in Canada by Thomas Allen & Son
Canada, Limited, Markham, Ontario

Library of Congress Cataloging-in-Publication Data
Hunter, Matthew.
The Kremlin armoury: a novel / Matthew Hunter.
p.   cm.
ISBN 0-8027-1211-8
I. Title.
PR6058.U538K74   1992
823'.914--dc20   92-8741
                                                  CIP

Printed in the United States of America
2 4 6 8 10 9 7 5 3 1

The Kremlin Armoury

1

On the Tuesday of what was to be his last week in Brussels, Marriner thought everything was over. His job. His marriage.

He walked as usual from the little hotel in the rue du Commerce, through the drab streets round the Berlaymont to the Musée des Beaux Arts. The exhibition was almost complete as he stood talking to Ritterman with the July sky outside the colour of washing-up water. His commission had been to prepare 'The Guns of Yesteryear', and the cases of arms and armour, neatly ticketed and labelled, marked the end of his efforts. Guns without gunsmoke since he came out of the Army – an expert now on past battles. Ritterman stood with the younger man, surveying the rows of flintlocks with a wash-'n'-dry look of satisfaction.

'Thank you, David,' he muttered. 'Such good condition.'

That was because we won, Marriner thought. HMG's Brown Besses, racked and oiled, had been kept under lock and key in Dover Castle; probably reissued to the Home Guard. Now that he was a professional on pikes and muskets he lived with this range of outdated lethal equipment that had shot and blasted in war across the face of Europe, carried, slung, holstered. History assembled in Brussels, home of the sprout and the Manikin Pis, occupied so many times that you might have said it was rented.

He had telephoned Celia the night before. There was a one-hour time difference and he could imagine her at nine-thirty, sitting alone after Katie had gone to bed.

'Hello, darling,' Marriner said cautiously.

'Hello.' Her voice was flat as marzipan.

Marriner drank whisky and sighed. In his charcoal grey suit he might have been a business consultant with a difficult client, but that was not what he felt. He was worried.

'Katie asleep?'

'Yes.'

No response. Silence like a wall, impossible to break through. A

1

terrible position for both of them, keeping up the conventions in front of Katie, but he tried, God knew he tried.

'What's the matter?' he enquired. 'Is something wrong?'

'Matter?'

Why did it have to go on like this, he asked himself, and knew the answer. Don't spoil it for Katie, darling Katie. He always patched it over for Katie's sake.

It had started as an easy marriage, in the Army; Celia had wanted a hero in a camouflage jacket, but Marriner had found soldiering tedious and retrained for this second career. He knew it was partly his fault, but the rest of the trouble was Celia, focused on private grievances that she was unable to share, residues from the childhood of a broken marriage.

'Oh go away. Look after your damned guns.'

'For God's sake, honey –'

Silence. Marriner felt tired, sensing the resentment at the end of the telephone. Unhappy Celia, who had slowly abandoned him. Something that did not fit with his preconceptions of home and duty, where women were warm and loving.

He tried again. 'What has Katie been doing?'

'Nothing.'

'Look, Celia, what's the matter?'

And then she had said it all, those words she had failed to produce when they were face to face but would now put in writing through solicitors, the bottled-up griefs inside her. Christ knew what lost opportunities she thought she had been denied.

'I want a divorce.'

The words he had dreaded, fought against, tried to pretend would never happen, for all their sakes. She had waited until he was in Brussels, and then made her decision.

'Don't be stupid, Celia. Don't.' His mouth was dry.

She laughed at him.

'I've seen solicitors. I want a settlement.'

'Celia, we've got to talk . . .'

'This is the only time I'm going to tell you, do you hear?'

'What do you mean?'

'I've told you.' Her voice had risen, full of nervous anxiety. 'After this, never. Not about the marriage, or the settlement, or the custody of Katie. Never. Until it's over. Do you understand?'

He groped at the threat. The condition was impossible; and he stood to lose his daughter.

2

'Now you listen to me, Celia. We've got to work this out. Try harder. My answer is no. I won't let you, Celia. No way. No.'

He heard her laughing.

'You'll get a letter . . .'

'I don't care how many bloody letters, how many solicitors, how much it will cost . . . I warn you, Celia, I'll contest it every inch of the way.'

Silence.

'Celia, please understand. Katie needs us both.'

A click at the end of the line told him she'd cut him off.

'You seem concerned,' Ritterman the curator said. 'Preoccupied.'

'Yes. Things on my mind.' He wouldn't tell a bloody Belgian, but he felt as tense as a man in a minefield.

'So. Let me introduce someone who will cheer you up.'

The glass doors behind them had opened and Marriner turned to see the security guard, accompanied by a woman. That in itself was unusual: they were behind closed doors, busy setting things up, and anyone wanting to visit normally made an appointment. In spite of his disturbed night in the overheated bedroom she took Marriner's eye. A blonde, with glasses and one of those interesting faces only a few degrees away from porcelain beauty: the mouth too wide perhaps, the eyes a shade too deep. Soberly, almost sombrely dressed in a dark red sweater and skirt, stylish without being extravagant. Her straw-coloured hair was short, cut to the oval face and her eyes behind the light glasses were quizzical and blue. As she walked across he noticed her legs.

'Good morning,' she said, in English.

Ritterman said, 'Allow me. This is Svetlana Malinkova, from Moscow. My dear Svetlana, I did not expect to see you today . . .'

'I want to see if I can help,' she said enigmatically. 'Europe no longer stops at the Berlin Wall. We work towards a single Europe, is that not right?'

'That is so,' Ritterman agreed with his prissy nod.

She smiled at Marriner modestly and something flowed between them that seemed to relieve his despair, for a moment at least.

'I'm here for Waterloo,' he said. The sentence appeared doom-laden. 'Last check on the exhibits.'

'Ah, so am I.' She frowned a little in concentration. Charmingly.

He began to feel better, his resilience returning. 'I didn't know the Russians were involved.'

3

'We can lend you a lot of material,' she said. 'The effect of the retreat from Moscow. The Emperor Alexander the First. The Congress of Vienna.'

Pull the other one, he thought. Her style began to amuse him, to erase, however temporarily, the dread of the night before.

She fluttered her hands, which were elegant and long-nailed. He saw the golden bangle slide on her wrist, arousing.

'We must co-operate. We have so much to share. Where do you work?'

'London,' he said. 'The Tower Armouries.'

She paused. 'Oh. That is splendid. An omen.'

'Why an omen?'

'I also work with ancient guns. We Russians,' she murmured in that faintly exotic accent, 'have always been part of Europe. Except during the war, when we stood alone.'

'Not quite alone,' he countered. 'Who was fighting in 1940? What about the Battle of Britain?'

She gave him that charming, twitchy-nosed smile.

'I understand.'

Ritterman left them and she suggested lunch. As Marriner collected their trays in the public restaurant she seemed to lurch too close to him. There was an edge of sympathy in her voice and manner, as if to signal she understood that he also had problems.

'You know, in my hotel,' she said disarmingly, 'there are funny noises in the wall.'

'I don't believe it.'

'Perhaps the wallpaper is listening.'

This organised man was looking at her as if she was not quite real. Wasn't that what they said about Moscow? Marriner was glad of the wine.

'Bad plumbing.'

'But you? You like Belgium?'

'Not much. No-man's-land.'

'Please? No-man's-land?'

'A dump. A good country for tank manoeuvres.'

'Ah.' But she didn't understand. 'Tell me, how many more days are you staying?'

'Three. I leave on Friday.'

She seemed disappointed. 'That is too soon.'

They walked away, under the pollarded trees in the Parc de Bruxelles, just across the road from the Beaux Arts. He found her a distraction from Celia, and an enigma. As if she knew he needed company she suggested a stroll along the flowerbeds. Their heels crunched on the gravel and she turned her face towards him. He was conscious of the lines of her cheekbones, the shaped head of fair hair.

'Your British guns,' she said seriously, 'were not things of beauty.'

'Our guns,' he said, 'worked.'

'Of course. But you have not seen the Russian guns to compare.'

Marriner brushed his hair from his eyes and smiled. 'No.'

'What do you know about Tula?'

'Not much.' He recalled that a small arms factory had been established there by Peter the Great. They had some muskets in the Tower, bearing the Emperor's cipher.

Svetlana paused. 'We Russians are proud of our past, but we do not always preserve it very well.' There was an edge in her voice. 'For example the monasteries . . .'

They passed a white-painted bench and the sun came out, warming the grass and the elderly women walking over-clipped poodles.

'Let us sit a moment,' she said, stretching out her legs which were golden brown with minute flecks of hair.

'Why do you look at my legs?'

'I'm sorry.'

'Oh. I don't mind. Men say I have good legs.'

He was charmed by her freshness. Celia had nice limbs too, but she would have hated it said.

'Where were you trained?' She was interested in this English-man; tall, thin, not unattractive, his brown hair ruffled by the breeze.

'I did a course at the Courtauld Institute in London. Applied arts.'

'So. And before?'

'I was in the Army.'

'Ah. I thought you looked a sort of soldier.' She stared at him. 'A nice one. Why did you leave?'

'No prospects.'

She seemed to reflect. 'The wars are over.'

Not for me, he thought, and asked, 'What about you?'

'I trained in Leningrad. I was brought up in Leningrad. My father was Director of the Hermitage. So it is in the blood.' She played with the bracelet on her wrist.

'But you studied at the Courtauld. Under the great Sir Anthony Blunt?' Her eyes sparkled with mischief.

'Before my time. Long before.'

'Do you think he was right?'

'Right? To deceive?'

'No. To put his political views above his service to the country.' Her English was almost perfect.

'No,' Marriner said. 'He did the dirty. You understand?'

Svetlana seemed amused.

She crossed her legs. Her court shoes were expensive, Italian, with just the right height of heel, neither too high nor too low. What was he playing at with her, Marriner wondered, with Celia trying to divorce him? He speculated on where her money might come from.

'What are you doing in Brussels?' he asked.

She raised her eyebrows, darker than the blonde hair.

'Contacts.'

'Contacts?'

She stood up and brushed her skirt. 'You are married?'

'Yes. Just about.'

He knew she was reading him, making herself available, and he tried to keep it professional.

'What sort of contacts?'

She put her hands to her hair in a way that excited him.

'I think I must know you better before I explain.' She hesitated, her head so close that he caught the exhalation of her breath.

2

Werndl called on the following day, his usual pain in the arse about the German contribution. Marriner thought that he should have worn black, the SS uniform. Oscar Werndl with his aquiline nose and sleek hair would have looked good on an aquasail, but he was one of those well-heeled playboys who for some reason chose to become a museum professional. Marriner watched him striding into the hall in his blue pinstripe and polished shoes.

The German surveyed with distaste the designer sketches produced by Charles Sablon, who was demonstrating last minute changes in Ritterman's office.

'Not colourful enough. Need more drama,' he pronounced in English.

'Real explosions?'

'Ha, ha. Little English joke, eh, Sablon?'

Sablon looked glum.

'The trouble is, old chap,' Werndl went on, in his boarding-school voice, 'there's not enough emphasis on the Prussian contribution. Blücher was the key element.'

'He was late for the battle.'

'Look, you know what I mean.' He strode up and down like an Obersturmbannführer, reorganising the cases.

'Marriner, why did you join the museum brigade?'

'To make a living.'

'Ah. So. In my case it was love. It was not the money.'

'Nor with me.'

Werndl smiled silkily.

'I see you are bewitched by the beautiful Svetlana. Be careful, she is a spy. From the Emperor of Russia. What does she want?'

Marriner found that he was choosing his reply with care.

'Nothing much. Some contacts apparently.'

'Ah. Glasnost. An exchange with the Soviets. Jolly good. But be warned.'

Warned, Marriner thought. The last thing he intended was getting tied up with Moscow. Everything in his training turned him off. It was exhausting enough trying to be a professional when your wife was unscrambling ten years of marriage.

Werndl was lecturing him.

'You know, you English. You have lost your role, so you create museums, is that right, no? In the old days what would you have been, Marriner? A district commissioner maybe, who would have hung five natives before the breakfast kippers, isn't that right?'

'After a fashion, Lord Copper.' (Prussian bastard, Marriner thought.)

'Who?'

'It doesn't matter.'

'But what about our designer, eh, Sablon? What do you say?

7

Have I got it right, in terms of popular appeal? The emphasis must be on co-operation. Wellington and Field Marshal Blücher.'

Sablon was Francophile, and shrugged. His hair was oiled like a salad, and he wore blue shoes.

'As you please.'

'Good. Then it is agreed.'

'Not by me,' Marriner said. 'Wellington won. I want the credits.'

Werndl's jaw dropped, his pale eyes seemed to be floating in Angostura bitters. He winked.

'I tell you what. You give me more space for Blücher, and I give you top rights in Svetlana.'

'What?' In spite of his pain and sorrow over Celia, Marriner felt the glow of interest.

'Oh yes. Your Russian beauty. She wants a man, you know.'

'Not me, sport.'

'Oh come on. Where is the British blood? Are you saying you are not interested?' Werndl's long Junker head, a base for a duelling scar, flashed and grinned. He picked up a handful of wood-chippings and ran them through his fingers.

'What do you know about her?' Marriner asked.

'Ah ha. I see you are twitching. Is she not beautiful?'

'She's all right,' he admitted. 'What do you know about her?'

Werndl sat on a packing case and swung his legs. The exhibition hall was nearly completed, but still resembled a casualty clearing station.

'The glorious Svetlana came to Berlin last year for the Tercentenary exhibition of the city. She was looking for contacts then. I think there is something or someone that wants to come out of Russia.'

'What do you mean?'

'How can I say? She would not tell me. Svetlana is different. She is unhappy, and, how you say, she is willing.'

'Save me from willing women.' He had always been faithful and even uxorious. Marriage was a long haul and now was not the time to change. There had been years with Celia when it all worked: he would not abandon her now. No way; remembering the good times on station in Cyprus and Germany, the early days in the museum.

'Ah, Svetlana. I took the dear girl out to dinner a couple of times,' Werndl said. 'No hanky panky, you understand?' He watched Marriner closely. 'She wants to leave Moscow.'

8

'Then why doesn't she?'

Werndl grinned. 'She fears they would not let her. She would want a job. And she wants to bring things out.'

'Things?'

'I do not know. She would not say.'

'Well, that's her problem.'

'You talk to her about it, eh? Maybe there are jobs in England for a girl like her. Thousands of museums, is that not so?'

'Too many bloody museums,' Marriner agreed. 'But I can't fix her up.'

'Well, she is looking for a knight in armour.' He made the invitation sound sensual.

'Not my business.'

'Now, don't be doggy on the woodpile. Svetlana needs a friend. Lonely. Lacking contacts in the West. You must understand how isolated the Soviets still are. I think she requires a husband . . . or, the very least, a man.'

Marriner tried to forget. Svetlana and Celia. He spent the rest of the day encouraging Sablon, talking to Ritterman, doing some souvenir shopping. In the Bon Marché he bought a T-shirt for Katie. And then he phoned Celia again.

Celia sounded drunk. He sat on the end of the bed, on the fourth floor of the hotel, and listened to her hiccuping, determined to limit the damage. The marriage and its consequences were too consuming.

Whether Celia still loved him or not, he wanted to be there for Katie and keep the home together. Nothing else mattered much: she'd moved out of his private life two years back when she'd started sleeping in the spare bedroom. She gave him little and wanted less. Companionship but not love. A fucking disaster.

'What do you want now?' she asked.

'Listen, Celia. I must talk about what you said yesterday. You can't do this.'

'I'm not discussing it. Ever. My solicitor is putting it in writing.'

'For Christ's sake, Celia.'

That freezing silence. Then she said, 'What have you been doing?'

'Setting up the Waterloo exhibition. You know that.'

'How do I know you're not running off with some blonde?' It

9

was not a suggestion she had ever made before; and she knew it was unfair.

'Oh come on. Have you ever seen a lady curator? A Belgian lady curator?'

Celia sniffed. 'When are you coming back?'

'On Friday,' he said. He always came home, always wanted to be home.

'I shan't be here. I'm going off to Pamela's.'

'Katie. What about Katie?'

'She's staying with her school friend. Janice Lanyard. You'll have to fend for yourself. I don't know when I'll be back. I've had enough,' she said. 'Phone the Lanyards when you return and see if Katie wants to stay with you.' Full stop.

'All right. If that's what you want,' he replied. He hoped that by agreeing he might buy reason, a little sympathy, but she kept after him. She wouldn't let him go, she wanted salt in the wound.

'And don't forget you're taking me to see the exhibition. I know you don't care, but I'm going.' To criticise and complain.

That was the other side to it: she was tired of the marriage, unable to respond in it, but would put on a silly act, as if to humiliate him. Marriner could have walked away, but what good would that do, petitioning for a decree-nisi and leaving her with the child? Katie didn't even know: in front of the seven-year-old they spoke to each other as if this slow estrangement, this dawning uncertainty, had not happened. Everybody makes mistakes; he had fallen for her prettiness at twenty-five, and she for him.

'Are you listening?'

'Yes.'

'I would like a weekend in Brussels. I've never been there.'

'It's a dump.'

'It's abroad. I don't get abroad.'

'OK.' He was pleased by the positive note. 'I'll fix it up.'

He could picture her now standing in the hall, leaning against the telephone table with its vase of dried flowers, dressed up to the nines. Probably that new two-piece suit in oatmeal, unless she had bought another one. Fresh from drinks with Pamela, a bitch who liked to meddle.

'What are you up to tonight?'

'I'm in my room.'

'Going out on the town?' He caught the suspicion in her voice. She didn't want him, but nobody else should either.

10

'I've got to eat sometime.'

'Don't spend a fortune.'

'I haven't got one,' he said, 'but Oscar has invited me to a reception tomorrow.'

'Oscar?'

'Oscar Werndl, from Berlin. He's organising the Prussian exhibits.'

'Um. Were they there too, at Waterloo? On our side?'

'For once.'

'Well just you be careful. And when you get back on Friday, I'll leave you to sort out Katie.'

It was better than cheese on sticks. Werndl had invited him to the German Embassy thrash in the Bundesrepublik Residence at the back of the Parc Leopold. A big grey building with flags out, and plenty of drinks on trays. A large and venal gathering of salmon-coloured men in blue suits, arms round each other's shoulders, talking deals. The drinks slid down to ease the pain. Marriner caught sight of one or two women, and there she was, coming across towards him.

He followed the curve of her figure, the shortish cocktail dress that showed off pretty knees and elegant legs. A black creation with a splash of gold on the corsage. He noted the wide eyes and the soft smile.

'Hello again,' Svetlana said.

There was pleasure in their meeting. She had the skills to warm him.

'This is a hot room. I'm glad to see someone I know,' she confided.

'Don't you know anyone else? There must be other Russians here.'

She shook her head. He admired the style in her dress. She could not have bought that tailoring and those Italian shoes in the GUM store in Red Square.

'No. On my own. A one-person mission.'

'Well. You look pretty good on it.'

'Thank you.' She hesitated. 'You like the clothes?'

'A million dollars.'

'Thank you. I know what you are thinking. These Russians they have no hard currency. Where do the francs come from?'

'It crossed my mind, but why worry?' He took more drinks from a passing waiter, a Campari for her, a Scotch for himself. 'Let's get out of here. There is a balcony outside those french doors.'

'A good idea. But if I tell you my dress is paid for by royalties, how do you like that?'

He caught her elbow as she almost stumbled. It had a warmth that shocked him as he touched the bare flesh.

'That's great. What have you written?'

'*The Illustrated Guide to the Kremlin Museums,*' she said. 'The foreign language edition. Doubleday in New York and Studio Vista Books in London. I will give you a copy.'

'Very kind, but I'm going home tomorrow.'

'Of course. But I give it to you tonight. Afterwards.' And she smiled.

He began to contrast her not only with Celia but with himself. She had even produced a book. A book that *sold*, unlike the pamphlet on eighteenth-century side arms by Marriner D., £1.75 each, twenty-eight pages, fifty-three purchased copies.

Outside on the balcony she stared at the back of the park. Houses and trees, a shut-in landscape, growing dark.

'Do you like museum work?'

'It's all right.'

'You don't sound so happy.'

She had again detected the flicker of his personal crisis.

'It's not the job,' he said.

Svetlana rested her hand on the stonework. Behind them the room babbled, and somebody else came out, a Belgian business-man smoking a fat cigar.

She touched Marriner's arm. 'Let's go.'

'Go? Where?'

'Let's leave this place,' she said. 'I can't stand the noise. The smoke. These boring people. Nobody will miss us.'

'I don't know. Perhaps we ought to stay on . . .'

'Oh, come on.' She turned her face towards him. 'Let me give you that book.'

Her hotel was an apartment block, the Paris Flats, near the Berlaymont. Again he was surprised, as they purred through the darkened streets, at the quality of her lifestyle: the hired BMW Series 5, then the fully-fledged flat with its bedroom and kitchen diner.

'I stay ten days,' she said. 'Research and a little holiday. To make contacts as well.' She stretched out her legs. 'I know. You think I have too much luxury for a Russian.' She laughed. 'But not everyone is poor. My father left me some money. And then there are my royalties, some of which I can spend abroad. And also I have a salary. Anyway I am not married so I spend on myself. Is that so bad?'

She gave him another drink, a cocktail of vodka and lime, green in the glass, and produced the book.

It was glossy, bound in white cloth and embossed, and full of colour photographs. The text was sub-scholarly, by Svetlana.

'It's very impressive,' he said.

'Thank you. It certainly sells. Especially in America. They have a kind of obsession, now that relations improve.'

'There's no biography.' He sipped his drink.

'Biography?'

'On the inside cover. A blurb about the author. Always in books these days you have to give personal details.'

'Ah. Not so in Russia. But you want my vital statistics?' Turning the phrases again, she was inviting him.

'Well. I am thirty-four. Figure OK I think. One sister in Sverdlovsk; she teaches there. Her name is Fanya. My father died when I was young, so we had to leave Leningrad. We lost our privileges. That is not so uncommon. Now, you want to know what I need?'

'Perhaps I shouldn't be asking.' What the hell was he doing there, he asked himself. He was in one crisis already.

'Please. I tell you.' She leaned forward and he saw her breasts, the dress suddenly low-cut. Her hands were round her knees, shapely bones in dark nylon.

'I need to get out of Russia. Permanently. And to bring out the things I have there. My private collection.'

'Your private collection? Is it that valuable?'

'Very valuable. You will see.'

Marriner finished the drink, feeling a shit.

'I'm afraid I can't help in that respect.'

'Please stay a little longer – I want to talk.' She fixed him another green goddess, and hovered closer. She smelt of summer fields. 'Am I boring you?'

'No. No. Of course not.'

'So. Look at my book. My *pièce de résistance*. I tell you it is a success, but I spend so much time on work that my private life suffers. I lock myself away. I need to have freedom.'

'Oh, come on.' Surely she could not be serious. She was fooling him.

'But it is true, David.' She raised her glass to the light. 'It is a long time since I have even had . . . an affair.'

'I have a wife.' That mixed-up bitch, poor Celia, and a kid who loved them both.

'I understand. I do not mean to go with you. I am talking in general. You follow?'

She stretched her arms, knowing he was mentally undressing her. His head felt muzzy with drink.

'A long time since I had a man.'

'I can understand how you feel.' Celia had taught him that.

'I know. You suffer too. Your wife is not a comfort?'

He got up to relieve the pressure.

'Celia and I have things to work out.'

'That is not always possible. Please tell me about her,' she said.

'There is nothing to tell.'

She sighed. 'You do not any longer love her?'

'I'm not sure,' he said. And in that admission realised that he was compromised, had given it all away.

'It would be nice to know you.' She was offering.

'I go back home tomorrow.'

'Listen, you must come to Moscow. To see me there. I send you a formal invitation.'

'Perhaps.' He remembered Tom Challenby's warning as he was chatting up Celia at the regimental dinner – Challenby was now somebody big in the M.o.D. 'Celia, watch him in Brussels. You never know what he gets up to. And keep me posted.'

Svetlana came very close to him then, and he thought that she would embrace him, but she stopped.

'I'm sorry,' she said. 'You must think that I seduce you.'

'No.'

'Well . . .' She held out her hand. 'It would have been nice.' She grinned. 'Some other time.'

He eased himself into his coat, looked around for his briefcase, remembered it was not a business trip, and swayed towards the door.

'I'll call a taxi,' she said.

'It's all right, I can walk.'

'Not this time of night. Impossible.' She waggled a finger. 'Wait while I phone the rank. They will be here in one minute.'

'You are very kind.'

Pleasantries. Superficial words of farewell and her eyes troubled. She didn't want to let go, and suddenly she was kissing him, her hands behind his neck, her figure tight against him. She was brief, uninhibited, passionate, and he saw tears in her eyes.

Blushing, really blushing.

'David, I'm . . . sorry. No, I'm not. Oh God.'

'I didn't think you believed in him.'

She coloured. 'Who?'

'God.'

'God? Oh yes. I believe in him.'

They were standing close together, only inches apart. A hot space in the passage.

'Must you go?' she whispered.

'I think I should.'

She stopped and fumbled for words. 'It is ridiculous.'

'Yes.' But looking down the passage with its jumble of furniture, her suitcases piled outside, this girl inviting him, he did not want to deny her.

'I must go, Svetlana.'

She touched him. 'I am really sorry.'

'Please don't apologise. It's just that . . . well, you know, it wouldn't be fair.' A funny, English thing to say; a defensive prod.

'Why not? I am experienced.'

'I mean I shouldn't.'

She gave him a sad smile.

'OK, I know. You go home. But listen, you must come to Moscow. To see the museums.'

'What do you do there?'

'I am in charge,' she said. 'Director of the Kremlin Armoury.'

She seemed so young, so interested, that he could hardly believe it. 'That's wonderful.'

'No, David, please. You must come.' She touched him again, then gave him a fleeting kiss as the intercom buzzed and a voice said the taxi was there.

'Thank you for everything,' he mumbled.

'I want you to come,' she whispered. 'One day in Moscow we talk.'

'No promises,' he said as he opened the door. He had a marriage to salvage first, he told himself savagely.

She smiled and shook her head. His last vision was of her standing there, waving.

'No buts. You must come.'

<h1 style="text-align:center">3</h1>

In London the weather had changed to a cold wind whipping the tourists in their plastic macs, as Tom Challenby parked in Horse Guards. He slammed the door of his Rover 820 and picked up his briefcase.

He crunched across the gravel and through the arches, incognito to the Life Guards. Another day. Last night he had found his wife riding an exercise bike. 'You have to reshape for these new swimsuits,' was what she said. He had forgotten they had a holiday coming.

Mountbatten's statue stared across the parade ground, looking for lost battleships. Dodging the Whitehall traffic he crossed to the M.o.D, showed his pass and took the escalator then the private lift to the rooms on the sixth floor. It had been raining and umbrellas grew in the corridor, black mushrooms drying.

A soft blip of typing as he entered his office, where Sandra was pummelling away at the IBM machine. She was small and sweet and Indian out of Kenya, with blue eyeliner on a darkened face and for the hundredth time he wondered how a Hindu could have been named Sandra.

It didn't make sense, he thought, taking possession of room 215/6: it must be some kind of nickname.

Sandra brought in the post. G4's translation of the assessment of Aeroflot in *Red Star*, a couple of computer print-outs of Warsaw Pact manoeuvre logistics, four or five internal minutes. Also a card from Henry Dibden who was away in Corfu, watching the topless beaches, a circular for a training course at the Civil Service College, and a trio of letters. One of them was marked 'Personal and Confidential', so Sandra left it in the envelope.

He slit it open. Inside was a handwritten sheet from David Marriner, dated the previous day.

Marriner. Marriner. A voice from the past, when they had worked together in Northern Ireland. David Marriner, with his problematic wife, who had talked to him at the reunion. Celia was one of those women who looked as if she ought to bed someone but would not give it any kind of priority.

> Dear Tom,
>   When we met I mentioned that I was going to Brussels, to set up an exhibition on Waterloo. I've now been approached by a Russian girl who wants me to visit the Kremlin. Are there any problems about clearance? I would welcome a bit of advice.
>   David.

Challenby sat back and smiled, his glance wandering round the room: the hard brown carpet, PSA desk, couple of squelchy armchairs, the bookcase, the eight-day clock, the conference table and chairs, the computer screen in the corner. In his dark pinstripe, double-breasted, he looked every inch the ex-lieutenant-colonel who had moved into military intelligence. Gentlemen in good suits, prowling a paper jungle where contacts were snakes in the grass. It could be that Celia had come up trumps. Marriner's recalcitrant wife, that woman with the wild eyes, had taken the message he had sown at the dinner. Marriner had said he was into museums, that was it, the Tower Armoury, Keeper of the Fusils or some such. Now he had an invitation to the Kremlin, exactly what they wanted. Challenby pulled at his cuff-links. It seemed like a gift from heaven.

Sandra brought him in coffee. The kind of dark-skinned girl that used to be called pretty, with a vulnerable face. She wore moccasins and made no sound as she walked.

'Thank you.'

'Mr Bullivant is calling a meeting at ten-thirty,' she said.

'Thank you. Have you got the report?'

She handed him the file marked 'Secret: Grade 1', slim as a menu. 'Chemical Weapons manufacture and stockpile: USSR.' Inside was the message from Vasily Borovik, the administrative head of the Soviet chemical warfare programme. The only other paper was the 'Report on Nerve Gases', the Sarin B derivatives, developed by the Baikal Toxic Research Institute. Borovik was offering details of Soviet chemical weapon production. All this, Challenby knew, was currently under discussion at the Helsinki talks, but Borovik was in possession of information that frightened him as much as Chernobyl had frightened the Politburo. The Soviet Union was

17

sitting on stockpiles of chemicals big enough to pollute the planet, yet nobody at the top was prepared to admit it, or to say where they were. Except Borovik. The last ditch paranoia of the cold war years still controlled the military, leaving lethal dumps all over the country. The Soviets denied they existed, but some of them were named by Borovik, the others were in his head. Challenby sucked his lips as he read. The report on nerve gas developments was pretty complicated stuff, and he wanted the technical assessment; but there was also an action slip on the Borovik papers, tagged 'Immediate', in Bullivant's hand, which said, 'He wants to come over.'

Challenby drank the coffee, trying to concentrate.

Glasnost was all very well but he had a job to do. The cold war was not quite over, in spite of what the papers said. The Reds might be pulling tank battalions out of East Germany but they still had their CW programme.

And in front of him was Marriner's letter, as clear as a demand from the Revenue. Black ink on yellow paper, a good firm hand, an address in High Barnet. He remembered now that Marriner had told him he had a daughter, an only child about Letty's age; and also a hint that the marriage had not improved. Not getting his oats. Challenby stretched and felt good. An unsettled background to work on. There was no better prescription for fieldwork than a man under pressure.

That pressure had started with Celia. Almost as if she couldn't let David out of her sight, she had reappeared when he returned. The prospect of a couple of quiet days went out of the window at once. Poor Katie looked miserable as her mother marched in and asked him to unload the car.

'I thought you were staying with Pamela.' A bridge fiend who lived in St Albans.

'I decided not to. Don't you want me back?'

'Of course, my dear.' At one time he had loved her, really loved. Looking at her now he felt a funny combination of compassion and resentment. Celia was still a smart woman, a little plump, but preserved. She had on a new suit, a blue two-piece with a spotted blouse, new shoes, too, expensive slingback sandals.

'You look good,' he said. If only she would come towards him, he would meet her half-way, but her eyes gave him no chance.

Katie ran over and kissed him.

'Oh Daddy, so glad you're home.'

Missed me, and all that stuff. She was his daughter all right, Daddy's girl.

'How was it with Janice Lanyard?' He hugged her close.

'She's got a puppy. Can I have one?'

'No,' Celia said. 'They make messes and chew things. Puppies grow up into dogs.'

Like glass slippers grow into old shoes, David thought.

'Well, are you or aren't you going to unload the car?'

Are you or aren't you going to ask how I feel? But he didn't. It was too far gone for that. If only he could keep Katie he might have cut the knot, but the courts favoured the mother, and he stood to lose too much.

When he came back with the suitcases Celia had taken off her jacket and was standing fanning herself in the front room.

'Finished in Brussels?'

'Yes. It opens next week.'

She ran her fingers idly along the back of the settee, facing the empty fireplace with its pot of dried flowers. All Celia's flowers were dried, she couldn't stand the petals falling.

She stared at him thoughtfully, her eyes enlarged behind the contact lenses, distancing herself from him. Katie had disappeared, unpacking in her room. He needed a cup of tea, or a stiff drink, but Celia stood there unrelenting, thick with suspicion.

'What did you do with your time? In the evenings I mean?'

Perhaps because she no longer loved him, and would not have him, she was always unhappy when he was away on his own, imagining he went on orgies, picked up women in bars, lost himself in fornication. Now she was pursing her lips and beginning the third degree.

'Who do you talk to over there?'

He tried to disarm her. 'A dreadful man called Ritterman who is in charge of the Beaux Arts and a German called Werndl. I'll introduce you when we go.'

Celia shuddered.

'How boring.'

What did she see in him now, he wondered. A thirty-five-year-old museum specialist, presentable enough, good-looking in a way that women thought sensitive, with a full head of hair; but none of that mattered to Celia who seemed to dislike being a professional

19

wife, being tied down in marriage, saddled with the child, the unwanted physical side.

'What about the women? There must be some women too?' She said it dismissively, her lips curled, but he felt she was nervous.

And he replied, 'No one I would run away with. Except a glamorous Russian.'

It was a stupid thing to have said, but she had needled him, and it was a matter of pride that Svetlana had made an offer. It betrayed him now. He tried to shuffle it off, as unimportant, inconsequential, but Celia shook out the facts, nothing could deflect her once she had a suspicion, a small fragment of evidence in which to sink her teeth. It was a long time since he had seen her so animated: her eyes became excited and there was a glow in her cheeks.

'A Russian, a spy?'

'Don't be absurd.'

'What's her name?'

'Svetlana. Svetlana something.'

'Svetlana.' Celia rolled it round her tongue, then she said, 'I'll have a drink. A gin and tonic.'

'OK.' He found the bottles in the sideboard and a couple of glasses. There was ice in the fridge and he shook out the cubes in a dish.

'Svetlana,' she said again. 'The name of Stalin's daughter.'

'I expect it's a common name.'

Celia stared at him over the glass which she held in both hands like a crystal ball. 'Svetlana. The glamorous Russian spy . . .' And she pointed a finger.

'Have you informed the authorities?'

'What authorities? Don't be ridiculous.'

But Celia had other qualities that he had come to respect, and among them was a cussedness, a doggedness. She would not let the matter go.

'Tell me about her.'

And so he had. So as to twist her tail. He had hinted at the blonde hair and the slim figure, the come-hither smile and the offer to visit the Kremlin Armoury. Svetlana, who had enticed him: and he let Celia know it, as a means of revenge.

And she in turn had said, 'She is a spy. I am sure of it. A Soviet agent . . .'

'Don't be ridiculous.'

'Ridiculous. I'm serious.' She would not let him alone. If there

20

was a risk, any risk, that he had a chance of comfort, a milligram of an affair, she would jump on it and exterminate it before it began to flower. In her obsessive way she responded to Challenby's warning.

'The Kremlin. You must tell Security.'

'Don't be absurd. What for?' She read too many novels, he thought. 'I wouldn't know where to start.'

'You start with the man you know, in the M.o.D. The one that we met at the Mess reunion. You know who I mean.'

There was no denying her. She had a memory for names.

'Challenby,' she announced triumphantly. 'Tom Challenby. You worked with him in Lisburn. He said he was in Whitehall now. Told me himself.'

He had tried to duck and weave.

'I don't know what he does, or where he is.'

But he remembered Tom Challenby looking into her eyes, asking to be informed.

'You write to him. Is that clear?'

And in the end Marriner had.

Even so it was with some surprise that Marriner heard Challenby's secretary on the telephone, a couple of days later, fixing up to meet him at lunch.

She made a preliminary booking and then Tom Challenby himself came on.

'David, old boy. Nice of you to write. Been wondering if we could meet again. How about the Athenaeum, one o'clock Wednesday?'

'That will be fine . . . Tom.'

'Where did you say you were?'

Marriner could imagine him, family portrait on the desk, already absorbed by some new puzzle.

As if he did not know.

'The Tower.'

'Oh, yes. The Tower. Ha, ha. Better mind what I say, eh, David?'

Tom Challenby was a dickhead too.

'Sure you can get across?' As if it was South Australia that he was telephoning.

'I'll make it, Tom.'

'Good. Good. Look forward to seeing you then.'

21

As he put down the receiver, Marriner found himself wondering why the other man was so bloody keen.

Challenby was waiting for him at the foot of the staircase, pretending to read the notices. As soon as Marriner appeared through the doors of the club he pumped him by the hand.

'Good to see you again, David.' He exuded a phoney good humour. 'I've got a table fixed up, and someone I'd like you to meet.'

Marriner found the doubts flooding in. Celia's dogged persistence had more than once manoeuvred him into situations like this.

'I thought we were just . . .'

'Of course. Quite confidential, old man. Bullivant's a chum of mine. My boss in fact. Knew that you wouldn't mind. Any problems always let us know. Anyway it's good to see you. Good to see you looking so well. Been abroad lately?'

'Only Brussels.'

'International travels, as well, eh, David? You chaps have got it made.' He sallied into the restaurant. 'Look. Let me introduce you . . .'

Bullivant sat at a window in the long dining room looking out over the shrubbery towards Carlton House Terrace. He rose to his feet as if he was balancing on them, a small grey-haired man who might have been a dancer, or a fairground owner with a tough life behind him: deep crease-lines over the forehead and eyes recessed into a face from which they peered with the benevolent suspicion of a defrocked bishop. There was something puckish and cunning about his presence, as he held out a hard, dry hand.

Challenby looked round. 'Let's eat and talk,' he said quietly. Bullivant selected a steak and Challenby settled for venison. Marriner seemed to disappoint them by ordering lamb chops. They paused until the waiter had gone.

'Bloody Italians,' Challenby said. 'Always hanging around.' He pushed aside the Club claret. 'Now. Tell us about this invitation to the Kremlin, David.'

There had been times when David Marriner wanted to join the Establishment, with its sense of running the show, but those times were getting fewer. He could not be sure whether Celia had soured him or whether he had just grown up, matured away from the club lunch and the old boy network. Sitting there in the dining room under the appraising eyes of Challenby and Bullivant, he felt

22

suddenly naked, exposed by his own confessions. Why had she led him on, and what was he trying to obtain, clearance or condemnation? He stumbled towards an apology for being there at all.

'Look. There's scarcely any need to bother you. At least I don't think so. It's just that Celia was so insistent that I should let you know.' And he had humoured her, partly for peace and quiet, partly because it was easier to take her advice.

Challenby leaned forward and Bullivant smiled sweetly, shifting about in his chair. The two heads confronting him: Challenby's dark and military, his suit scarcely creased, with just a hint of cuff; and his boss Bullivant, less well-groomed but warier. Those two heads, Marriner reflected, could have stood for the ruling classes in any BBC serial. Life imitated art, all the way, just as Svetlana had appeared from nowhere.

'Tell me more,' Challenby said, as Bullivant mashed up his potatoes. He looked around the dining room quickly, as if to impress on his guest that this was a hallowed place, sacred ground. Outside, the traffic in Pall Mall rumbled faintly in the summer air.

'I really don't think there's anything in it . . . but Celia asked me to make sure.'

'Good for Celia. And how is she?' Challenby said blandly. He knew, he damned well knew, Marriner could tell from his eyes.

'Oh, she's all right.' A statement like a Yorkshire pudding that failed to rise. If Challenby and Bullivant registered it they gave no sign.

'Still getting people healthy?'

So they knew that too: that she was a part-time secretary at Blades Health Clinic where businessmen went to dry out. 'A charming woman, his wife,' Challenby said to Bullivant, with just sufficient irony to make sure Marriner understood. 'Anyway, David. It came at the right time, your invitation.'

Marriner's lamb chops were congealing in a brown Windsor gravy suspiciously like his soup.

'What do you mean?'

'It could be important to us,' Challenby said. And Bullivant said, 'Absolutely. Spot on.'

'It would be a straightforward research visit to the Kremlin Museum,' Marriner explained uneasily.

'Of course,' Bullivant muttered. 'Most important to keep in

23

touch.' He leaned forward as if he were driving a car round a difficult corner.

'Tell me about this woman. The Russian woman,' Challenby urged.

They climbed the stairs to the reading room and settled into ancient chairs. Bullivant tapped off coffee from an urn and handed round little cups. In one corner an old man was asleep; the copies of Lloyds Register in the bookcase behind them stopped at 1937.

Marriner was impressed by their interest. The combination of Celia and some latent sense of duty had made him contact Challenby on what had seemed a trivial matter, but these types, they took it seriously, as if there was something in it.

And now Challenby, settling himself comfortably in one of the button-back armchairs, coffee on the table beside him, said, 'What does she want, David, this Malinkova woman?'

'She wants to get out of Russia. With some sort of private collection. She would like a job over here.'

Challenby's eyebrows rose.

'Ah. And what was your reaction?'

'I told her I couldn't help,' Marriner replied. 'That was all I could say.'

'Good. Right. And how did she take it?'

'I think she half expected it. Werndl the German says she'd been dropping hints for some time. Then she invited me back to see the Kremlin Armoury.'

'What did you say to that?'

'I didn't give any promises. Of course I'd like to go but I have duties in London. It's a fantastic collection: guns and armour, regalia, costumes, one of the great museums.'

'Attractive woman?' Challenby pressed.

'Well. I suppose so.'

'How old is she?'

'She told me thirty-four.'

'Ah. Isn't that rather young to be in charge of the main museum in the Kremlin?'

'I gather she's well connected.'

'We can check that out.' Challenby raised his elegant head and swivelled round but nothing stirred. The long room seemed suspended in a golden afternoon light.

'Look. I don't want to be involved in any trouble.' Marriner began to regret that he had listened to Celia: this was some kind of exercise engaging the professionals.

'Oh, certainly not. Nothing sinister.' Challenby smiled. 'All the same, it's most useful for us to know. Most useful.' He was looking at Bullivant, who bounced up on his toes and nodded.

'Tom, I must be going. Duty calls. Thank you for the lunch,' Bullivant said. 'Delighted to have met you, David.'

Challenby waved it away.

'So glad, Arnold, that you could come.'

They waited while Bullivant carefully removed the coffee cup and made his way out. Two elderly men picked over the magazines at the other end of the room, a solitary ex-minister from some past Labour government wandered in and out.

'I'd better be pushing off as well,' Marriner said. 'Kind of you to invite me, Tom. I take it that these days invitations to the Kremlin don't create such security problems?'

'Quite the reverse. We want you to follow it up.' Challenby's eyes were bright with enthusiasm. 'East–West relations are thawing.'

'What do you mean?' He knew there were no free lunches.

Challenby leaned forward. 'I want you to do us a favour, David. Perfectly straightforward business.'

Marriner's unease increased, but he was half inside the trap.

'I don't want to get involved in anything . . . you know . . . underhand.'

'Of course not. It's just that these new contacts, different contacts, outside the usual net, you follow me, can be very important. They could also be helpful to you.'

'I don't quite understand.'

Challenby laughed. 'We want you to go to Moscow as soon as possible, David. Write to this Svetlana. Keep in touch with her. Send her some museum stuff. I'll talk to Vic Burgloss in the Tower. Could be a breakthrough, research inside the Kremlin, a useful jumping off point. Keep up the glasnost, David, and follow up that invitation.'

'Look Tom. I was just asking about clearance. I don't want excitement.'

Challenby brushed that suggestion right out of the way.

'Of course not, David. Wouldn't dream of suggesting it. But personal contacts can be invaluable. Sometimes they are important for other reasons.'

'Well, I'm not sure . . .' Marriner was very doubtful, but this was the Athenaeum and Moscow was a long way away.

They stood up and shook hands. It was three o'clock and the club was emptying. In the marble foyer Challenby said, 'Don't forget, old man. Keep in close touch with her, and let us know.'

'Why?'

'Because,' Challenby said, standing to attention on the steps, 'Svetlana talks to a friend of ours.'

4

They met at the Royal Opera House. Arnold Bullivant and Denis Orford. First night of Verdi's *Nabucco*.

'Great stuff,' Orford said. 'Good to see you, Arnold.'

'Grand. Pavarotti's a bit tight.'

'Tight?'

'Unrelaxed. Not his usual.'

'Ah. Don't know, Arnold. Not a connoisseur myself.' Orford pronounced the vowels in his flat Yorkshire way. 'Guest of Mr Wanamake, Nissan Motors. Mr Wanamake, have you met Arnold Bullivant? He's in the government.'

'Civil Service.'

'Same thing these day.' You would never have guessed Orford was in it too. With his skull cap of red hair, almost like a toupée, cropped close at the sides, and the big pugnacious face with a pock-marked nose and untrimmed eyebrows, he could have been a football manager or a building site hard hat. His DJ was new and looked hired.

Mr Wanamake smiled politely.

'I am pleased . . .'

The Crush Bar lived up to its name, the white and gold décor submerged by the throng of first-nighters drinking champagne.

'How do, Lorna,' Orford said gruffly, recognising Bullivant's wife, sheathed in what appeared to be silver foil.

'Denis. How lovely to see you.'

'Right,' he said. He had no manners, she thought. None whatever. God knows how he'd got to where he was, wherever that was. Orford never made it clear.

'Mr Wanamake, this is Mrs Bullivant. I think she paints or something.'

'Sculpts,' Lorna Bullivant said icily.

'Well. I'm sure you two have got a lot in common,' Orford breezed, pressing the little grey-suited Japanese businessman on to her. 'Very artistic people in Japan. Lorna, darling, will you excuse us a minute.' And taking Bullivant's elbow, he towed him outside on the stairwell.

'We can't talk here, Denis.'

'Why not? You can't hear yourself speak.'

Bullivant sighed. He was used to the strong-arm tactics of MI6. He stood down his glass in a corner.

'Well? What is it?'

'Listen, Arn. This fellow Borovik, inside the Kremlin. He's taken risks with a message.'

'Another one?'

'Right. The guy is getting desperate. He wants to talk about Pripet.'

'Pripet?' The name rang a bell as the Soviet equivalent of Porton Down, the chemical warfare establishment.

Bullivant looked around carefully. 'For Christ's sake, Denis, we can't talk about that here.'

'I was going to call you,' Orford said, 'but now is as good as anywhere. Vasily Vasilyevich Borovik is the administrator of their whole damned CW programme. Serums, gasses, the lot. He's got it locked up in his head, and he's shit scared and wants to come over.'

'I know.'

'So. I'm looking for a safe-breaker. Somebody who can break in. A completely new face.'

Inside through the doors, Bullivant could see his wife making desperate conversation to the abandoned Mr Wanamake.

'I don't know about that,' Bullivant said thoughtfully. 'Safe-breaking is for professionals.'

'I want to get him out via Marriner.'

'Why not try a visa first?'

'You must be joking. They've got him on a ball and chain.'

'Look, Denis. We really can't talk here. That's the interval bell . . .'

'Arnold, all I'm saying is can I use this chap Marriner? I know he's a civvy, but he's the kind we need. Mixed-up, disillusioned, marriage breaking up. Ideal material – and he's been in contact with Tom Challenby.'

The sea of humanity swayed round them as for a minute or two they contemplated the destiny of David Marriner, linked now to Svetlana, whether he liked it or not.

Celia was out when David returned home late. When he found the house was empty his first thought was one of relief. As he opened the door the cat jumped at him hungrily, and there was a feeling of peace.

'Hello. Celia? Anybody home?'

The words had a hollow ring. There was an air of goodbye before he could even place it; and the bloody cat crying for food. He walked through the hall to the kitchen and saw the envelope.

It was lying on the breakfast table, propped against a jar of marmalade. He shouted for Katie, but Katie had gone too.

He made a cup of tea and slit the envelope with a kitchen knife. It tumbled out at him like a bad dream, a typewritten note on Celia's behalf from lawyers he had never heard of with a long memorandum attached, an affidavit. He read as if poleaxed. She was concocting lies.

The world stopped at nine o'clock. He was advised that the marriage had irretrievably broken down. Celia's petition went on and on. Ignoring her personal needs. (Jesus wept . . . ignoring her.) Failure to consult and consider her. Unwillingness to share. Rudeness. Laziness. Lack of commitment. Taunting and mental cruelty. A tendency to drink alone. Cruelty towards the child. (Jesus she was off her lid!) Obscene language. Desertion for work and duty. Extended absences abroad. Intolerable to live with. Suspected adultery with Russian woman in Brussels. Adultery!

He was shaking with a combination of laughter and rage at her lunacy. Celia's emotions had always been conditioned by her wrecked childhood but this was over the top. She had documented the dates during the previous two years: every little turd of evidence. The nights that he was away, the times he had been late home, what he had said or not said on the 7th, 15th, 23rd. The failure to offer her comfort: for Christ's sake, who was it suggested she slept in the spare bedroom, Father Christmas? A farce, a joke of a petition which didn't add up to a row of beans. The lawyers must be crooked to entertain it. Celia was disturbed, mentally and emotionally sick. He saw it now, the evidence was in his hands, and yet he wanted to help her, not break the whole thing up. He feared for Katie.

The tea was cold and the room had grown dark. He unlocked the kitchen door and wandered into the garden, stretching as flat as a football pitch. The cat came out and rubbed round his legs, feeling sorry for itself, so he went back inside and found a tin of food in the fridge.

'Jesus Christ.' The full horror of it struck him. He had a wife who wanted to leave, and if she should succeed with that lunatic divorce petition he stood to lose the house and Katie. She would be claiming maintenance, and custody of his girl.

'Katie!'

She had taken his daughter. Katie who really loved him, loved her father more than Celia. She had whispered as much to him one night when he had tucked her up after one of Celia's where-the-hell-have-you-been evenings. It would break his daughter's heart. No, Katie was not going to be a pawn between husband and wife. He renewed a decision. If she persisted with that half-baked petition he would defend it with his last penny.

He went to the drinks cabinet and poured out a double. That bit of evidence he would lay on the line: Celia drove him to drink. It was Katie who kept him on the straight and narrow.

Denis Orford was escorting Mr Wanamake to a large black Daimler at the end of the performance as Bullivant stepped out of the portico.

'Excuse me . . .' Orford said to the Japanese businessman. 'You wait here,' and hurried across, leaving the little man standing like a doll on the pavement.

The Bullivants saw him coming and knew deception was useless.

'Hello, Lorna.'

'Good evening again, Mr Orford.'

Orford grinned, and looked at the civil servant.

'Thought I might catch you. Missed you in the foyer. Got to tag around that bloody Jap, but you know what the tickets here cost. Seventy-five bloody quid. Did you pay for yours?'

'Naturally, but not such expensive ones.'

'Ah well. You know me. Always go for the best. I met the little bugger on a trip to Tokyo. We went round the interesting bits.' He grinned, then lurched close to Bullivant's ear.

'Any further thoughts about what I said?'

'What do you mean?'

'Come on, Arnold. I want a fresh face. A new contact. Somebody who might be moulded. No preconceptions.'

In a half-hearted way, Bullivant found himself defending Marriner.

'Surely you've got people in the field?'

'In my job,' Orford said, scratching his red thatch, 'you look for a different face every time.'

People were bumping into them and Bullivant could see Lorna getting agitated. She wrapped her cashmere stole about her upper arms.

'It's getting chilly, darling. I'm not dressed for standing about in the open air.'

'You look all right to me,' Orford said, unashamedly gazing at her corsage, red appliqué roses on black net.

'I think your Japanese friend is a bit lost,' she smiled between her teeth.

Orford said, 'Marriner. I use him. OK?'

'The man's an amateur,' Bullivant countered, then weakened. 'It's up to Tom Challenby.'

'Ah. Challenby.' Orford saw the excuses slip into Bullivant's face. 'Then it's OK by you?'

It had been a tiring evening, hot in the theatre, Pavarotti not on best form and Lorna for some reason out of sorts. Orford the bookie's runner hadn't helped. All that Arnold Bullivant wanted to do now was walk round to the car-park and drive back home to Highgate. Not talk shop in the middle of Drury Lane as the audience dispersed around them.

In a moment of weakness he said, 'Challenby and I talked to Marriner the other day. Bit of a queer fish.'

'No queers.'

'No. I don't mean like that.'

'I think your Japanese friend is getting into the car to go away –'

'Oh Christ,' Orford shouted. 'Mr Wanamake, hang on a minute. Just saying goodbye to my friends . . .'

Mr Wanamake smiled wanly behind his glasses and bowed.

'Bloody polite, these Jappos,' Orford muttered. 'Now, Arnold, how was that?'

And Bullivant was trapped.

'Challenby seems to think he's a starter.'

30

'I know.'

Bullivant caught his wife by the arm. 'Darling, I'm so sorry. You must be chilled.'

'In more senses than one.'

Orford grinned. 'Got it, Arthur. Night night, Lorna, look after the old boy for me.' Thrusting his hands in his pockets he lurched across to the patient Wanamake.

'Now let me take you to dinner. I know where there are girls . . .'

Lorna watched him distastefully, as his hands curved through the air.

Marriner was on to his third at ten o'clock and feeling queasy on an empty stomach when he heard the key in the door and went into the hall.

'Daddy. Daddy.'

Katie was running in and throwing her arms around him; and behind her was Celia, smart as paint.

Marriner hugged his daughter. 'Katie. Where on earth have you been?'

'Daddy. I love you.'

Celia said nothing, walking past him as if he did not exist into the front room. His daughter was clinging to him, and he still had his wife's petition in his hand.

He shoved it away into a pocket, and kissed Katie, who was laughing and crying.

'Don't cry, darling.'

'Mummy took me to the cinema. It was a funny film . . .' and then she said, 'Daddy, Daddy. Don't leave us. Please.'

She was sobbing now, in his arms as he tried to console her, feeling his world was crashing.

'Katie. Katie. It's going to be all right. Your mother's tired. We've got to talk things over. Don't cry. Understand. You must give us a little time. Please, Katie . . .'

'Don't leave me, Daddy.'

She wanted him not Celia, who had walked away like a zombie.

He kissed his daughter again, on the top of her forehead, conscious that she was his flesh and blood, his responsibility.

'Katie, darling, don't worry. Go upstairs to your room while I sort things out.' He was aware of the lounge door opening and Celia somewhere there behind it, listening and not moving, her old uncertain self.

31

'Say it's not true, Daddy. Say it won't happen.'

'Not if I can help it,' he said. 'Now, Katie, be a good girl and go upstairs. Please leave me with Mummy.'

Reluctantly she released him and he watched her run up to the haven of her room. She paused once and looked back, and then was gone.

He waited to see if Celia would come out, but she made no movement, so he walked into the lounge. She was sitting with her hands in her lap on the settee, facing the empty fireplace.

And she said nothing.

He held the letter towards her.

'Celia. For God's sake what is all this? You can't do this to Katie . . . or to us.'

There was a long silence, and he feared she would never speak. Celia just looked at her hands, carefully manicured, wearing her wedding ring, but not the engagement diamonds which had disappeared.

'Celia. What does it mean? We must discuss it like adults.'

Her hands were sideways in prayer, a Dürer etching, the frilly sleeve of her blouse edging them neatly. She had obviously had her hair done. He noticed her ear-rings were blue, like hard cold hatpins. Instead of answering she stared at the vase of artificial flowers mixed with dried grasses that decorated the fireplace.

David tried again.

Celia crossed her ankles. New patent leather shoes. She was able to spend his money, her money. Oh Jesus.

'Celia. For Christ's sake.' He waved the petition at her, moving closer.

And Celia stood up, as if he was threatening her.

'I shall not discuss it,' she said. 'Now or ever. You write to my solicitor.'

She had gone. He heard her moving into the kitchen and followed her there. His whisky glass was on the table, and she rinsed it in the sink.

'Celia. We must talk.'

But she ignored him.

'What have you said to Katie?'

Silence.

Marriner stared at her, facing the ruin of his marriage, his home, his family. It gripped him like an ache in the guts. He sat down wearily at the table behind her as she stood by the sink, and feared she would never respond, and yet he was tied to her, tied by Katie.

'Celia,' he said slowly. 'Are you listening?'

Her back remained towards him, frozen over the sink, looking out at the night.

Silence.

'Celia. Listen.' His mind was made up. 'I'm not giving up Katie. You hear me Celia? I don't think you're fit to take care of her on your own. I'm going to fight it, Celia, whether you answer or not. I could throw the book at you,' he said softly. 'I don't want to but I could. I'll answer you point by point, and I'll fight you all the way. Have you got that? For Katie's sake. This marriage is going to survive, in some shape or form, I don't care how, so that she has a home. It's Katie I'm thinking about, not you or me. We've got her future in our hands. For Christ's sake, let's try and give Katie a break.'

It was a long, hot declaration, and it exhausted him. Celia turned, walked out of the kitchen and went upstairs to her room without replying.

She left him standing there, looking at the bottle of whisky pushed to the end of the table. He could not touch it, his mind was whirling at the prospect she had presented, the fear of loss. Celia was unfair, impossible. She had the knife in his back and was twisting it round. Any sane man would have run, left home, given up, taken his chances on the rebound market. But Marriner wasn't made like that.

'It's my fucking home,' he said to the empty kitchen, 'and she's my kid.' And he raised his eyes to the ceiling where his wife would be in the spare bedroom that she had commandeered.

He was still there thinking, drinking cups of tea, unable and unwilling to face the stairs, when the telephone rang.

It was eleven o'clock, for God's sake.

He waited, half hoping Celia would come down to answer it, or that the thing would stop.

But the ringing persisted, and eventually he roused himself and picked up the receiver. He wondered if Celia would be listening on the upstairs extension, but he could hear no click.

'Hello. Is that David Marriner?' The voice was flat and faintly north country, Yorkshire maybe.

'Speaking,' he said wearily.

'Sorry to disturb you at this hour, but it's rather important.'

'Who are you?' Marriner said. In the background he could hear what seemed to be music, and the noises of people. The man seemed to be in a call box.

'The name is Orford,' the stranger said. 'Denis Orford. You don't know me, but I would very much like to meet you.'

5

'Good God,' Orford said, 'do you always have to push your way between so many bloody tourists?'

He stood in Marriner's office, clad in elephant grey, trickles of perspiration running down his large face, and added, 'No bugger knew where you were.' He looked with care at the room with its scruffy public service furniture and rows of books: at someone who was half scholar and half businessman.

'You came in the wrong way,' Marriner said. 'There's a staff gate.'

'Oh. Somebody should have told me.' Orford scowled. He remained staring at the younger man, and Marriner was irritated. Who the hell was Orford anyway, ringing up late at night when David had his private crisis, demanding an interview on the following day. Marriner did not offer coffee.

Orford relented, and smiled. 'Mind if I sit down?'

'Do.'

'Good.' He settled heavily in one of the interview chairs, while Marriner remained at the desk. The room was large and shabby, big windows opening on to Tower Green, and his eyes swept round it.

'They give you plenty of space here.' He noted the books and artefacts piled on the floor. A couple of old muskets; a swordcase; several framed lithographs.

'Yes,' Marriner said. 'These are the admin. offices. We're really quite a big museum. The old officers' quarters,' he added. 'Probably by Salvin.'

'Who?'

'Salvin. Architect.'

'Oh, yes. Right. Look,' Orford said, taking the plunge. 'I didn't

34

come to bullshit. I came to ask your help.' He gave a toothy smile, blew out his cheeks in the heat. His arms rested like two marrows on the arms of the big leather chair, his red thatch looked artificial. 'I'm part of the M.o.D, so you might say we work for the same outfit. Won't find me in the book though. Can we say for the moment I have an inside role?'

'How do I know? How do I know you're genuine?' Marriner retorted.

'Good point. You could ask Arnold Bullivant or Tom Challenby. You had lunch with them at the Athenaeum a few days ago.'

'I really don't know Bullivant.'

'But you wrote to Tom Challenby. Met him at that reunion.'

'Are you a detective or something?'

Marriner was youngish, thinnish, with neat brown hair. Looked as if he played squash and could be athletic, and Orford liked what he saw.

'No.' He leaned forward a little. 'Military intelligence.'

He watched Marriner's reaction. The younger man had seemed tired, distracted by something else, grudging about his time: now he was interested, but not quite as Orford expected. Moving in the murky waters of intelligence recruitment, Orford thought how varied the people he enlisted were: expatriates, the dispossessed or disillusioned, the ones who were in it for money. He tried to place Marriner now, and beamed at him over the table, all strong teeth and red face. Marriner was different again.

And Marriner said, 'Why should that affect me? I've bigger things to worry about. On my own plate.'

'Ah. But I've come to ask your help.'

Marriner looked round the room, from the muskets to the lithographs and the books.

'I've left the Army,' he said. 'No more orders.'

'I know. Tom Challenby explained.'

Marriner waved him away, as if it was a long time ago, a past he wanted to forget.

This was getting Orford nowhere, and he liked to make progress, to organise.

'Look. Can I take you to lunch?'

'There isn't time,' Marriner said, wrong-footing him again. 'And I usually go to the canteen, or across to the Trade Centre. I'm pretty busy . . .'

Orford stood up, held out his hand. 'In that case I'm sorry to bother you.'

Marriner's eyes followed him. 'Sorry if I wasted your time.'

Orford was a biggish fellow, six feet, broad-shouldered. There was also a touch of the ranker, bounderish, a lack of the social graces which was unusual. A good man in an alley punch-up, Marriner decided.

They stared at each other, fencing, feeling a sudden rapport; and Orford for his part liked this iconoclast who seemed to be a misfit in the museum trade.

'What did you want to tell me?' Marriner said.

Orford relaxed, but made his way to the door.

'Tom Challenby told us you have a contact, a Russian girl, Director of the Kremlin Armoury . . .'

'I think she is. So she says.'

'Anyway. She's asked you to Moscow. On professional grounds.'

'Things are easier these days,' Marriner said.

'Sure. Sure. But she works inside the walls.'

'The Kremlin's a museum. Anybody can walk in.'

'Correct. We know. I've been on the guided tour.' Orford paused at the door and turned. 'Listen. We want to make an inside contact. A top Soviet government man. Somebody who works and lives there, and has stuff in his head. Stuff that we need to know. And for that we must have a go-between. What we call a runner.' His concentration never left Marriner. 'You could do it.'

Marriner said, 'No way.'

Orford's pebbly eyes raked the younger man's face. Marriner gave him the impression of a man full of contradictions, firm one minute, uncertain of things the next. Fertile ground for implanted information or intelligence gathering, a potential instrument on which Denis Orford could play. His background was just about right: day school, neither good nor bad, somewhere in West London, then Cambridge and the Artillery on one of their pre-paid studentships, ending up as a Captain and opting out. Looking at Marriner now, as he tried to psyche him down, Orford thought it was a good face, regular and almost handsome, tougher than it seemed at first sight, a glint of steel in the eyes and firm lines around the mouth. Good height and well proportioned, would have looked smart in a uniform, perhaps why Celia had picked him, though Tom Challenby had said that at one time the marriage

36

was happy enough, before she went off the rails. What Orford saw now he liked, from the official viewpoint where he always began: the man had guts, an independent freakiness. In his way a tough bastard.

'Svetlana Malinkova is the contact point for this guy Borovik. You could use her,' he said.

Their glances met as the offer hung between them.

Marriner grinned. 'Get stuffed. I'm not going to use her.'

'We're not asking you to risk your neck.'

Marriner said, 'Oh, for Christ's sake, I've read about this in books. You pick up some poor bloody fool and use him as a pigeon. If he gets nicked, you don't know him.'

Orford's face was calm, the colour of old bricks.

'We're not that stupid. We know who is on our side. Think of it as industrial espionage, a kind of exchange of information. Look, why don't I buy you a drink?'

Marriner came round the desk, marched across the patch of carpet and said, 'I'll see you out. You might get lost again.'

Orford did not attempt to argue. He shrugged and walked through the door.

They clattered down the staircase and out into the sunshine. A beefeater was being photographed clutching two teenagers; people were eating sandwiches from plastic bags.

Orford liked him, that was the trouble. The old man had a soft spot and David pressed it.

'Sorry to trouble you,' Orford found himself apologising.

'I don't think you're sorry,' Marriner muttered, half to himself. 'I don't think you are at all.' In spite of himself he was intrigued, but he added, 'Look, I've got other problems, more important ones.'

Shielding his eyes from the glare, Orford sympathised.

'I understand. I gather from Tom Challenby that you and your wife . . .'

In the normal course Marriner would never have admitted it, but Orford was a confessor inviting confidences, standing there red-faced and smiling. It annoyed him.

'Jesus. Don't bother me now, that's all. My wife's asking for a divorce. She's trying to take me to the cleaners.'

Orford seemed genuinely sorry. 'What will you do?'

Marriner looked in the mood to pick up one of his muskets and run amok round the Tower, loaded with ball and primed.

'Fight her all the way,' he said.

Orford liked that.

Marriner was still in that mood when Tom Challenby telephoned a couple of days later. He had been out of his office, and had to phone back.

Now, in his own room, he heard Challenby's secretary, who sounded as if she was Indian, putting him through.

'David. Hope you don't mind my calling?'

Marriner was on the defensive, a guarded 'No'.

'Old Denis Orford came to see me. Said he'd been talking to you. After our little chat.'

'I told him no. I'm not interested.'

'My dear chap. I don't mean the Moscow business. Good God no. It's about Celia . . . I'm deeply sorry, old man. Deeply sorry. I had no idea that she was seeking a divorce. It must be awful for you. Denis suggested we should help.'

'Who?'

'Denis Orford.'

'Look, what is this: marriage guidance?'

There was a hollow laugh. A pause.

'Now listen, David. We're concerned for you both, and Denis has suggested – Denis is an old friend – a way in which maybe I could help.'

Marriner didn't seem to be listening. His head was bent, he could feel the sweat in his armpits. When the chips were down he still wanted to try and hold on, a kind of need.

'What?'

'Help. You need some help, don't you?'

'I don't know.'

But Challenby persisted. 'Denis told me that you intend to contest it.'

'Contest what?'

'Come on, David. The divorce. For the sake of your little girl.'

'Katie?' It was almost as if Marriner could not remember the name.

'Katie. Right.'

Another long pause, and noises in the receiver as if he had dropped the telephone.

'All right.'

'Are you there, David?'

'Yes.'

'Don't take this amiss,' Challenby said patiently. 'I don't want to intrude, but perhaps you need a good lawyer. If you really want to fight, that is . . .'

'Of course I do. I don't want to sell up, or lose Katie. Celia will get possession, the house, the kid, the lot.' Marriner sounded like a man who had weighed up the odds and decided he could not win.

Challenby sat back in his chair in the Whitehall office, feeling that he had made an opening.

'I know. I know. But I can give you a contact. The best divorce lawyer in the City of London. Personal chum of mine. I could ask him to take you on . . . defend the case. He could walk rings round Celia, whatever her chaps say.'

Marriner stared at his room, the books and photographs, the half-finished manuscript piled up on the side table, the second career at risk.

'What's his name?'

'Bob Edmondson. Sir Robert Edmondson. Have you heard of him?'

'Didn't he handle the Devonshire squabble?'

'That's right, David.'

'He'd cost a fortune. I couldn't afford it.'

'We use him from time to time, on official business. He owes us one.'

'I still couldn't afford him.'

'You misunderstand, David,' Challenby said patiently, with just the right nuance of anxiety. 'We could put him at your disposal for nothing . . . just think it over.'

At the other end of the telephone, Marriner laughed.

'What do you want me to do in exchange for that? Get somebody out of the Kremlin?'

'Of course not,' Challenby said. He was poised for the big push and it crept over the telephone like a warming breeze: the Establishment offering to help.

There was the girl too, at the back of Marriner's mind, Svetlana with her invitation, and that teasing between them that was almost erotic. Svetlana who had kissed him and apologised, a memory of the way she had touched him in the passage in Brussels, and of Oscar Werndl licking his lips, the Prussian bastard.

'She is a ready card,' Werndl had grinned.

'A ready card?'

'You turn her over and she comes up trumps.'

39

Werndl's jokes were beyond him but he got the message. Now he had Challenby hanging on.

'David, old man. You still there?'

'Yes.' Was Challenby really offering free legal advice, at a price?

'Edmondson is too big a fish.'

'Now listen, David. I know him. He owes me a trick or two. He would do me a favour. I don't want you and Celia to break up . . .'

'It's not that,' Marriner said, 'it's Katie.'

'Sure,' Challenby responded quickly. 'Katie. I know.'

He waited a long time. Eventually, Marriner said, 'All right. Can you . . . can I see him?'

Curiously it was Werndl who finally decided matters. The German turned up in London unannounced, and Marriner had a telephone call from the Connaught.

'I am here. Will you join me?'

'Where?'

'London.'

'I'm here too,' Marriner said. 'Which particular bit?'

'Please, you will meet me for dinner? And bring your wife.'

'She's not available, Werndl.'

'Call me Oscar, and come on your own. It is better.'

'OK, Oscar,' he said. 'Perhaps you're right.'

Werndl took him to a place in Soho which steamed with expense accounts. The service was cold-hearted and the food not much better, but Werndl was paying. The German's head was polished by the sun, a bronze that he never lost, varnished by sailing in summer and creosoted by skiing. He sat back in the red plush alcove, more like a businessman than Director of the Charlottenburg Museums. Head of the Kriegsmarine, Marriner thought: that's what he ought to have been.

Werndl called for cigars and selected one over a brandy with the air of an expert.

'You do not smoke, no?'

Marriner shook his head. 'No.'

'Is good. I kill myself.' He leaned forward and sucked on the end obscenely, until the cloud of corona wafted over David. 'But what the hell,' he winked. 'You know why I come to London?'

'Come on, Oscar, why should I?'

The Prussian stroked the lapel of his expensive suit. The smile was a leer.

40

'I come to give you a message.'

He puffed more smoke into Marriner's eyes, ordered two more cognacs.

'This Waterloo exhibition it is growing, expanding.'

'What do you mean, Oscar? I thought we had finished.'

'Of course. Of course. In Brussels, yes.' He swilled the brandy round his glass and sniffed its aroma. 'But the beautiful Svetlana, she has come to me again.'

'In Berlin?'

'No, no. In Brussels. She comes back with some more material. A lovely couple of pictures by Vorobyov of the retreat from Moscow.'

'Which one?'

'Napoleon of course.' The smile left Werndl's face like a cloud on the sun and then resumed.

'Svetlana returns, and says she has proposals for a major exchange. The Kremlin material for one of the big museums in London or Paris. That is her ambition.'

'Berlin not big enough?'

That brought the clouds back too, but Werndl was a professional, the war was over.

'Perhaps not. So I thought of you first. My friend David Marriner, I said. He could exchange the Tower for the Kremlin. And I saw her blush, David, I saw the roses in her cheeks. She is enamoured of you, you lucky chap.'

'She hasn't told me.'

'Perhaps she is more subtle. She works through me.'

Marriner began to wonder if Oscar had made it too, and the German read his thoughts.

He shook his head.

'In case you wonder . . . no luck. She has good figure though.'

'Hard cheese,' Marriner said.

'No, no. For me it is not so much women.' Werndl smiled, and not for the first time Marriner wondered about his preferences. 'She reserves herself for you.'

'What?'

Werndl watched his cigar smoke mingle with the ceiling.

'She invites you to go to Moscow.'

'I know.'

'She *wills* you to go. And when you do, it will be all laid bare. You are a lucky fellow, David. You have the chance to stage the biggest and best exchange in the history of Anglo-Soviet culture. Don't you see that? The bloody place is crammed with treasures.'

'I'm very busy.' With Celia, he thought grimly, trying to stop a disaster of my own.

'Well. If you don't get in there, David, someone else will.'

'Who?'

Werndl shrugged. 'Perhaps it will be me. I can put an act together. But I reckon the French.'

'The French?'

'Ritterman.'

Ritterman, that clown with the shooting stick, Curator of the Beaux Arts in Brussels; but then it occurred to Marriner that behind the façade Ritterman was a Francophile, and a French speaker.

Werndl smiled sweetly. 'He is after the Louvre.' He paid with American Express.

'Well, David. Great to see you. My advice is go for the big one, before somebody else does. Wasn't it your T. S. Eliot who wrote, "Uncorseted her Russian bust gives promise of pneumatic bliss"?'

'I don't know.' Marriner felt an odd stirring. Bliss was distinctly lacking in life with Celia, and yet it had started that way.

Werndl wafted his cigar through the restaurant and out into Greek Street.

'I knew this place when there were street girls. Now it is only clipper joints.' His hand touched Marriner's arm.

'How is your lady wife?'

It was a long time before Marriner replied, as they walked past the tourists and touts, and surmounted the black bags of garbage piled for collection.

'She wants a divorce.'

Werndl finished his cigar and trod it underfoot.

'I understand. I had heard as much.'

Rumours soon flew around on the museum grapevine.

'What do you do about it?'

'I'm fighting it. For my daughter's sake.'

'You have a daughter? How old?'

'Katie is seven.'

'Ah. I'm sorry.'

They passed a strip-show where a girl stood offering tickets.

'Alas my tastes are not catered for,' Werndl said with a smile. 'But yours should be.'

'Not here.'

'No. I do not mean here. I mean Moscow. You have a career to make. Brussels will be a triumph; and then the big one with Moscow. Don't be a fool, David. Women admire success: something to make her sit up.'

'She'll try and settle it quickly.'

Werndl began searching for a taxi.

'What kind of advice are you getting?' He stood very stiff, his figure like a lamp-post, and a cab drew up almost at once. 'You need a first-rate lawyer; they tend to be expensive.' As he climbed in, he added, 'Have you got a good man?'

'The best in London,' Marriner said. 'Bob Edmondson.'

'Ah.' Werndl paused. 'I used to play him at squash. Hurlingham.'

Marriner had said it in desperation, and partly to impress. From then on he was committed.

As Werndl drove away Marriner realised he still did not know why the German had come to London.

Edmondson was one of those very tall men who seem to be above the fray. Soft-spoken, polite, he talked into a notebook behind a mahogany desk when Challenby took Marriner to see him. His offices were close by the Law Courts, and his biscuits fit for a judge: expensive, Danish, thinly coated with chocolate.

'Hope you don't mind if I sit in,' Challenby had said beforehand. 'Scratch my back and we scratch yours.'

Marriner recognised the conditions laid down. Tormented by Celia's attitude, concerned for his daughter's faith in him, he no longer felt able to refuse Tom Challenby's manoeuvrings. He wanted to rescue Celia as well as himself: somehow the threat to the marriage made him fight to regain the long lost strawberry summer of their engagement when they had swum in the Med, and made love on the sand.

He shuddered now as he asked, 'Can you really help me?'

'Certainly. No problem,' Challenby replied. 'One of the advantages of knowing the rough end of the legal trade.'

In Edmondson's room he said, 'The point is, Bob, that David wants to contest a divorce.'

Scribble, scribble. 'What is your wife seeking to prove?'

'Desertion, infidelity, mental cruelty.' Marriner passed over the petition, which Edmondson read very carefully.

'Is any of this true?'

43

'Absolutely not. A tissue of lies.'

'There is no other woman?'

'Absolutely not.' Svetlana was a chimera, wish-fulfilment in another country.

Edmondson chose a biscuit and nibbled it with a surprisingly neat mouth. He adjusted his glasses but did not look up.

'She has a very good chance of proving unreasonable behaviour.'

'But I haven't been unreasonable.'

'The law is weighted in favour of the woman and child.'

'Look. I want to stick to Celia for Katie's sake.'

There was a stain on the carpet; then Marriner realised it was his own shadow.

'If the divorce is defended,' Edmondson intoned, 'the whole procedure becomes a lot more trouble. Have you tried to understand her, to excite her?'

'She doesn't talk to me.'

'Defence is a complicated process, just as it is in war. Always easier to attack, as your wife has done.' Edmondson smiled thinly. 'Divorces often start out being defended while the property issues are sorted out, and custody of the child. In the end the parties usually compromise.'

'I'm not prepared to do that,' Marriner said obstinately. 'I want to get her to retract.'

Challenby grounded his teacup. Edmondson, towering behind his desk, seemed as carved as a totem, scarcely moving. His eyes flickered over Marriner for the first time, appraising, small-mouthed. The quiet voice continued.

'To win her back you may need to strike a fresh note, something that really appeals.'

'That's not so easy.'

Edmondson rubbed his hands. 'No. Well. In order to construct a defence, I shall want depositions – from your friends. I think we can bring her round.'

More at ease, Challenby added, 'I want you to help him, Bob. All the help that you can. David is considering doing some work for us. He needs a bit of back-up while he decides.'

'What kind of work?' Edmondson's faded eyes showed a tiny enquiry outside routine.

Tom Challenby said, 'Helping to take advantage of the new climate. Glasnost makes it easier to pick up some of our contacts.'

44

Marriner saw again the price he would be asked to pay.

Edmondson said, 'Will you have more tea?' And poured himself a cold cup which he sipped thoughtfully. The room was heavy with bookcases. Marriner recognised the unspoken assumptions.

'No thanks.' They shook their heads.

'I have to say,' Edmondson pronounced, 'that my best advice would be to let the thing go through. The divorce, I mean. Less painful in the long run.'

Was he advising Marriner to pull out? But the younger man was shaking his head. Katie, Katie, Katie echoed through Marriner's mind.

'No way,' he said.

Messages were passing between Challenby and Edmondson confirming some previous understanding. A thin advisory smile.

'All right. I'll do what I can. We shall aim for a dismissal. My people will be in touch.'

As they walked away and climbed into Challenby's Rover, Marriner said, 'Thanks, Tom. What do I have to do for it?'

'Do?' Challenby's tie was deep blue with yellow stripes. 'My dear David. All you do is go to Moscow. Resume an acquaintance. Work up a cultural exchange.'

The car became stuck in traffic in the Strand, and Marriner said he would walk.

'We'll be in touch. No problems, David. By the way, how goes the exhibition, the one in Brussels?'

'Brussels? That's all set up.'

'Great.' He hesitated. 'Listen. This girl Svetlana Malinkova knows a man called Borovik. We want to brief you about him.'

Marriner's blood seemed to freeze. What the hell did they know? And Challenby seemed to anticipate the unformed question with a casual grimace. 'Don't ask,' he said. 'We have our contacts . . .'

As Marriner caught the train to High Barnet, crowded among the briefcases and mottled knees, he knew that his world had changed.

6

The kitchen had been carved out of the alcove on the stairs, little more than a cubby-hole, and Svetlana cursed it again as she went through to make coffee. The tap was still dripping into the stainless steel sink.

Dressed in the black slip that served as a nightdress, she carried two cups to the bedroom, and looked down at the pilot. He was half sleeping, but managed to rouse himself at the smell of the coffee, and squinted at her. This was Henrik, lying in her bed naked, his curly hair mussed on the pillow.

Henrik Asterharzy grinned.

'You look beautiful,' he said. 'Take it off.'

'No.' His assertiveness made her angry, but it was anger at herself. God damn this stifling Moscow flat, and the instincts that stooped to passing pilots.

She handed him the coffee and he sat up in bed, revealing a matt of black hair on his chest.

'Get back in, chicken,' he said.

Svetlana stood looking at him, and felt the bruise on her shoulder. Asterharzy made love like a bull.

'Haven't you got a plane to catch?' She felt that she wanted him out, out, out at any price. Let him take his pleasures with those flat-buttocked stewardesses, not with her. A passing flame was blown out as she saw him there for what he was, a predator who humiliated in the act of giving her pleasure.

Uncomprehending, Asterharzy showed white teeth interspersed with gold.

'My Tupolev is not flying today, so far as I am concerned.' He implied he had all day to spend with her.

She shook her head, flattened her hands over her body in the tight rayon slip.

'Too bad. I've got plenty to do.' She wanted to lever him out of that bed, her bed, feeling full of disgust – but instead he lay there smirking at her like a pig with a truffle. The room was fetid with body sweat which curdled in her mouth.

'Out, out, out,' Svetlana said. 'Get up and get dressed.'

46

Surprised, he sat up and stared.

'Oh come on. Let's have another game.'

'Game!' The thought of it made her react, a sudden flush of shame. She castigated herself for her own confusions. One part of her wanted this, said she could play the houri in an open society while she was attractive and well paid; the other half of her mind rejected the casual male as soon as she had achieved him. She placed her hands on her hips. 'I've got work to do. I want you to go.'

Asterharzy began to whine. 'You didn't say . . .'

'I don't tell you everything.'

She turned on her heels, barefooted, and walked out, past the little breakfast bar next to the kitchen, up two steps into the living room that she had created. Its mysteries worked to soothe her as she entered: a high, dark room with stairs leading up to a gallery crammed with pictures on the olive green walls. Automatically she flicked on the record player inside the door, a priestess into her sanctuary, which must be undefiled. The chorus of the Rustavelli choir surged out behind her as she switched on a light at the table in the alcove – the curtains were still drawn – and contemplated the paintings covering every wall. Icons, pictures of saints and images of the living God, row on row, the dark and sober memories of holy Russia that she had begun to collect, based on her father's inheritance, when she was thirteen. They stared back at her now, those deep-eyed masks of Christ and saints and holy men, which had survived the years of the Revolution and the State, visions of Orthodoxy, priceless heirlooms that she had been able to acquire quietly and privately from dozens of sources, in the closed monasteries, the emptied churches, the storerooms of provincial museums, the houses of abandoned priesthoods, farms and cottages where money counted, the black markets of Moscow, Kiev, Leningrad; drunken party men with a piece of booty, old women who saw in her someone who cared, and the tiny shops and secret barter houses where you traded icons for nylons and ball-point pens: all these she had visited, known, used, because she had the resources, and the calling behind her, and the obsessive urge to collect and preserve.

Forgetful of the night with Asterharzy, she stood in the great room now, the music booming around her, feeling the sensual pleasure of those images on wood and canvas, some of them beautiful, some of them simple daubs, but all suffused by serenity, a sense of holiness that to her was a mystery. She folded her arms together, willing them almost to speak, the berry-brown eyes of sorrow, the hands in prayer or anguish on the cross, the simple contemplatives who gave her peace of mind. The invisible choir reached a point of ecstasy and the walls in her mind crumbled. This was her Russia, her love, the old obsessions of a secret religion she neither understood nor abused, dark churches ringing with chanting. The faces were floating around her and she seemed to be standing outside herself looking in, watching a whore in a negligée who lived alone and slept with an Aeroflot pilot she had picked up on one of his journeys.

Svetlana shuddered, holding her hands to her head. In this room she had created, three tiers of pictures stared down, eyes and heads which seemed to follow her movements as she went to the alcove, sat at the table and lit a second lamp, a candle in an iron lantern. Now she could see it all between the dark green walls and the ruby curtains over the single window: every ledge and space covered with some memento of years of collecting, striving towards an inner peace that she could not obtain, part of the pain of Russia.

She buried her head in her hands, hair pushed through her fingers, body convulsed. The half-eaten remnants of last night's meal with Asterharzy, a half-drunk bottle of Georgian wine, reproached her from the table.

The music stopped, and the door slowly opened as Asterharzy entered, stuffing his shirt in his trousers.

'You'll wake the dead,' he said, still grinning, the bastard.

She roused herself, looking pale in the deep recess, a spectral woman, white arms, golden hair, black shift, a wicked queen in a fairy castle.

'Get out. I don't want you in here,' she said.

Finally, he took the message as she pushed him out of the room, her room. These were the hard knots within herself that she hated, when everyone conspired against her. The pilot looked at her in pained amazement.

'All right, all right, chicken. I know the signs.' He began to gather his things together in the bedroom as she watched, still in her slip, barefooted. There was an iron bedstead, painted white, and a big old armoire, three Empire chairs and a chaise longue, a theatrical setting. That too she had created. He picked up his uniform coat from the chair and dusted the badges of rank, the four gold bars on the sleeve. His cap had fallen off the table and had to be retrieved from the floor. He ran a hand over his stubbly chin and pushed back the wavy hair before cramming on his hat.

Standing in the doorway he made an attempt to grab her and kiss her goodbye.

'Will I see you at the weekend, Svetlana?'

'I don't imagine so.'

The pilot frowned, knowing there were other girls, not so difficult as this one, on his travels.

'Come on, pretty chicken.'

'Don't,' she said. 'I may be going away.'

'Away?'

'Oh go to hell,' she said, and propelled him out on to the landing.

His fingers fumbled for the cage lift, which slowly rumbled up four floors. She waited while it arrived, and then pecked his cheek briefly as he entered the tiny, two-person elevator, like a pig in a wire cage, she thought.

'Goodbye,' she said without emotion as he creaked out of sight.

Svetlana returned to the bedroom, stepped out of the slip and walked to the shower. The hot water rumbled and wheezed before it spurted with jets of steam, and used as she was to its eccentricities she had to jump to avoid being scalded. There was no curtain and she stood in the enamelled bath, looking at her figure as the water splashed over. She always felt like this, an emptiness, when the affair ended. All such couplings were empty, in her experience, but not wrong. Nothing in the State code said that she could not do it, so then why did it leave her so uneasy, with those residual pangs of conscience? Was it the images, the icons of a lost faith that both challenged and warned her? She thought of them coldly, the water running down her body.

Her mother was calling her, as a little girl, a precocious, fairy-headed, spoilt brat of a girl, in their Leningrad apartment. She had been nine years old.

'Svetlana, my darling puppy, come to me.'

She had been drawing, colouring a picture book, and her crayons and pencils were scattered on the settee. It was October, already cold, and a ghostly sun was shining through clouds over the Neva river, as they looked down from their apartment in the new block on Kutuzov Quay. Already the leaves had almost gone, leaving a brown carpet on the footpath below.

'Why?'

Her mother was very pale, one hand clutching her side, and with

49

her was Aunt Laura, who had suddenly appeared from the other side of the city. Anna and Laura were sisters, her mother two years younger, and Laura already a widow, smartly dressed in black furs, with a little astrakhan hat.

Seeing Aunt Laura, the little girl had asked, 'Is it winter already?'

Her mother had collapsed in the big chair in which her father usually sat, opposite the settee.

'Svetlana,' she had whispered, hands clasped in her lap, twisting and turning the rings on her fingers. 'Svetlana yes, it is winter already.' And in a voice so small it might have been a mouse in the skirting, she added, 'Your father has died.'

Svetlana felt the water trickle over her now, as she turned off the shower, in the same way that the cold had trickled through her then, twenty-five years before. She found a robe and stepped out of the bath, towelling herslf to forget, but always the image came back, of the little girl standing there before the two women, asking why and how and when, the endless questions, and feeling there were no answers.

She dressed herself in a dark green skirt and white blouse, as if in memory.

'A heart attack,' her mother cried, tears flooding her eyes. 'He was so brilliant, so young.'

And Aunt Laura had added, 'To be Director of the Hermitage before he had reached fifty. The State will honour him.'

Her mother simply sobbed and the little girl, understanding slowly, had thrown her arms round her.

'I will help you, Mama.'

She had felt the convulsions running through Anna's body, and was dimly conscious of others arriving until the room was crowded. Dr Stravinsky, the physician, who was fussing and opening a bag, old Olga the cook and Leonora, the assistant to Papa in the museum, all looking solemn and tired.

The little girl had kissed her mother and stood up to confront them, a clever little prig.

'I will take over,' she had said. 'I will become a director too.'

Now, she pulled on stockings and shoes, looked at her legs, absorbed herself in the mirror and brushed her hair. The hair needed resetting, blonding again. She frowned at the faint down running low on her cheek, smiled at herself, relaxed. The even features relaxed back: wide eyes under an unlined brow, a straight and finely chiselled nose, the full face and elegant lips, which she bit to engorge with blood. Her hands felt her hips and bosom: she was better than any man, worth more than that rat of an Aeroflot pilot, and already Director of the Kremlin Armoury.

She came back tired at eight o'clock after the day's work, clutching the bag of fresh carrots that Maria had queued for in the GUM store at midday. There had been no break in the routine: the morning meeting of comrade heads of departments, the inspection of the galleries, checking the warders were all on post, a meeting at eleven with Academician Sikhovsky who made the usual old man's passes at the late Director's daughter. He had even come round the table and put a hand on her shoulder, caressing it like a bed-knob.

'Svetlana, my dear, you are so like your father.'

'Thank you.' She had been at her most austere, in the green summer costume that the dressmaker Katya had made for her out of the cloth from Belgium and an old copy of *Vogue*. Knees tightly together, elbows on the desk, frowning over the memorandum that the Minsk professor had left with her. He bent over and sniffed her perfume, his eyes rheumy behind the thick lenses.

'Except, if I may say so, you are very much prettier.'

'My father was a handsome man.'

'Of course. Of course.' The hand was patting her shoulder and she resented the stench of tobacco coming from his clothes. 'But he was not a woman.'

'I am a scholar,' she said.

'My dear Svetlana, that is why I have come,' Sikhovsky wheezed. He was as squat as a water tub, with hands as soft as pastry, bald, short-sighted, a historian, a contributor to encyclopaedias.

'I would like to take you to dinner.'

Firmly, she had pushed him away.

'No. I am too busy.'

A hand came down lightly and touched her breast.

'Just for one night, my dear.'

Svetlana drew away. Why did they think she was vulnerable just because she was her own woman? She threw him off by standing up, in the great office which overlooked the inner courtyard. The red light was flickering on the intercom on her desk and it gave an excuse to break up the conversation.

'Good morning,' she had said, opening the door.

It had not endeared Svetlana to Academician Sikhovsky, but it established her authority, which she exercised throughout the day. She talked to Dobrynin, the pushy young deputy with his party badge in his lapel, and spent some time in the afternoon on correspondence with the Commander of the Military Academy in Kiev, who had asked for information about uniforms in the 1820s. Why did they assume a scholar who had trained on the history of art, and written about Bestuzhev and Orlovsky, artists and engravers, was also an expert on costumes and ballistics? God knew she had triumphed in Moscow, a junior from Leningrad, in one of those strange career moves that came out of the Byzantine system of Party preferment, supplemented by sympathy for the death of her father, and recognition of her own precocious and lonely talent. Alone again in the Director's room at four o'clock, drinking a glass of lemon tea brought in on a silver tray by that chunky fool of a secretary, bustling Maria Ulanova, she felt the passage of time. Her mother had left Leningrad as soon as her father died, dispossessed of the apartment, drawing a widow's pension, and resettled in Moscow, where she had been born. Withdrawing into herself, a ready-made widow protecting her two daughters. Both of them had gone on to Lomonosov University, and then when Fanya had married the engineer captain, Svetlana had branched out, inheriting her father's trust funds at eighteen and spending them not on clothes, but on collecting, always collecting: the images and resurrections of ancient Russia.

She felt the passage of time, the sixteen years since that stage, as she worked on in the big room with a green light at the desk like an editor.

A knock at seven o'clock. Timidly, Maria the secretary asked if she could go.

Svetlana looked up in surprise. She had not realised that it was so late. The summer evening was already almost over and this time there would be no dinner with a lecherous Aeroflot pilot, only a dish of fresh carrots, carrot tops in the string bag beside her leather briefcase.

'Maria, I'm sorry. I didn't realise you were still here.'

Maria had nodded. 'You must not exhaust yourself.'

Svetlana smiled. 'Do I look exhausted?'

That unexpected and regular beauty under the yellow hair looked pale in the half-light. The room was always overcast, in spite of the flowers, the curtains, the personal pots and souvenirs which belonged to the curator.

'You look tired.'

Svetlana watched her go, with a soft 'Goodnight', and had then locked the office, leaving the key with the security janitor in the outer room. The big clock on the Tsar's tower struck half past seven as she left by the Spassky Gate, and climbed into the official limousine for the short ride to her apartment off Arbat Prospekt.

Now she was returned home, if you could call it home, this theatrical hideout that she had constructed out of her talent for design. She emerged from the lift and unlocked the double doors. The apartment was old and grand, part of the past to which she knew she was in danger of becoming addicted. The doors opened into the narrow passage lined with books, and she switched on the light. Walking through, past the bedroom and alcove kitchen into the grand salon with its gallery, the icon room, the room of memories.

She crossed to the cabinet, poured herself a lime vodka and switched on the record player. Mahler filled the air with sad, mortal music. The great room crowded around her, the serious, holy faces and noble saints, faces blank with worship, or weeping for the lost Christ. It was a wave breaking over her, that room, those private pictures, which no one else understood. No one. A recipe for calm, perhaps for madness.

The vodka was strong and smooth, good quality from the hard currency shop with her royalty earnings. She pulled out the angular wooden chair at the head of the dining table in the alcove under the gallery and sat there, resting, looking at the images of God, and wished she knew how to pray. Instead of sleeping with men. But that too was a gift, and why should she deny it?

She did not feel hungry. Another drink first, then the music rising to a crescendo. There was a golden filter of late sun through the red curtains. The room was not a museum, it was a theatre for her soul, if she had a soul, she thought. And where did it take her, where was she now going? Svetlana Malinkova who had no more control of time than her dead father; all she had managed to do was tread in the empty footsteps of his unfulfilled career. Already Head of the Armoury, the next head but one of the Pushkin in Moscow or the Hermitage itself. Was that what she really wanted? The heads on the walls looked down and did not answer, but they were beautiful; and she was still young.

'Mother of Saints,' she whispered. 'Where are you now?'

The reply seemed to be a telephone call. The bell in the corner was ringing, on the press-button set. It was some time before she moved to lift it, standing with the empty vodka glass in her hand. It crossed her mind that it might be the tiresome Asterharzy, trying to suck up again, or perhaps Valentina Karpova, suggesting a night at the cabaret theatre she had discovered on Pilogorska.

But it was a man, speaking in English. She felt the muscles contract along the lining of her stomach.

'I am in Moscow,' David Marriner said. 'I wondered if we might meet.'

7

She had said she would collect him on the platform overlooking the Moskva River, outside the Beryozhka Shop, at the entrance to the Rossiya Hotel where he was staying. Her instructions were precise, specific, as if he might get lost.

'It is a horrible building, but it has a good tourist store,' she said. 'I often use it.' He noticed again that slightly hard air of competence with which she had first presented herself.

He waited for her now, wondering almost if he would recognise her in her native habitat. The oblong front of the hotel stood high over the river with the Kremlin domes glinting in the even light. A few people going in and out of the plate-glass doors, hardly a car in sight. Marriner walked to the parapet and leaned over. The river swam below, glassy and greenish, with one of the white tourist launches cruising by like a swan. On the opposite bank the Union Jack flew bravely over the British Embassy, where, Orford had said, 'You do not go.'

Somehow he had expected her to walk towards him, elegantly dressed as always, perhaps in a fur hat, holding out her arms, saying it was all wonderful. But the only women around were two of the chambermaids, smoking by one of the service doors, in blue nylon overalls and felt slippers. An Army man came out, accompanied by a large wife; a couple of crop-haired businessmen who might be Swedes; a dark-haired girl who was whisked away in a taxi; three elderly comrades who kissed each other and walked off separately; then the façade was empty and she was twenty minutes late.

He crossed over again and stared first at the river, sullen now as the sun went down, with only a refuse barge drifting by, then back at the sixties monolith of the hotel. Nothing. Almost as if she and Challenby between them had trapped him into some ludicrous mission, an escapade. He found a loose pebble and threw it into the bushes.

'Sod it,' he said.

And then she was there, almost before he realised. Svetlana, looking flushed and excited, driving a small cream Lada which swept round the corner and squealed on rusty brakes. She was out of the door almost before it stopped rolling, taller than he remembered, on high heels, those long limbs, clad in some slinky material, grey shot silk or shantung, close fitting to the figure, her face alive with excitement which seemed to widen her nostrils, a faint drift of perfume, her hair cut short and restreaked, fitting close to the head like a model in a shop window, and her arms were around him.

'David. David. David. Oh how marvellous. Why didn't you let me know that you were coming? But, anyway you are here.'

He found himself holding her, overwhelmed by the welcome, in front of the puritan stones of the hotel. She was so unlike Celia. She was interested.

And Svetlana was kissing him, just like that, briefly but firmly on the mouth, a kiss of a hundred promises, a thousand hours of wonder. He put his hands to her head and looked into her eyes. She hadn't even asked him why.

Instead she said, 'We must hurry. Get in quickly. I'm so sorry to be late.'

'Why? Where are we going?'

She had slipped back into the driving seat, and he saw again how good her figure was.

'The Bolshoi,' she said. 'It starts in twenty minutes.'

He climbed in and sat beside her as they rattled over the uneven surfaces round the corner of the Kremlin and into Sverdlov Square where she pointed out the theatre, a classical building with a portico, smaller than he had imagined, stained by the traffic fumes.

She smiled at him, even white teeth in a mouth outlined with lipstick. Celia never used lipstick, he thought, and said she disliked perfume. Svetlana, by contrast, in the moulded dress and softly

55

provocative scent had something unsettling about her, tarty almost, that pushed him beyond common sense.

She drove like an astronaut trying out a milk cart, skidding round islands and finally ramming the car into an obscure corner under the trees, two wheels on the footpath, scrambling out through the passenger door.

'I thought it was impossible to get tickets,' he said, as she urged him across and up the steps.

Svetlana grinned. 'We have our ways . . .'

He looked at the posters as she hustled him into the crowded foyer and took his elbow.

'What do they say?'

'It's Rimsky-Korsakov. A new production. *The Golden Cockerel.*'

The theatre was before him now, tier on tier of red and gold, and she had seats in the circle looking down. The orchestra was already in place, and as the conductor entered the buzzing stopped.

Why had she rushed him there? He'd come to talk about guns, unofficially about a defection, and here he was, he told himself, with a woman at the ballet. She was also flesh and blood, curved in the right places, a warm, attractive human being sharing his professional interests. What more did he want? He let the music flow over him as the gauze curtains, spangled with stars and planets, opened on to a fairyland of wizards and dancers, potentates and surreal cockerels, a haunting, impossible tale.

On stage the old wizard cast spells in a magical world of castles under cheese-rind moons. The dancers surrounded the lovers as a princess emerged, and there, beside him, Svetlana Malinkova seemed also to live in a never-never land, this dreaming, beautiful woman.

At the interval she took him to a bar where they had cake and soft drinks. Her eyes were as blue as cornflowers.

'I think it crazy that it is now so expensive to buy a bottle of vodka. Only Gorbachev could have worked such a miracle. But at home I have plenty.'

The invitation was reissued.

He sat on, wondering how he could define the unstable mission to which Challenby and Ormond had persuaded him, knowing he was in the classic position of compromise, risk and disaster. Sideways, Svetlana's face was a painting as she swayed to the music, entranced by the singing. A great clear lament from the tenor seemed to swirl in the air, and the silhouetted heads in the darkened auditorium might have been painted cardboard. It was a magical moment and he felt it should go on for ever, as a tiny movement by his side was made by Svetlana's fingers, her hand stretched out for his. Their fingers interlocked, and he felt at once the dreadful touch of desire. She turned her head and smiled.

In the darkness he was on fire, fighting to remember the rules of engagement. But she took no notice, her hand was stroking his, then resting on his thigh. Oh Christ, he thought, and tried to dredge up Challenby, but he could not find a face, only a blank in the mind. The woman who clicked into view was Celia, Celia sitting alone, trying to cry.

There was a finale at last, of fireworks and molten rain as the mystery world of the stage broke out into dancing figures and the golden bird died. Svetlana's hand left his as she leapt to applaud and the whole theatre reverberated with affection.

'Come on,' she said. 'Now you must come back with me, and we can talk.'

They walked down the steps and out into the warm night. It was after eleven o'clock, and she was offering a bed: he knew that, and he pulled back and wanted her at the same time. The whole evening seemed dangerous. He had never had it so easy, right from the first gropings of sixteen-year-old desire, as this night presented in Moscow.

'It's late,' he muttered.

She put her arm through his as she marched beside him.

'It is never too late.'

They were retrieving the car, and he watched the legs flick inside as she opened the passenger door and squeezed across.

'David. David. Why did you not come sooner, or let me know?' This was a half-starved alley cat, rolling over on her back. Disreputable. But also a beautiful dancer like the one on the stage. Oh Jesus wept.

'I've come on business,' he said.

'I'll drive you back to the flat.'

And if he got there inside the magic castle on a night such as this, he knew he might never get out. He fought the webs that she wove.

'I'm tired. It's been a long day . . .' he was mumbling. She started the engine, turned to embrace him again. In the intimacy of the car she was overpowering. Her tongue was in his mouth, tasting slightly of salt.

'Let's go,' she said, releasing him only because she had to drive. 'I feel so happy to see you here, after such wonderful music.'

He found his control at last.

'Take me back to the Rossiya. We'll talk about things tomorrow.'

She stopped the car, braking under the trees. Her voice was scolding him.

'Do you not want to see my collection?'

'Your collection?' Another way of framing the invitation.

'I have things you must see. Will want to see.' She stroked his hand.

'I'm sure. But it can't be tonight,' he said. Blindly, pricked by desire that he fought to deny.

'Why not?'

'It doesn't matter . . .' Sanity returning. 'It's too late and too soon for me to come back tonight.'

'You could stay . . .'

'I know. I know.'

'I have two beds. Or one big one.'

'I know that too.'

'Don't you want me?' she breathed. Her hand was under no illusion.

'It's not that . . .'

For the first time he heard the annoyance in her voice, and her English was strained. 'You do not so-called fancy me? I want to talk serious. Not a lay-out.'

He risked a quick return kiss.

'I understand. Me too. I have come here on business.' Celia, fucking Celia, at the bottom of this too. 'We can talk better tomorrow, when I'm less tired. Without this . . . complication.'

She sighed. 'You really want the Rossiya?'

'I don't want it. I think I should go back there, for tonight.' For Christ's sake how could he be sure that Ormond's assessment was right, that she could be trusted?

The car restarted and lurched along in the dark, round by the shadows of St Basil's Cathedral with its barley sugar domes. The streets were almost deserted, apart from a yellow truck, slowly sprinkling water.

'OK OK,' she said. 'Here is the damned hotel. I'm sorry.' It was the second time she had drawn back, just as she had in Brussels. Now she seemed confused.

They swept up to the entrance and he tumbled out.

'Can we talk tomorrow?'

'Of course. Of course. I will pick you up,' she said, 'and take you to the Kremlin.'

As he watched her drive off, a small, slim figure in the darkened car, he felt mad with desire, and yet released. And one of her rearlights wasn't working: he must remember to tell her.

It was a different car on the following day, and Svetlana was not driving. He found her sitting in the back of one of the black Chaikas reserved for officials, dressed this time in beige, a longer skirt and less provocative knees. She looked a little wan, her greeting circumscribed by the presence of a man in the front seat, who leaned across and shook hands. Ivan Kirilov, middle-aged, moustached, balding, cautious as any doctor, introduced himself in careful English as head of the museum directorate in the Ministry of Culture.

The car had been waiting when Marriner came down after surviving a breakfast of hard rolls and dry ham, and swept him into the Kremlin by the Trinity Gate. As they passed through, the militiamen on the guard post, shirt-sleeved in the sunshine, jumped to salute and he knew the thrill of arrival.

'This gate is fifteenth-century,' Svetlana said as if on duty. 'The bell tower was added two hundred years later.' She smiled. 'Since the fire of Moscow there have been no bells. They were burnt down.'

'Which fire?'

She waved a hand as they drove inside the walls.

'Napoleon. Your period.'

He looked up at the redbrick battlements and the yellow and white façade of the Arsenal where they had parked. He was prepared for this, had memorised the layout of the complex of buildings from the groundplan that Orford had given him but told him to leave in London. What he had not expected was the trees and the greenery, a maze of bushes, and the sparkling weather. He had a sense of foreboding, as if another magic curtain was about to be prised apart.

They walked across to the Armoury wing of the Kremlin Palace, already open to the public, and entered by a side door.

'It avoids most of the . . . what do you say . . . safeguards?' Kirilov muttered, wiping his brow.

'Security.'

'Ah. Like a prison,' Kirilov added.

Svetlana seemed well respected. Three men behind a wooden counter stopped reading *Pravda* as they arrived.

'Please come.'

He followed her ankles up an internal staircase, along corridors lined with prints: military engagements and scenes of Roman ruins. The walls were dull white and shone under electric chandeliers.

Her offices were a set of rooms, the outer one with a secretary and a tea-urn, the inner one curtained and cool. The blinds were still half-drawn to shut out the sunlight, and as his eyes adjusted he saw the trappings of her position: the large, rather plain, dark desk with its news-editor lamp, twin bookcases behind, glass fronted with leaded lights, a couple of armchairs in some kind of rexine, a conference table and a set of six solid chairs with red stars carved on the back.

She was introducing her specialists, gathered there, smiling awkwardly: Aldanov, weapons and armour, Marriner's own area, with grey hair and tortoiseshell glasses; Victor Larinsky, who looked like a jeweller and was keeper of gold and silver; Ulanova Someone who was in charge of fabrics; Captain Alexander Kursky, responsible for coaches and harnesses; and a young man, Leonid Pugachev, who had majored in Western Art.

He was inside a museum, inside the Kremlin, still feeling the heat of Svetlana's presence, inside a mind in turmoil. Kirilov stuck by his side and he had the impression that she would have liked to shake him off, and Aldanov the armour man, all of them, as they set out on a conducted tour, a posse sweeping through the galleries.

'What exactly have you come for?' Kirilov asked, ingratiating himself by positive little remarks about the collections in England as they swept along.

'To see the guns,' he said. That was at least part of it, and Svetlana let Aldanov, thin as a ramrod himself, show them the rooms of chainmail, battle-axes, muskets, wheel-lock arquebuses and flintlocks by Armoury gunsmiths. They gleamed in their cases, ornamental stocks of silver and ivory, curios, presentation guns, guns for the Royal Hunt, oriental display pieces, engraved, chased, finished in gilt and gold.

'What is it that you want?' Aldanov was repeating, inclined like a confessor as they moved on to the swords and sabres.

'Research into firepower,' he said. 'Comparative statistics.'

'OK, OK.' Aldanov seemed to expire once his section was over, and now they were following Svetlana like anxious boys with a mother as she steered them through room after room: armour, helmets and holsters giving way to superb exhibits of gold and silver, cups, jewellery, goblets, medallions, reliquaries, enamelled encasements, caskets inset with diamonds, sapphires, rubies, dishes of engraved gold, pendants, flasks and chalices, a storehouse of untouchable wealth.

There was a sadness about it. It did not make sense in Marriner's eyes. Svetlana was too young and much too attractive. How could she rule this roost, not just of arms and relics, but of the brocades and costumes through which they were now passing, the past luxuries of Church and State, the patriarchs and the Tsars?

It was then that Svetlana turned, as if she could feel his questions burning into her back. She flicked her fingers through her hair and stopped with hands on hips as if confronting him, Kirilov, Aldanov and the rest of them.

'It is exhausting,' she said.

'I agree.'

She laughed.

'The rest will wait till tomorrow. Now, I must let these people get on with some work.'

As she hustled them away, leaving him standing with Kirilov, was it a half impression that they were relieved to go?

His official tour was over and she was standing by a door into a private room.

'It is all right, Comrade Kirilov. We will talk business now. Technical matters: calibres, shot weights, rifling as it is called. Can you please leave us?'

Kirilov began to demur. Even inside the Kremlin he had to be a kind of minder, concern etched on his face.

'Please,' she said, and smiled.

'Perhaps I should sit in, to help translate . . .'

She showed that the room was tiny, dark and full of records, boxfiles and bundles of paper. All it contained was a table and just enough space for two chairs, a broom cupboard.

'The papers that our friend wants are kept in here. I shall be going through them. There is no need . . .'

Kirilov gave up.

Left suddenly on their own in the corridor by the archive room, he saw her eyes were cautioning him.

She waited, while Kirilov smirked uneasily and walked reluctantly off to join Aldanov's party retreating along the corridor. Svetlana watched them go: a warder sat on a bench in the cream and gold passage with its polished mahogany doors, but otherwise it was empty. Marriner realised that she had led him to what had once been the Tsar's apartments, not open to visitors, musty now, smelling of disuse and a certain loss of dignity.

She opened the door to the little room and slipped inside. He followed. It was a muniment store: the shelving contained papers marked with the Romanov cipher, carefully tied, many of the bundles sealed.

'Leave the door open,' she said.

He was squeezed at the narrow table with Svetlana on the other side, touching distance, and a boxfile of papers between them which she had selected at random. One elegant finger motioned him to say nothing.

She was writing on a slip of paper which she passed across to him. What she said aloud was, 'I can find you material here about Alexander's reassessment of the Army in 1814.'

How far can I trust you, he thought. On the paper he read, 'What do you really want?' in English.

'I should be very interested to see it,' Marriner replied slowly, grappling with the subterfuge.

He wrote, 'To talk,' and watched her eyes. 'And you?'

Svetlana was smiling, and began to direct him to papers as someone passed by outside. He saw that it was Pugachev, the Western Art man, no doubt another nark, the enamelled red flag of a party member glinting in his lapel.

Svetlana was scribbling again, passing the same note across, a proxy dialogue in an archive store.

'You,' he read.

Their eyes met, in hers that mixture of predatory interest and screwed-down emotion that she had shown from the start; Marriner's reflecting the uncertainty of his intentions, the compromise with Orford and Challenby. And she knew.

'Good,' she said, gathering up the single slip of paper on which communications had been conducted and tucking it in her hand-bag.

'Naturally, most of the material is in Russian, so you will need translations. One or two papers in French. For instance there is a table of comparative firepower: English, French and Russian cannon and demi-cannon. We might find the same for muskets. Would that help you?'

'Invaluable,' he said.

He was entering into a game, and she encouraged him, showing him sets of papers right up to the Romanovs' end at the bullet-riddled house in Ekaterinburg in 1918, the final sets stamped with a hammer and sickle. Once or twice she motioned with her finger to make sure they did not regress into their personal relations: the motives had been stripped out, and now she was engaged on the cover.

It took them three-quarters of an hour, in that small space, and he was conscious once more of her body, a different, more intimate perfume. Somewhere at the back of his mind those discussions in London with Challenby and Orford, and Edmondson the legal eagle, were all urging him to go on, and he had not even mentioned the name Tom Challenby had given him. He dared not do so until he was sure, and how could he be sure? The Russians might no longer be enemies, but how far could they safely be friends? As he looked into Svetlana's eyes, it seemed she was making an offer, playing games in her own back yard; it made him feel sticky and nervous.

As if she sensed his hesitation she glanced at her watch and said, 'David, it is after midday. There is a lunch for you. And then we shall go out . . . I shall show you our laboratories.'

As they emerged he saw Kirilov waiting, marching forward and smiling, at the end of the corridor where he had been talking to Pugachev. All at once they were arriving again, the stocky woman Ulanova, the Captain Kursky, Larinsky the precious metals man, as if they'd been awaiting a signal. Svetlana smiled at them all, apologising.

'Comrades, he wants to know so much,' she said, nudging David. 'I am so sorry to keep you waiting.'

They were out in the corridor now, the wall chandeliers switched on, moving on royal carpets along a suite of rooms where the doors were pulled back in welcome and staff in white coats appeared. There was a smell of cooking and she led him through to a dining room with a luncheon set out on a cloth.

'Please,' she said. 'You are our guest.'

That made it difficult too, in Marriner's book. The plates were white with gold rims and the Kremlin crest, and there was a spray of red roses. Twelve of them took their seats. Mineral waters and soft drinks were offered for the toasts and he drank to the health of the Kremlin Armoury under the triple portraits of Marx and Lenin and Gorbachev. In orange juice.

8

It was another two days before he could see her briefly in private, whether from design or accident. Two days in which she was around, but always with Kirilov, shadowing them like a dog after biscuits, often with one or two colleagues, and Aldanov or Kursky or Pugachev from the museum. They showed him everything – the store rooms, the labs, the model room, processing, printing, conservation, display, two other sets of archives – and yet he felt no closer to putting his case to Svetlana. How far could he trust her remained the terrible question in his mind. Orford's brash confidence and Challenby's Establishment calm both now seemed a long way away, leaving him very exposed.

'I'll see you soon,' she said, whispering in the company of comrades and parting with an enigmatic goodbye. At night he tried again to telephone but she was never available and he suspected that the line was tapped. The weather in Moscow turned thundery, heavy with rain and cloud, intimidating. His only contact was Kirilov, emerging in the hotel lobby in an open-necked shirt and sandals as if he had been there all evening, offering to take him to dinner.

Marriner began to start lying. Moscow was sitting on him, huge and alarming, like an undigested meal. He remembered those days at school when he had faced some terrifying test and chickened out with a made-up illness.

'Bit of a headache. Think I'll just turn in.'

'Oh, I'm so sorry. Do you need a doctor?'

Kirilov with his thin grey hair and indeterminate moustache gave a good impression of concern. They had a drink in the bar, two glasses of oily vodka and some biscuits, the price of friendship, before Kirilov would let him go. It occurred to Marriner later that they were probably tracing all the calls he was trying to make, so he stopped those too and wrote postcards to Celia, and to Katie.

The card to Celia was a picture of the Moscow underground.

'Hope you are better,' he said. 'I'm thinking of you.'

He sent Tom Challenby one of the Lenin Mausoleum, then stood himself more vodkas in the bar on the fourteenth floor.

He went to bed in a sweat that Svetlana would let him down, or even that she was setting him up. In spite of what London had said how could he be sure that she was the safe connection to this man Borovik?

The car came in the morning and delivered him back at night to the uncertain glories of the Rossiya Hotel, looking over the Kremlin's back yard. Kirilov was always in it, dressed in a shiny grey suit and patterned shoes, ready to please in his excessive way, anxiety sitting in his eyes.

'Ah. You are better. Rested?'

'Yes. Thank you.'

They would drive to the Armoury through the Kutafya Tower, under the Red Star, illuminated at night, on the Trinity Gate. One of the specialists would meet him, Aldanov or Pugachev, and Marriner would struggle to make notes on the cabinets of guns, and ask for translations of papers.

On the third day she was not there at all.

He felt another spasm of alarm, decoyed into a dubious mission, beyond the range of his experience. What was worse, they seemed to sense his anxiety.

Pugachev, thin, with a wispy beard, took him aside in the archive room and asked if he'd found what he wanted.

'Very helpful. Marvellous collection.'

Pugachev rubbed his chin, and played with the party badge he liked to sport.

'What exactly are you researching, Mr Marriner?'

'The retreat from Moscow,' he said, '1812. Assessment of the firepower of the French and the Allies.'

The Russian's eyes flickered with patriotism. 'You know, we had the best guns.' Just like Svetlana, when they first met. Marriner ignored it.

'I'd like,' he said, 'to send the Director some flowers. A thank you. Can you tell me where she is?'

'She has left Moscow,' Pugachev replied crisply. 'Temporarily.'

Then, on the fourth day, Svetlana was there again, waiting for him as Kirilov drove him inside the battlements and across to the Armoury. Marriner's heart jumped as she came forward smiling, dressed in a linen jacket. The uncertainties might remain, but she also diminished them, simply by being there.

Svetlana held out her hand, Western-style, standing in the sunshine with the wind ruffling her hair.

'I'm sorry that I have been missing you.'

'Me too.'

Aldanov the Weapons man was present this time, waiting with Kirilov.

'I had business in Kalinin; some help with an exhibition.'

But again there was no chance as she led him through the now familiar upper corridors of the Armoury building, surrendered him to Aldanov, and pressed his hand.

'You have been working too hard,' she said. This afternoon, I shall take you for a ride in the country.'

Marriner's heart was bumping over a rough road, the long road beginning with the break from Celia and recruitment by Challenby. There was no mistaking Svetlana's intention; he knew that if he wanted to move, she was providing the opening.

She took him to the Botanical Gardens at Prospekt Mira in the little Lada.

'Please. Not yet. Don't talk to me until we get there.' It seemed to him that Svetlana also was wrapped up with a secret that frightened her.

They rattled through the Moscow streets and drove through the gates to a car-park. The concrete was hot underfoot, and even the weeds had withered.

'First I show you the Alpine section,' she whispered. 'It is quiet there.'

It was a sultry afternoon, the sun high in an unclouded blue sky, and Svetlana took off her jacket and carried it over her arm. What looked like a batik shirt was in fact her own sweat. She had managed at last to give them all the slip, Kirilov and Aldanov and company, and Marriner sensed that she was coming to a private confession in her own time.

The gardens were large and uncrowded, the rockeries brown and deserted, the plants dried up. Only some straggling conifers at the end of the park made an attempt at shade. A family with teenage children trudged off in one direction, two off-duty soldiers wandered round in another. Otherwise the gardens were empty as they toiled over the grass.

Svetlana was glancing behind, nervous of shadows. As uncertain of each other as strangers, they walked towards the rock terraces and the trees: pines, cypresses and junipers scattering a carpet of needles on the baked ground.

One last look behind them, and then they were inside, in a dark, cool sanctuary of red-brown barks, fissured, scaly, grooved, like the enchanted wood that he had seen at the Bolshoi. She hugged him there.

He knew then that she was a witch.

Svetlana was clinging, and pleading, in that private world, dripping with perspiration, trembling against him. No words. Nothing but murmurs as she clutched him, obscuring the fixed points that he disciplined himself to remember: Celia, Katie, Challenby, the whole bloody balls-up of his married life.

He broke away, and they stood flushed and anxious, two animals watching each other.

'What do you want of me?' she asked.

The wood was silent around them. Only the far-off noises of a train, the thud of some building excavations, told him they were still in Moscow. He leaned against a juniper tree and the rust-coloured bark peeled away in his hand.

She found a space between the trees and motioned him to sit down, quietly, hands round her knees like a small girl, face half turned to him, unsmiling.

Thoughts flooded into his mind. How in God's name did he begin to explain? Challenby and Orford, Celia and Katie loomed before him. Easy to sit on your arse in Whitehall and proposition other people; still possible to chicken out now. Except that he had Celia to try and salvage, the price of saving Katie's happiness. That streak of love was like the sunshine through the trees.

Svetlana touched him gently on the arm.

'Well?'

He said, 'You tell me first what you want.'

She ran a hand down her bare brown leg, disturbing the blonde prickles, then pressed her fingertips together. Somewhere a siren wailed, a banshee howl as they sat in the private trees.

'That's easy,' she whispered. 'I want you to get my collection out of Russia.'

67

Her collection. He stumbled on to the word that she had used before. Marriner was not a man who found deceptions easy, and he feared he might have to deceive her as his heart hammered his ribs.

'Defection. Isn't that the right word? I want to leave my job in Moscow, and get everything out.'

Defect. Leave. He brought himself to understand. It was what he was meant to be saying the other way round. Svetlana saw the hesitation, and bit her lip.

'Help me.'

'What do you mean? Why can't you leave anyway?' he asked.

She stretched out her hands on either side, hunching her shoulders.

'You don't understand Russia, do you?'

'I suppose not.'

Svetlana began to cry, a tiny trickle of tears.

'I want to get out with enough money to survive.'

'Please don't,' he said. 'Look. You are well-off here. You have a good position. Money. Friends. What about your family?'

'My mother and father are dead. My sister, she is married. A long way away. I do not see her.'

'Then why don't you simply leave?'

She put her hand on his wrist.

'First, I have to get permission. Next, I have to support myself, to find a job. And then . . .' Her voice trailed off.

Svetlana was very close again, her head between him and the sunshine.

'Please, David. I do not tell you lightly. I have many things that I want to sell.'

'Sell?' he asked incredulously.

She nodded. 'Yes. I told you I am a collector. In my position you know where to buy. Many things in the Soviet Union have been almost thrown away in the past . . .'

'What sort of things?'

'Icons,' she said. 'Religious things. Beautiful paintings, little pieces of silver and glass. Chalices, reliquaries. But mainly it is my pictures, the memories of old Russia saved from the Revolution. Seventy years of neglect. I have over fifty icons,' she breathed. 'All of them are beautiful and many would have great value . . . in the West.'

He sat up like a man in a nightmare. How could he be sure that she was telling the truth, that this was not some dreadful double-game on behalf of the KGB? And yet in his book of conduct Svetlana was asking for rescue.

'I can't . . .'

'What do you mean?' She was on her feet, wiping away the tears, glancing anxiously around the trees as if there were gremlins in them.

'For Christ's sake,' he said. 'Hold on. What you say about leaving is dangerous.' He licked his lips, his mouth dry as a bone. 'How do I know I can trust you?'

'Me?' She stood upright and tense, hands on hips, glaring down at him.

'Yes. Why pick on me? I don't want to be a fall-guy.' He scrambled to his feet and faced her.

'Fall-guy?' She was puzzled. 'I only want your help. You are someone who understands these . . . obsessions . . . with the past.' She seemed confused, her face a high colour, the blue eyes worried.

'David,' she begged, fresh tears running down her cheeks.

He stared at her. It compromised his own proposal; and what did he really care, about her, or the past?

'Kiss me,' she said.

Their mouths met and hers was surprisingly cautious, as tentative as a young girl. He put his proposition then.

'You must help me first,' he said, his voice sounding thin and strange. 'To see someone else in the Kremlin. Not part of the museum.'

They broke apart. There was a long silence, as if each of them had gone too far. Fear and distrust on her face gave him a sense of reassurance.

'Who is it you want to see?' she whispered.

Marriner took the plunge. Now or never, his heart pile-driving like the noises off. 'A man called Borovik. Vasily Vasilyevich Borovik.'

She sucked in air, standing apart, her fists clenched, her face drained white, an alabaster saint.

'Who is he?'

He could feel his own nerves jangling as he repeated Orford's patter. 'The head of the chemical warfare programme of the Soviet Union. Knows everything about it: the stockpiles, the sites, the extent to which it has been declared in the SALT talks. Lives and works inside the Kremlin, and he wants to leave because he no longer believes that such a programme is right.'

Svetlana began to sob quietly.

'For God's sake . . .' Marriner said.

Between the snuffles she murmured, 'So you are prepared . . . to trust me?'

'I have to.'

'How important?' she asked. 'This man . . . you call . . . ?'

'Borovik. Very important,' he said. 'He advises the Central Defence Committee. Head of the *apparat* for the chemical industry.' He hoped to Christ that London's information was accurate; there had been too many cock-ups.

She shook her head. 'Why should I know him? The Kremlin is a big place. Many people are working for the Party there, the Secretariat and the Politburo, on the political side. And the Military. Why should I know them? I am only a scholar, an archivist.' She shuddered. 'I am feeling cold, David. Let us go back in the sunshine.'

And he knew she was lying. Orford had briefed him that Borovik was a frequent visitor to the Armoury, and that the runner who had passed on Borovik's appeal had observed him there, talking to the blonde young woman who was the museum director. Marriner distrusted her, and felt he had gone too far.

'OK,' he said, 'let's walk.'

They dusted the twigs from their clothes and emerged between the trees into the hot afternoon, as if parting a curtain. The rockery plants had withered, and groundsel, thistles and dandelions were overwhelming them, but in the beds dug in the borders he saw dying tulips, dark splashes of red. Two old women in head-scarves were cropping the heads with shears.

Svetlana and Marriner, Russian and English, walked slowly towards them.

'I'm told you do . . .' he said.

'Do what?' She stopped and faced him.

'Know him. This man Borovik. You have been seen with him,' he said. 'Why do you lie to me?'

He watched the colours change in her face.

'What do you mean?' she spat. 'What do you know about lying? What do you understand about me? About what I really want? Do you know why I am so unhappy?' She wiped her eyes. 'Russia is

70

too . . . full of lies.' She rubbed her hands around her neck as if she was choking.

He walked by her side, not touching, remembering the time when he had courted Celia much like this. Uncertain, fragile Celia. The women working on the flowerbeds did not even look up.

'You do not want me,' she said slowly.

'Svetlana. I have been asked to come for a different purpose. Because you know this man Borovik. That is all.'

Her voice was shaky now. 'No, it is not all. What about me? My icons for your Borovik. Is that not fair?'

He could not see how to make it work.

'I don't think that is possible, Svetlana.'

She dug a toe into the grass, kicking up a puff of dust. Fifty yards behind them now the two women on their knees were resting and watching.

'You must help me,' she begged. 'In the name of God.'

'I don't see how I can,' he muttered, not knowing how to respond.

'Please.'

'I'm sorry.'

'Swear to help me.'

'I can't.'

They were silent for a while together, as if the enormity of their admissions had shaken them, then they walked back over the gravel paths. More people about now, a couple of families, some young girls on an outing, the same drifting parties of off-duty conscripts that they had seen before.

'Why can't you help me?' she whispered.

'I will report it to London. After that it's up to them.'

'It cannot be impossible to find some way out. The system, it is not so strong any more.'

'I will ask my friends. It won't be easy.' Orford's plotting in London seemed not quite real.

It was very hot now. He wiped his brow on his sleeve.

'There is a café,' she said. 'Let's get a drink. It is not very good, but there will be tea.' He saw a glass-fronted building with a heavy slate roof, like a converted barn. Inside there were small tables, opposite a serving counter.

'I will buy the tea,' she said. 'It will be easier.'

He watched her as she queued for two earthenware cups and a

71

couple of cakes: slim figure, those fine legs, the blonded hair. Not Russian, but European, he told himself. Had not Gorbachev called it a common European house? If she really owned those things, why could she not export them to the West?

When she returned, he asked, 'How can I be sure these pictures are legally yours?' He watched her face.

'Because I tell you truth. Always.'

'And Borovik? How do you come to know him?'

'He is interested in beautiful things.'

'Such as you?'

She demurred. 'He comes to see the Armoury. Especially for the fabrics.'

'Fabrics?'

'Silks and brocades,' she said. 'Embroideries. You saw some of them. I showed you.'

Marriner stirred the lemon into his tea. 'Why should he come to see you about silks and brocades? Is he your lover?' he asked.

She frowned and shook her head, then put her fingers on the table as if measuring it. Two couples sitting nearby were staring at them.

'Make love?' she said softly, in English. 'Not with Vasily Vasily-evich.' For a moment she thought of the men she knew in that capacity, like Henrik Asterharzy the airline captain, and compared them to soft-featured almost feline Borovik with his beaky face and priest's hands, the glasses and the balding head. She smiled.

'Our interests are purely professional. Academic. Borovik is a homosexual.'

Marriner digested that further admission.

'And yet he comes to see you?'

'I tell you. He works nearby, in the Palace of Congresses. Why should he not walk across, within the Kremlin?'

And give someone a message. Within that great fortress Marriner began to realise, so monolithic to the rest of the world, beat all kinds of passion and human frailty, loves and ambitions and fears. Perhaps it was not so unnatural that some of them should find each other out, be drawn to each other by invisible wires.

As if to confirm, she said, 'One day, I talked to him.' Then a shrewd dig. 'You have a wife,' she said. 'For you it is different.'

She was reminding him, as if he could ever forget.

'I don't know.' He was back on duty, for Celia.

Surprisingly, with that revelation, looking round at the dull faces in the café, he felt suddenly confident that he could work something out, for all of them.

'What will you do now?' she asked.

'I think you'd better show me your pictures,' he said.

It was an astonishing sight to Marriner's eyes when at last she took him to her apartment. They went back in the evening after a drive to see Moscow from the terraces of the University on the West bank of the river. Mingling with the crowds in the warm air they might well have been lovers, hand in hand, instead of revolutionaries plotting each in their way against the State. As she led him into the block of apartments off Arbat Prospekt he did not know what to expect.

She had assembled a vision that made him gasp. He came up with her, as other lovers had done, and perhaps (he wondered) Borovik, in the rickety cage lift of the turn-of-the-century building with its ornate ceilings and high corridors, to the fourth floor. She stepped out in front of him and unlocked the heavy, white-painted double doors. Inside he saw a narrow passage, lined with books, a bedroom leading off with its door closed, a galley kitchen and store cupboard, bathroom, lavatory, and then the grand salon with its balcony, into which she led him, as small as a schoolgirl in front of him.

She stopped by the door and switched on the record player, a Philips from somewhere, and Bach's organ music, muted, swelled in the background. But he was stunned by the pictures, row on row, in that great serried room, her boudoir, her private escape. These were the haunted faces of the saints and saviours of pre-Revolutionary Russia, staring at the intruders, woman and man, joined in secret dealings. He had the feeling that similar thoughts were going through Svetlana's mind as she stood watching him, breaking open a bottle of vodka.

'Take your time,' she said.

He knew that these were great art, without knowing why. That she had an eye for the wonder, the suffering humanity, in those dark pictures on wood and canvas crowding the walls.

'St Saviour, St Jerome, St Simeon Stylites, St George, Christ in Mercy, Christ in Majesty, Mary Magdalene, Mary, Mary as the child of God, Jesus in the Temple, on the Cross, the Church of the Holy Sepulchre, the Hills of Jerusalem, the Seventh Station of the Cross from the Monastery of Tomsk, the Stable at

Bethlehem . . .' She recited them like a litany, taking him round them one by one.

'Don't you think they are beautiful?'

'Staggering. Stunning.' They seemed to leap off the green walls, those all-knowing faces singing to the organ notes of J. S. Bach, stacked there, rescued, she said, from destruction and decay. Svetlana refilled his glass and took his hand again up the wooden stairway over the dining alcove which led to the upper tier. Even more beautiful things were tucked away there: small Russian landscapes, harmonies of russet and yellow, and pictures of ancient churches, grey shadows across the snow. There too were the silver goblets that she had mentioned, beautiful holy cups that someone had thrown away, and boxes of carved wood, alabaster and ivory.

'Jesus,' he said. 'How do you expect anyone to shift all this . . . ?'

'Sssh.' She ran to the record player and turned up the volume. He knew that she feared she was bugged.

He made a survey with his finger, counting silently . . . over fifty items of rare beauty and value, many of them several feet square, heirlooms of the country. How the hell did she imagine they could get that lot out? Not to speak of Borovik. Her Majesty's Government was capable of many things, but not, he suspected, a house clearance from 17 Arbat Place.

But her eyes told him that she trusted him and somehow expected it.

She put on more music, Slavonic dances, as the organ notes died, and made him a meal of pancakes in the little kitchen. She showed him the rest of the flat, including the bedroom with its brass-knobbed double bed and pretty pink counterpane, but he did not go inside. Sooner or later the compromise moment would come and he wanted to put it off. Instead they went back to the salon, sitting opposite each other on the benches underneath the gallery with the big Ivan the Terrible armchair unused at the end of the table as if awaiting a further guest, whether God or the KGB, Marriner could not be sure.

They ate and drank, and he pieced together something of her past life: the happy childhood in Leningrad when her father had been so brilliant in the Hermitage, rising to become the youngest ever Director. And then the sudden death by heart attack at forty-three after which the privileges faded, along with her mother's health, as they moved from the official apartments and withdrew to a flat in Moscow. That had been twenty-five years ago, just as she was growing up, and both Svetlana and her sister had struggled to replace the father they had lost.

The drink was soaring round his head.

'My sister married,' she said.

'Why not you?'

'I don't know. I still have time. I'm not afraid of men.' She smiled.

'I realise that.'

More faces were looking at him, in addition to the saints. Celia frowning and Orford in some nook of clubland commenting to Challenby or Bullivant. 'The bugger is horny. All he wants is a woman who'll screw him, instead of that frigid wife.'

The heads and the music moved.

It was late. A clock struck eleven. Svetlana was tired, leaning back, the afternoon's sweat dry now on her shirt, the hollows of her armpits dark.

She yawned. 'You'd better stay here,' she said.

But Marriner stood up. He was not sure how he managed it but he stood up, his legs seemed firm and he knew that he was within distance of the Rossiya Hotel.

'I can't promise you anything,' he said.

'What do you mean?' She seemed to slump against the table, partially defeated.

Against the dance of the music he bent down and whispered, 'You must help us with Borovik, and I will ask London about all this —' he waved his hand at the eyes of the saints. 'But it's not in my power . . . you understand?'

'Please, don't go. Stay with me tonight,' she appealed. 'Please, David.'

Crazy, crazy woman.

He shook his head. 'One day, perhaps. But not tonight, honey.'

She looked up in alarm.

'Where are you going? David. Please! Where?'

He moved towards the door and opened it, switching on the light in the passage, knowing he had to bale out if he were not to be trapped for ever. But she came after him, throwing herself at him.

'David. No. Don't go.'

The faces stopped preying and praying as he left the room. The spell was broken; the colder air refreshed him. He turned to shake his head.

'I want you,' she begged.

'It would be impossible between us,' he said. 'Not this time, not tonight. Not ever. Don't you see? It would be stupid. Stupid. Go to bed. Forget it. Forget me.'

'Where are you going?' she asked desperately.

'Rossiya,' he said. 'Then London. They've got some work to do.'

9

'Good God,' Orford said. 'What are you back here for?' He squinted at Marriner across the polished woodwork of Tom Challenby's desk. 'What have you done with Borovik?'

Something in Marriner's face made him uneasy as they confronted him in Challenby's Whitehall office. Orford had come in a hurry when the Ministry of Defence man telephoned sounding agitated less than an hour before.

'Denis? I think you'd better get over here. He's home.'

'Home?' For a moment Orford, enmeshed in separate business over the Armagh ambush, did not register.

'Marriner,' Challenby said. 'Our chum Marriner. He's just back from Moscow. Flew in this afternoon and says he wants to see me.'

'What did you say?' Orford snapped.

'What d'you expect me to say? He's coming here at five-thirty.'

'Fuck it,' Orford retorted. 'All right, I'll be there.'

When he appeared, the red thatch matching his face, it looked as if he had climbed all the way to Challenby's deck on the sixth floor of the M.o.D. building.

'You OK?' Challenby asked, while Sandra brought in coffee.

'Yes,' Orford said gruffly, eyeing Sandra's back. 'Dusky little beauty. Is she safe?'

Challenby nodded. 'Double p.v.'d. Kenya Asian. More loyal than the Brits.' He passed over the digestive biscuits, but they hardly had time to nibble before Marriner was in the room, trailing a Globetrotter suitcase and bottles of duty-free which he dumped on Challenby's carpet.

'David? Nice to see you. What brings you back so soon?'

Challenby's eyes were unenthusiastic. 'We thought you had some research left, in the Kremlin.'

'I've done it,' Marriner said, perspiring. 'I've seen Svetlana Malinkova.'

Orford took his cup in both hands, as if he was warming them.

'What about our friend Borovik? Did you look him up?'

'I didn't see him, if that's what you mean. But there is a line through Svetlana.'

Challenby and Orford exchanged glances. 'We bloody well know that,' Orford trumpeted.

'Then why back so soon, old man?' Challenby asked smoothly, his voice telling Orford to play it softly.

'Because I've no idea how you can do it,' Marriner said.

'Do what, David?' Challenby persisted, resting his elbows on the desk and playing with a cuff link. His shirt had bold green stripes.

'Get out two people, and a private collection.'

He told them what he had found. What Svetlana had said about her relations with Borovik – 'she sounds a real fantasist,' Orford complained – and what she had to bring over.

Challenby stood up, put his hands in his pockets and strode over to the window, looking down from the rooftops over the Thames.

'Your pigeon, Denis.'

And Denis Orford growled at Marriner, who sat there in a crumpled suit straight off the Moscow plane.

'What did you come back now for, for Christ's sake? You could have tried a bit harder.'

Marriner stared at him as Orford combed his hair with his fingers.

'I thought you might say that. It's my neck though. If you want to get that fellow out, you'd better find a different lunatic to play the go-between.'

'Ah.' This was better, Orford thought: the same spunk that Marriner had shown before. Cross buggers with problems, they were the ones with potential, you could drive them.

'What about the girl?' he asked. 'You going to let her down?'

'I'm not going to risk the – what's it? The Lubianka – for anyone's sake. That's for sure,' Marriner retorted.

'David. Nobody was suggesting it.' Challenby came back across the room and sat down behind the desk. He waved his hands vaguely as if to show it didn't matter. Inside himself he was troubled. Arnold Bullivant had told him that they must get

Borovik, and get him fast. The problem was that he had to work through Orford, this was away team territory and Orford was erratic and old. He looked – Challenby frowned, trying to put words to his doubts – he looked half-cut.

'Not to worry,' Orford said. 'Plenty more fish in the sea. Can I have another biscuit, Tom?'

Distractedly, Challenby passed them over and Orford handed them round as if he was the vicar.

'Things any better at home now?' Orford asked, in the same vein.

'I'm going there to find out. I need time.' Marriner wanted to see their backs, all of them. He had a job and a wife to sort out, and Moscow was another world. Curiously, Orford seemed to agree, as he held out his hand. 'Well. Thank you for trying, David.'

'Is that all?' Marriner enquired defensively.

Challenby was at his smoothest. He might have come straight from his club and a game of snooker. The message was it didn't matter, and Marriner didn't either.

'David. We mustn't hold you up. Let me get Sandra to show you out . . .'

'No need Tom, I'll wander down with him,' Orford said cheerfully. He didn't even have a briefcase, Marriner noted.

They walked along the corridor and Orford said they'd take the lift. It was a small cage and he was a big man in a dark blue suit, so that they were pressed together as it shot swiftly down and deposited them at the south entrance, facing Richmond Terrace.

'Want a ride?' Orford said.

Marriner picked up his case, with the Club Class label still on it, and the plastic carrier with two bottles of vodka.

'No thanks. I'll get a tube.'

'Sure?'

'Yes.' All he wanted was out, he had the feeling that they were slipping a net over him even now, and he was not sure why. Surely they had other pebbles on their little beach to play with. The Whitehall traffic growled past, taxis and red buses, under the plane trees. Downing Street was opposite, only yards away, shut off by policemen and a pole barrier. There were flags out for a state visit, and, as he hesitated, Big Ben boomed the quarter-hour.

Orford looked into Marriner's eyes and still saw what he wanted as he paused to unlock his Volvo estate.

'Don't fuck me about, David,' he said.

Marriner glared at him. Bully boy tactics again.

'What do you mean? I gave you no commitment.'

'You know what I bloody mean. I want your help, David. Stop thinking about your skin.' He leaned closer. 'Concentrate on two things. One is your wife and kid, if you really want to see them home. I warn you, David, we can turn Edmondson on, and we can turn him on you. You follow me?'

'Are you threatening me?'

'For Christ's sake, David,' Orford said mellowly. 'You should know us better than that. I'm helping you. Helping you to the right advice, free of charge. Think of that, and your career.'

'What's the other thing?' Marriner asked, in spite of himself. A funny sort of help, he thought, spiced with threats and intrigue.

'Ah well, yes. The other thing is Svetlana. You'd be a fool, wouldn't you, to pass her up? And a shit, David, if you let her down.'

'I'm not having an affair . . .'

'My dear David, who mentioned an affair? I'm talking about integrity. And money. A share in the proceeds. Legitimate money, if that collection comes over here to be sold. Stand up and take your chances, David.'

'Her collection, not mine.'

'Oh come on. After you've rescued her on a white charger?' Orford grinned. 'Anyway, some other time. Got to be going now. Maybe I'll give you a ring. Hope things improve with Celia . . .'

He shook hands and started the car, as Marriner walked away to Westminster Underground.

It was a far cry from Arbat Prospekt to High Barnet. Marriner trailed back, suspicious of their intentions, Challenby and Orford and the ones behind them, including Arnold Bullivant, the white-haired bastard, who he suspected had set the whole thing up over lunch in the Athenaeum. He knew that they were manipulating him, that he was the expendable tool, worked over by the confident voices and the old boy conspiracy. He hated their guts: what he wanted was his own happiness, away from this murderous game, with enough cash for a decent home, and Katie's future secured. Instead of which there was Svetlana, her hair as blonde as wheat, begging him to help her leave Moscow. As the tube rattled northwards he sweated in his mind between two very different women, each of whom offered him something, and wondered what move he could make to resolve the impossible dream that somehow they would merge into one.

He took a cab from the station at the end of the Northern Line and the whole complacent suburb seemed to be shouting at him. In the summer evening it had a mock Tudor emptiness, as he came back to Celia. It never changed, that backcloth, that terrible dullness. Even the neighbours seemed permanent, unavoidable. He met one of them now, outside his own front door, a retired accountant named Bottomley walking his dog round the trees, a grey-suited wreck like some old pigeon.

'Hello, been abroad? Thought we hadn't seen you about.' Bottomley tugged at the dog-lead, 'Not there, Sam,' and eyed Marriner's duty-free vodka.

'Moscow,' Marriner said. No reason to conceal it, but all the same it sounded mad, a flight to a confused society offering women and secrets, pressed on him by those voices in Whitehall, on whom he was turning his back. And yet . . . and yet . . . he could not quite admit it.

Strangely, there was envy in Bottomley's eyes, as if he wished he were thirty years younger, as straight-backed and clear-headed as the returning traveller.

'You chaps get around at the tax-payer's expense.'

Standing in the evening light, fumbling with his door-key Marriner might have been a man coming home from holiday. 'That's right,' he said, unlocking the black painted door of number 34 with its little hard diamond of coloured glass above the letter box, one small opaque pane through which he could see her moving in the hall. Inside himself he hoped, Christ how he hoped, that this time it would be different.

Celia opened the door. Smart hair, dark sweater, black trousers, a glass of gin in her hand. He knew that it was not the first drink. She held it wide to let him in, without a word.

'I'm back, darling,' he found himself saying.

'So I see.' You tell me why, she implied. 'Come in.'

'Celia –'

'Yes?'

He dumped the case on the carpet and said, 'Forget it.' The hall had that empty look of people who had just moved in: in fact they

80

had been there eight years. She wasn't trying, apart from the vases of paper flowers. It hurt him to see her like that, as he asked, 'Is Katie in?'

'No. She's gone round to Tamsin's. We didn't know what time you'd be back.'

But he'd telephoned to say he was coming so it should not have been a surprise.

'There's a pie in the fridge if you want something,' she said.

'Great.' It was absurd, this play-acting between them that she kept house, the little woman who provided his shirts when all she wanted was to put him through the wringer. He walked into the kitchen, knowing it was no good saying, 'Darling, let's talk, let's be reasonable, think of the girl.' If he so much as started she would freeze into silence and stump upstairs.

Instead, she followed him into the kitchen and watched while he plugged the kettle in for a cup of tea.

'I'm thirsty,' he said. 'Must be the plane travel.'

She nodded. For God's sake what stopped her opening up?

'Did you get my card?'

She nodded again. 'Yes. Thank you.' The Moscow underground. Celia was hovering, half-interested, balancing her glass on the table while he found a cup and teabags.

'What was it like? Moscow?'

That was better. Marriner considered carefully how he should respond. 'I really didn't see much of it. We were looking at documents inside the Armoury. A lot of stuff about firepower, firing arcs from infantry squares. The average rate of fire was three shots a minute apparently.'

She sniffed. Technical stuff. 'The Armoury is inside the Kremlin, isn't it?' She drummed her fingers, scenting something. 'Who is we?'

'We? Oh. Various Russians. The curator in charge of weapons, a man called Aldanov –'

'What was he like?'

'Like? Well. You know, middle-aged, grey hair, glasses. Specialist on field guns, so he said, up to 1860.'

'What about the others?'

'The others? A whole crowd of them, just like the ones at the Tower. Difficult names to remember. Larinsky, Kursky, Pugachev. You know what it is. Would you like me tell you what they all do?' he said wearily.

But Celia wouldn't let the subject drop. It was like her, as always, to keep on enquiring.

'What about the woman?' she asked. 'Svetlana someone. Isn't she in charge?'

The kettle was boiling and he infused the teabag, prodding it with a spoon.

'Oh yes, Svetlana. Of course. She was the one who arranged it. Opened the archives for me. You need someone like that to circumvent the bureaucracy.'

But Celia came and leaned over him as he sat on the kitchen chair, drinking the tea. She began to use her presence like a lever, hands on the back of the chair, her body close and well packed.

'Did she take you out?'

'She gave me a lunch. An official lunch.'

'Did she take you out?'

'We went to the Bolshoi,' he said.

'Ah-ha!' There was a ring of triumph in her voice. 'What for?'

'What for? The first night of some new ballet.'

'What ballet?' The questions winged in relentlessly and he could feel from the presence of her body the essence of some sexual jealousy. He found it surprisingly exciting.

'*The Golden Cockerel*. A fairy tale.'

'Huh.' Celia's breasts were almost touching him as she bent over his shoulder. But she would not come round and front him face to face.

'Was it any good?'

He remembered the music, the dancing shadows, the suns and moons of desire and Svetlana stroking his fingers.

'Magic,' he said.

'And then I suppose she took you back to her place?'

'Look. What is this? An inquisition? I went back to the hotel.' Celia was jealous, and it worried him that she was still seeking evidence.

'That woman,' she snapped.

Marriner's antennae started to twitch.

'Svetlana Malinkova is my entrée to the Kremlin Armoury, like it or not. I don't see what it's got to do with you. It's a professional relationship.' Cutting Celia off again, he realised.

'Are you sure it's purely professional?'

'Yes.' He had had enough, but the inner voices were troubling, remembering Svetlana's invitations, and the walk in the botanic gardens. Also that high room, her private museum, where the music boomed and the saints' heads looked down, dark brooding eyes of Russia. He finished the tea thinking of her.

'What time will Katie be back?'

'I don't know.'

She had pulled away from him and was rinsing his cup in the sink, a ritual cleansing. Marriner addressed her back, conscious of the firm flesh. He wanted someone, and he dared not touch her.

'Look, darling . . .' he began.

'I'm not looking, and I'm not darling.'

'Of course you are, to me. Celia we've got to talk –'

'I'm not discussing anything tonight.' And with that parting shot she put the newly clean cup upside-down on the draining board and disappeared.

He went upstairs to what was now his bedroom, carrying the case, and dumped it on the bed. The contents tumbled out at him, used shirts and dirty socks, the detritus of foreign travel, and the mohair scarf that he had intended to give her. Something fell from the coverlet, where he had failed to see it, and he retrieved two envelopes from the floor.

One was in Katie's hand. 'Daddy.' A childish drawing of two waving flags: the Union Jack and the Hammer and Sickle, with a brown blob, presumably meant to be a bear, running around between them. Or was it him? 'Welcome home' it said. Katie knew what she was doing, and what she wanted to preserve.

The second was from Edmondson, answering her cussed solicitors. Edmondson the legal eagle had kept his word, and frightened the shits out of them. 'Whereas it has been brought to our notice . . . suggestions of immorality . . . physical and mental cruelty . . . etc . . . etc . . . all utterly refuted . . . my client denies absolutely and categorically that any breakdown in the marriage has occurred. He is able and willing to support, sustain and cherish . . .' Marriner let the jargon flow over him. So that was it then. Edmondson and Boughton, Law Practice Limited, had done their stuff, as Challenby had promised. A sense of relief slowly and gradually unthawed him, until he began to realise how tense he had been. It was over. It was done. He had found a way of keeping the home together, and for the next ten years that was the key objective, ten years until Katie would be independent.

He whistled between his teeth. He owed Challenby something.

Life went on for a while as if nothing had happened. Celia's solicitors must have had the original of the Edmondson letter but no word on it passed between them. All these legal flurries might have been pure fiction as they sat down to meals, asked Katie about her schooling, went shopping together on Saturdays. He wanted to confide in the neighbours, the Bulmarshes next door or the Lanyards nearby, but circumstances drew him back, as if he could no longer trust anyone. Celia's conduct still forced him to live apart, and she remained reclusive, unwilling to open out. A façade of a marriage, and the only people who knew, apart from that Whitehall cabal, were his sister Patricia and Victor Burgloss his boss in the Tower, both of whom opposed charades. What they meant was to give it up, let the divorce go through, strike out on his own. And yet he still searched for a key that might unlock her affections.

'I have to say,' Burgloss counselled, over a drink in his office, when Marriner tried to explain, 'have to say it sounds like a busted flush.'

'A what?' Marriner was not even listening. What Burgloss said was irrelevant.

'Dead duck. Finished. Not repairable.'

But there was always Katie, who wanted them to do things together. Katie was small and pert, and sharp as a pin. Aware of too many divorces among her friends, determined to keep her parents together, scheming in a half-cunning way to overcome the barriers. 'Let's go and have a picnic this weekend,' or 'Why don't we go to the seaside? Zoë's parents have a chalet that we could use . . .'

Until even Pat swung round, on the receiving end of Katie's charm. 'I see what you mean, David. I wouldn't want to hurt her.'

'Hurt her?' he said. 'Katie's everything.'

Patricia hunched close while Celia was out of the room. 'David. Could it ever work again? As a real marriage, I mean? Aren't you kidding yourself?'

His thoughts seemed far away. 'I don't know. What's eating into us?' he said.

She suspected there was another woman, and the knowledge was a form of torture. When they were children she remembered them finding a cat, a wild, abandoned animal that he had wanted to keep, but their mother said no. He had crept out and fed it for

84

weeks until one day it disappeared. David had cried and cried for something he had set his heart on but could not succeed in taming.

Celia came back smiling, as if nothing was wrong. 'Patricia. Do try this cake. I baked it specially.'

And his sister covered up, as confused as he was, as she accepted a slice.

A fortnight later there was a further letter. He was at home when the post arrived, and it was extraordinary the way Celia played it, as if such exchanges of broadsides were part and parcel of marriage. They had seen Katie off to school and shared a late breakfast because he had a meeting at the British Museum. Without a word, Celia handed him the envelope from Pitt Rivers and Fawley, her solicitors, and returned to the *Daily Telegraph*.

Marriner put the letter by the side of his plate and tried to savour toast and marmalade.

'I might be back early tonight,' he said.

'Oh. Right. I shall be out. Katie has a key.'

'Out?'

'Yes.' Nothing to do with him of course. 'I'll leave you something to eat.'

'Look, dear . . .'

But Celia was gathering her skirts, pulling the housecoat round her and smiling blankly at him. 'I must get dressed.'

When she had gone he stared for a long time at the envelope before slitting it open. Somehow he still hoped it was all going to go away, this subterfuge, the silences, the ritual of two people going through the motions; but he knew it wouldn't, the thick envelope told him as much. Celia was surface normality, her complexion clear and her eyes blue, well manicured, dressed and coiffured like a partner in a successful business. But the firm was his marriage and between them the partners had turned in a loss.

He unfolded the letter slowly. It was a new petition, and Celia was crazy if she thought it would work.

He knew as much from what she alleged. Every domestic detail remorselessly catalogued. Five minutes late was an insult, forgetting an errand a crime, failing to invite her – God knows she would not have gone – to some official function was a personal humiliation. And there were allegations which set his word against hers: attempts to molest and disturb her in the night; running after other women during his trips abroad. Above all failures: failures to understand, consult, support, finance, agree, accept, along with a refutation of his whole defence. Marriner in short was unloving, a self-centred, scheming, devious, sinful bastard.

And this was his wife, taking him to the cleaners. He could hear her now, moving about upstairs, waiting for him to go out.

He found himself staring at the suburban garden, and wanted to open the window, to find some air. But it was only a lawn with a few straggling bushes and the apple trees, and even that seemed constricting, shut in by wooden fences, surrounded by similar houses, overlooked. He walked outside, pacing to the end and back like a prisoner in an exercise yard, and as he turned he caught a glimpse of her face at an upstairs window. Watching. Waiting.

She was not going to get away with it, but he wondered why she still tried, why Edmondson's dry catechism of rebuttal had not been enough.

Celia, for her part, saw him react and decided that Werndl had been right. Oscar Werndl, who had invited himself one afternoon by telephone, and asked for a private visit. Werndl with his slick hair and sunburnt skin, tall, hawk-like and patrician, with something commanding about him when he came to her door, like an ex-pilot or a cavalry type. She fell for extroverts and soldiers – David had seemed one such – and liked the German at once. Not sexual interest but rather his air of well-heeled courtesy – a skin over a blade of ruthlessness – was what had singled him out.

'It is so kind of you to see me, my dear Mrs Marriner.' He kissed her hand, and smelt of expensive toiletries.

'Not at all. How can I help you?'

'I come, you understand, in the strictest of confidences.' He had looked around the little front room as if he expected someone to be hiding behind the settee. His legs seemed too long for the seat and nudged awkwardly against the paper flowers on the coffee table. He noticed the portraits of Katie.

'Charming. Beautiful girl. Your daugher? So like you.'

Celia was flattered, and Werndl accepted coffee. She had begun to wonder what he wanted, when he would disclose himself, why he was so insistent that he came on his own, when Werndl picked up the photograph and seemed to hesitate.

'Even now,' he said, in his correct boarding-school English, 'even now I wonder whether I should have come. But your daughter reminds me that it is not just two people's lives, but the child too, whose happiness is at stake.'

And Celia had fallen for it, that mixture of charm and deceit, when he had reluctantly informed her of Marriner's 'renewed affair' with the beautiful but treacherous Svetlana. He hesitated, of course, oh how he had raked his conscience before deciding to come, an outsider, disinterested, concerned only for the welfare of a colleague whom he had known for years, and with whom he was working in Brussels on 'The Guns of Yesteryear'. Would she, could she, understand that he, Oscar Werndl, was not an informant, a fly-on-the-how-you-put-it-wall, but a perturbed observer, a friend, and almost how-you-say a kind of confessor of David Marriner's sins? An associate with their interests at heart.

She heard, she grieved, she thanked him, cool in her own reactions, as reserved as Werndl had expected, after what they had told him, Orford and Challenby. That evening when Marriner came home she had left him a note saying she was out on business, and could he fix Katie's supper.

The second petition had followed, and as Marriner saw her face at the bedroom window he knew he would continue the fight.

He went to the British Museum, upstairs and along corridors not dissimilar to those in Moscow. All museums were the same, like airports and railway stations, once you were past the exhibits and behind the closed doors. As Marriner sat through a meeting on domestic loans policy he thought again of Svetlana and her requests, knee to knee in that cubby-hole in the Kremlin stacked with the dusty archives of the Tsars. Somehow she would not evaporate from his mind, a presence more real for the contrast with Celia and the mess he was in.

White wine and sandwiches, cream cheese and lettuce, tongue and lettuce, egg mayonnaise and cucumber, the diet of the museum gourmet. And a message, in the middle of it, on a silver salver.

Marriner broke off from bubbles of conversation that he was drifting through, his mind elsewhere.

'A Mr Orford downstairs would like to talk to you,' the messenger said.

They were waiting in the central lobby, two of them: Orford the prop forward with his ill-combed red thatch, growing white at the edges, and Oscar Werndl. Werndl carrying a packet, as if he'd been buying a souvenir from the museum shop.

It was too late to duck, and Marriner walked into their greetings.

'I think you know Oscar,' Orford beamed.

'Of course. I didn't know that you did.'

Orford said, 'We have our contacts,' and Werndl was more specific. 'Denis is an old acquaintance, from his days in Berlin. We always keep in touch. I visit when I come to London.'

'Ah. I see. You seem to come pretty often. For the shopping, I suppose.'

Oscar smiled, and waved the package at him. 'Head of a boy. Greek marble reproduction. Very good quality. Good price.'

Marriner was not playing ball. 'I was in a meeting,' he said.

He found Orford clutching his arm. 'I know. They told me where you were. Your excellent lady in the Tower. But I understand it's broken up. Hope I haven't spoilt your lunch. Too many oysters not good for you.' Once again that spark of rapport, in spite of their difference, between two wrestlers. 'We ought to move somewhere less crowded,' Orford said, as they were jostled by tourists trying to buy postcards. 'How about the Elgin Marbles? Nobody stays long there.'

He led the way as if he knew the layout well, on to the echoing emptiness of the Duveen Room. A few students sat on benches; the Marbles looked abandoned and lost, out of context on the walls.

'A miracle,' Werndl said. 'A miracle they are preserved.'

'Pretty good quality, eh?' Orford ventured, wrinkling his pug nose. 'Pity they're so bashed about. Still, we've got 'em. That's the main thing.'

Marriner turned round and confronted them, the thick-set M.o.D. man and the German aesthete. He was in no mood to play toy soldiers after that morning with Celia.

'Look. What do you want? Why are you here, Oscar?'

Without lowering his voice, Orford said, 'Now come on. You mustn't let the side down. We want you to go back to Moscow, David. Have you decided yet?'

He stared at them. Was the world full of lunatics leaving him sane, or the other way round? Well, let them try.

'You must be joking. Send Oscar, since you know him so well.'

Werndl looked down his nose. 'I'd love to go, old boy, but I'm not *persona grata*.' His hands waved delicately.

'Ah. With the KGB?'

'No, no. With Svetlana.'

'She wants you,' Orford said. 'She's already told Oscar that, in Moscow.'

So Oscar had been there too, in Moscow, nosing around, maybe trying to establish whether he could get the big one, the Kremlin Exhibition for Berlin, as he had once suggested. And Svetlana wasn't interested in a man's man with a duelling scar and an all-over tan.

They were walking slowly along the side of the gallery, looking at the sculptures rather than each other, as if addressing libations to the warriors and horses. Torsos and severed heads and spear thrusts that reminded Marriner of his home battles.

'Listen,' Orford said. 'Our big man there is getting panicky. Borovik. Oscar knows all about it.'

'Nothing to do with me. I've never even met him,' Marriner told them, aware of the old uncertainties he felt about Svetlana.

'You will. You will.' Orford admired the bodies with their damaged appendages. 'Well hung lads, eh Oscar?' Then turning to Marriner he added, 'Svetlana is ready to arrange it. A meeting between you both. We got a message and we think we can work things out.'

It made Marriner angry, these constant assumptions that he would jump when they said so, and that he wanted her; and Orford spotted his confusion.

'Oh come on, David. What more do you want? You've got her on a plate.'

'I don't want her,' he said stubbornly.

'Don't you?' Orford grinned. 'Wish I were twenty years younger. Jesus Christ.' He suddenly exuded sympathy. 'By the way, how is your wife?'

It was an unfair shaft, below the belt, and Orford knew it. Werndl managed to look sheepish.

Marriner glared at them. He was sick of the Duveen Room, sick of museums, and sick of Orford's festering, artificial concern.

'Much the same.'

'Much the same. I'm sorry to hear that.' Orford's response was tinged with a nod of regret. 'I thought Bob Edmondson would put a stop to her nonsense.'

'He tried,' Marriner said awkwardly. 'But she's come back again. A second petition.'

'Ah,' Orford said enigmatically.

'My dear fellow,' Werndl muttered, 'I am appalled. I had no idea. How could things happen so?'

'Have you met Celia?'

'Well . . . no, of course not. But I've always assumed . . .'

'It doesn't do to assume anything about a marriage,' Marriner retorted. 'Celia's ill, and trying to break up my home.'

Orford touched him on the arm. They had come to the end of the room and were staring at the damaged tympanum. 'Tough titty.'

'I'm not going to let her.'

Orford seemed genuinely sad as he shook his head like some old actor, slowly and theatrically.

'You still intend to fight it?'

'Of course.'

Orford smiled. 'Good man. We'll wheel up the guns again for a counter-attack. I'll talk to Tom Challenby, and see that Bob Edmondson keeps going on your side.'

'Don't think you're going to buy me.'

'Buy you? That's not the point, Dave. We don't want you to worry about what is happening behind you, in your absence.'

'In my absence? For Christ's sake, who do you think you are?'

They had begun to talk loudly, attracting the attention of one of the warders, who was staring across. Lowering his voice to a conspiratorial edge, Orford added, 'Want you to help us, David. One more time. That's all I ask.'

'I told you no a couple of weeks ago. You are a persistent devil,' Marriner countered. He began to inspect some bas reliefs. Celia, Celia, Celia. And a vision of Svetlana.

'Understood, Dave, but things have developed.' His sharp change of tone froze Marriner's blood.

'Why? What now?' Marriner snapped. He could feel the screws being tightened. His questions echoed.

It was Werndl who supplied the answer. 'I have a personal message.' He sighed and paused, looking awkward. 'From Svetlana. I fear that she says she is pregnant.'

At first he did not believe it. 'Oh, for Christ's sake . . .'

Everything seemed to have stopped.

'I am afraid so. Unfortunately, there is a further complication.' Werndl managed to seem embarrassed. 'She suggests that you are the father. After meeting her in Brussels . . .'

Marriner began to laugh, causing the shocked warder to hurry towards them.

90

'Brussels. Jesus, I've never even touched her.' Yet Svetlana, his dream woman, had never seemed more real, a vulnerable flesh and blood beauty.

'Well. I'm terribly sorry, old man, but that's what she told me,' Werndl said firmly. 'What is more, she intends to write. Asked me for your home address.'

The bastards, the bastards, the bastards, Marriner thought in fury, and knew they had worked this out. The detail that could clinch Celia's revised petition. Then he began to cool down. Surely Svetlana would not be so desperate or so stupid. She was too smart for that . . . and even if it was true it could not be his child. Both of them knew that. It was a put-up job. A plot, a piece of crude blackmail; but maybe it also showed how much she wanted him.

So what did they expect him to do: disprove a paternity suit brought by a blonde in Moscow? He seemed to see the gods on the wall leering at him.

'It's rubbish,' he said. 'A pack of lies. Absurd.'

'Alas, that's what she said. She told me she would put it in writing to your wife,' Werndl added, his long nose high in the air. How far was he telling the truth or embroidering on her fantasies, or simply playing Orford's game?

'If Celia throws a letter at you, just tell her it's not true. She wouldn't accuse you of philandering, would she, David?' Orford said smoothly.

Once again he could feel them trapping him, closing in.

'I can't tell Celia anything. She doesn't communicate.' Marriner recognised a signal from Svetlana that could be a shout of despair. But it worked like a kick in the balls.

'Ah. I know. I'm sorry.' Orford offered condolence in his fatherly way. But he had a more concrete suggestion.

'Listen, David.' His face loomed hot and earnest. 'If she is pregnant you will need a denial. But it won't be plain sailing. Blood tests and all that. Not so easy in Russia.' He paused. 'If you ask me, Svetlana's inventing a reason to get you back there. She wants your help, David.'

'Help! For Christ's sake she's out to get me.'

'No. No. She wants you to go back. Oldest trick in the book,' Orford said. 'You hear me? Listen. She's sending a message: come and get me or else . . . OK, then. We take her on. You've got plenty of guts, David. Go back and we'll bring her over, her and her

91

bloody icons and our defector friend Borovik. All in one go. You read me?'

Marriner still did not know whether they had set this up or were simply taking advantage – Orford the opportunist.

'I don't know.' It was an insane proposal.

'Yes you bloody well do. Go back and get her out, and you get your evidence. A simple denial.'

'Whose idea is this?'

Orford's face was bland as ham. 'Mine. Get out of the rut, David. Do something useful for once.'

'You bastards,' Marriner said. They were prepared to use any persuasion, any weapon, he now realised.

'Now, don't say that, David. Let's do a deal. One more visit would tie everything up. As safe as houses. You can get in and out with nobody blinking an eyelid with a chum like Svetlana. Scratch my back and we'll scratch yours, including paying for Edmondson.'

'Svetlana's not my problem. I'm sticking with Celia.'

'Before you decide on that, I suggest you think carefully,' Orford said.

'Is that a threat?'

They stopped admiring the statues and walked through the Roman rooms. Marble and terracotta frozen in dignified silence, and Japanese ladies taking Polaroid photographs. Underneath Hercules, struggling with a snake, Orford said, 'We'll use Edmondson against you, if we have to.'

A cold impotent anger, mixed with the terrible feeling that Svetlana was truly desperate, drove him to ask, 'What do you really want?'

'Simple. Go back and see her. One more time. Official visit, bit of research.'

'And?'

'Ask her what the hell she's playing at, and do a deal.'

'A deal?'

'She denies that you've screwed her, and helps us to get out Borovik. We transport her collection.'

'Why? Why should I?'

'To help us and help you.'

'What else?'

'That's all, old man. You can end up in the money. Celia would like that.'

'I'm not interested in money.'

'Come on, David. I'm talking about opportunities. Sales of icons on the free market. Sotheby's, Christie's. Think of it, David: take the chance when it comes.'

'Right, well, listen to me,' Marriner said. 'If you think you're going to get two people and two or three crates of goodies out of the Soviet Union in broad daylight without anyone noticing, you need your little heads examined.'

'Lay off it, David. I tell you we can fix it. Russia's not the closed book it was. Svetlana needs you and so do we.'

Svetlana, the golden witch.

Marriner looked round the frozen sculpture in the long gallery with the chilling realisation that in the long run they were all dead, and perhaps he wanted to do something before that happened.

'So I do it?' he said. 'Just like that?'

'That's right. You do it.' He smiled. 'And we defend the divorce. Come on. Enough of culture,' Orford said. 'I'll buy you a drink at the Bunch of Grapes over the road.'

10

'I've got a couple of tickets,' Challenby said, on the telephone. 'Felicity and I would simply love you to come. You and Celia.'

'Well. Yes. Thank you very much Tom, but you know Celia –'

'Try her, David. Tell her that we insist. It's the new production of the English Theatre Company: *Antony and Cleopatra*, at the Queen's.'

Marriner sat in his office and tried to concentrate. Too many things going on, not least this pressure for him to go back to Moscow.

'I don't think Celia would –'

'I'll send them anyway, David. See if you can persuade her. If not, why not bring Katie? The ETC have got a tremendous fan club. Crashaw and Susan Lawrence make a wonderful team.'

He was selling them like a new car, hymning their praises, and when the tickets came by special messenger they were the best seats, £30 in a box.

Marriner showed them to Celia at supper with Katie who talked and talked between their silences as if she was frightened that the world would stop. Celia seemed more relaxed than she had been for some time, almost as if she enjoyed the process of recrimination that she had set in train. He was sure that the letter from Svetlana had arrived – something in Celia's manner showed that there was a new secret, an extra nail in the coffin so far as she was concerned – but of course she would never show him, she merely gave him to know.

'I've had further information about your lady-friend in Moscow,' she had said earlier, as soon as he came in and before Katie appeared.

'My what in Moscow?'

'That's all. I'm not discussing it. I'm just letting you know.'

'What information?'

A secret smile and no answer. 'How about a drink?' she said, as Katie blew in and gave him a hug. 'A whisky maybe?'

It was absurd, humiliating, and yet strangely comforting that they could live this charade as if the marriage meant something: perhaps in a way it still did. But even so he had not expected that she would accept Tom Challenby's invitation when he mentioned the tickets, tentatively handing them across the table.

'Oh. *Antony and Cleopatra*. That sounds marvellous. Why not?'

Perhaps she was still thinking of Burton and Elizabeth Taylor, but she agreed. It greatly surprised him that Celia should be so willing, and almost excited, as if the allegation of a seduction in Brussels, in which she hardly believed before Svetlana's revelations, added appetite. Certainly she seemed more cheerful, as she said yes. And Marriner began to hope, for the first time in years, that there might be a streak of sunshine through the clouds which had darkened their relationship. Celia was nodding at him.

'What am I going to wear?'

'Wear?'

'Yes. I can't go to a first night without a decent dress.'

She looked pretty chic as it was, he had to say, but the mood was encouraging.

'Get yourself a new outfit.'

'Can we afford it?'

'Oh come on, darling,' he ventured.

She seemed to be so happy with the idea of an evening with the elegant Challenbys, able to hold the same ground, that he could not help but respond.

'OK. I'll tell him. We'll go.'

'I'll look forward to it,' she said.

No hint then of the barriers between them; whatever its objective, however real or false, the impact of Svetlana's letter had been the reverse of intended. Celia still would not mention it but she began pulling down the Berlin Wall in her mind.

'You go and enjoy yourself, Mummy,' Katie urged, sensing a compromise.

Patricia was persuaded to stay for a couple of days, partly to babysit. She forced her brother into a corner with those unblinking eyes of hers.

'Is it really changing? Getting better?'

'How can I tell?' he said. 'There's been another petition, but I'm defending it.'

'Do you think that's really wise?'

'It's what I want,' he said.

Celia was coming downstairs in her new dress, black chiffon and lace, cut tight to the figure, taking away the plumpness, causing him to feel good. Even her face seemed changed, as if life had come back, giving her a vividness that had been missing for years. Her hair had been reset, and offered a glossiness, an animal thickness that made him want to stroke it. And she seemed to respond, aware of this new interest, as their eyes met.

As he started the car to go back into town she sat beside him, in the passenger seat of the second-hand Audi.

'Why has Tom Challenby asked us?'

'I'm not sure.'

'You told me he tried to pressurise you about the Moscow business.'

Not merely was she interested, she had been taking notes when he had tried to communicate over the barbed wire. Marriner's spirits soared.

'Not so much Tom Challenby. Another prick called Orford. Him Big Chief Intelligence.'

She chuckled in her throat. 'You've got yourself in a fix.'

Was that an oblique reference to Svetlana's accusations, Marriner wondered, but prepared to let it pass.

'*Antony and Cleopatra*,' she purred beside him, warm and perfumed, as if reflecting on it.

Antony had his problems too, he thought, driving into the traffic flowing round Archway. He looked at his wife's head, turned away slightly, smiling. Life needed to be lived. Perhaps she thought Svetlana was his Cleo.

There were six seats in the box and as soon as he saw them Marriner smelled trouble. The theatre was in Shaftesbury Avenue, and he parked in Carlton Gardens, close by the Athenaeum where this conspiracy had hatched. It was a fine summer evening, warm without being humid, and they could almost feel the city, a tangible London of food and entertainment. Eros was in Piccadilly, along with the punks and the drop-outs. 'I like you in a dinner jacket,' she suddenly said.

Tom and Felicity Challenby were waiting, Tom as sleek as a penguin, Felicity in a red creation that was wired and expensive. Celia was wearing better, Marriner thought, as he saw the outline of her figure.

Challenby shook hands as if they had scarcely met. 'So good of you to come. Gather you've had a long chat with Denis.'

'Sort of . . .' Marriner eyed the two additional chairs.

'I'm hoping he'll join us,' Challenby said, beaming, his complexion shrimp pink. 'Celia, I'm sure you'll like him, and his friend.'

Marriner knew them, well before they arrived. Orford and Oscar Werndl, that curious partnership made clear to him in the BM. They slipped in just as the curtain was rising, allowing only hushed introductions. If Celia had any intention of saying she had met Oscar, he gave her no opening, only a quick, murmured hand-kiss. 'Your husband speaks so much of you. Delighted, dear lady.'

The curtains parted on a sand-pit and an arch. 'Look where they come.' Marriner heard the once familiar words as Antony and Cleopatra, gleaming with gold and oil, entered with their retinue.

> The triple pillar of the world transform'd
> Into a strumpet's fool.

He felt for Antony, who tried to prove himself between two women.

At the interval, in the bar, Challenby elbowed them to a corner where he'd reserved a table. His attention seemed rooted in Celia, as if he wanted to seduce her.

96

'We need your husband, Celia.' He produced a bottle of iced champagne. 'Has he told you that I'm trying to borrow him?'

Celia looked at them sweetly, Challenby and Felicity, and the attentive heads of Orford and Werndl.

'What for?' she asked.

'Another trip to Moscow.'

She considered, sipping the champagne. 'Really.'

'And I hope you'll help me persuade him . . .'

Marriner suddenly realised Tom Challenby was not sure. He did not know – such were the ways of his world – how far his man was committed. Orford was the centre of power, so far as trips were concerned. The evening seemed aimed at Celia, a means of softening her up. 'There are one or two little items of business there, Celia, for which we need a new face. David could be the answer.' He smiled at Marriner as if he was being recruited, quietly and privately, into a new profession.

Looking at Celia, Marriner tried to read her mind, confronted by this assault. And Celia was animated, as if new doors were opening. Who was it had been left behind by Antony's little excursion in Alexandria? He scanned his programme quickly. Octavia, that was it, Octavia betrayed in Rome.

'It's his choice,' Celia was saying above the conversation as the bell rang. Werndl, he noticed, had also locked eyes on her, and he wondered from Celia's attitude whether she had found an excitement inspired perhaps by the thought that he had a new role, that these men needed him. He must nullify Svetlana's letter, and he would go to Moscow. Orford had already recruited him. Celia's new enthusiasm as she chattered and laughed was far from a woman betrayed: it had the high pleasure of someone who herself aspired to be a Queen of Egypt.

As if he had discovered a key, it unlocked sentiments in her that he had never recognised. Celia at last was happy, engaged in the attempt to prove herself. Not yet to keep him, he was sure she had not moved that far, but at least seeing herself as a woman being asked, considered and consulted by Tom Challenby.

'We must get back,' he said as the second bell rang.

And then she put her hand on Challenby's arm.

'What you are saying is, you've selected him?'

Challenby, with Orford beside him, and Werndl inconspicuous in the rear, escorted them from the bar.

'One more time,' he said.

She glanced at David, and he knew from her eyes that she was daring him. Perhaps she wanted him out, and hoped for a betrayal, but there was also an interest, as if she herself was pitched against the other woman.

'It's up to David,' she said.

Marriner was looking at Orford, who already knew, the bastard, following the BM meeting. He seemed like some red spider, in the middle of a web where Marriner was now dangling.

'I've said I'll go.'

He heard the intake of his wife's breath.

'When?'

'I don't know, dear. We have to work that out.' He could see the emotions in her eyes, Challenby smiling, Oscar Werndl stroking his cheek, Orford standing behind them.

'It will take a few weeks to arrange,' Orford said. 'We'd better resume our seats, or else we shall miss the deaths.'

The lights came up as the final curtain dropped, and Challenby said, 'I've laid on a supper in Greek Street.'

Celia laughed with pleasure, but there was a delay.

'Ladies, excuse us for five minutes,' Orford announced out of the shadows behind them. 'Must just take David backstage. Someone for him to meet. Oscar, you coming too?'

There was no doubt that Werndl was primed.

'What about Celia?'

'Give her a chance to powder her nose. Backstage is grease-paint and underpants.'

'Will you excuse us, Celia?'

She seemed reluctant, in her new-found energy, to part from David's company, but then released him.

'A necessary part of the show,' Orford muttered, hustling them down a staircase and into the wings.

'Get a move on,' he boomed, pushing past the stage crew and actors opening cans of lager. 'Well done, lads.'

He was ushering them, Werndl and Marriner, into the crowded passage connecting the dressing rooms, a channel already cluttered with debris: boxes, panniers, containers, unused props. People were dashing by whom Orford appeared to know from some past reconnaissance.

Orford banged on a door at the end. 'Stage manager' was pinned up, handwritten on a postcard.

'Hurry up,' he bellowed.

A curly grey head popped out, anchored to a thick-set body in a cable-knit sweater and green corduroys.

'Brzezinski,' Orford announced. 'Daniel, I want you to meet the bloke I mentioned.'

Brzezinski was dark-eyed, his skin had piebald patches and the wrinkled appearance of someone from underground, but his handshake was firm.

'Daniel is the man to know,' Orford said. 'Want you to get alongside him, understand how he ticks. These Poles are bloody complicated, but good blokes, eh?' He slapped him on the back.

They crammed into the sweaty room, sitting on packing cases. Brzezinski produced some glasses.

'Can't stop now,' Orford intoned. 'We've got the women waiting. But you two are going to talk.'

Marriner liked the look of the Pole, but already it was a question of how far he could rely on anyone.

'I don't follow . . .'

'You will. You will.' Orford pointed at the clutter. 'Look at this mess, eh? Look at it, Daniel.'

'It's touring,' Brzezinski said.

'Too bloody right it is. How many truckloads, Daniel?'

'Four,' Brzezinski replied. 'Four container lorries to get this stuff on the road.'

'Big buggers too?'

The tough little man nodded his head.

'Forty-eight feet long. Two thousand items, and four hundred costumes for five plays.'

Orford turned to Marriner.

'Fancy carting that lot round. Enough to equip a small army. Don't know how you keep it all together, Dan.'

Brzezinski grinned.

'Organisation,' he explained.

'OK. Smashing. Where you going to take it to next?'

'Kiev and Moscow,' Brzezinski said, 'in October.'

They drove back to High Barnet, Celia and David, after Challenby's supper, wrapped in their own thoughts, the usual marital silences. But Celia was humming quietly to herself, as if the evening had not faded. Her face was shadowy in the dark of the car, the green dials glowing like jewels, and he thought she was smiling.

Pat was sitting up, waiting.

'How was it?' she asked uneasily.

'I enjoyed it,' Celia said. 'David even went backstage.'

It hadn't seemed possible to him that she would swing round like this, under Challenby's charm, yet here she was, smart and seductive in her new cocktail dress, offering him a night-cap.

'Katie in bed on time?'

'Sure. No problem.' His sister stared, perhaps beginning to realise this was a change of mood, under the pools of light from the standard lamps in the lounge.

'I think I'll go on up.'

They watched Pat gather her bag and say goodnight, waited while she went upstairs to the spare bedroom. Then they were alone in the room, on either side of the fireplace, drinking a night-cap. Celia slipped off her shoes and stretched out her legs on the settee, a slight furrow of concentration creasing the tip of her forehead.

'Well. What's it about?' she asked, without any resentment, as if the call to duty had impressed her.

'I'm going back,' he said. 'I promised Orford.'

'Who is Orford exactly.'

'Military intelligence. So I believe.'

'Do you trust him?'

Marriner shrugged. 'How do you know who to trust? He's Ministry of Defence, reporting to No. 10. He has his reasons.'

'I wouldn't buy a car from him,' she said.

He did not follow her, but her talking delighted him. It was as if they were sharing things that he had long since written out: an interest in his situation, and in hers.

'Can't you tell me?' she asked.

That was the hell of it. Say nothing, Orford had instructed, nothing to anyone, wife, lover or mother. Was that understood? And he had agreed.

They trapped you with their cunning, the mesh they wove. He saw it now, as his wife tried to communicate: but his lips had been sealed. Marriner kept his word: one of the reasons why Orford had selected him.

Celia's skirt had pulled up above her knees and she leaned back to arch her breasts. Perhaps she had drunk too much, but it was not the reason that she was talking. He poured himself a second drink, but she shook her head. Under the reading lights it was almost as if they themselves were on stage, examined from the silent corners of the room. The petition, the second petition in which she had numbered his sins, the trivia of a tired relationship, still lay undiscussed between them and he knew better than to try and discount it, but she was *talking*.

'I'm not allowed to say why.'

She was drawing on fresh reserves, salted away by training, boarding-schools and family loyalties.

'You're going to see that woman.'

'Yes. It's part of the job.'

'I've had a letter,' she said.

'Show me.'

'You might destroy it.'

'You know me better than that.'

'Do I?' she asked. 'Anyway, I haven't got it. It's with my solicitors.'

'They were trying to put pressure on me,' David said. 'Werndl went to Moscow and put her up to it. It isn't true what she says. I give you my word.'

She stared at him for some time before replying, a quizzical smile on her lips. It was as if she did not care, one way or the other; but the old bitterness, the churlishness, had died.

'No woman would send a letter like that to someone she did not know, unless she was a fool.'

'Svetlana's no fool,' he said. 'She knows that I've never touched her.'

Celia sat upright and watched him closely. 'Who is she?'

'Head of the Kremlin Armoury.'

She hesitated. 'I suppose she's clever and cunning. What does she want from you?'

It was his turn to hedge. 'I'm not sure, in the end.'

'I sometimes think,' Celia said, 'that you would respect me more if I had a degree, and a string of phoney letters.' It was a resentment she harboured against the academic world. She cradled her neck with her bare arms. 'So you won't tell me anything?'

'I can't. But so far as Svetlana's concerned, there is nothing to say.'

'Then why are you going back? Why did you disappear with that man Orford when the play ended?'

'To see the stage manager,' he said. 'They are touring in Russia.'

'What has that got to do with things?' Her face was bright with interest.

'I don't know yet.'

'But there's something going on. I can see it in your eyes. You're not good at lying, David.'

'I'm going to visit the Kremlin,' he said.

'You'd better take one of those kits,' Celia retorted. 'Pregnancy kits. I bet she can't get them in Moscow. Only abortions.'

It was the first time they had laughed together in months or even years. Celia stood up, and rearranged her dress.

'I'm going to bed now, David.'

David. Used as a term of endearment it startled him for a moment, and he wanted to reach out and hold her, but he knew that would be the wrong signal, disturbing the fragile ecology of this new plant.

'OK. Me too.'

She switched off one of the lamps and preceded him to the door.

'When are you going?' she asked.

'In a couple of months, they tell me. Some time in the middle of October.'

'That's when the ETC are due to go as well.'

Celia was sharp as a knife when she was interested. As if they were engaged, all over again, she seemed to be lingering near him and for one moment he thought she would come to his room, and share his bed. But she stopped on the threshold, and he wondered if Pat was listening in the next room.

'Are you going to work tomorrow?'

He shook his head. 'I've got to see a man called Brzezinski. Someone I met tonight.'

'I thought so.' She sighed, almost as if she might kiss him as tentatively as on a first date. 'You be careful,' she said.

11

The October wind gave a premonition of winter. There was a promise of snow, and the long nights to come, as it whipped the remaining leaves into spirals of brown flakes, leaving the trees bare. It was blowing a gale as the black Volga delivered Svetlana to the door of the apartment block in the narrow nineteenth-century street off Arbat Passage. The cutting edge from Siberia battered through her coat as she stumbled into the foyer, where the furnace fumes smelled of anthracite. Her boots echoed across the marble floor.

The pilot was waiting for her. Asterharzy, inside, grinning, in his dark Aeroflot uniform with the four gold rings on his sleeve, carrying his cap.

'Hello, chicken,' he said.

It set her teeth on edge. She hated that term of endearment which he used with such abandon.

She was cold as she peeled off her gloves.

'What do you want?' It had been three months since she last saw him, decorating her bed, and she hoped he had gone for ever.

'To see you,' he said.

She stamped her foot. 'I told you not to come back.' There had been the panic last time, when she had gone to the clinic for the urine tests, just as that fool Werndl had arrived, and she had the problem of trying to shake him off.

'Oh come on, Svetlana. Don't be like that.' Asterharzy gave her one of his charming smiles, and she could smell the scent of his expensive unguents, duty free, picked up abroad. He was holding out a bunch of flowers, hot house freesias from somewhere in white paper with a red ribbon.

'I thought you had gone for good.'

He shook his handsome head of dark hair.

'No way, darling. Why should I desert my chicken?'

'It's finished,' she said.

He looked her over carefully. The tailored double-breasted top coat, belted, with gold buttons, that had not come from Moscow, the high tooled boots and that cropped head of blonde hair under the silver fox fur. A desirable, unusual creature in the Kremlin desert. He wondered for a moment if she was someone else's mistress, and then decided to chance it. He wanted her, and used his relaxing, pilot-to-passenger voice.

'I need to talk to you . . .'

'You can say what you want here.' In the echoing foyer at the foot of the lift cage.

'It's not the right place,' he replied. Their hushed voices seemed to whisper round the stairwell, echoing up the shaft to the listening floors above. She knew if she took him up there into the sanctuary it would be a capitulation, a defilement, even more than in the bedroom. Asterharzy looked around. 'We can be –' and he touched his ear, to show he feared an eavesdrop.

Svetlana shrugged. He had caused her enough trouble, this big buck with the ready tool. It had been fun once, in a moment of weakness, but Mother of Saints she regretted it when her periods stopped and she had flown off in a panic to the Women's Clinic. Oscar Werndl, the Director of the Charlottenburg Museums in Berlin, who happened to be chancing by, had been unusually interested when she had mentioned it as a reason for not meeting him for dinner.

'Are you unwell, my dear?' Werndl had that solicitousness, the understanding of women, that marked out a bisexual.

'No. Just a check-up.'

'Is everything all right?'

'I think so.'

And something had clicked in his mind, she had seen it register, although she did not know what.

Now, standing there with Asterharzy, she decided enough was enough. No way was he going upstairs; he had no hold on her. 'Thank you for the flowers,' she said, accepting the bouquet still thrust towards her. 'They are lovely. But as far as I'm concerned it's over.'

He gave her a mock salute, then pointed quickly out through the high, black doors of the entrance which she had closed behind her. A waft of male perfume, Old Spice aftershave, as he clutched her elbow and whispered in her ear.

'I've got a car outside. I want to warn you.'

Alarms went off in her mind. It could be a ruse, but she doubted it, his eyes seemed troubled. He nodded vigorously and put a finger to his lips. 'I'll take you somewhere.'

'Where?'

'A ride,' he smiled.

She felt her stomach contract, the feeling that events were closing in, the half recognition that things could not go on as they were, living too close to luxury and wanting to cheat the system.

'All right.' She fumbled in her pigeon-hole to make sure there were no letters, then turned to him. 'I can't be long,' she said. 'I'm tired.'

He crushed his hat on his head, and pulled at the heavy levers controlling the front door. The knife-edged wind caught her breath. How she hated the winters, never growing used to them in spite of a lifetime there, in Leningrad and Moscow. It was a pessimist's country, she had decided, a continent at the limit of endurance, only kept sane by drink in the long barren nights of which the wind was a harbinger.

'It's just round the corner,' he said. 'The blue Skoda.'

She gathered her coat and ran for the shelter of the car, another one of his privileges. It was new and shiny, and the plastic trim had not yet started to fall apart. He slipped the key in the ignition and the engine started roughly.

'Bastards,' he muttered. 'I want to get a Mercedes.'

Asterharzy was pulling out into Kalinin Prospekt and shooting down the traffic lanes as if he was taking off.

'What's the hurry?' she asked. 'I don't want to go far.'

'Sure, chicken, sure.' A hand accidentally-on-purpose brushed her knee as he changed gear and waited at the lights leading to the Tchaikovsky section of the Sadovaya Boulevard. He was glancing in his rear-view mirrors.

'Didn't you know you've got a tail?' he said. 'They are behind us now. No, don't look around. You can see in the mirror. The black Moskvich with the white patch on the bumper.'

There was a stream of traffic as they headed round the ring road and eventually crossed the river by the Krymsky suspension bridge. At first she could not see the Moskvich, lost in the stench of exhaust fumes from the growling trucks he was passing, but as she watched it seemed to be gaining on them, swinging dangerously past the trolley buses.

'Where are we going?'

Asterharzy laughed. 'To give 'em a run for their money.' He glanced back and cursed. The bent white fender was distinctly nearer, she could make out the two men inside the car. Plain-clothes, in dark overcoats. He was into the southern suburbs now, dull avenues she did not know, lined with the faceless post-war housing and factory blocks that she had come to hate. Asterharzy stepped on the gas and they lurched forward, weaving between two oncoming trucks and into a side street. The black car followed inexorably, faster than the underpowered Skoda.

Suddenly, he braked, pulling in to the footpath underneath an elephantine tenement.

'Give me the flowers,' he said.

She handed them back to him and followed him out of the car, into the front of the building just as the Moskvich drew up. A quick glance through the doors showed that the unmarked police car was sitting there puzzling.

'I've got a grandmother,' Asterharzy said. 'Lives here with my aunt.'

He was bounding up two flights of stairs and pummelling on a door in the corridor. Svetlana stood behind him, panting. The narks were not coming, perhaps their orders were only to trace her movements. She wondered for a fleeting moment if this was another trick by Asterharzy to decoy her to some bedroom, and then dismissed it. As the door opened the room behind smelled old.

Asterharzy presented her to a grey-haired woman living with an ancient lady in a single cluttered room. The grandmother was sitting in a chair by the radiator and scarcely moved, a crone so old it was hard to tell she was living. The withered hands and worn out face made Svetlana shudder as she touched her, a *memento mori*, a used up and futile life. The pilot kissed the old woman and called for glasses of tea, then peered from the lace curtains at the cars parked below. 'They may be there for some time,' he remarked grimly.

Svetlana unfroze in the fetid warmth of the room and thawed in their kindness: they thought she was Henrik's girlfriend, and an exciting catch. She listened, bored, to their snatches of conversation; behind the glamour of his uniform Asterharzy was a hard-working professional who had climbed a difficult ladder to pilot the big jets. Perhaps he even hoped that this would impress her, too, from beginnings so unlike the Leningrad luxury of her father's advantages.

She accepted the lemon tea and a square of honey cake, balancing them on her lap. The two elderly women gazed at them with pride and awe, in that peasant way, at once protective and enquiring, that showed they had come in from the country a generation back. Her country, her soil, and yet she had been stretched out of it, educated, eviscerated, until she found it impossible to relate to their simple needs.

Instead she said, 'How did you know?'

'Observation,' Asterharzy replied. 'I came to see you twice before tonight. I couldn't get through on the telephone, so I called. Each time there was a car there, watching the entrance, so I watched them. I would say you have been under surveillance for a couple of weeks.'

The fear froze inside her: she knew what that meant. Fleas were on bigger fleas. Someone had shopped her: her mind raced to find what they knew, or could be after. No doubt they had inspected her rooms, defiling the collection, pawing her private cupboards. It made her nervous. Worse, they might have identified her meetings with Borovik – yes, that was more likely – they could be watching Borovik, poor vulnerable Vasily Borovik with his fantasies – and he would have led them to her, in those murmured conversations standing before the galleries of costume and textiles. There was even – the realisation was evident, once she started considering – even the Englishman, to whom she had put her proposition, and the German Werndl, who was floating in and out.

'You must never underestimate the KGB,' Asterharzy whispered. 'Perestroika hasn't reached them yet.'

She put down the cup and stared cautiously out of the window. The black car was still there: she could see them smoking inside, two young men in dark coats. Asterharzy was looking at her with a mixture of hope and concern.

'What have you been up to?' he asked.

She shook her head. The aunt brought her more tea, and the old woman went to sleep. Svetlana and Asterharzy were like two alien beings from another, more successful planet who had suddenly appeared and were talking their private riddles. Even the aunt lost interest as they sat knee to knee, running over the problem, a position, she realised, which the pilot found more acceptable than she herself. And yet she could not tell him, could not begin to articulate the fears inside her.

'I don't know,' she replied.

He shook his head. 'Chicken, you've got to be careful. When they start watching like that, you know what it means.'

'Yes.' An informant, a suspicion reported. Everyone inside the system was at risk. Things had not changed that much, the freedoms were still curtailed. She should have known Borovik was a marked card.

'It can't be because of me,' he said uneasily.

'No. It's not you.' She smiled in spite of herself, grateful to him and his schoolboy enthusiasm. 'It's me. Perhaps the people I see in my professional duties.'

His eyebrows rose. 'Ah. Who are they?'

She shrugged. 'Like you, I go abroad. And I meet strangers. Some of them visit me in Moscow.' Asterharzy grinned, assuming the worst, and she ignored the innuendo. 'They visit me in the Armoury.' She made no reference to Marriner.

'What sort of people?'

'Foreigners,' she said. 'A German and an Englishman.'

'Ah.' He waggled a finger at her. 'Careful, chicken.' And he was right. Russians were suspicious, insular, jealous of their patriotism; and she despised them for it. But in a sense Asterharzy seemed to give up pressurising her as soon as she told him, relieved almost at having to look elsewhere. She hoped that she appeared too complicated, too unstable for him, that perhaps these enmeshments warned him not to be stupid in going after her. The car was still there below, but he seemed to have had enough.

He stood up and said his goodbyes, to the sleeping grandmother and the aunt watching television. She realised they had been four hours stuck in the cramped apartment. The evil wind blew through darkened streets as they emerged.

'Come on, chicken. We've paid a family visit. Now I can take you home.'

Without the flowers, he drove her slowly back and deposited her by the doorway of her own building, still watched by the Moskvich. When he had left her, and she entered her own apartments, she found that she was shivering. At first she half expected to find the place turned over, but there was no sign of trouble. The rooms were as she had left them early that morning. But in her heart there was fear, fear that they'd marked off her name on some long list of 'unreliables' in the Lubianka files. It was not an efficient machine, the KGB, but it was dedicated if it picked up a scent. The problem was you never knew. Should she try to clear herself by mentioning the approach that the Englishman had made about Borovik? To condone it was an act of treachery, and she did not know that there was any chance of getting him out. But more than that she wanted out herself, if only there was a way.

She slumped in the heavy chair at the end of the dining table in the alcove. The mysterious iconography stared down at her bowed head and she ran her hands through her hair, too tired to undress, too weary to be hungry.

12

Marriner stared at the Kremlin from the snack-bar at the end of the corridor in the Rossiya Hotel. Now that he was back there, half a world away, he wondered if he was mad, but the last summer in London had been crazy enough. The redbrick Kremlin walls were lined with fir trees, above which soared the cathedrals, and the green dome of the Council of Ministers. Lenin had lived and died there, where Svetlana and Borovik now worked. He selected a table close to the well of the stairway and tried to examine the minds of the two people inside whose future was in his hands.

'Put yourself in their shoes,' Orford had urged. 'And don't take too much notice of all this glasnost crap. Borovik is at his wits' end. Top scientist suddenly hits doubt, like a bishop with a crisis of faith. You think that you've got problems? What about that poor bastard who wants to spill the beans about the extent of their stockpiles? Life and death, David, old man. You can't detect gas stocks like rockets: ask the Yanks. And germ warfare's even worse. All you want is a few spare canisters of the bloody things. Low technology these days. Borovik has the facts in his head. But fortunately for us he's also got emotional problems, personal ones that the bastards in the KGB know all about, you follow me?'

Marriner chewed his bread roll, and swallowed the tepid tea while he remembered. Orford had sent him away, two weeks in a country house lost down a lane in Wiltshire, for briefing about the uncertainties within the Soviet Union and Borovik's state of mind, as much as they knew. Not once but several times Borovik had been seen in restaurants outside the walls where he had been joined by young men, crop-haired, blond, with far-away wistful expressions, and soft moustaches. Their heads had been close togethers, whispering in public, the informant noted, as had the KGB men wearing raincoats at another table.

A gay on his own at the top of the pile looking for friends was scared, Orford said. Accidents could still happen in the Soviet Union to that sort of bugger, maybe would have already if Borovik hadn't been so important and indispensable. The West knew he had been thumbed, reported by anonymous men who were part of the apparatus of State Security. Borovik had become uneasy, and put out feelers to leave, one of them through an Aeroflot pilot who slept with Svetlana.

'You with me, Dave?' Orford had come to see him in the Wiltshire mansion one August afternoon, sitting in the library as they went over the maps. 'Don't take them with you. Memorise. The Russian ones are no bloody good.' The smell of cut grass wafted through the open window and birds were singing in the trees: it was all so absurdly natural that it had been hard to realise that the business was serious. But Orford said it had to be done, pointing a finger which he jabbed first at the map, then Marriner.

'Don't worry about Brzezinski. He's a bloody Polish exile. Hates 'em and knows his onions. He won't let you down.'

Marriner thought about that now, on his first day back in Moscow, without the faintest idea of what Brzezinski was up to. 'You'll work in the dark,' Orford had confided, over a cup of tea and walnut cake. 'Concentric circles. You'll know when they intersect. It's much safer that way than carrying a plan in your head.'

'Are you sure there is a plan?'

'Oh, come on. Of course there is. Have another cup of tea.'

It was not exactly reassuring to be watching the Kremlin now, peering at the wall of the fortress, waiting for Svetlana.

'How do I meet him, this Vasily Borovik?' he had asked Orford.

'No problem, David. All you have to do is contact Svetlana, and follow instructions,' Orford had grinned.

Marriner had left for Russia as if it was a package holiday, that was the way it was done. Orford had sent him the tickets, Club Class out, pre-booked return via Leningrad, British Airways. Celia had pecked his cheek but no one had seen him off as he humped his bags to Heathrow on the Piccadilly line, and now he was stuck in Moscow as if he had never left it three months before after his tryst with Svetlana in that strange room in the ornate building off Arbat Prospekt.

'Take care,' Celia had said, and that at least was something.

Denis Orford had telephoned, the day before. 'I don't mind what you get up to, as long as you do what you're told, and we spring Borovik.' It had sounded as if he was in a call-box. In other words, they didn't care, they didn't fucking care about him or Svetlana, so long as they could be used to bring Borovik out. And but for that meeting in Brussels, none of this might have happened; yet

110

Marriner began to wonder how much chance there had been in Ritterman's introduction on that overcast morning in July when she had walked into the exhibition hall, a woman in a dark red sweater. Thinking of her made him realise he still did not understand her. What had seemed a diversion, a burst of emotion after the struggle with Celia, had suddenly become confused, more complicated. And, even as he set out, Celia was shifting her ground.

Marriner finished his breakfast. The queue remained by the counter, shuffling forward. One of them was buying smoked eel. No one seemed to be watching him. He walked back along the corridor and gave the key to the desk girl, a fish-eyed woman who nodded and slowly put it away. To maintain his tourist credentials he tried to ask for directions, but she would not or could not understand. He spent a tedious morning at the Museum of the Revolution inspecting the horse-drawn machine-guns of the First Cavalry Army and looking over his shoulder.

In the days after Asterharzy's warning Svetlana was a cat on hot bricks every time she saw a strange back. The pilot had disappeared and it was hard to believe that she had been so naive as not to see the men in doorways. Now she seemed to glimpse them everywhere, except when she was at work within the Kremlin itself. It was as if she was safe there, sacrosanct, but as soon as she drove outside her car was shadowed, usually by the black Moskvich. Inside, at her desk, Maria the secretary became concerned, her face contorted with half-suppressed hero-worship.

'Are you feeling well, Director?' The heavy-hipped girl hesitated. 'I think you work too hard.'

Svetlana looked at her nails, and shook her head. The green light glowed on her desk as she worked late to forget, and to catch up. She was as trapped as Borovik, and struggling to find a way out.

'I'm fine,' she said. Maria was a dedicated girl, a group leader in the Young Pioneers, who sublimated her instincts and devoted herself to the office. Man trouble again, she wondered, and dared not say, but Svetlana read her thoughts.

Maria frowned as she cleared away the debris of the meal taken at the desk: a pot of yoghurt and a small cup of black coffee. 'You ought to go home and rest.' Find yourself a husband, her eyes implied, or live with someone, as long as it's not a buffoon like the schmuck I settled for.

'Thank you, Maria. Goodnight. I'm leaving now. Tell the car to come round.'

She fiddled with the tasks in front of her, unable to think clearly. Staff reports to be countersigned, a plea from Aldanov to be allowed time off to see a museum in Hungary, two dissertations for doctorates on which her views were requested, the small change of memoranda between departments. It had grown sour on her, and she was lonely; but she was also frightened. She had come too far too fast, and there were people against her, some of them in her own museum: Leonid Pugachev the party man for example.

Svetlana felt she wanted to cry, but there was no one to cry to, only a duty militiaman in the now deserted building. Dragging herself to her feet, she locked the door of the office and handed the keys as usual to the security guard who was reading at his desk in the corridor. He slipped it into a drawer and she walked down the back stairs to where the car would be waiting in the shadows by the walled garden. Even with her winter coat on, the air was bitter: a first frost sprinkled the ground and soon it would be winter. The stars punched holes in a sky as dark as murder and the driver waited with the engine running.

She stood for a moment, frozen, tempted to run away like a small girl again. But it was no good: she was a prisoner inside a fortress, the buildings looming around her. A floodlight played on the golden domes of the Cathedral of the Assumption and the red stars glistened above the Kremlin gates. In its way it was beautiful, and made her shudder.

The driver had seen her come out and shunted across. He was a new man, from the car pool, and she did not know him.

'You'd better take me home,' she said.

It was striking ten o'clock as they drove through deserted streets the short distance to Arbat. Along the river road, near the water tower on the south west corner, she thought she glimpsed the black Moskvich but when she looked again it had vanished, and she settled back with relief.

The official Volga drew up at her apartment and the parked cars lining the pavement were empty: only a single figure huddled in a doorway against the cold. She was conscious of the man watching, prying eyes in the dark, and the sense of foreboding took hold of her again. Up and down the high buildings, shuttered against the night, the chill wind rattled, flapping the plastic bags left on a building skip against the opposite apartments. The figure seemed to crane forward as she stepped from the car and wished the driver goodnight. Out of the corner of her eye, as she searched for her key and saw the Volga's tail-lights disappear, she was conscious of the figure approaching, the looming hand on her shoulder, and shrank back involuntarily as if expecting arrest.

'Good evening,' he said in English. 'Svetlana, it's David Marriner.'

She rocked on her heels in the doorway, unable for a moment to comprehend. Her first thoughts were ones of panic: who else was there with him, why should he want to approach her in this way? In a country of doorways no entry was safe, as Asterharzy had shown her. But it was the Englishman, returning as he had said, weeks after she had ceased to hope.

The key was in her hand and she stood shivering. Marriner was in a dark raincoat that the wind must have cut like a razor, but he did not seem to notice.

'You'd better come inside,' she said. 'Quickly.'

He followed her into the foyer and she pressed for the lift cage. As it ground upwards to the fourth floor she asked, 'Who sent you?'

'No one. I came on my own.'

'Was anyone following?'

He seemed very calm as he said, 'I don't think so. I've been walking round for two days, visiting places; there's been no one that I could see.'

The lift came to a halt and they stepped out before the high doors of her apartment.

'It's not safe to come here,' she said.

They were inside now – Svetlana hesitant as if she expected to find an interloper, or the signs of a search, but there was nothing – the internal passage with its overspill books, the tiny galley-kitchen in a corner, the bedroom on the left, and her gallery of icons. She walked quickly through ahead of him and switched on a single light by the music box inside the door. Their shadows stumbled across the curtained room.

Svetlana's first need was music: Beethoven's Third symphony, its familiar sounds reverberating round the walls, the volume turned up until it boomed through the speakers as if they were in a concert hall. She was taking off her coat, and pulling off her walking boots, becoming at once in his eyes smaller and more vulnerable. She switched on a second light, at the alcove table, and he could see her blonde head, sleek like the back of an animal, as she turned towards him. She motioned him to the table, not to the easy chairs which stood in front of the television, and he sat down to face her with his back to the room.

Svetlana leaned across, her cheekbones highlighted by the table lamp, her blue eyes wide with uncertainty.

'They watch me,' she whispered. 'We must talk quietly. Perhaps they are recording us. It is not good to come here. You will have been seen.'

He remembered their conversation by notes, crushed into that archive cupboard of her own museum. He saw the fear in her face, and bent forward to hear her, so that they were almost touching. He could see the pores in her skin, and a tiny mole on her cheek.

'It doesn't matter,' he said. 'You are entitled to visitors.'

Visitors. Asterharzy, and the others before him. Her unhappiness welled up, and brought tears to her eyes. He did not realise, this simple Englishman who came like a knight in armour, or thought he did.

'You have a visa?'

'Of course.'

She put a hand on his arm. He felt her tremble as she contemplated the impossible, wrenching herself away from a country she both loved and hated, dreaming of a life elsewhere, safe from these grim limitations of the socialist state. She was trying to hope.

For a few minutes they sat in silence, staring at each other's faces. He saw the faint lines in her skin for the first time, a tautness about the eyes that came from pressures inside her, no matter how calm her hands were. And she, in turn, glimpsed in him complex matters, and knew there was more to this return than an attempt to see her.

'What are you doing here?' she whispered.

Marriner shrugged. 'I have some work to do. I remembered what you said before.'

'It's crazy to come like this. I am not ready.'

'It doesn't matter,' he said. But first he had something to establish, a puzzle burning his mind. He could not dissemble.

'Svetlana. Tell me the truth. Are you pregnant?'

She did not seem to comprehend, or perhaps the directness of

114

his question stunned her. How could he know? For her part, Svetlana felt he was researching into her private life, and in that she was vulnerable. She stared at him, and said fiercely, 'Why do you ask?' What did he want; how could he begin to suspect the panic she had had when the Asterharzy affair broke up; those ghastly journeys to the clinic, trying to keep her identity secret.

'Svetlana, I want to know. Are you pregnant?' he repeated, so close that she could feel his breath and see the stubble on his chin.

She looked at him more calmly, and said, 'No. Of course not.'

He pushed his head even closer.

'Then why did you write to my wife? Why accuse me?'

Her eyes were blank with confusion, as Marriner began to realise the significance of that faked letter, while the music pounded their ears, as she replied, 'I have never written to your wife.'

Marriner stood up, and paced across the room. At that moment he did not care about the KGB, or the entire Red Army; what upset him was that Orford and Werndl, his own people, were trying to fuck around with his marriage. Svetlana watched as he circled the room, angrily stamping his fist into an open palm.

'There is a letter,' he said. 'To my wife, on your notepaper, saying that I made you pregnant. That we slept together.' He was raising his voice and she came across to stop him, catching his coat and telling him to talk more softly. Her face seemed as white as paper in the uncertain light.

'It isn't true. You know that can't be true. Where is the letter?' she said. 'Have you seen it?'

'My wife has it, in London.'

She clutched at her throat.

'I have never written to you. Someone is tricking us.' She searched her mind for a reason: a plot by whoever had put her under surveillance, and yet what purpose was served? Or Asterharzy, trying to get his own back – but that was not his way. Someone in the Armoury perhaps, trying to work off a grudge, with access to her files. Someone, more likely, who knew she had been to the clinic when her period was late. And then she remembered Werndl, the long-headed, elegant German who had appeared that day, and seemed unnaturally interested in her indisposition.

'If you didn't write it,' Marriner said, 'you'd better think who did.'

115

She told him the possibilities, running through the options, ending up with Oscar Werndl. Marriner was sure they had tricked him, determined to get him back.

'The bastard,' he swore. His legs felt shaky. With friends like Orford and Werndl . . .

She found glasses and a bottle of vodka.

'David, forget it.' Her slim figure moved towards him. 'Let us make the most of our time.'

The music had suddenly stopped as the tape clicked to an end. She whirled round and silenced him with her eyes and he saw her as a small child, suspended in the big room in her simple russet dress. Darting across to the record player she pushed in another cassette, Russian music this time which he did not find soothing. The faces on the walls seemed to observe their tryst with dark eyes that followed their movements.

'I have almost lost hope,' she said, 'since I last saw you. David, I gave up living.' Svetlana in despair. She raised her glass and swallowed the vodka in one slug, her eyes wide with new fears. 'They must have wanted you to come. This German. Your own people.'

He drank more slowly as she recharged and the music surged.

'They wanted me to come for their own reasons.'

She stood close to him now, in the middle of the room, grasping the eggcup-sized glass, almost as if they were dancing.

'What can I do?' she whispered.

'Help me,' he said.

'Help you?' It seemed to be a new concept, as if she had forgotten their conversation in the trees. And then hope entered her voice.

'Will you take me away?' She swept her hand at the icons, the ancient saints on the walls, and he nodded.

'There is a plan,' he said. 'That is what I came to say.' The commitment appalled him.

Her arms were round his neck, her fingers entwined in his hair, as if they were locked in combat. He half-pulled, half-carried her across to the cushioned settee, and tried to disengage there, but she clung to him, smiling and crying.

As he loomed over her, pushing her into the chair, he said, 'I can't promise a future. But I can try to get you out, with some of these things, if you help us.'

116

'Yes. Yes. Yes,' she cried, her mind steadying on the objective that had so long been a dream.

'I have to find Borovik first. To check that he is ready. I need you to contact him.'

She seemed to relax, stretching out her legs.

'That is no problem. I can arrange that you meet him. It is known we are friends.' She suddenly understood something more clearly. 'Perhaps that is why I am watched.'

If that was so, Marriner decided, their chances were less good: he had to rely on Borovik still being a free agent within the confines of Moscow.

Svetlana shrugged. 'Maybe. But I can always talk to him without arousing suspicion.'

Marriner pressed her. 'I've got to contact him personally. There is an opportunity . . . what we call a window, for him and you . . .' he said. 'But it won't be there for long.'

Her eyes were shining. 'Tell me, please, what you want.'

But he denied her, he was still not certain how much it was safe to confide in this strange, emotional beauty.

'Not yet. Borovik first. How quickly can I meet him?' He stood against the icons on the walls.

'Soon,' she breathed, as the music throbbed on, creating a devil's cave of sound and fury.

'Tomorrow?'

'Tomorrow? It is nearly here already.' But she shrugged. 'It is good. I telephone his office. He will come to look at the costumes in the Armoury.'

Telephone across the Kremlin, he queried, and then he thought, why not. Her contact with Borovik was known: both held positions of trust.

'All right,' he said. 'Arrange for him to meet me tomorrow.'

She said, 'Give me more drink,' and he rescued the bottle and carried it over. The alcohol made her flush, and he wondered if she drank too much. 'So. What will you do?' She looked at him as if he wove spells, a miracle man, and he knew it was not that easy, nor could he explain in detail, not until he was sure.

'Let me meet Borovik first.'

'But how, David, how? I want to know.'

He told her no, the plan was not yet agreed, but she would understand soon. A clock chimed the quarter hour and he realised it was nearly midnight.

'I've got to go, Svetlana.' It seemed that he always frustrated her. He saw the pain in her face as he retrieved his raincoat and struggled to the door.

'Where are you going?' Svetlana was clinging to him.

'To my hotel.'

'Oh David, you are a fool. Why do you not stay with me?'

'I'm sorry.' He tried to deny the offer. 'We have a business deal.'

'It is cold outside. Do you walk the streets at night? Perhaps you have a car?'

'No. I walked here, and I'll walk back.'

'That is ridiculous. If you look in the street, there will be someone watching.'

'I don't believe it.'

She laughed. 'You do not understand, do you? Come and see.' Very cautiously she doused the lights in the big, echoing room as if she was going to bed, and edged open the curtains, the heavy crimson brocade concealing a nylon net.

He peered down with her into the deserted street, four storeys below, at the parked cars under the street light. At first there was nothing there, until she said, 'Look. The one over there by the building site. You see it has a white bumper. Wait, you will see them inside.'

Marriner craned forward, and saw the puffs of exhaust smoke where the engine was idling. A sharp white frost was icing the parked vehicles, but this one was still alive. And as he watched he saw the strike of a match as one of the minders lit up.

'It will be cold out there,' Svetlana said behind him in the darkness. 'And dangerous.'

He turned to try and locate her in the blacked-out room, stumbling across a chair, and her laugh was behind him.

'Put on the light,' he growled, above the music.

'Why should I?' she said softly. 'They think we have gone to bed.'

He thrust out a hand to find his bearings and she was there in front of him, soft and scented and warm. 'We do not need lights,' she said, 'and you are safer here. Your visit can be explained if you stay the night.'

His senses were draining from him after their drinking and he found himself accepting the excuse that she offered, even though he protested.

'Svetlana. This is madness.'

118

'Is it?' Her voice came back, tempting him in the dark and he pushed out his hands again, this time making contact, and realised she was undressing.

Or nearly so. He heard the zip in the dark, and desire fought against common sense, the movements of her body against the fear of compromise.

'No, Svetlana, no.'

'Come to bed,' she whispered, the music still pumping and swelling, organ notes rolling round. He felt her body in a slip and bra pressing against his. In the dark she became a succuba, clutching his clothes like a bat, a bat with a subtle perfume and that strong, spiky head.

Marriner broke away, crashed into the settee and found his way to the door. There was a light in the passage and it illuminated them both, Svetlana small and neat, standing on stockinged feet in her black lingerie, smiling at him.

'It's no good,' he said.

She came along the corridor towards him, running fingers through her hair. He saw the hollows of her armpits.

'Don't go, David.'

'It wouldn't work,' he said. 'It never would,' and saw her crying. He turned.

He wanted to seize her and kiss her as she crumpled in his arms.

'Take me away,' she said. 'Take me away.'

He was tempted to throw the whole thing up, but for her vulnerability, and his own sense of duty to those shits who had enlisted him back in London.

'I'll do my best,' he promised, holding her in the corridor by her apartment door, 'but you must do what I say.'

Her mouth found his in one last, appalling kiss.

Marriner released her and pulled back the door chain. The door opened on to the empty lift cage with the stairs circling round and he ran down before her mood changed.

The empty foyer echoed with his footsteps and as he opened the night-bar on the outer door the freezing air took his breath away. It was a foretaste of the winter to come, and in that moment he loathed Moscow, loathed this humourless city with its terrible emptiness, and the sense of eyes on his back.

He turned rapidly, hands in pockets, and began to walk away, using his sense of direction from Arbat into Kalinin and round Red

119

Square. At his back he heard the car doors slam as they came after him, just as Svetlana had said, but he quickened his pace and refused to stop. The bitter air rasped in his lungs, causing him to pant, as he tried to hurry, and the pavement was slippery with ice where puddles had frozen. The footsteps behind him were nearer.

A voice behind him in Russian called out sharply and there were hands on his elbows as he turned round. Two of them had followed him from the parked Moskvich, young men in tough grey overcoats and fur hats, as if it was already winter, propelling him round now back to the waiting car where a third man was watching.

'I don't understand,' he protested. 'British citizen.'

He learned the Russian for 'shut up' as they bundled him inside, one minder on either hand, and the car edged out into the road. They kept their hands on his arm.

The Moskvich shot through some lights, and took a bridge over the river which glimmered below them in the night. He was hustled through a series of streets, an area he did not know, trying to measure the distance by the blocks racing past, and the time they were driving. A big railway station, with a few all-night figures huddled inside the glass doors, then darkened streets and a forecourt into which the car turned.

The minders levered him out, up three or four steps and into an unmarked building, so dark that he could not see how many storeys it had.

Angry Russian commands, and then he was in a room bursting with light, green-painted with brick arches and round-headed windows. Big box radiators stood against the far wall giving off waves of heat, and in the middle a small man sat at a desk of brown wood.

They were asking crisply for his papers, and he fished out his passport from an inside pocket: the embossed blue and gold command of Her Majesty to afford the bearer all necessary assistance and protection began to seem a bit thin. The small man studied it carefully, his fingers flicking the pages and staring at the visa photograph.

'Sit down,' he said. They pushed a wooden chair behind him and switched off the overhead light, leaving the room illuminated by the two small lights on the desk which swivelled on flexible stalks. He turned these now towards Marriner, and said in passable English, 'What were you doing there?'

Marriner's mind lost its usual urbanity in the fierce light of the room and the frowning faces. The interrogator – some kind of desk officer, no doubt in the KGB – seemed to live behind the lights and be a creature of habit. He opened a packet of cigarettes and began smoking.

'Visiting a friend,' Marriner said.

The small grey head was furrowed, clipped hair and sharp brown eyes.

'Who?' Smoke curled between his fingers, and hung around in the air.

'Who?'

'Svetlana Malinkova. The Director of the Kremlin Museum. I am a professional colleague.' It sounded ludicrous, even to himself, remembering her third attempt to seduce him.

The grey head nodded, and rose behind the desk. In his hand he carried a ruler, which he prodded at Marriner's chest.

'So you visit . . . eh . . .' One of the men who had brought him spoke rapidly in Russian. 'At ten o'clock. You leave at midnight. Why?'

Marriner pushed the ruler away. 'Why not? Do you expect me to stay?'

The small man laughed, and the others took their cue from him. 'What do you say? Discuss?'

'Museum business,' Marriner retorted.

The KGB man was puzzled. 'What business?'

'Exhibitions. Collections,' Marriner said.

The ruler came down again, pointing at his chest. 'You fuck even?'

It made Marriner angry, and he shouted at them. 'Do you think I am that stupid?'

'You fuck,' the ruler repeated.

'No. I left.' He realised the half-admission but the Russian did not seem to notice. Instead the desk officer laughed.

'We watch. We notice,' he said.

Marriner wanted to ask why, but the ground was too risky. The desk officer picked up the passport and returned it.

'Be careful,' he said.

The interview was over. They had his face now, and were pushing him out again, into the car, back to the monstrous shape of the Rossiya hotel, illuminated by a floodlight against the tower. One of them pushed him in the back, a soft punch into the kidneys as if to warn him again. He found himself inside the swing doors of the north entrance as the police disappeared.

His heart was pumping heavily. For the first time in his life he felt a wanted man, but there were also others depending on him to act. It was as if he rode a rocket which might blast off successfully or blast them all to hell, himself and Svetlana and the unknown Borovik.

The room service girl at the darkened desk in the corridor gave him his key without speaking and resumed reading, but he knew she would mark her book. It was a city of covert signs. He wondered again if his bedroom was wired, but did not care. He found his hands were shaking, and poured a glass of dusty-tasting water from the brackish carafe. A tiredness was pounding his temples, it was difficult not to feel helpless, against the odds, manoeuvred into a position not of his own choosing by fate and other people. Life in the Tower Armoury would never be the same again, he thought grimly, kicking off his shoes and rolling on to the bed. He switched on the television but the picture was talking heads, interrupted by static.

This was his last opportunity to pull out and give up, whatever Orford said, and Orford did not own him. But something held him there – the memory of Svetlana, the need to prove himself, even a sense of duty that came from way back – and the KGB made a mistake if they thought they could scare him. The television flickered to the end of the Moscow transmission, and he was almost asleep.

They reported back to the desk officer – a KGB colonel called Kazakov – that they had delivered him to the Rossiya.

The smoke still curled from another cigarette in the colonel's fingers.

'Was he frightened?'

The senior minder shrugged.

Kazakov called for more coffee, and paced about the room.

'Why should he go there? Why? At that time of night, unless he wants to sleep with her?'

The other man looked tired himself: it had been a long duty on a cold night, sitting in the car waiting. He shrugged.

'Maybe she did not want him. She has her Aeroflot pilot.'

Kazakov considered his fingers, flexing them as if they were acrobats, and cracked his joints one by one.

'Maybe,' he said curtly. 'She goes abroad too much. Who is this woman?' he asked angrily.

'They say she is the daughter of Nikolai Nikolayevich Malinkov who was the Director in Leningrad, at the Hermitage.'

Kazakov fretted. The name rang a distant bell, and he would check with records.

'The Hermitage?' Then why should his daughter be suspect, reported for talking with Borovik, a known queer, when she slept with macho men; and why were the English involved? He would need to know more about the blonde who lived in that apartment. 'Malinkov? Director Malinkov,' he brooded. 'What happened to him?'

The lieutenant was chosen for brains, and he had done his homework.

'There was a mistake,' he said, 'at the time of Khrushchev's reforms. Someone reported him for abuses of the State –'

'Abuses of the State?' Kazakov frowned and lit another cigarette. 'What sort of abuses?'

'Living in luxury. Misappropriation of property. He was accused of theft.'

Kazakov's antennae were quivering.

'Theft, from the museum?'

'It was a trumped up charge, by a jealous professional. Malinkov was a brilliant man.'

'Ah, so.' The colonel scratched an armpit. 'And what happened?'

'He was garrotted,' the lieutenant replied, 'by accident.'

Kazakov whistled. 'How old would the girl have been then?'

The lieutenant consulted a notebook.

'Eight or nine I suppose. There were two daughters and a widow. It was a terrible mistake, a botched job in an alley, and it had to be hushed up.'

In spite of himself the colonel shuddered, suddenly seeing the body, pitched out of a car somewhere, blood speckles staining the snow.

'Was it ever explained?' he asked.

The lieutenant snapped the notebook shut. He wanted to go back to barracks. 'I don't think so, sir. But amends were made later in Moscow. The girl was helped.'

'Ah.' The colonel let out a long sigh and flexed his fingers again. It could explain what had puzzled him: why she had risen so fast, but, more important, it might explain the instability in her affairs.

He yawned, pleased with himself. Svetlana was one to be watched, and the Englishman too.

13

Red Square was round the corner. In the morning he walked there, up the wet cobbles, the sun dispersing the ice, and the tourist buses, rear-engined, curtained, already offloading. Frost lingered in the depths of the Kremlin walls, touching the tips of the blue firs which shadowed the graves of the heroes. Orford had said that Stalin was buried there.

The duty tracker was worried as he followed the foreigner. All too easy to miss him, merging in the visiting groups; it would be a disaster to report that he had lost contact outside Lenin's tomb. No: there was the Englishman, the tall figure in the dark raincoat, inspecting the Roman-style busts that lined the walls and staring at the mausoleum. The sky was a glacial blue and parties of young pioneers with bright red scarves were lining up for photographs.

Marriner tried to imagine what life was like for Svetlana, behind those brawn-coloured battlements, a butterfly in a box. He tried and failed, hopeful that the apparatus of repression within the Soviet State would have outlived its time in these days of easier access, of democratic reform. But it did not do to be careless, last night was also a reminder that life in Moscow was dangerous. He was trading on the human frailities inside that monumental wall.

He walked away past the drum of the former scaffold and St Basil's Cathedral, locked and shut on its island. He inspected them each in turn until he had identified the young man who was tailing him, hunched in a fawn greatcoat. There was no doubt: every time Marriner stopped to admire the golden domes his new friend stopped too, fifty or so yards behind.

Towards the river and the Moskvoretski bridge, a footpath ran along the embankment below the Kremlin. It was less crowded there, with only the rumble of traffic and a few families on foot enjoying the autumn day. The overcoat was plodding behind him, watching the boats on the river.

Marriner took his time – all the time in the world – until he reached the Borovitsky Gate at the south-west corner. More coaches were drawn up there in the parking bays under the trees and suddenly he was lost between them. The overcoat broke into a trot and began to run round the buses, but people were standing about and the stranger had disappeared. The militiaman on the gate swore that he'd seen no foreigner. A straggling crowd of tourists was already forming a crocodile, talking and joking, waiting for things to open: busloads from Smolensk and Kaluga and Kalinin. Why worry, the militiaman said, nobody goes inside here unless we let them. That would be stupid, wouldn't it? But Marriner had taken his ticket, hunched over and joined the queue. The overcoat squinted inside, and told the guard his problem. He had to report back. It did not even occur to him that he could have broken orders and looked for the foreigner inside: that would be for Kremlin security, uniformed and plainclothes branches, and while they were discussing it Marriner had gone to ground.

He followed the white lines, keeping with the group from Smolensk who pressed about him with puzzled indifference. The great cathedrals in the central square, restored emblems of the old religion, seemed to draw them like magnets. Workers on holiday, families with eager children, old women in black coats who crossed themselves at the threshold, all of them explored the Church of the Assumption. There was no singing now, no music and no priests, and yet the echoes lingered in the limestone vaults and the painted frescoes, in all the abandoned saints still clinging to every pillar.

This was Svetlana's Russia of dark Byzantine reds and golds. He stood in a corner unnoticed, closer to understanding the pictures that glowed from every wall in her apartment. The smell and touch of a secret obsession, that patina of age and mystery which signified ancient places, holy shrines of gold and silver, metalwork and carvings. Svetlana, in the Armoury Palace, in charge of the secular treasures and secretly hoarding her own. Marriner tried to read her mind, aware that they were linked together in a terrible chess game.

It was one o'clock when he emerged. The sun was warmer now on the sandstone paving. What was it that Lenin had said about preserving art for the people? Still no sign of the militia: provided you kept to the painted lines, art for the people was good.

He walked back in the sunshine, past the Victorian façade of the Kremlin Great Palace, its cream and yellow plasterwork gleaming with new paint, towards the Armoury. Outside the Palace railings a crowd watched a ceremonial guard, like tourists at the end of the Mall. He was beginning to sweat, but the Armoury was a public building abutting the Kremlin wall. It was elegant in yellow stucco, with carved pilasters and round-headed windows and a pitched green roof. On his previous visits Svetlana had used the staff entrance and taken him up the back stairs, but today it was a different rendezvous, if she was true to her word. He came to the public entrance, followed a party of schoolgirls and slipped in behind them. The single policeman on the corner of the Borovitsky Gate glanced up the avenue towards him and turned away into the shade. There was no sign of a manhunt.

He was inside now, inside Svetlana's building, approaching countdown. The ground floor rooms with the firearms and armour should have been his specialities, but he headed for the ornamental staircase, just as she had said, past the trophies of the Swedish wars, with the labels that he could not read.

The jewels of the Tsars were surrounded by admiring crowds but elsewhere, in the fabric gallery, the atmosphere was more relaxed. She had not brought him through here on his previous visits and he saw for the first time the silks and brocades of mediaeval Moscow and the Russia of Peter the Great, the sacerdotal robes of the Church and the Imperial kaftans. Magnificent silken fabrics stitched with gold and silver were displayed along both walls and mounted in a series of cabinets. A woman's high-heeled boot, encrusted with pearls, the shoes of Catherine the First, embroidered gloves and cuffs in intricate, hand-worked patterns. A gallery of the past extravagances of human pride, and largely unfrequented. A single wardress, a formidable, uniformed bruiser in the dark blue serge of her trade, was stationed by the door as he entered.

He walked between the cases, closely inspecting the objects and looking through the glass: three young women pointing at a decorative cape, a man and a girl holding hands, two teenage girls giggling at the corseted day dress of the Empress Ivanova, a group of Chinese tourists, and the small man in the corner, sketching in a notebook, who might or might not be Borovik.

Marriner had a description, learned by heart in London, which this man had to fit. 'About fifty-five,' they had told him, Orford and the man with the dossier in that panelled house in the Wiltshire countryside, surrounded by the greens and golds of an English autumn. Centuries ago. As soon as he made this appointment, Marriner knew he had committed himself, irreparably and finally, like the first shot in a war. 'Small-featured, thinning hair, brown eyes, no scars.' They were describing Borovik like a passport photograph, perhaps where the information came from.

At the end of the gallery he found the small man waiting, dressed in a shiny gun-metal suit and matching grey shoes, meticulously drawing the entwined fruit and flowers on the sleeve of a robe edged with silver lace and patterned with quilted satin. Marriner approached the display case, his heart pounding, but the other man continued sketching as if he was completely alone. They were now remote from the wardress who guarded the far door. Marriner edged casually closer, until he stood next to the artist, so close that he could see the dandruff on the shoulders of his coat, and the man knew he was watching.

The artist began to write a caption under the half-finished pencil sketch, in clear Roman script as if describing the drawing for his own and Marriner's benefit.

'Possibly English.'

Marriner knew he had found him, but Borovik had changed since his passport years. Now he was a fragile man who looked older than his mid-fifties, as if strained by an ulcer, with a hard rather furtive mouth and nervous eyes. The movements of his hands and arms were like a small jumpy bird, and the tendons in his neck showed how much he was on edge. His face turned to stare at Marriner.

'Very good,' Marriner said.

The other man nodded, slowly.

'Thank you.' His voice was surprisingly firm, a fluted tenor, adding to the air of strain. It even had a touch of contempt, or bitterness against some barrier.

Marriner was speaking softly, but he had little fear that they were being observed. It was safer inside the Kremlin than outside in the Moscow streets.

'My name is Marriner.'

Borovik resumed his sketching, his hand as erratic as a tachograph.

'I was expecting you.'

Looking round, Marriner could see no interest in their conversation: between the display cases of the gallery they had at last linked up. Svetlana had told him the truth. Now it was up to him.

The Russian completed his sketch, and they walked through the gallery together, back to the four-square wardress. More people were filing in now as the afternoon crowds thickened.

'Do you go back to work?' Marriner asked.

Borovik nodded, his eyes nervous in the pale face. For a moment Marriner wondered if he could be a plant, a decoy from the KGB, and as if to disabuse him Borovik said, 'I was asked to meet someone here . . .' He hesitated, then added, 'By Svetlana.'

'A friend of mine too,' Marriner said.

They passed the wardress and could feel her staring. Borovik nodded to her as if he was a familiar, no doubt why she had not bothered them, out of sight at the end of the gallery.

'Today she says she is busy.'

Marriner felt himself moving between two worlds: the security of life in London now caught up and disturbed by this strange rendezvous. At the foot of the staircase they looked at each other, the unhappy Russian with the details of chemical weapons, and the Englishman whose wife had driven him into proving himself. Or had he really been driven, Marriner wondered, by Svetlana? The fear in the little man's eyes told him that they were all on short time. The window of escape from the Kremlin would not be open for long.

They stood together in the entrance hall and Borovik said, in precise and careful English, 'I wish to go.'

It was an appeal for help in the clearest possible terms, within spitting distance of the Politburo.

'I know.'

Outside, back in the sunshine, Borovik began to edge away, as if anxious to return to his offices in the Council of Ministers Building. This was still visitor-land, thronged with people, whereas Borovik's work, and the secrets he carried with him, were confined to the central offices and his small residential flat in the secretariat, out of bounds to all tourists. Borovik was still a prisoner within the system, and Marriner saw his haunted face.

'I am sending Svetlana some tickets,' Marriner said, 'for the English theatre. I would like you to be her guest. Will you be able to come?'

Borovik's eyes were dull, but his lips fluttered a thank you.

'I will come.' And he was gone like a shadow towards the roped-off barrier that marked the security zone.

Marriner turned and walked back towards the Borovitsky Gate.

He could see the slots for the drawbridge. More police now, smart in their mid-blue uniforms and flat, red-banded caps, who stopped talking as he approached. Like a tourist he followed the arrows, his mind mainly on Borovik, the possessor of secrets which could put a stain on the world. What was it Orford had said? 'He knows about the whole bloody stockpile, the chemical warfare cover-up.' There was Svetlana to think about too, Svetlana who would be the courier, but what kind of future for her if she abandoned her roots in this unhappy society? His own feelings were equivocal. She offered him a sexual promise and yet there was the smell of brimstone. The idols and the icons of an ancient Russia.

He saw the policeman step out from the edge of the tower and hold his arm up, the sign language very clear. The policeman was young and nervous, standing there red-faced at the sight of the man he had been told to identify. He was asking for papers.

Marriner handed over his passport, with the entry visa stamped in London. 'Academic research,' it said in Russian and English.

The man was perspiring, and caught Marriner's arm, beckoning him into the guardroom. They were drinking coffee in there, four men who looked up suspiciously.

'*Anglishki,*' Marriner said hopefully, controlling the urge to panic, confronted by sullen faces. Even the tourist phrases deserted him as he waited, his mouth dry. The sign languages began.

They motioned him to sit down, on a wooden bench inside the door. He could see the human traffic out there, flowing through the Kremlin gates, and the narrow line between detention and freedom. From their resigned impressions, he might be there a long time. One of them was on the telephone, asking for instructions.

Marriner rose to his feet, and they waved him back. Uncertainly. Young and untried militiamen on what was an easy duty, suspicious but not unreasonable in these days of new freedoms.

He pointed to the telephone. They shook their heads. He took out his passport again, which they had returned, and pointed with anger to the royal coat of arms. Never had it seemed so useful, so impressive, the golden heraldry on the dark blue cover, as when he waved it at them.

'Telephone,' he growled. That at least was the same word in Russian.

A senior policeman appeared, a stocky man with a brush haircut who seemed to be friendly. They all stood and looked him over, apparently without orders, other than to pick him up. Marriner decided it was time to call for help.

'Telephone,' he said again. 'Kremlin. *Oruzheinaya Palata.*' That was how she had told him it was to be pronounced and he hoped to God it was right, trying to keep calm. He refused to let them see he was rattled. It was crowded in the box-like room, a square lodge with a desk and benches along the wall on which the militia stretched out. 'Dr Svetlana Malinkova.'

The Palace of Arms. The Armoury. The words seemed to ring a bell, and they looked at him with new interest. The senior policeman, three chevrons on his arm and a gold badge in his lapel, shrugged and pushed the telephone across the little desk.

Marriner began to dial the number she had given him, direct into her office, praying that she would be there. It was a curious feeling to have his future in her hands, dependent on the way she would handle this. The bell seemed to ring and ring. He leaned on the linoleum desk top, with the policemen watching, trying not to seem concerned.

A woman's voice was answering. Businesslike and unintelligible. He could not begin to make her understand and tried to reason with her. 'Dr Svetlana Malinkova. Malinkova. Marriner. David Marriner. I must speak to her.'

The sergeant policeman was nodding. He understood who she was, an important official within the system. He took the receiver from Marriner's hand and carefully explained the problem. '*Da*,' the woman said curtly, and he heard her receiver click.

They handed back the telephone and he had to wait. The woman on the other end, a secretary he guessed, gabbled what he took to be an explanation that they were looking for her. A series of further clicks and then at last he heard Svetlana, unmistakably Svetlana, saying in her cool, clear English, 'Hello? David, is that you?'

He tried to keep the nerves from his voice, as if it was perfectly natural to be detained by the militia, but he knew they were watching him sweat. The adrenalin was pumping his veins, as he found he was now in her power, asking her to bail him out. 'They seem to be detaining me at the Borovitsky Gate.'

She knew that a bond had been forged.

'I'll be there in five minutes,' she said. 'Hand me back to the police.'

Their attitudes changed at once, he could see the light jump in their faces. The sergeant policeman smiled, and one of the others brought coffee from an urn in the back room, weak coffee, syrupy with sugar. Marriner found he was parched. He fought hard not to rattle the cup as he drank the sweet brew. The fact that she had come to his rescue seemed to jeopardise his own independence, his power to determine her future.

Waiting. Waiting for what seemed a lifetime as the minutes ticked by. He asked himself again and again how he had got into this mess, how he had been persuaded, and knew it was the spell of Svetlana, the magic she seemed to cast, as he saw her cream Lada draw up. He watched her slip out of the driver's seat, dressed in a navy costume and matching shoes, instantly recognisable by that small head of short, blonde hair. Standing in the sunshine, talking to the outdoor guard who was pointing in his direction, she looked more Swedish than Russian, a visiting star out of some Bergman film.

She was walking across the cobbles, then inside the doors towards him, smiling.

'David! What are you doing here?' She held out her hand in Western fashion. No bearhugs now, she was the Director of the Kremlin Armoury and those boys knew it. A hint of the old, authoritarian Russia. She turned to the police and spoke curtly, with gestures that made her displeasure evident, acting out his freedom. He could follow it clearly, from the puzzled frowns on their faces to the high colour in hers. What orders had been given; why had he been detained? A note of anger, carefully controlled, crept into her questions.

They seemed to be apologising. No one knew why he was there. They had just been asked to find him.

'To *arrest* him?' Her voice was full of contempt.

The sergeant shook his head.

'I think it is a mistake, no? Some confusion,' Svetlana said. She turned to Marriner as if they had only just met. 'I am sorry.'

One more sharp exchange with the desk, who shrugged and began to disengage. The sergeant was opening the door and Marriner walked the path to freedom. He felt now that he owed her something, as well as having something to give, but the words were not easy to find.

'I'll drive you back,' she said, as if she understood.

He climbed into the little Lada and found himself still shaking as they drove out through the gate with the police saluting them.

'Don't talk about it,' she said.

It was a short drive up past the Alexandrovsky Gardens, left into Kalinin and then left again to her street off Arbat. She was pulling into the footpath, where the KGB car had hovered last night when they picked him up. Svetlana seemed cool as ice.

'You were stupid last night,' she said. 'You should have stayed. Then there would be no questions asked. In Moscow it is better to sleep with someone than to be suspected of spying.'

'Are they watching us now?' he asked, as she locked up the car and removed the windscreen wipers.

She shrugged. 'Probably. Once they start they don't stop. Sometimes they steal these things.' Standing on the pavement, she added, 'It keeps the secret police, our internal security, fully employed.'

'Employed in theft?'

She shrugged. 'One day things will be different. But now –' She grimaced, a wicked smile on her lips. 'Everything in short supply. You'd better come inside before I vanish too.'

It was three o'clock, an assignation on an October afternoon with the leaves turning brown and little puffs of dust that might almost have been pollen spiralling in the sunlight. 'Take my arm,' she said. 'Probably they are parked down the street, or it may be that man on the corner, or they have a window somewhere. They would know I have a lover.'

He could feel her power to demand him as they went up in the gilded cage, and he watched her unlock the doors to her apartment. The cream doors opened into the narrow corridor cluttered with books, and he followed her once again into the great room with its paintings stacked on the walls, row on row, a miniature version of the frescoes before which he had stood in the Cathedral of the Assumption. The red curtains were half closed, and the gauze netting behind them diffused the light, giving the room the darkness of a church.

She put her arms around him, as he tried to take charge. He felt her tongue in his mouth as he held her there. There was no music now, just the sense of two people, and he found her as determined as he was.

'You are a fool,' she whispered. 'You should have waited for me. You must make love to me now.'

This time there was no excuse. Svetlana was overwhelming, outside his experience. He kissed her and swung her round. Her bright hair shone in the room.

'Pull back the curtains,' she whispered. 'Let them see you.'

Marriner went to the window and parted the nylon netting, so that he was silhouetted, seen from the street below. There was a man on the corner, glancing up, or perhaps it was an illusion, he looked too old and decrepit, but in Moscow the Chinese puzzles went on and on, and no one was what he seemed. He refastened the nets and closed the main drapes, a pattern of leaves on a dark ruby ground. The only light now was from the lamp in the alcove, which threw them into surreal shadows.

She slipped off her shoes and held him, her arms round his neck. Svetlana seemed to have no doubts.

'Come into the bedroom,' she said.

The bed had brass headrails, and a blue quilt on a white coverlet. The lights were brighter there, a décor of soft blues and pinks on the wallpaper, the dressing table and the thick Islamic carpet.

'I like to keep the lights on here,' she said. 'The other room, it is different.' As if it was a private church. Svetlana sat on the bed. He found her hands were cold. His reason said this was madness, the folly he had fought to avoid, but instinct was stronger. She had a cool white body, and he wanted her.

'Come into bed,' she said.

She was naked between the sheets on a Moscow afternoon, and he made love without regret. But her coldness surprised him: the iced hands, cold feet and thighs. It was as if she was shivering and she seemed to have little pleasure, as they turned in the bed.

'What is the matter, Svetlana?'

'I don't know,' she whispered. 'Give me time.'

It occurred to him when it was over that the performance might have been recorded by the KGB.

14

There was a letter from Edmondson in the morning. They gave it to Marriner with his room key, and he wondered if it had been opened, but was unable to tell. The envelope looked untouched, posted in London three days before, and he took it along to his bedroom. Sitting at the little wooden writing desk he read the brief message on Edmondson's cream paper.

'Pitt Rivers and Fawley have been instructed for the time being to take no further action on the second petition. Accordingly I am not for the moment pursuing the further measures we discussed; but I regard it as imperative that you obtain a written disclaimer on the matter which has so complicated the proceedings.'

Edmondson was careful, Marriner noted, not to drop names. It really began to look as if Celia was coming to her senses, renewed by his mission to Moscow, a catharsis in their relationship. But there was also Svetlana; Marriner could picture her now, another of those dispossessed Russians whose older versions he met at private views. He decided that Edmondson's letter should not be left around; it conveyed ambiguous messages if anyone came looking. It needed to be burnt, but he realised he had no matches. Downstairs in the lobby there was a desk selling cigarettes, but of course it was closed. With the letter in his pocket, he strolled outside, on to the stone terrace where Svetlana had come to meet him on his first trip to the city. The autumn was shutting down now, a grey mist on the river and people muffled in coats. He was glad of the heavy Burberry which he had brought from England, and thrust his hands into the pockets, walking round the hotel and under the flyover into Razin Street. In Moscow he was nowhere anonymous, the foreigner was always suspect, and the letter was now an embarrassment. He was gripped by the paranoia of a visitor in a strange city attempting a dangerous game, walking without direction, trying to order his thoughts. They were waiting for him to deliver, both London and Svetlana. Svetlana who had made love as if there was no tomorrow. Svetlana who had then gone back into that great double room where the icons glimmered and danced with him in the gloaming, at five o'clock in the afternoon, her hands round his neck, her body swinging against him as he ran his fingers over her head. Svetlana who had put on records deep from the soul of Russia, Glinka, Tchaikovsky, Mussorgsky, while she danced with him, naked, in the shadows.

When he left her she had cried a little, wrapped in a dressing-gown of black and gold dragons. 'I need you,' she whispered.

He had stood with her on the landing, waiting for the little cage lift. 'You have your alibi now.'

'Alibi?' The word had puzzled her.

'To show that we are lovers, to the security boys.'

She frowned. 'Oh, that. But, David, we are.'

He pondered that problem now, and found he had walked in a

rectangle, along the business district of Kuibysheva Street, almost back to Red Square. The GUM store was on his right and if anyone was following – again he could not be sure – that was the place to lose them. He entered the glass arcade and was submerged in the shoppers queuing for morning bargains. It was eleven o'clock, and he had a day to kill. As he wandered between the shop fronts he knew that he must soon draw back from getting too close to Svetlana. A casual liaison was one thing, she had hinted that there had been others, but a permanent affair between them was out of the question, for her sake as well as for his. Yesterday afternoon he had nearly cocked everything up. Shit. He fingered the letter from Edmondson which was burning his pocket. Somewhere inside the GUM store he came across a refreshment stall and sat down to try and think. There was a chrome samovar and a woman in a white turban who tapped off a glass of lemon tea. Perched on a rickety stool he slowly sipped the drink, reliving his decisions. He had let Challenby decoy him and Denis Orford buy him, for the sake of his marriage, for Celia and Katie's sake. But Svetlana had also arrived, Svetlana who was fire itself, like the Golden Cockerel that she had shown him on stage, a bird of magnificent plumage, but signifying what? The golden bird in the end died along with the fantasy world when the lights went up. . . . Somebody jostled his arm, and he realised that others were waiting, queuing up for his seat. But at least there was a waste bin, a battered cardboard drum half full with cigarette packets and old copies of *Pravda*. He tore Edmondson's letter into shreds and stuffed it in with the rubbish.

When he had gone, the man in the corner showed a card to the woman and took away the bin.

Sverdlov Square was shining under the street lights and full of traffic as he walked to the Maly Theatre on the following evening. The trees in the public gardens were almost leafless now, and a wind was blowing the leaves like a carpet of giant cornflakes around the bust of Karl Marx. Across the road the cream columns of the Bolshoi gleamed under the floodlights as if to detract from the posters at the Maly's smaller façade. The English touring company, fresh from a triumph in Kiev, were opening in Moscow on schedule. Excitement enfolded both buildings on a night of double firsts: *Boris Godunov* at the opera, *King Lear* at the theatre, in English. In the dusk, as Marriner entered the Maly, the ornate nineteenth-century building seemed to float in spangles of lights.

He began looking for Svetlana along the reserved seats for which Brzezinski had sent tickets, complimentary tickets, two of them passed on to the Armoury. But she had not arrived, no sign of her or Borovik, and the unease began. It had to be tonight, he told himself, tonight when they had the excuse, so that she could be his guest, and he could introduce Brzezinski, while there was still time.

He edged along the row of seats; two empty ones on his left. A hand touched his back, and he turned to see Kirilov, flat-faced and anxious-eyed, blinking at him. Some bastard had given the man from the Ministry tickets two rows behind and he sat there with his wife, a cottage loaf in a floral frock.

'Delighted to see you,' Kirilov muttered. 'I think you await some friends?'

A complacent voice stepped in before he could respond. 'Don't you worry, old chap. People are always last minute here.' He held out a hand. 'Charles Wootten-Smythe, British Embassy. You should have contacted us.' There was a hint of caution in the introduction, and Marriner had the feeling that he was under surveillance from more than one side. He turned and smiled at the Kirilovs, and sat down to wait for Svetlana. The curtains were beginning to stir as the music started and the house lights dimmed. 'Oh Christ,' he found himself praying, 'don't let me fuck it up now.'

And then she was there beside him, squeezing in just in time, with Vasily Borovik in tow. He caught the breeze of her perfume, a hint of spice and desire, and scarcely had time to admire the rich folds of her gown before in the semi-darkness she had touched his hand and whispered hello. The taffeta dress, dark green edged with gold, rustled as the pressure of fingers conveyed conflicting messages: on her side God knew what assumptions about the afternoon they had spent, on his the confused signals of what he had to perform for the sake of conmen like Orford. If Marriner turned his head he could just see Borovik now, a blurred head on small shoulders, like an old-fashioned photograph, sitting on the edge of his seat.

He knew that he had to be careful, conscious that Kirilov was behind him, and the Russian was not there by accident. Kirilov had been looking for him, his little eyes almost reptilian, trying to piece together this jigsaw just as they had the fragments left in the GUM wastebin. What Kirilov could not understand was why if they were so important the Englishman had not burnt them, or flushed them down the toilet. They had been resurrected, painstakingly, like a puzzle, by Colonel Kazakov. What was 'the further action', 'the further measures discussed', and for the moment shelved, he pondered? Ivan Kirilov was anxious, trying to solve a conundrum in the darkened auditorium with the translation headphones clamped to his ears.

Kirilov bent forward to concentrate as the curtain went up. His English was fluent but rusty but the storyline was familiar: the old King betrayed by his daughters with Crashaw and Susan Lawrence as Lear and Cordelia. They rang strange notes in his mind, a parable of the powers of the state, but in front of him was the Englishman, and he still wondered why he had come, and why he had invited Borovik. Marriner was a fool if he thought that making love to Svetlana – as reported by the KGB – was a means of reaching the scientist. He watched their heads in front of him, Svetlana's slightly inclined, and smiled to himself grimly.

In the interval Wootten-Smythe led the way to the bar, and took the brunt of the Kirilovs, who happened to be there too. Marriner and Svetlana seemed to make a handsome pair, as she caught his eye and threw back her head and laughed. Both of them were under pressure but Svetlana might have been a filmstar. She seemed a creature from the stage itself, hair shining under the lights, but to Marriner she was no Cordelia. There was something cold-blooded about her that reminded him more of Goneril.

'I did not realise you knew Dr Borovik,' he heard Kirilov saying. 'Strange that he should be here with you.'

'We met at the museum,' he replied.

Svetlana drank a mineral water. 'Vasily adores the theatre. The costumes and the designs. Is that not so?'

The little Russian's brown eyes, dogged, huge behind horn-rimmed glasses, blinked uncertainly.

'I study Shakespeare,' he said.

Kirilov regarded him coldly. 'But you must have so little time . . . ,' he said in English.

'On the contrary,' Borovik replied, his slender hands brushing more dandruff from the lapel of his coat. 'I have almost too much.'

Wootten-Smythe found that funny; he stood against a pillar and laughed, while Marriner edged closer.

'Charles,' he hissed. 'Take care of Kirilov and get him off my back.'

The final act seemed endless, as Lear's ravings mounted. He could sense Svetlana beside him, her fingers fluttering to his and then away again, a kind of promissory note, while Borovik sat there unbending, absorbed in the drama of the king who went mad. The tight-packed theatre was tense as Lear carried in Cordelia, howling like a dog. Svetlana hesitated. She understood they were meant to move as soon as the curtain came down, and leaned over to whisper, 'When?' He saw her full mouth and wide eyes close to his, and resisted the stirring, the urge to touch her.

'Not long,' he said.

Then Lear himself was dead, and Edgar's farewell brought home to him the risk.

> We that are young
> Shall never see so much, nor live so long.

It might have been a reminder of how much he had at stake, as the curtains swished down and the applause began. Crashaw and Susan Lawrence were in front of the audience, throwing kisses, receiving bouquets. Everyone was on their feet and Marriner could feel Kirilov's eyes spearing into his back. But the Kirilovs were trapped in the stalls, two rows behind them, talking to Wootten-Smythe.

'Now,' Marriner said. 'Hurry.'

He was pushing past the rest of the row before they knew what was happening, with Svetlana and Borovik following, as if they had a train to catch. Then he was in the aisle, remembering Orford's trial run in London as he made for the exit nearest the orchestra pit. An usher sitting on a stool looked up in surprise.

Brzezinski, for Christ's sake where was Brzezinski? He saw two doors to their left leading backstage, marked in Russian, and charged into one of them, Svetlana and Borovik in tow. A passage back to the wings with the sounds of applause still coming from the stage. John Crashaw was speaking, a thank you in English spiced with laborious Russian: they could hear it amplified. A woman in a pink woollen costume was waiting in the corridor.

'Where the hell is Brzezinski?'

She understood. He hoped to God that Wootten-Smythe was containing the Kirilovs on the other side of the curtain. Svetlana's face was white with tension, while Borovik brought up the rear, bemused by these cramped corridors smelling of old polish.

'Through there –' the woman said. 'In the main storeroom.'

They pushed through another door and entered a world of chaos where the weary stage manager was sitting surrounded by boxes, discarded props and used clothes. As he saw Marriner he jumped up and embraced him.

Marriner said, 'This is Vasily. Vasily Vasilyevich Borovik. And Svetlana Malinkova. When can you package them?'

The dark Polish eyes sized up the proposition that they had discussed in London as an academic exercise.

'In two weeks time,' he said calmly. 'In Leningrad.'

'Two weeks?' Marriner exploded: two weeks would be a lifetime. The Pole shrugged. 'It cannot be done before. It must be when we fly out.' He waved his hand and grinned at Borovik who seemed to have shrunk even smaller, like a deflated doll, his colour waxen as he realised the risks.

'It will not be a problem.' He heard Svetlana's voice, and saw her holding Borovik's hand. 'David will do it,' she said. There was certainty in her eyes. Svetlana Malinkova was either in love with him, or a very good actress, he thought when he had time to consider.

'Sunday the twenty-sixth,' Brzezinski said. 'You must travel to Leningrad.'

Slowly, like an automaton, Borovik nodded and found his tongue. 'I ask permission,' he said. 'But can you arrange the rest?'

Brzezinski said, 'Guaranteed,' as if leaving Russia was child's play. There was no pussy-footing, this was a man who meant business. He turned to Svetlana. 'You fly out separately. You have an overseas visa?'

Svetlana was flushed with happiness. 'Of course. Of course.' She caught David's arm and kissed him, in front of the bemused Borovik.

Brzezinski was like a general who had arranged his battle plan. 'We will be ready,' he asserted.

'How will I know what to do?' Svetlana asked.

'Through your friend here,' the Pole replied.

Marriner had a gambler's instinct to assess the chances as even, provided that they weren't stupid, or the KGB more efficient. But Svetlana's relations with him now seemed to be a bigger problem, and he feared for the longer term. Borovik's doggy eyes were looking to him as a saviour, flattering but untrue. It was like falling in water, once he had taken the plunge he felt himself going deeper and deeper.

On the other side of the curtain the applause had stopped. Brzezinski understood the danger. 'Sophie,' he said to the woman in pink, who was sitting on a tea chest, waiting. 'Fetch Johnnie-boy quickly.' They could hear the last ripples of clapping dying away, and with them their backstage time.

'Drink?' Brzezinski asked, flushing out a bottle of Scotch. He poured four generous tots into some waxed paper cups, as if he was saluting the future.

Sophie came back with Crashaw, who was looking exhausted. He did not seem to register who they were. 'Fantastic people. Anything you say, Danny-boy.'

He scribbled on Svetlana's programme, then on Borovik's.

'Put on "with love",' Brzezinski said. 'And hurry up.'

Crashaw bowed and complied, and Brzezinski handed to Marriner the two scribbled-over programmes. 'Get back on-side,' he said. 'And let's all forget we met.'

Marriner was left with a fortnight to explain away, and as they came back from the wings a very worried Kirilov, standing in the outer corridor, was arguing with the usherette. Wootten-Smythe was hanging in close, trying to calm him down.

'Ah, there you are,' he said, as if he'd lost them on a picnic.

'Collecting autographs.'

Svetlana and Borovik showed their programmes. 'What a man,' she said smiling. 'Such physical presence. I like a man with that.' Her eyes were again on Marriner.

Kirilov looked concerned. 'You should not run away like that. You might have disappeared.'

'No chance,' Marriner said. 'I wanted them to meet the cast. Only way to get his signature . . . Svetlana was so keen.'

The theatre was emptying. Wootten-Smythe said he'd drive them back, but Borovik was being collected by a car from the Kremlin, and Svetlana had her own. She turned to Marriner, slipping her hand through his arm as they stood in the foyer, with Kirilov smiling.

'May I offer you a lift?'

Marriner knew what that meant, and he could not afford it. Svetlana was as much a problem as the KGB, he was not sure which he feared worse. He shook his head, and opted for Wootten-Smythe's Sierra. Disappointment clouded her face, again noted by

Kirilov, with his wife on his arm. 'Some other time,' Marriner said. Svetlana turned away, her unhappiness obvious.

There was an autumnal mist now in Sverdlov Square, cold fog swirling like smoke, as they came out to the air. The pavements were full of Muscovites watching from either side, just as Kirilov watched him. Wootten-Smythe was going to the Embassy, on the river opposite the Kremlin, and would drop him off on the way. As Marriner climbed into his car he caught a last glimpse of Svetlana walking across to her Lada parked in a nearby bay, observed by the envious faces and the stone wall of the Kirilovs' displeasure. He saw her slip off her heels and slam the door: those same elegant legs that had snared him in the beginning. What did she feel, he wondered, really feel, about the events she had started and now could scarcely stop? Who was she at bottom, this beautiful, floating woman who was searching for happiness and offering love in return; moreover, if he got it right, and spirited her collection from Russia in payment for her help with Borovik, what was the price he would pay?

'Pretty good show,' Wootten-Smythe said, in that tone that might have referred to a workmanlike fifty at Lords on an overcast afternoon. 'Get what you wanted?'

'After a fashion,' he said.

Wootten-Smythe turned his head, well-groomed and fed. 'We're all trapped here. I don't know what you're up to,' he said, 'and I don't want to know. But for Christ's sake be careful. That's official.'

Marriner saw the stars on the Kremlin as he dropped off by the hotel.

Kirilov made a report, by telephone that night, if the Englishman had only known, and it perturbed the KGB colonel still on duty in the grey barracks over the river.

'There were two people at the Maly, on his complimentary tickets. Svetlana Malinkova and Vasily Borovik.'

He heard Kazakov whistle. He knew that Svetlana met Borovik from the observation reports.

'Did they go away together?'

'No,' Kirilov said. 'We sent the car for Borovik, and she drove off alone. The Englishman went back with a man from the British Embassy. Wootten-Smythe.'

Kazakov sketched out the names, sitting at his desk in the

middle of the plain room where he had interviewed Marriner. He also had a report that Marriner had spent an afternoon with her in the Arbat apartment a couple of days before.

'She sleeps with him,' he said. 'The English researcher.'

'I know.' Kirilov was conscious of his own wife, her face set into a rat-trap, listening as he spoke from their flat. 'She sleeps with anyone.'

Kazakov sighed. 'Let's hope it's as simple as that.' His pencil tapped the desk. 'We shall have to make sure.' He even made a small joke. 'At least she won't sleep with Borovik. What is it that they have in common?'

'Tapestries,' Kirilov said. 'He is always sketching the clothing, the embroideries in the Armoury.'

Colonel Kazakov frowned. Why should the Kremlin's top man on chemical warfare stockpiles and controls, a scientist they could not replace, a man who came trailing degrees from Moscow and Akademgorodok, also be interested in art? And women's art at that. He scratched his groin. 'Anything else?' he asked.

The man from the Ministry hesitated. 'I think she's in love,' he said.

'Love!' Kazakov banged the desk top and his pencil rolled on to the floor. 'With Comrade Borovik?'

'With the Englishman,' Kirilov muttered, half-embarrassed.

Kazakov said, 'They are both fools. What future is there in that?'

'I don't know.'

The colonel sucked his teeth and pressed the bell for his aide. Over the telephone he said to Kirilov, 'All right. We'll increase the surveillance. How long is this man here for?'

'Two more weeks. On research.'

'Keep him away from Svetlana if you can. We don't want any complications.'

Afterwards he turned to the lieutenant, and ordered a drink, Sitting back in his chair, with his boots on the desk, he pondered the situation: Marriner had a line to Svetlana and she had a line to Borovik. That much was clear. Whether there was more to it was something he would now find out. He smiled to himself: he certainly wouldn't help her sex life.

15

Brzezinski had told him to wait. The English Theatre Company played to packed houses but the players in Marriner's life – Svetlana and Borovik in Moscow, Celia and Orford at home – seemed shadows he could not catch. None of them made a move, and for two long weeks he acted the museum professional. Tuesday a raincoat was monitoring, Wednesday he had disappeared, Thursday a face was back again watching the places he visited, the Army Museum and the glass panorama of the battle of Borodino. Aldanov came there with him, and deplored the lack of consumer goods.

'In the West you would have proper shops. Replicas of old guns.' He shrugged. 'You see we lack expertise. We do not have a market.'

Marriner nodded. If he survived this venture he would have enough material to write a book on free trade. Aldanov's shadowy companionship did nothing to diminish the worries in his mind over why Svetlana failed to appear and how soon Brzezinski would contact.

Aldanov took off his spectacles and explained the retreat of Napoleon. 'We were on the same side then.'

'Of course.'

'And now again.' They seemed to be circling each other as the October days hardened into frost and storms.

Aldanov peered at him closely, through his heavy glasses, not unfriendly but quizzical, mindful of a question from Kirilov, before they had started out, when the Ministry man had appeared unsolicited in his office. Kirilov had wrung his hands and handed him a copy of *Pravda*. 'English triumph at the Maly. The greatest contemporary actor of Shakespearian drama,' Kirilov read out slowly, 'has had an acclaimed success before a Moscow audience.' He rubbed his moustache and made a face.

'Well?'

At first Aldanov had not really understood.

'Marriner was there,' Kirilov had explained, 'with the Director on the opening night. Together with Vasily Borovik.'

'Ah yes. He met her in Brussels.'

Kirilov had grown agitated. 'Don't you see? He's acting like a tourist. But he's not one.' He paused. 'What has he really come to the Soviet Union for? Take him around and find out.'

So Aldanov had begun to accompany Marriner on his visits, and watched him while he took notes enough for a supplement to his opus on eighteenth-century firearms. Aldanov solved the language problem and provided authenticity as Marriner studied papers and looked at the snaphance mechanisms of early flintlocks.

'I hope you are enjoying your trip,' Aldanov said, standing on the Borodino platform as they viewed a hundred metres of painting, the attack on Napoleon's guards, the cavalry in the cornfields. 'You are learning about things for science, or something else?'

'Pure science,' Marriner replied. Unable to elude the system, he decided he might as well join it.

Aldanov, a professional pressed into service by Kirilov, the Ministry official who monitored East-West relations, smiled a little as they paced the viewing level, the battle pieces under their noses: grenadiers, bayonets, cossacks charging. This ultra-nationalism, the chauvinistic patriotism, Marriner found hard to take. They built a brick wall against strangers, except for Svetlana. But he had a learning curve there too. He put away his notes in the briefcase, and asked to go back to the Armoury.

Aldanov had a small room at the top of the building, and they went there to look at more papers. The Keeper of Weapons came in with Kirilov as Marriner was writing up notes: unexpectedly he had found a subject that was unexplored and absorbing, the firepower of various muskets. But Kirilov did not seem pleased.

'How much longer are you staying?' He knew that Marriner's visa was valid for a month.

The Englishman shrugged. It was hot in the cluttered office full of green filing cabinets; their coats were hung over the chairs.

'About another week now. Depends on how quickly I finish. Not before the twenty-sixth.' Brzezinski's deadline, when the ETC left Moscow. He was worried by Kirilov's tone, more acid than before, implying he was being bollocked by someone higher up. For the past week he had avoided Svetlana and had heard nothing from her, as if by mutual agreement they preferred to dissemble, but now he wanted her cover, her authority. I e asked to see her.

Kirilov shook his head.

'She is not here.'

'Not here?' The information tripped him up. If Svetlana wasn't there, he had no line to Borovik when Brzezinski came through, other than the risky option of another chance rendezvous, this time under surveillance. What if they had intervened to get her out of the way? He sensed their hostility as he leaned back in the chair and stretched. 'Where has she gone?'

'On holiday,' Kirilov said. Under the drooping moustache his mouth closed like a trapdoor.

'Holiday?' Without letting him know. Marriner could scarcely believe it. He felt the disappearance was threatening.

Kirilov smelled of tobacco. As he came closer it reeked from his hair and clothes and his breath was bad. 'A small holiday,' he said. 'It is entitled to her, is it not? I believe she has gone to Georgia.'

'Georgia?' He did a rapid calculation from schoolboy geography. A thousand bloody miles away, to the south. 'When will she be back?'

Kirilov ducked his head, yes and no, and Aldanov was no more helpful. 'Who knows?'

The room was unbearably stuffy and Marriner wanted fresh air, but the windows were shut for winter. He tried to conceal his anxiety but those men in the grey raincoats were beginning to add up now, together with Aldanov himself and Kirilov the Ministry 'guide', into a wall of death, this obsession with internal security. He hoped to God she had registered Brzezinski's date of the twenty-sixth.

Marriner picked up his coat.

'OK. Let's hope I see her, before I leave.' He was standing up to go home, back to the scuffed cell in the Rossiya Hotel with the television on the blink.

'Of course.' Kirilov smiled, capped yellow teeth.

'You would like dinner tonight? I would be pleased to take you. Or find some company.'

Was that a hint of an escort service, Marriner wondered. Or a joke at the expense of Svetlana? 'No thanks,' he said. 'I'll do some work in the hotel.' There were letters to write, and photographs for Celia and Katie, and he might try to phone them. Also a postcard for Orford at the address supplied: a picture from the Borodino gallery of a pug-faced, red-haired Frenchman half-skewered by a bayonet.

Kirilov was again convoying him, down the stairs to the door,

145

where an official car would be waiting, the driver fiddling with its radio, to run them back to the hotel. All at once he was sick of Moscow, Kirilov, Aldanov, the grey men in overcoats lingering in grey doorways; he was no longer even tuned in to Svetlana's wavelength. He stood in the Kremlin grounds watching the last leaves flake from one of the plane trees on the road to the Borovitsky Gate. And shuddered. He felt the vulnerability of the operator on his own, and he wanted to play safe. Better to take a quick meal in the Rossiya restaurant and turn to the wall in his room than have another sad evening trying to be jolly with Kirilov's half-trusting eyes in some lugubrious watering hole. The sooner this was over, the better.

'No thanks,' he said. 'I'm turning in.'

Svetlana was uncertain as well. Alone in the Arbat apartment she was torn between affection and fear. The work was no longer a fall-back, something had shifted inside her as she understood Marriner better. Even the icons seemed unable to pacify, and she turned up the music in vain, wondering what was in store if she crash-landed with that collection for sale at Heathrow airport. Moscow was a frightening place as the days grew darker and colder and the watchers remained in the streets. She would have dearly loved company, but dared not telephone Marriner, and she waited for him in vain. She came home late and cooked herself basic meals, or asked for cold meats to be left by Alexandra the maid. Fanya was in Sverdlovsk, but her sister was older and settled, tied up with a teenage family and a civil engineer for a husband. They had little in common since they had drifted apart but she would have liked to confide now if only they could have spoken. But Sverdlovsk was nine hundred miles in the wrong direction, stuck in the freezing Urals, and her number was unobtainable. Svetlana sat on the bed, in the room with the wallpaper roses: sat on the bed and shivered.

Moscow had never been her city. She pulled on a dressing-gown and re-entered barefoot the great theatrical room with the heads of the saints lining the dark green walls. As if it were a church. The eyes in the varnished faces seemed to stare without pity as she thought about drinking and then pushed away the bottle.

But the Englishman refused to telephone, as if he had his own problems; nor did he come to her office inside the Armoury. Kirilov was there instead, telling her about Marriner's visits all over

146

Moscow, to the Army Museum, the City Museum, the Pushkin, the Borodino. What was he researching, Kirilov asked, and she knew he was probing and covered up, like a mother with a naughty boy, or, she admitted, a lover. She went to restyle her hair, and had it bleached again, and felt no better. A bitterness erupted inside her that he could be so callous, leaving her for so long, and yet she invented excuses and all the reasons for confusion.

In the end, after days of anxiety that seemed to have stretched for years, when the telephone finally rang she found that her voice was trembling.

'Yes – ?'

'Hello, my chicken,' he said. 'I've got a Tupolev waiting.'

For a moment she did not understand, thinking perhaps he'd learned Russian, but it was Asterharzy, macho man trying his luck.

'What do you mean?' she replied, her throat husky, brushing away the tears. He recognised the symptoms at once, but did not say so.

'I'm flying down to Tbilisi,' the pilot said. 'How about coming along?'

Mother of Saints, why should she? She had dismissed the man. The black dressing-gown fell open and she glimpsed her half-naked body, both desirous and ashamed. He was a first-rate prick, and that was all.

'I'm sorry Henrik. I've told you.'

Asterharzy was comforting. 'Chicken, are you all right? You sound unwell.'

'I'm fine,' she replied, unconvincingly.

'You work too hard,' he said, 'and need a break. A holiday.'

She held the telephone between her head and her shoulder and firmly refastened the robe, as if he was there in person, instead of in some airport call-box, by the sound of it.

'Perhaps. Some time. But not now, Henrik.'

He seemed to be laughing. 'Now come on, Svetlana. Remember I pointed out a few of the facts of life for a young lady like you in our present state of society.' It was a veiled reference to the men in the street below, and she was grateful to him for warning her, that afternoon when he had pestered her, and taken her to the old women in the tiny flat in the south-eastern district. 'Chicken, are you still there?'

'Yes,' she said quietly.

'Come away with me,' he urged. 'A weekend in Georgia would

do all the good in the world. I'm flying there tomorrow, a final-leg tour of duty, and staying for the weekend. I can arrange your flights.' He paused to let it sink in, then added carefully, 'I can arrange any flights. You ought to know that.'

What did he know, she wondered? Or was it just a coincidence? But then he said it again, more specifically, 'Leningrad for example, if you want. The weekend after this.'

That was Brzezinski's deadline.

'I think you'd better come,' he said.

Her head took charge of her heart again, and in some ways she was thankful. However he had come to know, or to guess, he was offering her the price of her passage, and she decided to buy it.

'All right,' she said slowly. 'When?'

His pleasure at the other end was almost audible.

'Meet me at Unukovo, inside the terminal. Three o'clock, tomorrow. I'll have the concessions ready.'

She found herself at the airport in the afternoon, received with a bunch of roses presented by a uniformed girl when she called at flight enquiries. There was a little white card with 'Captain Henrik Asterharzy' printed on it, and three kisses in green ink. She was taken to a VIP lounge with glass coffee tables and brown woollen carpets, away from the crush in the booking hall, and waited on by the hostess. A security policeman came in.

'Everything all right?'

She nodded and smoothed her knees, feeling her skirt was too short, but, hell, why had she come if she wasn't prepared? The policeman seemed to sense she was nervous.

'It's a good flight,' he said, admiring the roses. 'All quiet down there now. Somebody meeting you?'

'I'm not sure,' she admitted.

She hardly expected to see Henrik, of course, if he was flying the thing, but crammed into the aircraft she found her stomach contracting as it lurched down the runway, bumped and seemed to skim the trees. As if he was showing off. She tried to read a magazine but found it dull and poorly printed. She was used to a better diet, a Western bill of fare, she thought, as they brought round the in-flight service, water in plastic cups. The plane soared into the clouds and headed steadily south and she wondered why she had weakened.

Then he was coming towards her – Asterharzy – resplendent in his dark blue uniform and white shirt, smiling broadly, other

148

women admiring his dark curly hair. He had an easy charm, and even the glassy-eyed peasants in the opposite seats stared at him with respect. He was bending over her, a big man, an Austro-Russian from Minsk, smelling of Old Spice: Henrik too went abroad.

He pulled up her hand and kissed it as she sat with the flowers in her lap. She thought of the plane flying on with no one at the controls and felt the same way herself.

'When we get to Tbilisi, wait for me in the airport.' He winked. 'It's a romantic city.'

She said, 'I've never been there.'

'Well, you should. I will show you around. We have three days.' Three days, she thought, when she should have been organising, three days waiting for the Englishman, one of them a working day when Kirilov would notice her absence, but looking at the brute leaning over her with his handsome brown eyes she realised she was not so sure. She had clawed her way up like an actress and now she was tempted again.

Conscious of the eyes on her she gave him a polite smile, a message passing. 'I'll wait,' she said.

They came in over the mountains in the dusk and the necklaces of lights were strung out over the hillsides, thicker and thicker towards the city centre. The air outside had the warmth of a heated room, a pleasant contrast to Moscow already padding up for winter, and it seemed to relax her. Asterharzy knew how to pull strings and she was met by a car which whisked her across the tarmac. More flowers while she waited there and after a while he came, carrying his in-flight bag, a hulking man in crisp uniform and a gold-banded cap.

The hire car took them into the city along a palm-fringed road, with Asterharzy in the back, his arm already round her shoulders. She hated this sense of possession, as if he was buying her, and she had compromised by letting him. They swung round towards the river and he elbowed her into a tower on the bank of the Kuva, a modern hotel looming above in the darkness, Intourist accommodation.

Her heels clicked across the parquet, following him, conscious of the eyes on their backs. Were there still men in raincoats, she began to wonder, among those reading the papers between the potted plants?

'I've reserved a double room,' Asterharzy smirked.

She nodded. What it was to be young and free and fitted with a cap.

Nothing upset him now, no matter how distant she seemed, she was conscious of his self-confidence, the sense that she was in his power, as they dumped their bags in the bedroom looking down over the water, twenty storeys below. The air was oppressively close, a Mediterranean humidity, and the costume she had worn from Moscow was too thick for the climate, but somehow she did not want to change in the room with him watching.

'I'm going to have a shower,' he said.

'I'll wait.'

She sat on the edge of the bed, trying to read a guide book as he padded backwards and forwards in his underclothes. The water gurgled in the bathroom, and he made loud yodelling noises which she took to be singing. Perhaps he would try to seduce her there and then: why, oh God, had she agreed? But Asterharzy was more cunning, he came out still in his underpants, selected some casual clothes and disappeared again. He was a strongly built man with heavy biceps and calves that he had trained on weights: he reminded her of a bull.

Svetlana went into the bathroom, and watched him under the shower, looking more ludicrous there, his genitals bobbing about as he splashed in the cubicle.

'Come on in,' he urged.

'No thanks. Tell me something,' she said, remembering all too clearly why she had come. 'What did you mean by saying, back in Moscow, that you could arrange any flights?'

He stepped out of the shower and grabbed a towel: a hairy great brute and she felt happier when he began to dress.

'Flights to anywhere?' He looked cunning, his eyes were too close together.

'Yes. What made you say that?' She was unrelaxed, taut as a bowstring.

He tucked his shirt in his trousers, and zipped them up in front of her.

'Don't be a fool, chicken. I can read you like a book. You don't want me now, do you, with your *Anglishki* lover boy? I say to myself maybe you like a flight out, with some of your goodies, eh? Isn't that what you think?'

She coloured in spite of herself. Asterharzy studied his women and perhaps she had said too much. She loathed his guts, more so

150

because he divined that she was up to something, under surveillance. Bastard, she said to herself. He pressed home the advantage.

'Don't worry about me.' He pulled her close and felt her breasts, putting his hand unashamedly under her jacket. 'I won't give you away, as long as you play ball.'

She stood there and let him touch her for a moment, then she pushed him away. 'Later,' she said with hard eyes.

He went back into the toilet and she sat on the bed again, considering her position. Should she run away now, lock him in the room and vanish, take the first flight to Moscow? But if she really did that he might be tempted to shop her, when all he wanted was bed. She had had him before, and she could have him again, in spite of his little obsessions, it would be safer that way. She crossed her legs. Moreover he could help, in a way he was on her side. A flight captain had privileged status and could arrange tickets, just as he had brought her there, to the room with its colour TV and basket of oranges on the occasional table. Her hand strayed to his flight bag, thrown carelessly on the bed. He was still in the bathroom, shaving for his evening's fun with an electric razor that he'd taken from the bag. The lock was already undone and she opened the clip. Inside was a wad of money, the standard flight crew revolver and what seemed to be a whip.

She closed the bag again quickly as he re-emerged, blowing debris from the cutters, and stowed them away.

'OK, chicken. Let's eat. How do I look?' he asked.

'Vain,' she said, and he laughed.

She knew that she had to use him, while he was in this mood, for her ticket and Borovik's on the twenty-sixth.

'Listen,' she said. 'Before we start. Can you get me two tickets to Leningrad? For the twenty-sixth of the month?'

He stopped by the door and stared, his eyes wide open with interest.

'Ah. Of course. If I know the names.'

'One is for me,' she said. 'I want to see the Englishman off. He flies back from there the next day.'

'I see. So you want to go with him?' His heavy face was impassive.

'No. I go to see him off. As for me, well who knows? Maybe I have a reason to go to the West again. There is an exhibition in Brussels that he is working on.'

'You are in love?' he enquired, rubbing his jaw.

'He helps me professionally,' she said.

He paused, then said, 'OK. And who is the other one for? I must have names. Is it for your sexy friend?'

'No. A man called Borovik. Vasily Borovik.'

'OK,' he said again, no questions asked.

'You will arrange it tomorrow? Confirm the bookings and have the tickets sent to me?'

He nodded cheerfully. 'By hand,' he said, 'to Arbat Prospekt.'

A wave of relief surged through her, but she looked at him without pleasure. Now she must pay the price and there was lust in his eyes.

But Asterharzy wanted enjoyment as well as sex and they took a rattling taxi back into the town, to a restaurant on Rustaveli Boulevard. There was food and good wine and he was determined to drink, away from his tour of duty. As the evening wore on he swayed at her across the table, scrambled by too many bottles and the lights and the music.

'You're a real find, my chicken. I love your short hair.' He began to rub her arm, then to play with her fingers as if she were a game. His suggestions became obscene, and she bore it all, smiling bravely, her heart like ice, determined to get through the night and make sure that he ordered those tickets in the morning. Asterharzy called for more drink and fuelled himself up on peach brandy.

'I'll give you an evening,' he said. 'A night of love, my chicken, that you'll remember for ever. You can tell your lover boy that.'

She faced him and said, 'The tickets. Promise me you'll fix them tomorrow?'

A pained look on his face. 'Would I forget it, my queen?'

'I hope not,' she smiled.

'Let's drink to it,' he said.

'Haven't you had enough?' Other tables were looking, and even by Georgian standards he was laying it back.

'Why? Do you want to go?'

Shuddering, she said, 'Yes.'

Then they were driving back, Asterharzy comatose in the taxi while she prepared for the worst, hoping he would keel over with three bottles of wine and the best part of two of peach brandy tucked inside him. And she hated him.

He slammed the door of his room, their room, and locked it behind him, throwing the key on the writing desk with an air of satisfaction. His face was clammy with sweat, his chest heaving in the heavy air. She put the lights full on but he turned them down again and stood there gawping at her.

'I'll have a bath,' she said.

'You won't.' He was swaying like a punch-drunk boxer, standing with his feet splayed, a new hardness in his tone. 'You want me to help you. Now you help me.'

'What do you mean?' she whispered, a little girl again, fearing her first violation.

'Get into bed,' he said.

She shrugged. 'All right.' He would not last the course, she thought, but then he seemed to energise. He pulled off his clothes in a fury, purple-faced, and stood there facing her showing what he could manage. She felt sick.

'Lie on the bed,' he said.

She was in her underclothes, and he ordered her to take them off. Never in their couplings before, when they made love in Moscow, had she seen him so mad, as if the knowledge that she had jilted him was burning into his mind, and now he would get his revenge. His face was suffused with a kind of sweaty anger, his lips puffed up and his eyes pink as a pig's. She smelled his body sourness.

'You don't want me,' he raged.

'It's not that . . .'

'You cheated me,' he swore. 'You threw me out for the Englishman.'

'It was over before he arrived so far as I was concerned,' she mumbled into the pillow, between her tears, expecting to feel him claw her, force her, humiliate her.

Crack. At first she did not feel the pain, but then it cut into her skin as the whip from his bag licked at her ribcage and made weals on her buttocks.

'Henrik, no,' she screamed.

Crack. He hit her skin again and she flung herself round to confront him.

He stopped and stared, the whip poised in his hand as she faced him on the bed, holding the airline revolver, which in his drunken rage he had not seen her take from the bag.

She lay on the edge of the bed, naked, the weals on her back a reminder that underneath the charm and machismo there lurked a sadist.

'If you don't stop, I'll kill you.'

He paused, snorting like a champion bull. 'Don't be stupid,' he said. 'I don't want to hurt you, chicken. It's a game.' But his words were slurred and he became confused.

'Put that thing away,' she ordered.

'Of course, chicken.' He threw it on the floor, suddenly seeming ashamed.

Still covering him with the gun, she said, 'Now get into bed.'

He obeyed like a dog, sullen, wordless and confused. She would have taken him then, drunk and gross as he was, because she was still frightened, terrified out of her wits and she wanted his help, but all he was capable of was a kind of pawing, squeezing her breasts, his fingers in her groin, as if she was a piece of meat. A piece of meat. That was what he should be, she told herself, as she tried to keep sane, until he collapsed beside her and snored away into the night.

16

Sunlight filtered through the shutters of the overheated room as she awoke, to see his greasy head beside her, one arm half over her body. She was tempted to get the gun, there and then, and drill a hole in his complacent smile, but trying to move his arm disturbed him. His eyes opened, and she felt the pressure of his muscles: he had that Slavonic defensiveness, a cruel kind of suspicion that at one time had made her receptive, mothering almost, she who never doubted her self-confidence and superiority. Now the beast was in charge, a great hairy monster rearing up in the bed as she struggled to get away in the hot, damp room.

His great thighs pumped at her.

'Turn over.'

'No,' she whispered, the tiny girl again, abused, penetrated.

'Turn over,' he roared, a mad creature in the bed, a minotaur from the sea of her sleep, and pushed her downwards. She fought, she kicked, she screamed that she would kill him but he was insatiable, now that his stupor had cleared. 'You bitch,' he said, forcing her head down on the bed, dragging himself behind her,

Svetlana so important in Moscow and now so impotent with him, her pilot, her raging bull.

'You're hurting,' she shouted, but his lust was beyond redemption, the cruelty in his heart was real, as he saw the weals on her back, her buttocks.

'Bitch.'

When he had done he seemed to collapse on top of her, both of them slippery with sweat. Defiled and exhausted she crawled into the bathroom to wash away the stains, and saw that there was blood. She felt ashamed, a bitter anger inside her that she should have come to this.

The water ran over her body as she stood under the shower, in the enamel bath, trembling.

'Are you coming back?' he bellowed.

Mother of God, did he want her for more? She did not answer.

'Are you coming back?'

She returned, draped in the bath towel and he looked at her grinning. 'That will teach you,' he said, 'to give me the run around.'

She gathered some clothes to dress, away from him in the other room. She could not look at his face, the hirsute chest and great forearms. He was a monster.

'I'm very sore. You made me bleed,' she said.

'Cunt,' he replied.

Even then her mind was cooler, clearer than Asterharzy's. Now that he was spent he was cheerful, full of muddled goodwill.

'I'll send for breakfast,' he said.

She surveyed the stinking room, with the coverlet pushed to the floor, the sheets stained with her own blood and Asterharzy's shaggy presence like King Kong in the bed. The bedroom reeked of their odours and she wanted to fling open the shutters and breathe fresh air. She pulled on a skirt and sweater and unfastened the windows, stepping out on the tiny balcony. Her hands were still uncontrolled as she gripped the rail and stared at the scene below: the river sparkling in the hazy sunshine, a clutter of cars parked in the court, ant-like people on their errands while she had suffered her punishment. In her memory the walls of her room in the Arbat apartment were crowded with those strange faces glaring and staring when she had humped him before.

And one of the faces was changing, becoming lighter and paler; the face of David Marriner.

She turned and looked at the animal watching her from the disordered bed. Asterharzy had been rough before but never so sadistic. In their struggles they had overturned the coffee table and the bowl of apples and oranges had spilled over the floor. She bent to pick them up and straighten the carpet, one thing in her mind very clear. She had to make sure of those tickets that he had promised.

'I'd rather eat downstairs. This place is a pigsty.'

He scratched his head, then agreed.

'OK, chicken.' His moods seemed to change like slides and she wondered if he was really sane. Asterharzy was out of bed and retrieving his clothes from the pile of the night before. Already there was a stubble on the line of his mouth and chin but he did not bother to wash. 'Let's go,' he said. She found that her legs ached and her joints seemed to fail to connect. Asterharzy held her arm.

They came out of the room into the empty passage and went down in the lift like lovers but in her heart there was murder. No one seemed to have heard them, all her shouting and screaming had been lost to the world that was now made up of tourist parties at red and white checker-clothed tables.

Asterharzy lurched over and told them to hurry the service. He seemed to be cock-a-hoop, as if he had scored a triumph, a decisive victory in the warfare between them, but her eyes were hard as flint.

She drank the coffee thankfully, gradually more composed, and ate a sour cream pancake while Asterharzy wolfed everything that he could find: breadrolls, wheatflakes, cold meats, slivers of fish and cheese. She waited until he had finished and then she said, 'You promised me, Henrik.'

He belched and asked, 'What?'

'Tickets,' she said. 'Tickets to Leningrad, on the twenty-sixth.'

At first he seemed not to remember, growling, 'I want more coffee.'

She poured it for him and he began to look cunning.

'Leningrad? What does my chicken want there?'

'You know.'

He grinned, a strong mouth with gold-filled teeth.

'Ah yes. Your *Anglishki* lover boy. You tell him where you have been, eh? You show him your marks?'

She quivered as she pressed her fingers into the tablecloth, to stop herself spitting at him, controlling herself because she still needed to use him, aware of the restaurant watching.

'Tickets,' she said. 'He is going away. I want two tickets to see him go. For me and Borovik.'

'Borovik?' He twisted her tail. 'Has the *Anglishki* slept with him too?'

'You bastard,' she hissed, hating his handsome face, the hair of a Greek God, the nose of a Roman Emperor, the eyes too close together.

Asterharzy demurred. 'I love you, my chicken.'

Love, what was love, she wondered, if it ended like this? Was there any such thing, apart from self-interest and some cravings of lust?

'You promised me tickets,' she whispered.

He held up his hands towards her.

'Of course. Of course. I ask no questions. I promise. I get them for you.'

'Now,' she said. 'Before we go any further.'

'Plenty of time.' He looked at his watch. 'I will take you sight-seeing, maybe I buy you a dress. This is a beautiful country, full of lemon trees.'

'Now,' Svetlana said. 'I want to know for certain, now.'

He raised his eyebrows, the brown eyes expecting trouble.

'Does it matter so much?'

She nodded. 'Yes.'

For a while he did not answer and she feared another outburst. Instead, he finally sighed.

'OK.'

'Now?'

'Yes, yes. I order them now.'

She looked at him, this bleary-eyed monster shovelling toast in his mouth, with his red-veined nose and barbed-wire chest in the open shirt front, and wondered how she had ever succumbed. She must have been crazy and she loathed him for finding her weakness, hated him for the humiliation that he had inflicted. Even now she still had to beg, with the wounds sore on her back.

'Come on, then. Let's go.' She had a consuming urge to run away from the confusions in her mind and this troubled, terrible country, to the West she had seen and envied. She felt she had sold her soul. Asterharzy's coarsened power, a kind of perverted manhood, a pilot of fast machines who treated her like a dog, was the final clinching admission that she had lost her way. All she wanted now was her revenge, and then to run.

He sank more cups of coffee and signed the chit: a big man full of confidence, dominating the room as if to say that he'd had her, this white blonde in the two-piece green costume, hair cut short like a boy's.

'What's the rush? I take you, show you the sights. I show you where people were killed in the demonstrations.'

'The tickets first,' she said.

He was difficult then. 'What do I get for it?'

'You've had your price.'

He leered. 'No way, my chicken. I brought you here and you're mine.'

She was Head of the Armoury, a career woman with a confident past, an even more confident future, and she had demeaned herself, tried to make a lover of him and ended up as a whore. The inside of her throat seemed scarlet, she wondered if she tasted blood.

'Please,' she begged. 'I want to make sure that we get to Leningrad quickly, on the twenty-sixth.'

They left the restaurant together, his arm in hers as if he had right of possession.

'Internal flights are no problem. You order your tickets yourself.'

'Listen,' she said. 'For Borovik it would not be wise. You understand? I am under surveillance. Borovik must not leave Moscow without permission. If I order tickets myself the authorities will be notified: I am on the security listings. Now do you understand? But from here it is different. In your name.'

His eyes opened wide, the shrewdness she had once admired, and taken for honesty.

'You are in trouble,' he said. 'I knew it. I told you about the police.'

'Let's not stand here talking,' she reminded him, as they argued in the lobby. 'I want you to go to Aeroflot.'

Asterharzy grabbed her and kissed her. 'Anything you say, at a price.'

He bundled her into a taxi and walked into the airline offices in Lenin Square. In five minutes it was done, and she had the two precious tickets, reservations in his name which would not now be queried because of his security clearance, the prefix on his papers as a senior captain on the international flights. One was for S.

Malinkova, occupation curator, the other for V. Borovik, scientist. Nowhere was rank mentioned. Georgia was another country and they did things differently there from the twitchy, hard-faced desk clerks reporting to the Moscow KGB: reporting, if she had known it, to the likes of Colonel Kazakov. But even so she was still trembling as they came out from the office, and stood watching the trolley buses swirling round Lenin's statue in the tree-lined square.

'A glorious day, my chicken,' Asterharzy said, in good spirits, pointing out the seminary where Comrade Stalin had started. Now it was a museum full of golden treasures, more relics of the old religion. She ought to have had a professional interest, but her body ached and Asterharzy had other plans. The weather was crisp and clear, the sky seemed a painted blue and he wanted to show off.

They climbed back into the taxi and threaded along the river, out of the city. She did not know this lush, southerly country wedged in between the mountains, where palm trees grew in the streets and there were grapes on the hard, dry, dark green hills. He was taking her into them now, sitting in the back seat fondling her, his paws on her thighs already, as if it did not matter, as if she was his chattel. She tightened her body and held her bag on her knees as the first line of defence.

'No,' she said.

'Shut up. You do as I say.'

But he wanted to show her something, some place he had been to before, as the car climbed laboriously along the roads of the valley, and she prepared for her fate comforted that at least the taxi-man was there to intervene.

It was a beautiful day now, a serene blue over the hills where the trees were like tufts of green wool as they reached a rocky spur and he told the car to pull in, on the edge of a ridge.

'There,' Asterharzy said, pointing down the valley, a toy landscape with model trains, the meeting place of two rivers, a confluence of the ancient trails that led from China to Europe. And nestling at the bottom, in the V of the rivers, the domes and roofs of a town.

'Mtskheta, the old capital,' Asterharzy said. 'It's in a mess,' he grinned. 'Like you.'

'Up here,' he said, beginning to scramble up the cliff from the road, and she saw there was a church at the top, an ancient cruciform edifice with a tiled rotunda. There was no one to see them, the driver waited in his cab, and she sweated after this monster like a hot bitch following a dog. They climbed three hundred feet, out of sight of the road, to the deserted building, which she now saw was in ruins. Asterharzy kicked open the door.

Peering inside she saw the round drum of the cupola, and the four cruciform arms. Light filtered from high windows, dust swirled in the air like snowflakes. The church had been cut from rough stone, and left to deteriorate. There were carvings over the door, mysterious carvings of lions and round-headed birds, but what drew her most was the stillness, a sense of loss.

Asterharzy had jumped on a window ledge, four feet above the ground. He stood there in the dusty light swinging his arms like a windmill. She gripped her shoulder bag and faced him, staring up from the floor. The damp-stained church, abandoned and left to rot, gave out messages that she tried to decipher, from the pitted roof marked by lost paintings to the floor worn hollow by pilgrims.

Asterharzy shouted, bellowing with his lungs, the howl of a chieftain beating to arms, and the ugly discordant notes echoed round the empty building that had been built for plainsong, and bombarded her ears. A howl that went on and on, as if he would split his sides, a primitive tuneless noise, discordant and barbaric. And then he spat: spat down into the chancel where she stood, his saliva glistening before her feet.

When he stopped, exhausted, Svetlana called out to him, 'Why did you do that?'

The reverberations had disturbed more dust and now he was almost veiled by a curtain of yellow particles, suspended in the air between them. He looked like a god up there, and she was afraid.

'Why did you bring me here?'

'It is a church,' he called. 'A goddamn fucking church. Isn't that what you want?'

'It's a dead church,' she said. 'Abandoned. Empty. Look, there are holes in the roof.'

He laughed, a chilling, echoing laugh that screamed at her: she held her hands over her ears.

'You like churches,' he said. 'You live in the past. Why don't you like this one?'

'Because it's disused,' she replied.

Again she fought against his manic, cackling laugh. He was teasing her, tormenting her, destroying her.

'There are piles of shit in that corner, if you want to look. People come here to shit . . . and to fuck,' he shouted.

160

He jumped down and ran towards her, catching her before she could flee outside down the precipitous hillside to the waiting taxi. He caught at her jacket and ripped it, she felt the stitches part and fresh pain in her shoulder. 'Come here, pretty chicken. I'll show you what I think of your churches and your relics and icons.'

'No,' she screamed, hitting him with her fist, and running towards the door.

'Oh yes, sweet legs. I'll show you what I think.'

She managed to escape at last as he stumbled on the broken floorblocks, but he came after her with his bull-like strength, pushing her to the ground. They rolled on the rough grass, on the path outside the door, and she saw the sky wheel above her as he tore at her fastenings.

'No. No.' She hammered and kicked at his groin, but he was too tough, too powerful, and pulled her into the bracken that grew alongside the track up which they had climbed. She caught her clothes on bushes, thorns tore at the skin, his head was on top of hers and she gasped at the weight of his body.

'Fuck you, chicken,' he laughed.

She pushed and shouted to stop him but there was no one to hear. The driver was asleep in his cab three hundred feet below and birds were the only witnesses. He was trying to press into her now, her back and buttocks still sore where he had thrashed her before, and she felt it would never end, that she could never stop him. Her shoulder bag was somehow still there and she touched it lying by her hand. Asterharzy was winning now, his body pressed on to her legs, her knickers torn off, but in the bag she could feel the hard outline of the service revolver, the small automatic that she had seen in his flight-bag and taken in self-defence.

'Don't, please don't,' she yelled.

'Shut up.' He was grunting like the bull he was, absorbed in his own requirements and her mind was blank with fear as somehow she pulled out the revolver and cocked the safety catch.

She had warned him like this before, on the previous night, and he treated it as a joke: she was a thing he despised. Now she shouted again, as he tried to find entry against her wriggling, kicking body.

'Stop, or I'll kill you.'

He did not seem to hear, he was past the point of control when the gun suddenly exploded, tearing a hole in his skull and spattering his brains on her face.

Svetlana sat up on the grass and felt the weight of his body fall away. The hole seemed huge, the back of his skull blown in, the bullet cleaving the plates at the top of his head. His blood and brains dirtied the grass as he rolled over on to his back, his eyes open in astonishment. She still had the gun in her hand, hot with the stench of explosive, and her mind reeled. She managed to wipe her face and then found her stomach left her as she realised what had happened and did not know what she intended. She vomited across the dead pilot and collapsed.

When she came to, the scene was still there. She was lying across Asterharzy's legs and his blank face stared at that blue, unrelenting sky. Around her the heather and bracken were crisp and high. Still nothing moved, the only faint sound was the wind, rattling the wooden shutters of the broken church above them. She found the gun on the grass and her eyes travelled from there to the body of the pilot, legs thrown loosely like a broken doll, one arm across his chest, the head draining of its colour as a mass of blood seeped into the ground behind it. She was on her knees now, looking at the stains on her jacket, fortunately not very much, and she rubbed them with a handkerchief from the shoulder bag, little specks of bone and tissue. There was blood across her face and nose, and she had to remove that too, sitting beside his body, half hidden by the ferns. Her head was singing with horror, and the first thoughts of self-preservation. Dear God, she had killed him. Had she intended it? Or only to frighten again, as on the night before? Her own mind shook with confusion but she fought to get away, the instinct to escape now paramount. On her knees she began cleansing desperately, hands, legs, skirt, face and hair, each of them dishevelled, sticky and stained with his blood. Poor bastard, she thought, and retched, but no longer sick, her nerves coming under control and her own self-preservation, that ruthlessness which served her so well, taking over again.

Under that plain blue, deadening sky, the sun high up at midday, she struggled to make sense of this thing, this lump of carcass beside her, the body that had beaten and dominated and still could revenge by his death. For the first time in her life the prayers she had never admitted, never understood, were crawling round her brain like the flies that had appeared from nowhere, blowflies and midges awaiting their own deaths and given a few hours' pleasure by this grisly execution. Oh God, she prayed, let me escape, take me away, don't let them get me now. Fingerprints on the gun. Her marks would be on his body. He had been seen with her, they were in the hotel together. And in a week she had planned to be free, Marriner had promised it to her, in one week she could be away, out of this terrible country where the winters shut down like ice and even in summer there was a soullessness, a sadness she found oppressive, where lovers made love in their socks; Mother of God, let me get out, give me time to get away.

Her head was much calmer now, the crisis had been surmounted and she wiped the pistol carefully with a second small handkerchief from the pocket of her coat, then forced it into his hand and closed the fingers round it. She began looking around, at the empty hillside and the square little church behind them. The big, empty country said nothing. How long, she wondered, how long, before he would be missed? Two or three days perhaps, before they became alarmed, when he did not return for duty with Aeroflot. And then they would begin to check, trying to establish his movements, verifying his trip to Georgia with herself. But it would take them weeks to find him, if she was lucky, out in this wilderness of scrub and rock. She realised she could hide a body, if only she could carry off what had happened that morning. Strengthened in her new resolve, she looked again at the church, standing on the edge of its spur over the steep gorge. The old stone building had been built at the top of the cliff with a path curving up to it, along which they had toiled. So they were at the cliff end too, although she had scarcely realised. She tottered to her feet, terrified and feeling the soreness of all the beating and pummelling, but conscious of what she must do. She clawed her way through the bracken to the edge of the rocks and stared down. Hundreds of feet below them was the curve of the Kuri river towards the Mtskheta confluence, she could see the huddle of red roofs and the domes of its churches, like a painting on the far bank. If she could only get him there, Asterharzy, to this edge, he would tumble down into the bushes and might never be found. Hope compounded with fear as she ran back to his body and, taking him by the legs, pulled him round, inert as a sack of potatoes. He was too heavy for her, a twelve stone deadweight, but desperation drove her on, and she was moving him, slowly but surely moving him.

She paused, gasping for breath and listening. The wind still flapped the church door that he had kicked open. She must remember to shut it. The driver would be in the taxi, bored, waiting, probably asleep, she guessed. Too idle to climb up and find them. How long had they been gone? Astonishingly, less than an hour, glancing at her wristwatch. She picked up the legs again and heaved him towards the last line of rocks, leaving a thin trail of blood from the congealing ooze on the back and top of his head, disturbing the flies which settled as soon as he was still, this thing, this terrible thing. One more heave and she was there at the edge, with the great broken doll, and staring down at the slope. But if he rolled there, he could still be seen, he might wedge on the rocks below where nothing grew. Oh God, she prayed again, help me, help me to cover him. And then she saw there was a ledge, fifty or so feet down where some small shrubs were growing, juniper or myrtle trees clinging to the hillside. If she could tip him there, she could scramble down and conceal him, not for ever but with luck for a week.

She heaved his legs over the edge and shut her eyes so as not to see the blown-in back of his skull, white splinters of bone and black hair in a blood-soaked porridge. One desperate push with her remaining strength and he was gone, while she stood gasping and rocking on the edge of the cliff, watching his body tumble, arms and legs flailing at nothing, the revolver falling somewhere apart, until Asterharzy slowly settled among the bushes below. There was a scatter of dust and earth, a few stones rolling further downwards, and then once again that ominous, pervasive silence, as if only the fates were watching. But she could see him clearly, his light blue shirt and brown trousers, spreadeagled in the bushes, and his face was turned upwards as if he was mocking her.

She would have to go down and cover him, down that steep cliff herself, but terror made her determined, because she wanted to live. She took off her flat shoes, so as not to scuff them too much, and the torn green jacket and her skirt. It was warm enough to work in her underclothes, and easier to clean up afterwards. Hand over hand she was working her way downwards, dislodging chips of rock, a small landslide of earth, edging from foothold to foothold on the precipitous cliff. If she fell and missed the ledge she would pirouette hundreds of feet and smash herself against the boulders, but she thought of nothing but the need to get down there. Then she had landed beside him, saw that ghastly face again, and said, 'Oh God, forgive me.' There was no time to rest, she was tearing at handfuls of branches, brown ferns and elephant leaves and pulling them over him, covering his face and hands and the rest of the body. The ledge was some two metres wide, heavily overgrown where the plants had self seeded; peering below it she saw a series of shelves, each one shallower, all the way down the cliff. Perhaps she should have tried to roll him down to the next in line, but that one would be unreachable, if the body was still exposed. She tried to dig in around him with her bare hands, pulling the undergrowth over, cracking the branches and twigs, which snapped and scratched her flesh.

And then it was done. Over. She paused, tired out, and realised she had buried him completely under the mass of foliage. Here and there his clothing peeped out, but it could not be seen from above. But what if the branches blew off? She found stones and weighted them down as best she could. In the process his shoes poked through, and she took them off and threw them away. She watched them flutter down the cliff face like two wheeling birds, until they disappeared. Her underclothes were damp with sweat, her chest rasping for breath, but Asterharzy was concealed. Exhausted, battered, she hauled herself up again, struggling over the edge and back to the safety of the place from which she had tipped him. Only then did she realise how dangerous it had been as she stared down at the ledge where nothing now could be seen, and beyond it to the bottom of the valley and the grey snake of the river.

Asterharzy was dead, and buried, as far as she could arrange, and she was alive and unseen. For that she thanked her new-found God. She was trembling and dizzy as she recovered her clothes and dressed again. The green jacket had a torn shoulder but it could be concealed if she did not move her arm, the skirt was creased but unmarked, she had taken care with the shoes. By the mirror in her handbag she combed and smoothed her short, blonde hair, put on a dash of lipstick and checked that her face was clean. She breathed in heavily to calm her nerves, took one final look at the ground marks where they had rolled and fought. There were bloodstains on the bigger leaves and she pulled them up and threw them away. The crushed grass needed straightening out, but it was not so difficult, once Asterharzy had gone. The blood had seeped into the soil. Unless you were really looking it was no more than a nest in the undergrowth, a place for lovers. She shuddered. The stone church behind her was black against the skyline, a pepperpot on top of the hill. She saw the straggling path back to the road and the car. It was time for her to go.

The chipped black Moskvich that they had hired had rolled into the shade of some trees, and at first she could not find it as she came round the corner of the rocks.

For a moment she panicked again, thinking that it had abandoned them, but then she saw it parked close to the road, like a dead beetle. There were no other cars on the dirt track in this lonely spot and the driver must have wondered where the hell his passengers were. Now only one was returning, and he did not even look up.

When she reached the car she saw why. He was stretched out on the back seat, *Pravda* over his head, taking a midday nap. On the front passenger seat were the remains of a roll and a half-eaten apple.

She tapped on the side of the car and his head appeared: a middle-aged taciturn Georgian with blue stubble on his chin, who spoke poor Russian.

'OK,' she said. 'We go.'

He scrambled to his feet and climbed out, looking puzzled, blinking in the sunshine. Down here she could hear the crickets, still buzzing in the grass. At the first frost they would die too.

He jerked his thumb behind her. 'Where is the other one?'

She shrugged. 'He is not coming.'

'Not coming?' His forehead tried to work that out. 'It's twenty-five kilometres back into town.'

'We had a quarrel,' she said.

He inspected her white face, noticed a scratch on her bare leg. Somehow she did not look so smart as when she started out with that big guy with the dark hair.

'What's going to happen to him?'

'He's sulking,' she said. 'He'll make his own way back.'

'It's a bloody long walk,' he said.

'He'll get a lift on the road.'

He opened the car door and jumped into the driving seat, relieved to be going at last. The remains of the bread and apple were thrown on to the grass.

'Shall I come back for him?'

'No need,' she said. 'Just take me back to Tbilisi. He can do what he damned well likes.'

The cab driver nodded slowly. He'd seen this happen before. Wouldn't mind betting he'd got her up there in the bushes and tried to have a poke. She was reacting now as if she'd bitten his cock.

'OK,' he said. 'It's his funeral.'

17

Sometimes he was sure they were following him, sometimes not. In Moscow the winter seemed to have come already: wind out of Siberia chilled Marriner to the bone, scattered the shrivelled leaves and brought dark in mid-afternoon as hailstones battered the streets.

Kirilov became quite friendly, as if this raw cold was a test of stamina that his stocky frame relished. Back in the Armoury Marriner and Aldanov finished examining the guns, the long black muskets that had decimated Napoleon's cavalry.

'When will you be writing about us?' Aldanov asked.

Marriner kept up the pretence, no longer feeling a shit but more and more the field operator that Orford had seen in him. Aldanov showed him the plans, the despatches and other relics, but the Russian texts defeated him, as he bluffed his way through the second week.

'When I get home,' he replied, sitting in Aldanov's study, drinking tea. Aldanov had set up a desk for him in the corner and the room, already crowded, was now an obstacle course, where they climbed over cardboard boxes to reach the chairs. Rain ran down the windows in silver beads.

'Good,' Kirilov beamed from the doorway. 'You must send me a copy.'

It was easy to believe they were friendly, and not just keeping him tagged. He was tempted at times to pull out and leave it all to Brzezinski, forget Svetlana's problems, let Borovik find his own solution, but something always stopped him. In part it was the Russians themselves, who never left him alone, suspicious as well as concerned; in part his own conscience, a sense of commitment to Orford and the recognition that Celia was now in a way on his side. He smiled at his minders on the top floor of the Armoury.

'I need time to write up my research.'

'Of course. Of course. Please do not let us disturb you.'

They pressed on him new maps, statistics of battles, tallies of trophies acquired, taken from mouldering records in the muniments room. A girl came to help him translate them, a dark-haired interpreter who said that her name was Saskia, and that she lived with a girlfriend in a concrete bottle-crate on the Outer Ring.

'Kusutzov was better than Napoleon,' she said glibly. It was always the way. That tight, nationalistic pride was ganging up against him again, as suspicious of foreigners as ever. To get people out of this country, two senior Kremlin people, one of them with her icons, still seemed a tough proposition. Marriner shrugged, pushing aside the maps, deciding he had had enough. The heating in the dark, high-ceilinged rooms was hot enough for a stokehold.

He said goodnight to Saskia and Aldanov and gathered up his papers.

'I'll call for you at seven-thirty,' Kirilov said.

He was being taken to Kirilov's home, a rare privilege. An apartment near the Kiev station where he lived with his wife and two daughters, blushing, shy teenage girls in gingham dresses. Irena Kirilova was determined, on her home ground, and fed him as if he was starving, an orphan from some strange country, on borsch and meat stew and pancakes, while Ivan Kirilov beamed and sweated at the end of the table that dominated their living room. Three clocks chimed each quarter hour: Kirilov was obsessed by time and spent his spare cash repairing them. Through the curtained windows they could hear the swish of traffic, rumbling in the rain-washed streets. It was a night to be indoors, fuelled up on wine and vodka, but he knew it was more than a gesture, the motives were concealed in the warmth.

'You have enjoyed Moscow?' Kirilov was pressing, his bald head shining under the centre light, brushing crumbs from his moustache.

'Very much. A lot to see and do.' His answers were as bland as possible, and he had to seem grateful.

'And you go back on the twenty-sixth?'

'To Leningrad, yes. I have to change planes there.'

Kirilov nodded sadly, offering more vodka. 'British Airways, better planes.'

'It's just a question of flight times,' Marriner lied, calculating the problems Brzezinski would have to overcome if he really was to get freight out of the airport unchecked.

'I understand.' That sucked-in, crushed smile while his wife made them coffee and the daughters giggled. Kirilov took off his glasses and polished them.

'You like Svetlana, eh?'

It was a sniper shot, tried in the dark, and Marriner jerked in reaction. Kirilov used the intimate name.

'She has been very good.'

The Russian contemplated his glasses, holding them up to the light as if he was reading the future.

'What you think of her? A beautiful creature?'

'Certainly. Very attractive.'

'A sexy girl, eh?' Kirilov grinned at his wife's square back as she went out to the kitchen.

Marriner put up his guard, unsure how much they knew, wondering whether their love-making was already a KGB tape on general release.

'I suppose so, yes.'

Kirilov leaned his elbows on the lace tablecloth and picked his teeth. 'Oh. There is no doubt. She has had many lovers.'

Many lovers? What was he trying to tell him, or was he just fishing?

Marriner stirred uncomfortably and gulped his black, sweet coffee. 'I can't believe that,' he muttered. But he was unwise with women, he knew that too, and Kirilov's eyes seemed to say so, flashing a half-drunk message.

'Oh. It is true. Where do you think she is now?'

Marriner was concerned at her absence that weekend, and had made careful enquiries, which must have filtered back. Kirilov's daughters' faces showed they were unable to follow the conversation in English. They smiled and left the table like young Victorian ladies.

'I've no idea,' he said.

Kirilov stuck a plastic toothpick into a piece of bread, like a small boat with a mast, sailing on the white cloth. His face was as bland as a family doctor's, full-mooned and serious.

'I will tell you. She has gone to Georgia for a holiday with her lover.'

'Her lover?' The words fell away from Marriner, and seemed to spin in the air. Kirilov knew that his shot had gone home.

'Of course. Do you think a girl like that, unmarried, successful, beautiful, does not want to have a lover?'

Marriner considered the situation, as his blood ran cold. Somehow he had not expected that she would cheat him so, although she had mentioned lovers in the past. Why should he assume that he was the one and only, or even the first in line? But it was a revelation.

'I was told she was going on business. Aldanov said so.'

Kirilov moved the toothpick and resumed probing his molars.

'Of course. Her business. With an airline pilot.'

'An airline pilot?' If they knew so much about her how much did they know about him, Marriner wondered. And when would she be back? He would have to find Brzezinski and warn him.

'Yes. It is known to us all,' Kirilov said, smiling. 'It does not matter.'

Doesn't matter? Marriner's mood was bitter, remembering the forged letter, the protestations of innocence. If she could deceive him thus she could have deceived him before, about the pregnancy and the letter in conjunction with Werndl. He felt sick and cheated.

'Who is he?'

'Does it matter?'

Marriner subsided. 'No. I suppose not.'

Kirilov was leaning over. 'Do you . . . fancy her?'

'Impossible,' Marriner said.

Kirilov was wagging a finger, pointing the toothpick.

'Ah, but be careful, my friend, she can bring you bad luck.'

It was as clear a warning as the KGB could give, if Marriner had known.

Monday and Tuesday dragged by, and the countdown was now five days. He had to see Brzezinski, to warn him of what was happening in the dark, closed-in city.

He rang up and asked for tickets. The Maly was sold out, they said. At the Embassy Wootten-Smythe was unavailable and the man who replied seemed to think he was cadging a favour. In despair he turned to Aldanov, and asked if he knew a way in, but the Keeper of Weapons lost interest. So he telephoned the Ukraina, where the ETC party was staying. At first it was almost impossible to make them understand, but he persisted and at length reached a girl called Rosalind, who said that she was in costumes and would give Danny a message. All this, by telephone, in Moscow, he knew was courting trouble but the news about Svetlana, and her prolonged absence, seemed to give him little choice.

170

'Daniel Brzezinski is busy,' Rosalind said, as if it was Marriner's fault. 'We're in the last three days here. He's got to sort the whole show out.'

Marriner hoped as much, but he needed to talk to the Pole, and that meant he had to take risks. Half an hour before the performance he tried to cross Sverdlov Square and found it was ringed by police. The pavements had been roped off and no one was being allowed near unless they had valid tickets, but Marriner suspected the worst as they waved him away. The grey men were back in the doorways, watching where strangers were going.

Instead he found a restaurant, a Hungarian-style place near the Square, and ordered a meal; it took as long to get fed in Moscow as five acts of *Othello*. He wrote another postcard to Katie saying he hoped to be back before it actually arrived; and then, on an afterthought, sent the spare one to Challenby. 'Trying to get sorted out,' he wrote. 'Lots of confusion but expect to have seen the light before I come back. Returning Monday, Yours D.M.' Let the smart arse see what he made of that. Turning over the back, it occurred to him to study the picture, another one in the series on the Moscow Underground. Belyayevo Station in snow: the end of the line.

At eleven o'clock he stepped outside again, into the freezing air. The wind had strengthened as he walked back across the square, towards the bright lights, but the traffic had slackened and the police had departed. Even so he felt conspicuous: the trouble with being alone in a city like Moscow was that all strangers were stared at. He walked past the Bolshoi portico as the lights went out, then across the street and down by the side of the Maly. What was 'stage door' in Russian? But he need not have worried: a handful of hopefuls, students, theatre buffs, Anglophiles, were crouching under a canopy, clapping as people came out, waiting for the great John Crashaw. He had learned enough Russian manners to push to the head of the queue, ignoring the complaints. There was a woman on guard, a formidable square-shouldered attendant who glared at him in the half-light of the single bulb.

'*Anglishki*,' he said.

'*Nyet*.' Her arm came down like a barrier.

Some of the spear-carriers emerged, hurrying back to their hotel, a couple of young ETC actors whose names he never knew. He grabbed their coats as they slipped past.

'Listen, for Christ's sake. I must see Daniel Brzezinski,' Marriner hissed. 'It's important.'

The English message was clear-cut, and they reacted at once over the babble of argument that had broken out. The dragon's hand flailed 'no entry'.

'You carry on arguing, I'll go and get him,' one said.

They stood on the icy pavement, Marriner, the Russians, the guardian, until he came. Marriner could not be sure whether he was still observed, somewhere in the parked cars, by men with night glasses, but this queue clamouring for autographs was not a part of the system. All of them whipped by the wind, huddling for shelter along the theatre wall.

Brzezinski came after five minutes, smoking a cigarette, wearing a leather coat. 'Let's walk round the block,' he said, 'and make it quick.' He pulled on a flat cap as if he was dressing for a point-to-point.

'Where's Svetlana?' were the Pole's first words.

Marriner fought against the cold, which was already eroding the warmth of his meal and brandy. His raincoat seemed made of paper.

'I was hoping you'd tell me.'

'No way,' Brzezinski said. 'She should have been at the Armoury yesterday.' He withdrew his hands from his pockets and rubbed them together. 'Hurry up. I've got to go back. How do you know the buggers aren't watching us?'

'I hope they've all gone home.'

'Huh. No bloody hope. And no Svetlana, no deal eh?'

Marriner shivered, as much at himself as the cold. What a bloody stupid fix, the whole bag of tricks collapsing if she did not turn up.

'Can't you get Borovik out without her?'

'What do I fucking do?' Brzezinski asked. 'Ring up the Kremlin, ask if he can come to play?'

'But if she's disappeared there must be a reason.'

'Of course there's a reason,' the Pole snapped. 'It's probably the KGB.'

'I don't believe it. They can't have anything on her.'

They stood on the corner of the street, before walking on. A militia van trundled by, looking for trouble.

'Time is getting short,' Marriner said. 'She must come back. She may have been delayed on that trip to Georgia.'

'Sure. Sure. You're an optimistic bastard.' Under the sodium lighting, Brzezinski shrugged. 'All right, I'll give her a day. We don't move out till Sunday.'

Marriner pulled the Pole back as he turned away. 'But if she contacts me what the hell do I tell her?' This was what he needed to know. 'What do I say?'

'Say?' Brzezinski stared at him. 'Just ask her if she's ready for the decorators. That's all.'

'That's all?' Marriner repeated. It was like every spy book he'd read, but now for real.

'Right,' Brzezinski said. 'If you can raise her, give me a ring at the hotel. 2294072. Got that? Someone will take a message, probably Rosalind.'

'The decorators?'

'That's right.' Brzezinski burrowed his head tortoise-like into the thick collar of the leather coat. 'She'll know what it means. And mind your hide.' He held out his hand in a formal goodbye. Marriner grasped the stone-cold fingers, and wondered if his own had frostbite, then Brzezinski was gone, swallowed up by the night.

But when the telephone rang, as he was shaving in his hotel room on the following morning, it was not Svetlana but Celia.

The line was not very good, and he heard a buzzing and clicking as if it was being recorded. He responded with caution, but Celia seemed to have continued the recovery that he had noticed in London. Her voice had a freshness that he had not heard for years, and he found genuine pleasure in talking to her.

'I'm putting Katie on to say hello.'

They must have been up with the dawn, to catch him at that hour, but his daughter increased his happiness and told him what he was missing, in small talk more private than all the arrangements for Borovik's defection, and Svetlana's freedom. He listened, knowing it would fool them, those secret decoders, as she babbled about Janice Lanyard's rabbit and the class visit to the zoo.

'When are you coming home, Daddy?'

The sooner the better, he thought, even if empty-handed; surely it couldn't go wrong now, with Svetlana or Borovik . . . ? He supposed in their way they were traitors, but neither saw it like that: Svetlana too full of self-interest, Borovik a man with a conscience.

'Are you still there, Daddy?'

Yes, he was still there. Just. Nervous of what was happening but unable to pin it down.

Celia had repossessed the telephone. 'Darling?'

Was he hearing aright: had they got a crossed line? She hadn't used that tone for years. It was as if the parting, the sense of mission that Denis Orford had conveyed to her in his blunt Yorkshire way, had given her new respect. 'Is everything all right?' she said. 'We got your postcard, but we want you home.'

We want you home. What had changed her, he speculated. So much for the second petition, and the letter from Svetlana filed with Pitt Rivers and Fawley. His hopes soared. Sitting by the side of the bed, in a plastic, button-backed chair with a tear in the seat, he said, 'Do you really mean that, C?'

There was a tiny cry of admission.

'What about her?' she said. 'That woman?'

Over the indistinct line he was having to hammer out a position that could incriminate Svetlana.

'There is nothing between us.' But he had slept with her, against his common sense, and Celia could almost feel it.

'How do I know that?' The old cautious edge had returned to her voice.

'Celia. I can't discuss it now.' Oh Christ, what would they make of that, those line-tappers somewhere? 'But I promise you, darling. I swear to God.'

'What about the letter?' she said. 'The letter that she signed?'

'For Christ's sake, C, I can't sort that out now, over the telephone. Don't ask me now. Please, C. Don't press me,' he begged.

'I told you that I believed you, before you left,' she said. 'Just hurry back, and prove it.'

Desperately, he tried to turn the subject, asking about Katie, whether she had visited her friends, the details of life in High Barnet, remote and foreign. And Celia played along. In her mind she was beginning to see that it might not be a perfect match but it might be the best of the options.

Marriner was in a different country, another world, where two lives hung in the balance. How could he forget Svetlana, after what had happened between them? He was pulled apart by conflicting demands.

'Are you still there, David?'

'Sure.'

'I want to tell you something,' her voice said over the crackling line. 'I'm withdrawing my petition.'

The second petition. Edmondson had done his stuff, or perhaps she was really contrite. Marriner's heart was pounding.

'Celia, that's wonderful.'

'How much do you love me?' she asked.

Love. Love? A kaleidoscope. She hadn't used the word in years, yet now she was screwing him up, two thousand miles away, in a Moscow hotel room. He needed that question on notice, but she was pressing him.

'It's been a long road . . .' he said.

'I know. I know. I'm sorry.'

Sorry. Celia, sorry? Another bridge had been crossed, a milestone passed, and he ran down the road to meet her, scarcely crediting his fortune. All that he had once believed in came back to him now.

'Celia. We can make it. I'm sure we can.' And not just for Katie's sake. It was only a sense of duty that kept him in Moscow, once his wife had swung round as if a coma had ended; but two lives still precariously depended on the contacts he made.

'Yes, David. But how much do you love me?' she insisted.

In his head was a terrible confusion between what he desired and what he had recently done. Svetlana's white limbs on the bed, the open invitation on a Moscow afternoon, the commitment he had entered into for her sake and Borovik's, and now her disappearance before he could settle anything.

'All the way, Celia.' The words brought increasing assurance. 'If you can only meet me.'

She really was crying now, he could hear her sobs on the telephone, and it perturbed him.

'Don't. Celia. Please don't.'

The trooper in her took over.

'David. Just come back safely.'

When she rang off he sat for a long time worrying. There were only three days to go.

18

'The Director wants to see you,' Kirilov announced, sliding into the room at the top of the Armoury where Marriner was sitting with Aldanov.

'The Director?'

Boris Kirilov was smiling, like a country physician whose patient had miraculously recovered. 'Dr Malinkova is back. She has been for a few days in Georgia, and please could you come to see her?'

Marriner felt a surge of relief that drained to the end of his toes, and then returned as concern. Concern that he should get it right, concern at a relationship that cut across Celia's call earlier that same morning. He nodded at Kirilov and edged past Aldanov's table, where the Russian was writing letters in longhand for a copy typist.

'OK.'

He followed Kirilov along the familiar corridor lined with coloured lithographs. Sand-coloured walls where the carpet began. This was where she had received him on his first visit, in the Director's suite with her stone-faced secretary guarding the samovar in the outer office, ushering them through to Svetlana's high-ceilinged room.

Inside, he did not see her, only the empty desk with its green-shaded lamp, the bookcases, the table and chairs carved with the red-star motif, and wondered if it was a try-on to test his nerve.

'Please sit down,' Kirilov said. 'She will not be a moment.'

He waited with mounting anxiety, oppressed by the strangeness of this room, a strangeness he could not pin down. It smelled of reports in bookcases that had been there too long. And through the far window he could see the golden onions of the Kremlin churches. Churches. That was it. Cathedrals inside the fortress, gleaming with fresh paint, a crass, uneasy coupling of the sacred and the profane. Like Svetlana herself.

For a moment he thought he had seen a ghost as she came in, dressed in black velvet with high lace at the neck of the white blouse beneath, and a single gold clip on the lapel. Her face was the colour of paper, a strained, chalky white which seemed to show the tension lines across her forehead. She held out a hand and smiled, with Kirilov closing the door.

The hand was cold to the touch, as if she'd been out in the street, but he knew she had been in the building and in that room shortly before he arrived: her top coat was on the couch.

'Are you all right?' he asked. 'You look very pale.'

Svetlana smiled again, and suggested that they should sit. He had the impression that Kirilov was monitoring them both, and Svetlana was keeping her distance, plagued by some inner crisis.

'I had to go away . . . for a few days. In Georgia,' she said. 'I have been a little . . . unwell. I needed a rest.'

Marriner tried to signal to her that time was running out, and still no certainty how Brzezinski would move, but she did not seem to care.

'Are you sure you are fit? Perhaps you should be on sick leave.'

She looked at him sharply, thinking how little he knew. Kirilov sat there between them, frowning, brown-eyed like a china dog. Maria, the secretary, bustled in with cups of tea and small plates of sweet biscuits. A little colour returned to the boneline of Svetlana's cheeks, and she stretched out her legs.

'I am recovered. I was away longer than I intended. I had . . . a problem.' She accepted the tea and put a biscuit in the saucer of the china cup with its gold band and gold star.

'How has your research gone? Do you have all you want now?'

It was a loaded question, and he could have answered it several ways, wondering what had happened. He found that his reactions had modified, looking at her now, older, less sensual, more enigmatic than ever in widow's black.

'Yes. Nearly all,' he said.

Kirilov rubbed his hands and looked forward to reading it, but his pouchy little eyes never left Marriner's face.

The conversation came to a halt, as if she was very tired. Marriner began to tell her of his trips out of Moscow and about the researches in the Army Museum. He mentioned the Botanical Gardens at Prospekt Mira, where she had driven him once, on that lost afternoon in the summer, but he raised no flicker of response. Did she still want to escape, or was it all over, another charade? In which case if Brzezinski moved the whole thing could be a fly trap, and they would stick on the paper. Yet Svetlana was still smiling at him, seemingly more relaxed, her skin less milk-white, a better colour as she talked, as if the worst was over. What had she feared, he speculated, that had made her so frightened when she entered the office, her work-room with its musty smells. As if Maria thought so too, she suddenly removed a vase of flowers, tut-tutting as she sniffed them; and Marriner realised that Svetlana had only just come back. She had not delayed in seeing him: something or someone had detained her, and frightened her to death. Kirilov was making small talk, but Marriner was not listening, he watched Svetlana's hands, one in the other as she twisted a small gold ring on her little finger. The pregnancy, he wondered? Oscar Werndl's little joke? Had it had a basis in fact: had there been an abortion behind the scenes in a city where she was anonymous? But surely it would be too late, surely she would not have slept with him, or lied to him, in that case. Marriner stared at this woman to whom he was contracted, and found that he could not read her. Yet something had happened . . . something.

Svetlana said, 'I am so sorry, I have not given you much time.'

Kirilov, the little shark in his double-breasted suit and grey shoes, was watching for his reply.

'It's been sufficient. I found out what I want to know.'

This was her Directorial role, abstract, feminine, on duty and remote, as if she was acting the part. Svetlana rose to her feet, and the interview was over.

'I'm so glad.' She paused, coming closer, that faint scent of French perfume. 'I would so very much have liked to invite you for dinner . . .' He was conscious of Kirilov half-smiling, clocking up the nuances of another rendezvous at that magnificent apartment off Arbat Prospekt. 'But I fear it will not be possible before you leave.'

'Of course. I understand,' he muttered.

'No. No.' Her hand fluttered into his, standing by the double doors. 'It is simply I am in a state of . . .' she stumbled over the English, then said, 'confusion. No, chaos, is that the word? You see, I am waiting for the decorators.'

The decorators. She was now signalling to him. She was urging him to tell Brzezinski, in front of Kirilov, and he shrugged and smiled in relief.

'I understand. I quite understand, Svetlana.' He risked her first name; once again they were professionals talking.

She opened the door, and squeezed his hand, one sharp finger-nail biting into his palm.

'Goodbye,' she said. 'And thank you.'

Marriner walked down the corridor, followed by Kirilov.

'I think the Director looks ill,' the Russian said.

Marriner agreed.

'Why do you think that is?'

'How on earth do I know,' he replied almost angrily, as if they assumed he had caused it. What mattered now was Brzezinski, and to set that in motion he had to make his apologies and get away from this over-insistent chaperone in the top wing of the Armoury. He began to invent excuses.

'I really ought to do some shopping. I'm going back to London.'

'Ah, so. You leave for Leningrad on Sunday? There are better shops there, if you have time.' Kirilov came up to his shoulder as he gathered his raincoat and papers in Aldanov's room. 'In Moscow there is nothing worth buying, outside the Beryozhka shop. No soap, no chocolate, no sanitary towels. My wife says so.'

'I don't want any of those. I prefer a fur hat,' Marriner said. 'It is so bloody cold.'

'Yes. There you are talking. We have the best hats in the world. You would look good in one.'

'I'll go and buy one.'

'Please. I will come with you. To get a better bargain.'

'No need. I'll use the hard currency shop in the hotel. It is stuffed with fur hats.'

'Ah. But too expensive.'

'It doesn't matter,' Marriner said desperately. 'I want to go back there, and write up my notes.'

'But you can write them up here.'

'It's not the same. I need to be on my own.'

'Then we will clear the room.'

Christ, he thought, these persistently obtuse minders: perhaps it was another way of trapping the outsider. A difference of cultures, an inability to take a hint, or a more devious cunning.

'Listen,' he said. 'I just want to do my own things. Some personal shopping. A walk round the GUM store, then back to the Rossiya. Is that allowed?'

Kirilov looked sheepish. 'Of course, if you do not want me to come . . .'

'That's right. I'd like to be on my own. Incognito, Greta Garbo.'

'Of course, David. OK. But please be careful.'

Was that a hint or a warning, Marriner wondered. Eventually he escaped, out through the Spassky Gate and into Red Square. Easier there to lose anyone who was following – he dared not look round to check – in the crowds shifting round like pigeons, but he was still uncertain how best to alert Brzezinski. A telephone call from the Kremlin might well have been safer than the bugged lines from his hotel, but it seemed tempting fate.

Where were the public phones? He saw some on a street corner, but moving into a phone box might itself seem a suspect act. He bought himself a hat instead in the department store, an astrakhan pork-pie that made him look like a sheep, but Kirilov was bound to ask. He would wear it next time it snowed in central London, and come to work like a cossack on Tower Hill. If he survived. He bought himself a scarf too, and wrapped up against the hailstones spattering the cobbles, then walked past the chocolate Gothic of the Lenin Museum into the gardens of Sverdlov Square. The Karl Marx monument was a god-like head in the middle. That was Svetlana's problem, that was all of their problems, he reflected grimly. They didn't dare risk the afterlife, but it crept back in their memorials, and perhaps in her fantasies.

Nobody seemed to be tagging him, and he passed the back of the Maly, where he had talked to Brzezinski a few nights before. It was too much to hope that the Pole would be there in the afternoon, but he saw the British transporters parked at the side, ready to move out on the Saturday, perhaps already part loaded. It jolted him to see the English registrations on the four trucks flown out, big Leyland articulateds with 'English Theatre Company' stencilled in royal blue and white. A policeman was standing on duty, as he walked up.

'*Anglishki,*' Marriner said.

Surprisingly the man nodded and touched his red-banded cap. The ETC had moved hearts in the Soviet capital; the question was could they move Borovik and a hundredweight of icons.

There was the usual minder, at an alcove inside the main door, and a queue of hopefuls sheltering under the archways. No way would they let him in.

Marriner stood in front of the big trucks, at the side of the theatre, looking for someone to trust. And then he saw the driver, eyeing him from the third cab, where he had been left on duty, to keep the ETC's own watch on their precious hardware. He was reading the *Daily Mirror*.

Marriner tore off the astrakhan hat and called out, 'Afternoon.' The man put his paper down and responded to the English voice.

'Christ,' he said. 'Who are you?'

'A friend of Daniel Brzezinski's. Don't look surprised,' he said. 'Can you give him a message?'

'No dodgy stuff,' the trucker said.

'No way. I just want a message passed on. Do you know Brzezinski?'

'Course I bloody know him. He forgot to give us overcoats.'

'Where is he now?'

'Dunno. He'll be back if you hang around.'

Marriner had the feeling that it would be a mistake to wait.

'I can't stop,' he said. 'Just tell him something from me. From Marriner. You got that?'

The driver nodded.

'Tell him she's ready for the decorators. Is that clear?'

The driver stared down from his high cab.

'I got that,' he said. 'OK, mate. You're on.'

In the chilly, mind-killing half-light of Friday afternoon, Svetlana left the Kremlin for the last time. Since she returned she had ached with exhaustion and fear, shutting herself away in the office where she had seen Marriner. Now, locked in the Arbat apartment, she was shaking with apprehension as she slumped in the great room hung with the icons of Russia, her own collection. What did she really want, what was she going to do, she asked herself. The room with its blood red curtains drawn against the night, the pools of light from the standard lamp and the candle-light on the table, the strained and holy faces on the walls, the room she had created to give expression to something, a groping for lost faith, a morality outside the bedroom, all of it now seemed tawdry, theatrical and false. In her mind was the other picture, the memory of Asterharzy with the top of his skull blown away, his popping eyes glazing over, the revolver in her own hand; and then the way she had hauled him despairingly up to the cliff face. His body was tumbling head first in a slow motion replay, crashing into the bushes, dislodging rocks and earth that plummeted far below him into the inaccessible valley. She had seen it caught there, fifty odd feet below her in full view of anyone who looked over, and been forced to scramble down – heart in her mouth for she hated heights – and landed on the ledge beside him to begin the terrible business of trying to conceal him. She had wedged him with rocks and loose bushes, covered him with soil and leaves, and left him there to rot.

Those had been frightening minutes, and she had lived the nightmare ever since. Now she sat in the alcove in her own room, and listened to the plaintive horn-notes of Mussorgsky's *Night on the Bare Mountain* eating into her soul. The painted heads whirled around her as she drank to forget, and prayed to the unknown forces – could she regard them as fate? – which had protected her since childhood. She had bluffed her way back to Tbilisi and paid off the hired car, then steeled herself to stay on in the room the pilot had booked, scattering his clothes around so that it seemed occupied. She had paid the bill for two and flown back to Moscow to collect the tickets he had ordered. She had them in her hands now, turning them over and over: Aeroflot to Leningrad in two days time. If she could get this far, and the Englishman took the message, surely she could escape, and leave this tragedy behind? Her mind began to blur as the vodka took hold on an empty stomach, her head seemed punished by spears, but she struggled to think her way through. 'Svetlana,' her mother had said, 'never forget you can win.' Svetlana the spoilt child, bright-eyed for the next adventure in Leningrad where she had started.

It depended on Marriner now, and whether she had persuaded him. God knew that he had been difficult, harder to catch than an eel, but in the end she had triumphed – the contract had been made in bed – and he had sworn to help. Marriner and Brzezinski, if Brzezinski got the message. But she had felt so ill when she had last seen Marriner in that final meeting in the Armoury that she wondered if the magic held. The spells that she cast were sexual, intimate and invading, but the Englishman's fall had been incomplete; even so he offered a lifeline beyond the confines of Moscow, the rat-trap faces of winter, the hardline Communist mouthings about the creation of plenty in a desert of consumer goods. David Marriner. She breathed the name while the drumbeats of music sounded to arms in her mind. They must not find Asterharzy's body. It must lie there for ever, a skeleton under the stars. But she knew that it could not be: there would be enquiries, searches, as soon as his presence was missed. Aeroflot had lost a pilot, the grandmother and the aunt that he had taken her to see in the southern suburbs of Moscow, they too would want to know. What had happened to Asterharzy would be a question for the authorities, as soon as they understood. She gulped another slug of vodka, nibbled at a piece of bread and some of the vegetable salad that had been left in the refrigerator. The door did not close very well, the rubber seal was coming apart and the inside was scarcely cold. It was a tiny symptom of a much wider malaise, which had corroded her being, as she travelled on privileged passes to the West. She had been corrupted, seduced, she who seduced in her turn, by the affluence her skills could buy there, the life she could otherwise lead, poor little lonely Svetlana, rated by Asterharzy as less important than a new Mercedes. If only she could escape. Escape. Escape from Asterharzy, from the inevitable uncovering of his body, and sooner or later, the enquiries, the trial, the sentence. Condemned to imprisonment for manslaughter, shut away in an asylum, a penitentiary or a labour camp, the whole dream crumbled.

They were clearing the courtroom now as the black-robed judges gave verdicts, and she could hear the bells. 'Guilty . . . Guilty.' But it was not a courtroom, it was the room she had created, the secret collection in Arbat, where she was. And the bell was her telephone, in the corner by the record player.

She switched off the music and in the sudden silence heard Brzezinski's voice.

'Are you waiting for the decorators?'

'Yes,' she said. 'Yes. Yes. Yes.'

'That is good,' Brzezinski said in Russian. 'Be ready tomorrow morning.'

But she was ready now, in a burst of electric energy that cleared the wires in her head, as she began to pull the pictures, her precious memories and icons, from the olive green walls. They came off the hooks and she stacked them in three rows on the floor, leaving a pattern of darker squares where the stippled paper had not faded. St Julian, St Jerome, St Mary, Christ in Majesty, in Sorrow, St George, St Sebastian, St Luke. The regiment of old men and holy faces, impenetrable eyes of Russia. She stacked them all, together with the silver cups, and the landscapes of winter churches, and lastly two family portraits, of her mother and father, painted in Leningrad twenty-five years before. What did they amount to now? Everything she had built up had been destroyed by Asterharzy's death, and she must be prepared to run. The pictures would be her passport, investments in a new future, forty-seven pieces of board and canvas that she had horded like gold. But she could part with them, they were the means not the end. She finished the bottle of vodka and her head was raw, as she stood in front of them laughing and running her hands through her cropped hair. Stripped of its décor, the room had already lost the purpose for which she had created it: it was no longer a haven, a sanctuary, but only a set of walls needing redecoration, and in that change her past could be shed too, like an old skin. However much she loved Russia, there was one basic problem: she could never avoid its shortages and limitations, its sense of inferiority. It encompassed her, it swamped her and in the end it would kill her, unless she found a way out.

19

They came for him that same night, Marriner, as he emerged from the Baku on Gorky Street, the restaurant recommended by Kirilov. He had started out thinking that he would call on Svetlana, to warn her it was all arranged, but rapidly changed his mind. The danger time was approaching and there was nothing more he could do. It was now up to the Pole. Instead he had walked on and dined alone on mutton balls wrapped in vine leaves, washed down with Armenian brandy. At first he had not noticed the car as he left the restaurant, but then it was running alongside him, just outside in the street, and the two young men climbed out.

'Get in,' one of them said in English. 'Police.'

He sat between them, wedged in the rear seat, protesting innocence, his stomach turning to iron. But this time it wasn't the small colonel smoking his cigarettes in the grey building south of the river: they weren't taking him that far.

'Papers?' they asked.

He showed them his passport again, and the visa expiring in six days time.

'OK. We take you back.'

He was puzzled by their behaviour but the unmarked car drove round the nearly empty city and headed back towards the Rossiya; then, when it should have swept up the platform to the hotel, it accelerated, shot to the end of Red Square and across the Moskvoretski Bridge.

Marriner said, 'Hey. Wait a minute,' but they only smiled.

The black car was turning off, at the other end of the bridge, braking suddenly in the darkness of the great stone arches where the boulevard ran underneath it.

'Out,' they said.

His bed was just over the river, in the hotel. The river road was deserted and silent at eleven o'clock: Moscow was not a late city. He seemed to be equidistant, walking distance, between the hotel on one side of the river and the British Embassy in its old merchant's house, further along on the other.

'Why bring me here?'

'Out,' they said, and one of them had a gun. They were levering him from the police car, which then reversed at speed and disappeared back on to the bridge. He found himself in the underpass, stepping over piles of sand and granite road setts where they were repairing the carriageway. Figures came out of the recesses where they had been waiting, two shapes with wooden staves, bundles in ragged coats. His reaction was automatic. He began to run, then turned, ducked behind a cement mixer and hurled himself at the first pursuer. Marriner's weight, launched like a torpedo, cannoned him against the machinery, the man's head hit the drum of the mixer, and he slid to the ground. Number two was coming to get him, but Marriner kicked at his shins, and pulled him down. Blows rained on Marriner's neck and shoulders, and rocked his senses, but he held on. He had purchase on the other man's legs and rammed his attacker's groin, clawing himself on top as they rolled in the dirt. His combat training tricks came back. His fingers covered the second man's throat and he pushed his thumbs into the windpipe. The figure had to drop the weapon as he tried to break free, but Marriner was pressing downwards, cutting off his efforts to breathe.

Then the bridge fell on Marriner as a third figure from the shadows hit him across the back of his neck, the earth came up to meet him, and he collapsed on the sand pile.

The first sensation was in his mouth: as dry as a brick oven. Then giddiness, a swaying motion as the sun became clearer. Not the sun, but a light bulb in a ceiling, looking down on a bed. A small, bare, cubicled room with stains on the walls, brown and grey, and hand-prints. He realised he was in the bed, with a head like a punchbag. Twisting, he could see a window behind him covered by a rolled-down blind, and a door at the foot of the bed. He was lying there in half of someone's pyjamas, coarse striped cotton, no bottoms, staring at his surroundings, trying to remember the night before. He assumed it was the night before. His watch was on the locker, next to a glass of water. That was all. His clothes and his identity had vanished.

Marriner struggled upwards, on to his elbows. The back of his head wasn't sober, but he had a hard skull. The worst part was raging thirst, the sewage in his mouth, compounded of alcohol and whatever they'd shot in his arm where he could see a plaster over a nick in the flesh. As he was working that out the door opened and a doctor came in, a severe-looking woman, mid-forties, with a stethoscope for a necklace and her hair drawn back in a bun.

She walked across and peered at him, looking worried, then said something in Russian. He realised where he was now, in some Moscow hospital eleven hours after the attack, and shook his head. The doctor sighed and withdrew. He fiddled around in the bed, feeling his strength return and the pulses in his head slacken, waiting for the next move. He put out a shaking hand for the water, which was warm and sweet, as if it had been carbonated and drank it thankfully.

There were noises outside the door, and suddenly the room was full: a uniformed, bare-headed policeman, the doctor and a nurse and another man he did not know.

'I'm sorry,' the stranger said.

Marriner groaned. The policeman sat on a chair inside the door as if the patient might make a run for it.

'Where the hell am I?'

'The Botkin Hospital, Botkinsky Prospekt,' the stranger replied. 'My name is Commissioner Peresvetov, Moscow City Police,' he said in English. 'I am sorry you have been attacked.'

'Attacked?' Marriner's head finally cleared. They were after him, trying to nail him: that attack had been set up. 'I was dumped out by your police boys, under the bridge. There were three other bastards there waiting.'

Peresvetov frowned. He sat on the edge of the bed, thickset and toad-like, an old bruiser's face. The doctor began to fuss, and put a thermometer in Marriner's mouth.

'Please try and think back,' Peresvetov said solicitously. 'What were you doing there under the bridge at that time of night? A patrol car found you unconscious.'

Jesus Christ, Marriner thought, shaking his head.

'Moscow is a safe city. Safer than your streets in London. But you

186

should not go walking at night in that area if you are on your own. There are sometimes undesirables. Petty criminals.'

It made Marriner angry, listening to this smooth talk. The policeman was making notes, and the nurse was watching. Presumably they spoke English too. The doctor retrieved the thermometer and Marriner found his tongue, as he sat up in the bed and felt the back of his head.

'Listen. Your boys took me there and left me. They showed me their police cards.'

'Oh, come on now, Mr Marriner. Was it a police car? Were they in uniform?'

Marriner's head started hurting. 'You bloody well ought to know.' What were they after, he wondered. The doctor shook the thermometer and talked to them in Russian.

'Good. She says you are better. No temperature and no concussion. You have been very lucky,' Peresvetov smiled. Then his boxer's face, puckered under the eyes with a nose knocked about in some fairground, pushed closer to Marriner's until he could smell his hot breath.

'What were you doing there?'

'I told you, I was going back to the hotel when your boys picked me up.'

'Who were you visiting?'

'Visiting?' The question sounded sinister. 'For Christ's sake I'd been in a restaurant. On my own.'

'Why?'

'Why? Aren't I allowed to eat?'

But Peresvetov was not amused. 'What are you doing in Moscow?'

'Historical research.' Come on now, Marriner thought, you know that.

This man was officious and awkward, unlike the silky colonel smoking cigarettes in the underground room.

'I want to discharge myself,' he said. 'I have to get ready to leave on Sunday.'

'All in good time,' Peresvetov replied. 'We have your passport.'

'Then look at the visa,' Marriner retorted.

'I have. Where are you working?'

'The Kremlin Armoury.'

A slow smile broke on the stoic face, as if it was an admission that they wanted.

'Ah. You have the authority of the Director, Dr Malinkova?'

They knew. They knew all about it, the bastards. The men in the grey raincoats, in doorways and parked cars, had made their contributions. Marriner's mind went into gear. Did they know about Borovik too?

'Yes.' He held his head and groaned.

'Were you thinking of visiting her?'

Oh Christ, he thought. The decorators. 'At eleven o'clock at night? Don't be crazy,' he said.

'But you have visited her?'

'I saw her in the Armoury.'

'And in her apartment?'

'Once or twice.' He began to realise that they were fishing, setting him up to see what they could find, uncertain of what was happening, suspicious of why he was there. Thank God he had not telephoned, or tried a surprise visit.

'You were there one afternoon. We have a report,' Peresvetov said. 'The afternoon of the 15 October.'

Marriner's heartbeat jumped. The same afternoon that he had met and enlisted Borovik. If they knew of that meeting they might well make the connection.

'Why did you go to Arbat with her?'

'We'd been working together in the Museum.'

'Why did you go there at three o'clock in the afternoon?'

'Look, what is this? An interrogation? How about finding the bastards who jumped me in the dark?'

But Peresvetov was not interested, and Marriner's head was singing.

'I want to call my embassy. The British Embassy.'

Peresvetov's battered head was eyeball-to-eyeball with him, with light-coloured, freckled eyes, like a fox.

'Why did you go back there?'

'She invited me.'

'To sleep with her?'

Marriner said, 'None of your business. I refuse to answer. I want a telephone.'

Peresvetov smiled, a crack across the wall of his face. 'You would not be the only one.'

'It was a business meeting,' he began to say, then knew that would make it worse, and Peresvetov saw through the excuse. The doctor was telling him to stop, and he drew back reluctantly.

'I understand. You sleep with her because she likes you. She is attractive woman. OK.' He lunged forward again.

'Do you meet Asterharzy?'

'Who?' Thank God he did not mention Borovik: that episode seemed under wraps, as far as he could tell.

'Asterharzy. Flight Captain Henrik Asterharzy?'

'Never heard of him,' Marriner said, as the policeman's eyes hovered on his face. He remembered Kirilov's warning about the pilot.

'No?'

'No.'

A sigh. 'He was another caller, at the apartment.'

'So?'

'So. He has disappeared.'

'Don't look at me.'

'You must leave him now,' the nurse was saying.

Wootten-Smythe bailed him out, late in the afternoon after endless waits on the telephone, and drove him straight to the Embassy in the comforting red Sierra.

As they turned into the forecourt the uniformed police in the boxes covering the road outside saluted half-heartedly.

Wootten-Smythe was furious, his pink young face like a scuba-diver coming up for air. 'You've buggered up my weekend.'

Marriner got out of the car and stood under the Union Jack flying from a pole on the porch opposite the Kremlin on the far bank of the river.

'I was told never to come here.'

'Too right,' Wootten-Smythe muttered. 'But when you get picked up by the KGB, we've got to show that we care.'

They mounted the steps and were in a gloomy hall, cluttered by the duty desk, dark mahogany woodwork and carved funereal stairs. Wootten-Smythe was nodded through and took him out to the rear where what had once been a garden was built over with prefabricated huts.

'Our quack has a surgery here for Brits like you. You'd better have a check-up to make sure they haven't infected you with anthrax or something,' he said tersely. He unlocked the door to a room full of utility chairs and out-of-date magazines, *Spectator*, *Time*, *New Statesman*. It had the inescapable air of being directly descended from all the British war films Marriner had ever seen:

189

RAF fighter bases, incident rooms in the blitz, *Carry On* consulting rooms. Suddenly it was all there, that dozy, seedy Englishness as much a part of his soul as icons were to Svetlana. He sat down with weak legs and felt the lump on his head.

'Bad?' Wootten-Smythe said.

'No. Much better.'

'I'll rustle you up a cup of char.'

He vanished and left Marriner to read the world's news in the *Economist*. When Wootten-Smythe reappeared with two paper cups of tea from a machine in the corridor, he said, 'Half the Moscow security corps must be watching you now. What the hell is going on?'

Tell them nothing, Orford had instructed. Least of all our own people. Don't go near the Embassy, it's always the kiss of death. Unless you want to be bailed out, that is.

'Nothing.'

Wootten-Smythe grinned, and handed him a bowl of sugar with a plastic spoon stuck in the middle.

'OK. That's your problem. But they're after something, you know. That mugging was set up to try and make you panic. Routine procedure: shake the other bloke's nerves. Give him a going over and then pump in the questions. That's why we want a blood sample, to see if they've tried any drugs.'

The Embassy doctor appeared, a bespectacled Scotsman called Richardson, who busied himself with his black box while Wootten-Smythe waited, sipping the powdery tea.

'Ah. Just the sleeve, Mr Marriner. This won't take long. Now let's have a look at your eyes.'

The examination was careful, longer than he had expected, before they pronounced him fit, subject to the lab results.

'My advice is, go home,' Richardson said, a neat man in a tweed suit. 'Once they start, you're in trouble.'

But Wootten-Smythe was not finished. 'What did they ask you?' He was now making notes.

'About what?'

'Oh come on, Marriner. We weren't born yesterday.'

'They asked me about my research. And my contacts.'

'Who did you name?' Wootten-Smythe said quickly, and Marriner began to wonder if they too knew more than they said. In this hall of mirrors, you never knew which face was real.

'Svetlana Malinkova, Director of the Kremlin Armoury,' he said.

'Ah. That sexy bitch. And . . . ?'

'That was the only name I gave them.'

Wootten-Smythe nodded, and stacked their two cups together, one in the other.

The doctor was packing his bag. 'You'll be all right,' he said.

'Are you sure?' Wootten-Smythe added, more concerned about names than the state of Marriner's head. 'If you're OK I'll run you back.'

'No need,' Marriner said.

'Oh yes there is. Safety first. Anyway they will be watching so we must show the flag. What time is your plane to Leningrad?'

'Ten o'clock tomorrow,' he said, 'from Unukovo airport.'

Wootten-Smythe nodded. 'On the Kiev road, about twenty miles out. That's OK. Stay inside the hotel and keep your head down. Take a cab there in the morning.'

It was almost an order, and Marriner had the feeling that Wootten-Smythe was not pleased. 'Come on. Let's get moving. I've got theatre tickets for my wife tonight.'

Marriner decided he never wanted to see a theatre again.

The red Sierra purred along the river boulevard and he stared across the green water to the walls of the Kremlin, exposed now by the leafless trees. Maybe he would never go inside there again, and that would be no loss either. Svetlana had become a siren, luring him on to the rocks at a time when the break-up with Celia seemed to make adventure desirable. That was the trouble. The Sierra rumbled over the bridge where they had done him over, and he saw a police car still there. Did they think he might go back, down those granite steps, and wait for another mugger?

Wootten-Smythe cut across near St Basil's Cathedral, looking slightly surreal under the frosty blue sky, and drew up outside the Rossiya. He shook hands.

'OK. Remember what I've told you.'

'There was one other name, by the way,' Marriner said. 'Not one that I gave them, but one they asked me about. Some guy called Asterharzy. A captain in Aeroflot. Apparently one of her lovers.'

Wootten-Smythe's pink complexion turned a darker red. 'Oh Jesus,' he said. 'Why didn't you say before? What did they want to know?'

'If I had ever met him.'

'What did you say?'

'I'd never heard of him.'

Wootten-Smythe blew out his cheeks. 'Why did they want to know?'

'Apparently he's disappeared.'

'Fucking hell.' Wootten-Smythe's calm had broken. His hands beat a tattoo on the steering wheel. He stared at Marriner. 'Listen. Go inside. Keep your head down. Pack up. Shut up. Get away on the morning plane. You know nothing. You understand?'

Marriner nodded, slammed the door, said goodbye.

'Why?'

'Why? Asterharzy is one of our contacts. Is or was.'

20

There was a buzzer, somewhere at the back of her brain. Svetlana opened her eyes and found herself in her own bed, and remembered she had crawled in there, shaking with drink, after that terrible evening when she had been told they were coming. She shuddered and pulled up the coverlet, but the buzzing went on. The digital clock by the bed told her it was eight o'clock. The central heating was gurgling and the bedroom was stiflingly hot. She sat up and covered her shoulders as the buzzing persisted, then found the black and gold kimono and clawed her way to the intercom.

'The decorators,' Brzezinski said.

A huge sense of relief. Of joy, as she realised it wasn't the police. 'Can I come up?' he asked.

She signalled yes, and ran back into the bedroom, dressing hurriedly in slacks and an orangey sweater, slipping her feet into the Nike trainers that she had bought in Brussels. Her cropped hair fell neat and child-like around the elfin face.

Brzezinski was there in the lift as the cage appeared, a short man with a pitted face, a miner's face she thought, with curly grey hair and deep-set, careful eyes. His fingers were blunt and professional, and his handshake firm as he introduced himself.

'Don't say too much,' he said before they entered the apartment. 'You got the message? You're ready?'

She nodded, in a daze of release from the tensions of the last few days, those dreadful moments in Georgia, clinging to the cliff face of her own sanity, and the questions in Moscow.

Brzezinski walked through to the bedroom and opened the window. The cold air whistled around as he peered down to the inner courtyard, four storeys below. He nodded and shut it quickly.

'Big window,' he said.

She switched on the clock radio and turned up the volume. Martial music for Muscovites, to cheer them on Saturday morning.

'What about the police?' she whispered. 'There's probably someone down there in the street.'

Brzezinski shrugged.

'Stupid bastards,' he said. 'They'll do what they are told, and nothing more. They sit there and watch the front door. The van is coming in at the back. Through those gates. Can you get 'em open?' he asked. His Russian was easy and fluent.

'I don't know. I've never tried. I haven't got a key.'

'Make me a cuppa,' Brzezinski said, suddenly changing to English. 'It's a cold morning.' He grinned, and fished out a pair of bolt cutters from underneath his leather coat. 'Made in West Germany. Bloody strong.'

She zipped into the cupboard-kitchen on the landing and filled an electric kettle. This had to work, it had to, she told herself, hands shaking. There was fierce frost on the kitchen window, which looked down into the street, and she could see nothing. But who was he, this thickset man with bad teeth, and where were the watchers?

'Don't worry,' he said in Russian again. As if to reassure her. 'Your friend came through with the message OK.'

She nodded: recollecting the nightmare that stretched behind her from the first days of decision to leave this country, the realisation that every promised reform, every putative freedom would not give her what she wanted, right up to Asterharzy's death. Henrik. She shuddered. Henrik who had abused her, a tiny spot in her mind admitting that she half-courted him and hated him at the same time; Henrik whom she had killed, half-deliberately; Henrik who had been the first one to mention Borovik. Of course, that was why he had been prepared to get tickets, without demur. She remembered their conversation one day in her own bed.

'Do you like your work, my chicken?'

Svetlana had said it was lonely, at the top, for a woman especially.

'Aren't there men in the Kremlin?'

'Political animals. Commissars. Party men on the make. Not for me.'

'Ah. But some of them have weaknesses.'

'I don't go to bed with anyone.'

'I know that, chicken. But you may need a friend one day, inside the Secretariat.' And then he had said, 'Do you know a man called Borovik? Vasily Vasilyevich Borovik?'

'No.'

Asterharzy had scratched himself in that great, lazy macho way that drew her, in spite of her judgement.

'Well. I'm told that he visits the Armoury many days. Lunchtime. Looks at the clothing and embroideries. A poof,' he said. 'So you ought to be safe.'

'What's that to me?'

'The English are interested. He carries in his head the secrets of our chemical warfare stockpiles. Chemical weapons are not good.'

'I'm not a traitor,' she said.

'I know that, chicken. But these things are useful to remember, if you want to leave yourself.'

It was the first time she had realised he understood her frame of mind, and it had not occurred to her then, naked in bed beside him, that his knowledge of Borovik was too precise, too clear-cut to have been picked up casually. She had been stupid, assuming that Asterharzy, persistent and regular Henrik, had only been after her.

She made the tea and walked back to where Brzezinski was standing by the side of the bed. He did not seem to have moved.

'Who are you?' she asked.

He put a finger to his lips.

'The stage manager,' he said. 'I've come to arrange the packaging. Tomorrow we spirit you away. You got the Leningrad tickets?'

'Yes,' she whispered, feeling her head spin round.

'And you have passed on the other one?'

'Yes.' One of the reasons that she had gone back, into the Armoury, feeling like death on the morning she had seen Marriner, was to find Borovik too. She had even risked a telephone call to the Council of Ministers building to locate him, to suggest that he came to see a special piece of cloth, vestigial sleeves from

Iran, and when he appeared like some shy ferret she had passed over the ticket.

'Good,' Brzezinski said. 'Now, don't worry. Everything is in hand. Just show me where the stuff is.'

She led him through to the room she had stripped in her frenzy of the night before and he inspected the rows of pictures stacked against the wall. Brzezinski whistled. 'Music,' he said.

She put on the record player. The last time she would use it. Everything was changing around her, like the shape of the room which now seemed so sad, so empty. It had given her comfort and she felt exposed.

The record she chose was Rimsky-Korsakov and it reminded her painfully of the night at the opera with Marriner, the first time that he had come, the Englishman picked up in Brussels.

Brzezinski seized her arms and suddenly twirled her round, in rhythm to the music.

'Cheer up,' he said. 'It's going to be all right.'

But she was worried. 'The police will be watching you.'

'Two puddings in a Volga. They note that I come in. They note that I go out, an hour later. What does that tell them, eh? Maybe they ask who I am. I am member of English Theatre Company, visiting to ask advice on costume design. But don't worry, they will never stir themselves, the stupid pillocks.'

'But they will see everything, if you take these pictures out.'

He laughed, and shook his head.

'They will see nothing. Except the decorators. Now let's get the gate unlocked.'

They came in unobserved, at the back as he had promised, through the service gate into the courtyard from the other side of the block. An unobtrusive back entrance normally choked with rubbish. Brzezinski had broken the padlock with the bolt cutter and made certain the gates were loose before taking himself off. The van appeared at nine-thirty: a battered, green-painted truck with a Moscow registration and two men in overalls, one of the Saturday enterprise units now officially encouraged, so they said with a grin. Nikolai and Ivanovich.

Svetlana went down the fire escape inside the courtyard nervously, clinging to the flaking rail. They had already pushed open the doors and nosed in the ancient vehicle after waiting for Brzezinski five or six blocks away. When he emerged they moved in. The truck pottered up to the fire escape and the doors were closed again. It stood in the central courtyard, a place of rubble and rusting, junked equipment from the flats overlooking the dingy well. Someone had jumped from a window once and killed themselves on the cobbles, and few people ventured there now. These were expensive apartments and people preferred to look outwards, towards the street scene, not down into the rubbish pit. She scanned the blank windows quickly, but could see no staring faces from the other floors on three sides. This was their downside view, protected by curtains and pot plants, which sealed off bedrooms and lavatories. With luck the quiet would hold early on Saturday morning as the two workers in overalls carried their paint pots upstairs, using the iron staircase and coming in at her bedroom window. They seemed a cheerful and proficient pair, like the American comedians she had once seen, Laurel and Hardy, a thin one Nikolai and a fat one Ivanovich, part of the emergent culture of the commercial underground.

Ivanovich stared in amazement at the luxury of the room, compared with his hovel in Frunze District. A large, white-painted bed, its coverlet matching the flowers on the wallpaper and curtains. 'A film star's room,' he said. 'Like Hollywood.'

'Not exactly,' she murmured, conscious of the linoleum that only just covered the boards, and the woodworm disguised by the tallboy in the corner.

'Where is the stuff then?' He stood there awkwardly, his paint pot looped over his arm.

She took them along to the big room that she had devastated, showed them the stacked pictures.

'Holy Mother Russia,' he said. 'These are beautiful.'

'Can you package them safely?' she asked.

Ivanovich grinned like a clown. 'No problem. Just wrap them in paper.'

She had already started, and they brought more wrapping with them: newspapers, old copies of *Trud* and *Pravda*. She had a supply of masking tape, and they had purchased more. Within a couple of hours the pictures, the silver, her caskets, were sealed and packaged, lying around on the floor like a surplus of New Year presents.

'Sorry about the room,' Nikolai said. 'It looks a bit of a mess. It shows you need us professionally. What about the record player; and the furniture?' He eyed it greedily.

'You can have what you can carry,' she said. It was a kind of payment, in the land where barter was commonplace. How she hated it, she hated this peasant subsistence.

Their eyes shone.

'Let's get the stuff down,' they said.

They roped the pictures together by sizes and lowered them in groups of five, straight out of the window, storing them in the green van in the deserted yard. The big ones they carried down, and the small parcels in bags, so that it might have been debris from their decorating.

'Pity about the furniture,' Ivanovich said regretfully, admiring her refectory table and the Ivan-the-Terrible chair. 'But we can manage the electrics.'

They separated the components of the imported Philips music centre which had given her so much happiness, and carried it down. It disappeared into the van.

By midday the work was finished.

Then they began to redecorate, stripping her precious paper and reducing the room to chaos.

'Leave the curtains up,' she said. It gave a better cover from the street.

They bundled the old wallpaper into piles on the bare boards, with the carpets rolled away. It seemed that they were stripping her own life, her past, as they did so. This was the real price she paid, the price of evacuation, but whereas she had once had a choice, she knew that she did not have one now, with Asterharzy dead on that hillside. The old sense of nausea, of vomiting, caught her again as she watched them.

'Are you all right, Madame?'

She inclined her body slightly, and went back to sit on the bed, but they kept coming in there, depositing their spoils through the window. There seemed to be no rest, no escape, and she wondered if that was her fate now, driven always to run. In the end she fled to the kitchen, and made them cups of coffee.

Ivanovich came and stood with her, she could feel him sizing her up, wondering how far he could go.

'You going to sleep here tonight? On your own?'

She nodded. One more night. Only one more night, dear God, before she could get away. One more night undetected, she prayed, without that echoing knock that would mean the KGB.

'Lonely spot. That empty room and all.'

'How long will the decorating take you?'

Ivanovich shrugged. 'We were only paid to do what we could today.'

Brzezinski had not told them much, she thought; and that was wise. Enough to get the stuff clear, assuming that she could leave tomorrow, first to Leningrad, then on her open visa by air from there to Brussels. If that failed she was finished, she had burnt her boats, but it would be death to stay. Ivanovich was looking at her, his face red with exertion, as if he had half a mind to offer her a bed for the night. As if she took any man: Svetlana drew away, a pale woman with eyes that were misting over. She sniffed, and suddenly realised she could not stay there after all, in the desecrated flat, once those things had gone.

'Where will you take them now?'

'We got to deliver them to a comrade. He's going to look after them for you.' Nikolai, the thin one with the sardonic face, winked at her. 'You know. The Pole.'

Brzezinski. She knew. The Pole she had hardly met who was chancing his life to help, enlisted by the Englishman Marriner. What was in it for him, she wondered. Marriner she could reward, Marriner she could love, but Brzezinski? Was he in it for money, or some kind of revenge on the whole retarded politics of Eastern Europe? It was beyond her now, she was too tired to care. All that she could do was try and get out herself: in the last resort, she realised, even her precious collection would have to be sacrificed. As long as she saved her skin.

It was hard recognition.

Ivanovich wandered back to take one last look at the big room. It was an empty stage, littered with paper, the rolled-up rugs in the corner, the chairs piled on to the table.

'OK,' he said. 'We've finished.'

They went down the fire escape for the last time and she watched from the bedroom window as the van drove away. Nikolai reappeared in order to shut the gates, and they were gone, taking her past life with them.

She was left with the empty shell, and a new wave of fear: arrest, imprisonment, decay. She could not stay there. In a panic she pulled a suitcase from the top of the wardrobe and crammed in a change of clothes, a few cosmetics, a handful of personal things, letters, her passpart with the overseas visa, and her small stock of hard currency. There was a wall-length mirror in the tiny bathroom and she was shocked to see herself. The blonde hair was coated with dust and she seemed ten years older, almost frail. Her hand pulsated as she brushed her hair, saying goodbye to herself. Then she picked up the case and closed the double doors of the apartment behind her without a trace of regret. She wanted to live in the future, not the past; above all she wanted to live. Going down in the cage lift for the last time she felt she was changing identities, reaching the end of a road that had started when she came to Moscow with her newly widowed mother, twenty-five years before. Dispossessed in Leningrad they had started again, and she had worked and worked to climb up inside the system, a bureaucratic labyrinth that she also found choked her, frustrated her, denied her very Europeanness. She slammed the cage shut, determined to begin a new life.

It was already growing dusk. A hard, clear night, frosty with stars like diamonds. The parked cars were misting over and she looked to see if any had their engines running or the side windows scraped, but without walking back again on the other side of the street she could not tell. Even the KGB had limits on their manpower these days, and she suspected they were watching her callers, not herself.

She walked on quickly, and took a 23 trolley-bus in Arbat Square along Kalinin and over the river into Kutuzovsky Prospekt. Halfway down she changed direction and caught the underground back to the Kiev Station, where she booked into a small and undistinguished hotel. Only then did her heart stop racing.

Colonel Kazakov, Moscow internal security, was reading the situation reports in the grey building south of the river, not very far away. There was a note from Kirilov in the Ministry about the Englishman's research, and the way that he had talked to the Director of the Armoury in that last fleeting visit. It mentioned that she had seemed ill after disappearing for several days. 'Tense and disturbed,' Kirilov had written, 'when she said goodbye to Marriner.'

Well, well. Kazakov was forty-three, and had been through the Intelligence School after transferring from Signals; he held a sharp-shooter's badge and saw life as a cryptogram to be decoded. Women were more difficult to read and they interested him especially, particularly if they were powerful. There were women in the apparatus, in his section of the KGB, who looked like used combine harvesters, but Svetlana was pretty as a flower, and, it appeared, available. He lit another cigarette and perched himself on the radiator under the round-headed windows, the warmest part of the basement where he had his office. He liked to have weekend duties, it gave him a chance to think, being a single man.

There was also the second, more puzzling, report from Peresvetov of the Moscow Police, who had been requested to pick up Marriner: a statement on his interrogation of the Englishman, attached to a separate note from the Flight Staff Directorate, Aeroflot International, at Sheremetyevo Airport. One of their pilots was absent, having failed to turn up for duty. A reliable, senior captain, no reason given but known to have flown to Georgia. A friend of Dr Malinkova.

Kazakov crossed back to the desk and went through the papers again: a single yellow slip which reported the disappearance. Not abroad but in Georgia. He scratched his head. He could understand a defection abroad, there were a lot of temptations, that was why positive vetting was so important; but it was almost impossible to vanish in the Soviet Union. The system should have been foolproof, and he was annoyed when it wasn't. Asterharzy, that was the name. Senior Captain Henrik Asterharzy. One of Svetlana's lovers.

He pressed the bell on the desk, which brought his clerk at the double.

'Get me Dr Malinkova's file. Whatever we have on her.'

The duty clerk was puzzled. 'She's the Director of the Armoury.'

'I know that,' he shouted. 'Get me the papers on her.'

The clerk came back at a run, carrying a slim folder with her name on the cover, under the reference K. He flicked through the pages greedily. Svetlana Malinkova, thirty-four, Museum Directorate, Level 2A. Overseas visas for Brussels and Berlin. London refused, because she was known to be seeing the Englishman Marriner, as well as the German Werndl. Numerous contacts, inside and outside the Kremlin. Unmarried. No close attachments. Last full security clearance 1986. A long time ago. And then the scribbled upratings on a sheet at the end. Known to have several menfriends, lovers who stayed the night. He stubbed out the cigarette and whistled between his teeth. One of them was Asterharzy, reported telephoning there a week ago.

Kazakov smiled to himself though his face was devoid of emotion. It would be interesting to talk to the Director about Asterharzy's disappearance. It might be even more interesting to have someone pay a visit. He would have a perfect excuse in enquiries about Asterharzy, and it was also said that she lived in style. Why not pay a visit himself: a short ride in the car and a break from office monotony? He would very much like to see if she was quite as attractive as various reports made out. There was even a black and white photograph smudged from a street camera, which showed her in boots and a hat accompanied by an unidentified man.

Arbat was not very far, and the car took him there in ten minutes. A long dark feeder street, cars parked on either side. Grade 1, reserved apartments, he noted at a glance. There was still a car on the corner, with a young man looking cold. He showed his pass, and the photograph.

'Has she come out?' he asked.

The plainclothes boy nodded. He was young and not very bright, and the presence of Kazakov unnerved him.

'I think so, maybe.'

'You think? What do you mean?'

'Just as we changed cars,' the minder said, 'a blonde came out, carrying a small case. I think it must have been her.'

'Did you check?'

'No, sir. I wasn't told.'

'Told? Don't you use your head?'

The boy was silent.

'Did you telephone in?'

'No . . . no, sir. My instructions were to observe.'

'If we sit there observing long enough, we'll all be dead,' Kazakov said bitterly.

He walked over to the apartment block and opened the outer door. The inner door was locked but he had a selection of pass keys and soon found one that fitted. There was a marble staircase, running round a cage lift with gilded walls. A fancy place indeed. He saw her name on the index and pressed the button for the fourth floor. There was no one about.

The lift opened on to a landing, and he saw a pair of white doors ornamented with filigree panels. He rang the bell, and knocked. When there was no reply he tried the pass keys again and opened that lock too.

A corridor lined with books, art books in Russian and German, imported paperbacks in English and French. A lavatory, a small kitchen, a bedroom with chintzy curtains and feminine, expensive coverlet. Also a smell of paint, which led him to the big room at the end, cream double doors pulled shut. He turned the handle and entered. A scene of devastation, with every wall stripped of paper and the carpets rolled back from the floor. Undercoat on one wall, but the job scarcely begun. And everywhere paper and tape, as if someone had been packing to go away. A table fitted under an alcove, with chairs stacked on top.

Kazakov was several minutes taking in the scene, then he walked back to the bedroom and began to look in drawers. Her clothes were still in the wardrobe, expensive Parisian styles and several pairs of Italian-made shoes. There were some bottles of perfume, make-up, nail varnish. But her hairbrush had gone, and he could find no toothbrush or personal bag. She was not coming back that night. She was not coming back, he decided.

21

Daniel Brzezinski sat in the cab of the leading truck, the big Leyland articulated, and watched the road. In front of him the red Sierra of Wootten-Smythe, in front of that the police escort with its blue winker bar across the top of the white Volga. It was foggy in the early morning and the dual carriageway out of Moscow was comparatively free of traffic. He had the four trucks to get north; the company had travelled ahead on the overnight train, exhausted by their tour, the long grind in Kiev and Moscow. As John Crashaw had said, 'Thank Christ the show's over, darlings,' posed on the steps of the sleeper in his fur hat.

Not quite over for me, Brzezinski thought. Five hundred miles still to go and God knew how many inspections, checks, forms and questions, before they made the plane. But it had worked out so far. Borovik had his air ticket as far as Leningrad: after that he would join the company. The icons were in their cases, along with the rest of the scenery, in the four trucks on the road. And Svetlana: well she should make it. She had an external visa and the other ticket to Leningrad. Within just over twenty-four hours it should be all over.

The cab driver passed him a packet of Opal Fruits.

'Still got a few left,' he grinned. 'Brought them out for the kids.'

Brzezinski chewed an orange flavour thoughtfully. It was all a bit too neat. He didn't trust assignments that smooth, remembering the time in Czechoslovakia when some fool had tried to stow away in one of the property hampers. This time it would be better worked out: they must not lose Borovik now.

The police car was pulling in, and the Sierra was following it. 'Fuck,' his driver said, grinding down through the gears. 'What's the bloody matter now?'

The convoy edged into the grass verge of the road, already soggy with mud, taking care not to bog down. The last thing I want, Brzezinski thought, is to have to offload the crates in order to dig the trucks out.

He opened the cab door and jumped down. Wootten-Smythe was walking back, dressed in a sheepskin coat and lightweight Dunn's trilby. He waved his hand.

'All right. No panic. End of the Moscow limit. The police boys are handing over.' The end too, if he had known it, of Colonel Kazakov's command.

They sat around grumbling, stamping their feet to keep warm as mist rolled in across the beet fields. The truck drivers brewed up tea and shared it with the Russians, who gave them packets of cigarettes. A traffic patrol stopped for a chat and Brzezinski talked to them in Russian. Wootten-Smythe looked annoyed that his own languages were less good. They were not very far from Kalinin but at this rate they would not be in Leningrad until past midnight.

After half an hour a second police car came, a road patrol to take them all the way, and much to his relief they restarted. He was comforted by the normality, the steady state inefficiency which showed that there wasn't a manhunt, and he settled back with satisfaction inside the heated cab. Never take anything for granted, with two containers of contraband and an illegal emigrant in the offing.

The truck ground on through the straggling city of Kalinin, then to Torzhok, and finally on to Vyshny-Volochek, where they pulled in again at an apology for a service station. The drivers had tea and chips, but he contented himself with a bread roll and a sliver of jam: his stomach was too tight for grease. Wootten-Smythe came down the line again.

'I'm going back now,' he said. 'It should be plain sailing from here.' He looked at Brzezinski closely, not wanting to know too much. 'I hope that it is,' he said.

'Sure.' Brzezinski detected a slight unease in the other man's farewell. Wootten-Smythe did not want to be around, in case something blew up. Nevertheless the stage manager watched the red car disappear with a feeling of regret.

They were refuelling the trucks now, pumping in diesel from an overhead line in the service bay. Brzezinski walked across to make sure that the padlocks were still intact on the rear doors.

'I hope that this bloody diesel isn't crap like the Kiev lot,' one of the drivers said.

'So do I,' Brzezinski agreed. There had been chaos in Kiev when water contaminated the feedline and the trucks broke down one by one. They had had to strip down the engines to sort out the problem, delayed two days on the road.

As they waited, long-distance buses came in, dusty and down-at heel, and bleak faces tumbled out. Brzezinski smiled at them but they shuffled away, not daring to come across with the police car there. He felt a pariah in his leather coat and brown boots. Waste paper blew across the parking bays.

'OK, let's go,' the interpreter in the second truck said, hurrying them along. Brzezinski was pleasant to him: they didn't need language help, Brzezinski's fluency was picked up from a Russian mother, but the interpreter was not there for the ride. He was almost certainly an implant, and Brzezinski treated him as such. In the faint, hazy sunshine of midday they strolled back to the vehicles and rolled back on to the highway.

Thin birch forests stretched on either side between the towns and patches of cultivation, monotonous, grey-green country. He tried to settle down to sleep, but the ruts in the concrete jarred the suspension and interrupted his dozing.

'Christ almighty,' the driver said. 'I hope we bloody make it. This stuff could bust an axle.'

'In that case we lodge a claim with the British Council,' Brzezinski said. But the British Council wouldn't be so happy if they thought that the stage props included a couple of million quid in illegal pictures, and a conjuring trick to po· Borovik into if the poor bastard made it. The Svetlana woman puz led him as he pondered the future. Why the hell should she bother with Borovik, except that it was the price extracted to get her stuff out as well? He guessed as much, and guessed also that Marriner was a factor in her calculations. Some screwing going on there, he decided.

The truck bounced again, and unsettled him. A roadgang,

tough-looking women, stared in amazement at the little convoy, and then they were in traffic once more, threading into the outskirts of Novgorod. Trolley-buses ran down down the roadside in separate lanes, people stood patiently waiting on the verges, apparently depressed. The police car ahead began to flash its blue lights.

'I tell you, I'll be glad to be home,' the truck driver said. 'This country gives me the creeps. By the way, that bloke who came up in Moscow when I was waiting at the back of the theatre and asked me to give you a message, did you know him?'

'An acquaintance,' Brzezinski said, and thought of how close they had run things, waiting for Svetlana's return. Where the hell had she been, he wondered, and did it really matter, could it have been significant? It was covering worries like that, eliminating the chances, that had kept his nose clean so far, but the fact was he did not know. Tough shit. He looked at his watch. Less than twenty hours now and they should be in London.

They seemed to be arriving at last, past the long spillage of industry and satellite townships on the Leningrad outskirts. He was desperately tired. The industrial wasteland straggled on for miles, the flat, dull delta of the Neva marshes, where mists crept in from the Gulf of Finland. The police cars were shepherding them over the Nevsky Bridge and drawing up outside a milk-crate hotel calling itself the Moskva. Brzezinski disliked the name: he wanted to get away, arrange the transport and go, BA freighter to Heathrow. They tumbled out of the trucks in the darkness and clapped their hands against the wind off the river. It was time to leave Russia.

He supervised the parking of the trucks, and checked the locks again. The actors had already settled in, and people were crowding in doorways hoping for autographs, so that he had to push through. As he booked in he wondered about the trio who would be coming out with them if things went according to plan: Borovik, Svetlana and Marriner, but he dared not ask.

Mars Bars imported from Finland were on sale at the kiosk: he was getting closer to home.

Marriner was checking out of Moscow with similar thoughts of relief. It was up to Brzezinski now, he told himself, as the Aeroflot bus headed out to Unukovo airport along Leningradski Prospekt, but Svetlana had worried him, at their Kremlin meeting. It was almost as if she was cracking up, and the last thing he wanted in London was a neurotic, expecting him to find her a role. He stared grimly out at the tower blocks lining the carriageway. The last thing he wanted, in fact, was Svetlana. He cursed himself for getting caught up, and cursed Denis Orford, with his pug face and red hair grinning on the edge of his memory, for dropping him in this hole. Once they were home, once she had her icons on sale at Sotheby's, Marriner would have done his bit. There was no long-term between them. He hoped to God that Celia had begun to understand at last, that absence had increased her fondness and confirmed her change of heart. That also was to be tested.

Moscow in autumn chilled his bones. The city was penetrated with a web of intrigue in which he was only a cog, a contact point for desires, but he still felt unsafe. The monotonous, elephantine buildings, unadorned by advertisements, loomed on either side of the boulevards like film sets for the Revolution. A few cars, a few slogans, a liquor queue, groups of girls in flat shoes, there was a human face somewhere underneath this monolith but it was a confused country, not least in its hopes and dreams, and Svetlana was as foreign to him as the unidentified pedestrians on the pavements. Celia, for all her faults, at least he could comprehend, but these sad, watchful faces, they told him nothing.

The airport bus went through the gates and deposited its collection of Swedish students and East European businessmen in the departure lounge. Marriner had chosen the bus as less conspicuous than hiring a taxi, and now he seemed on his own in the jumble of passengers at the check-in.

'Mr Marriner,' the voice at his elbow said. 'You should not be queuing like this.'

He turned to see Kirilov, the ubiquitous man from the Ministry, with the eyes of a plaster saint.

'There was no need for you to come out this far on a Sunday . . . ,' he said, disturbed.

'Oh. Why not? Of course we must see our guests off,' Kirilov muttered. 'I missed you at the hotel when I arrived with the car.'

'I'm so sorry. It is extremely kind.'

Kirilov was pulling him out of the queue, which parted like the Red Sea.

'Please, you must come upstairs. To the private lounge.'

It sounded ominous, as Marriner followed his blue-suited figure up the open-plan staircase to the quiet rooms on the first floor.

There were guards in the corridors now, airport security police in navyblue uniforms, one of them outside the door of the room to which he was led. A waiting room for VIPs with a glass coffee table and black and chromium plastic chairs.

'Please, to sit down,' Kirilov said.

A girl appeared with cups of coffee.

'We are waiting for some other guests,' Kirilov added.

Marriner knew then that it was going wrong, and he began to sweat. Kirilov's face was as bland as a football as he rubbed his moustache, talked of the weather, the interest in Marriner's research, whether Moscow was colder than Leningrad, and the meaning of glasnost. He smiled like the angel of death, and Marriner kept asking himself why.

A large Army General walked in, the flat red tabs on his shoulders showing he was a Staff man; but Kirilov ignored him. He might have been a piece of the furniture. The coffee cups were removed and Marriner waved away more. Outside through the windows he could see the white jets loading up.

'I'm sorry. There has been a delay,' Kirilov said. He disappeared to make enquiries and returned with a shrug. 'One hour.'

Who were they waiting for? Marriner picked over his actions, comforted by the fact that he had not told Borovik or Svetlana when he would be flying to Leningrad.

'I hope you like Russia,' Kirilov was saying.

Before he could reply she was there. Svetlana as white as paste, her hair the colour of lemons, in a dark green long-fitting topcoat with an astrakhan collar. And Borovik in tow behind her, the same small indeterminate man with thin mousey hair and glasses whom he had met in the Armoury, and taken to see Brzezinski.

Kirilov rose to his feet.

'You will have company,' he said. 'I saw from the flight list that the Director goes to Leningrad also. A coincidence.'

Why had they come on this flight? Why hadn't they taken the train? And then he realised the tickets were controlled by computer, and he had only confirmed his twenty-four hours before. If Kirilov was clever enough, he could have directed his booking on to a flight preselected by Svetlana's name on the list. The cunning bastard, he thought, remembering now the uncertainty of the Aeroflot counter girl when he had checked in. He had wanted a Saturday flight, and been told after some hesitation that they were fully booked.

Vasily Borovik was sitting quietly on the opposite seat, as if it was irrelevant that he was there. Svetlana merely nodded to him.

'Of course, you know each other?' Kirilov asked, enquiring from her to Borovik as the little man read a leaflet.

Svetlana replied in Russian, and the conversation left Marriner but he understood she was explaining that the acquaintance was casual, one or two chance meetings in the Tapestry Room, guest tickets at the Maly. Borovik was looking bored, and began to flick through the tourist magazines lying on the coffee table. There was no rapport between them, and Marriner admired her efficiency as a liar.

Since there was no effusion, Kirilov seemed satisfied, and turned his attention to Marriner.

'And naturally, you two are good friends. How convenient you travel together.' There was a new air of authority in his voice as he added, 'Why exactly do you fly to Leningrad at this time, Director?'

Svetlana smiled tensely. 'I have some business there, in the Hermitage.'

'Ah. I see. Going back to your father's museum?'

'Yes,' she said. She refused to look at Marriner, and he could imagine her emotions, compounded of hope and fear, tense as a bow-string; she would not be easy to live with, perhaps why no one had tried.

A message came over the loudspeaker and the General got up to leave. They sat on in the *huis clos* lounge, Svetlana, Borovik, Marriner, with Kirilov trying to find the connections in a jigsaw.

Marriner opened his briefcase and pretended to read his notes, but the words jumbled up in front of him. For Christ's sake hurry up with the plane. Trip-hammering in his mind was the thought that everything could blow in the last few hours.

'Are you sure I can't get you more coffee?' Kirilov was solicitous as always.

They shook their heads.

'How long will you be in Leningrad?' Marriner decided to ask her.

She shrugged. 'Two or three days, perhaps.'

'I did not know you were going there,' Kirilov said sharply.

'A late decision. My flat is being decorated.' Her fingers were drumming along the edge of the black settee.

'Well, I wish you a pleasant journey back to London,' Kirilov said, returning to Marriner.

208

London. The word was a rock of sanity after these closed-up faces. Could he really be getting out, after all? But the Russian was in no hurry for him to leave.

'I'll wait until your flight departs.'

'But please, there is no need . . .'

'It is my duty,' he said.

A second hour dragged by, then flight control said they would soon be off, according to Kirilov. Even his conversation seemed to be drying up, and Svetlana read a book. Borovik might not have existed, sitting on the other side working at some of his papers; when he went to the toilet they noticed that he took them with him.

'It is long time delay,' Kirilov applogised, gazing out at the nearest plane. 'I think that is your flight. The others have boarded.'

They could see the glazed faces peering from the portholes of the Tupolev.

And then at last, after two-and-a-half hours, a series of further announcements. Kirilov scrambled to his feet, Svetlana began to put on her coat; only Borovik was passive, as if he was waiting for a different destination.

'Nearly ready to go,' Kirilov said.

Borovik was on his feet now, small and neat as a dancer, in a grey suit and polished shoes. The loudspeaker in the corner said Flight 1072 was at last ready to depart, with apologies for the delay, at least according to Kirilov, who held out his hand in farewell.

Borovik went through the doors, and Kirilov held them open for Svetlana. But there were three men coming down the corridor in the other direction, three men in police uniform, the gold stars in their caps shining with reflected light. Instinctively Marriner drew back, but they were not coming for him, or for Borovik, who moved ahead and past them, down the stars to the bus waiting to go to the aircraft. As they came closer, Marriner's card-index mind fumbled to place the one that he half-recognised, a slim-featured man with dark eyes. Under the flat cap and in the official coat it was difficult to be sure, but he felt he had seen him before. And then the man's eyes caught his, and he knew: this was the KGB man in civilian clothes whom he had last seen perched on a desk in a smoke-filled basement when the police had picked him up, and driven him to a grilling in the barracks in Moscow, two weeks before.

But Colonel Kazakov was not interested in him now. He was addressing Svetlana in Russian, and dearly as he would have liked to wait, Marriner was forced to walk on. Walk on and leave her, as he went down the steps to the airport bus, with Kirilov in close attendance.

Before he boarded the bus, Kirilov suddenly clasped him in a Russian bear-hug.

'Goodbye,' he breathed, 'my friend.'

Marriner looked for Svetlana, but she did not come, and Kirilov understood.

'They want to question her,' he said hoarsely. 'She will not be on this aeroplane.'

Leningrad was below the aircraft. A sprawl of worker high-rise, marshes and lakes of water, matchstick trees, factories along the shoreline and the railway tracks as they banked to come in. Down there should be Brzezinski and the ETC trucks. He wondered if they had made it, or if the KGB were on to their tail as well. In that case it would be curtains, for all of them.

Ahead of him in the plane he could just see the back of Borovik's head, the neat bald patch on the skull. The little man made no move.

'Fasten your seatbelts.' The sign was in Russian and English. As he did so Marriner had the feeling that he was in for a bumpy landing.

22

Brzezinski had left him a message in the Leningrad Moskva, Sunday night, suggesting they met in the foyer. It was crowded with Intourist groups but Marriner saw him by the cigarette kiosk eating a Mars Bar.

'Bloody expensive,' the Pole said, 'but I've got a sweet tooth.' He took Marriner by the arm. 'Can't talk in here. Let's walk.'

Brzezinsky was travel-stained. 'You looked tired,' Marriner said.

'So would you after twelve hours' driving,' the Pole retorted.

They elbowed their way through the scrum, out into Nevsky Prospekt, the great wide backbone of the city, Marriner edgy and hungry, feeling very disturbed. Cold froze the bones in his fingers, wind off the Neva cut like a razor blade into his exposed hands. No gloves. At home his raincoat would have been good till December, but out there in that northern coldstore of stucco palaces it seemed useless. He stumbled along with Brzezinski, who was like a large parcel in a leather coat.

'Let's jump on a trolley-bus,' Brzezinski said. 'They go right up to the Square.'

'I want a meal,' Marriner replied. He wanted to get drunk too. Pissed. Stoned. Pulverised, to keep out the cold, the misery of his thoughts, and that last sight of Svetlana, her back pressed against the wall.

Brzezinski nodded. 'Marvellous city,' he said, enjoying himself as if there was no tomorrow. 'One last night on the town. Restaurants up this end.'

They tumbled out of the trolley-bus and clawed their way against the wind, under the triumphal arch leading to Palace Square.

'Know what this is?' Brzezinski asked.

Marriner thought he meant the Hermitage, the Winter Palace opposite, where the Kerensky Government had finally thrown in the sponge, the monumental museum which Svetlana said her father had run, but Brzezinski shook his head, and indicated the archway.

'No. This bloody great stone hoop. Ought to be up your street. Commemorates the Russian victory in 1812.'

Marriner had forgotten his muskets, the dry bones of his research, which seemed to belong to another being. He stood in the darkness, hands in pockets, and stared across the cobbled square that had seen so much bloodshed: the mob mown down on 'Bloody Sunday', the palace gates stormed at the start of the Revolution. It was like an Eisenstein film. The wind rocked across the parade ground and his head ached. Whatever his feelings had been he could not associate his future with the mysterious Svetlana who had once lived in that palace, and been brought up in its luxury, if not to own it at least to have it around her. He understood a little more then what made her tick.

'OK,' he said. 'Let's eat.'

Brzezinski led him back to the Nevsky, leaning against the wind, and found a moderate restaurant where they could still get a table. It had good bread and cheap wine and Marriner unthawed in a corner, dining on soup and shashliks in a scuffed, smoky room. Only then did he tell Brzezinski.

'I think they've got her,' he said.

Brzezinski did not seem surprised, and certainly not perturbed.

211

'It was always a risk,' he said. He contemplated his wine. 'But I don't think she'll crack in a hurry. There's nothing we can do tonight,' he said fatalistically. 'Why should she tell them anything?'

'Then why did they stop her coming?'

Brzezinski shrugged. 'I don't know. But they didn't stop Borovik, did they?'

It was true. Borovik was so unassuming that Marriner had almost forgotten he was the one that counted. Svetlana was the means not the end. But he was still concerned.

'Don't look so worried,' Brzezinski said. 'The system is bloody confused. Even if they're on to something it'll take them days to find out. Besides, don't forget she's Director of that Armoury Museum. She'll have her friends in high places.' He grinned. 'The Kremlin is a girl's best friend.' He began to wade through sweet dumplings filled with strawberry purée. 'Eat up and forget it.'

They reminded Marriner of blood, but the Pole had an iron stomach. He seemed completely at home in the Russianness of the restaurant, shabby paintwork offset by flowers on stained table-cloths. He rested his gargoyle head on his elbows. Why wasn't he running scared now, Marriner wondered; why was he enjoying this game?

As if to reassure him, Brzezinski said, 'You think I don't care, eh?'

Marriner drank black coffee that tasted of grounds and brandy. 'No. But I worry about the girl.'

Brzezinski shrugged. 'It is a hopeless place; but things take time. They will move very slowly. Listen, I know. I understand. My mother was a Russian girl, transported to Poland by the Nazis. So I am displaced, eh? After the war, in Cracow, she marry Polish guy, but no house, no work, no food. And then we get place in England because he had been with Mikolajczyk in London, and Polish Armoured Division in Normandy. So my parents are grateful to England. I am grateful.' He seemed to raise his head. 'It is my country . . . so, when they ask me to help . . .'

Help. It might well have been the same plea that Orford had made to him, Marriner thought, but he did not enquire further. They drank more brandy until the fumes rolled in their heads with the room noise like a sea in the background. It had been seven years, Marriner reflected, since he had done anything significant, worthwhile in his own terms. Seven years since the Army, and a deteriorating marriage, which had nearly driven him on to the rocks. Until Orford had recruited him there had been little to show for them except his work on firearms in the Tower Armoury. He owed the UK something too, his country by birth not adoption, or was that now regarded as sentimental drivel? He did not think so. The tears were in his eyes as they staggered back into the night.

'We've got to make this work,' he said. 'They need Borovik in London.'

Brzezinski stood in a doorway, pulling at his coat collar and looking up and down the street. They were back on the Nevsky Prospekt where they waited again for a trolley-bus. The street lights shone on the wires as the double cars clanked by. The shop fronts along the boulevard proffered their half-hearted consumer goods in the freezing night. It was this northern hardness from which England had saved him, offering instead the enjoyment of ill-funded, chaotic arts ventures which took him back into Europe under cover. And the Pole was grateful. Marriner by his side, stamping his feet to keep warm, anxious to get home, to rebuild, saw the same thing in different terms, a huge and impersonal state against which individuals like Svetlana struggled to be free. Leningrad was full of fine buildings and nothing for people to buy.

'I want to go home,' he said.

Brzezinski had found a bus. 'With a bit of luck,' he replied, 'you will.'

Colonel Kazakov was no amateur. He said very little to Svetlana after cancelling her flight, and she found herself now in a basement, a room with round-headed windows and green-painted brick walls; he sat at a desk in the middle, isolated like an altar.

'Please sit down,' he said, this uniformed policeman who looked slightly less formidable as he removed his cap and unbuttoned his blue tunic. He had brush hair and dark eyes, a sharp nose in a thin, almost emaciated face.

She sat uncomfortably on a hard wooden chair.

'Why have you brought me here? I have business in Leningrad. I am Dr Svetlana Malinkova, Director of the Kremlin Armoury.' She tried to keep her voice calm but inside she was shaking.

'I know who you are. This is an interview on record, Comrade Malinkova.' He nodded to the two men behind him, in the shadows by the radiators, one of whom was making notes.

'You have no right to detain me . . . ,' she began, but he held up a hand to silence her.

'You can protest later, if you wish. I have a right of arrest.'

'Am I arrested then?'

He smiled like a ventilator suddenly being pushed open.

'Of course not. It is only enquiries. At this stage.'

She might have panicked then, beginning to explain that she hadn't meant to kill Asterharzy, that it was a terrible accident when she had fired the gun which had forced her to decide that she must flee the country, but Kazahov did not wait.

'I understand that you know Captain Henrik Asterharzy?'

You know him. They had not found a body; they did not know he was dead. She flushed and nodded. Kazakov put his boots on the desk and tipped the chair back. Two reading lights like tiny cranes pointed towards her, outlined his head behind them.

'I find the lights obtrusive,' she said.

'I'm sorry.' He adjusted them towards the ceiling. 'Now. Please tell me when you last saw him.'

'About a week ago,' she said. 'We flew to Georgia together for a weekend. He is an Aeroflot pilot, and so he has special ticket rights.'

Kazakov lit a cigarette and she watched the smoke curl upwards in lazy spirals. Her mouth went dry but she dared not lick her lips.

'Is he your lover?'

Svetlana considered carefully before replying. 'Do you mind if I take off my coat?' It gave her time as he waved his hand; she knew he would examine her figure, and crossed her legs carefully.

'We have quarrelled,' she said, unsure still whether they were also bluffing, and had found his remains on that hillside near Mtskheta. 'The weekend did not work out.'

Kazakov leaned forward, his cigarette probing the air; the room was stiflingly hot but she sat rigidly upright, in her grey skirt and jacket.

'When was this? Which day?'

She calculated. 'The eighteenth.' Exactly eight days ago, and she prayed that they had not found him.

'What happened?'

'He walked out on me. I told him to go.'

Kazakov's voice was tougher now, icily polite. 'What was the problem?'

'He was a sadist,' she said.

214

The voice behind the lights said, 'What happened?'

In that small girl reversal she was admitting the things that ashamed her.

'He abused me.'

'I want to know what happened.'

'He tried to beat me . . . with a whip. And then he forced me . . . anally.'

Kazakov chainsmoked. 'Did you report it to the police? Or see a doctor?'

Tight-lipped, she whispered, 'No. It was not necessary.'

'But you told him to go . . . this lover?'

She shuddered. 'Yes. I hated him.'

'You hated him. So you told him to go. What happened? Where did he go? I have to warn you we are investigating his disappearance.'

'Disappearance?' She seized on the word as if it was a new idea.

'Aeroflot have reported that he is missing from duty. He has not been seen for a week. Yet you stayed on in the hotel for two more days. And paid the bill for both of you. Is that not so?'

'Yes.'

'Why was that?'

'I was very tired. I needed a rest.'

'In a double room, paying someone else's bill?'

'The difference was not very great. I did not want to move.'

'So he walked out when you told him. After forcing you?'

'He knew that he had gone too far. That it was over. He packed up his bag and left. I assumed that he went back to Moscow.'

'You assumed? You did not bother to ask?'

'No. I just wanted him to go.'

Colonel Kazakov sighed. 'How long have you known Captain Asterharzy?'

'Two or three years.'

'How did you meet him?'

'At Sheremetyevo Airport. He tripped over my legs.'

Kazakov was looking at them, as she expected, but he did not relent. 'And then?'

'We talked. He was amusing, well-travelled.'

'You like travelling outside the Soviet Union?'

'I have a Grade 1 visa to visit certain countries.'

'Such as?'

'Belgium, and West Germany.'

215

'The United Kingdom?'

'No. I have never been there.'

'But you would like to go, eh?'

'Why do you ask that?'

'The Englishman, Marriner. He sleeps with you too?'

'That is a personal matter.'

'It is State business,' Kazakov almost shouted, thumping the desk. 'Is he your lover as well?'

Svetlana cringed. 'It is nothing to do with Asterharzy. I am a single woman. Responsible. I take precautions. It is not illegal.'

'It is a risk to the State, unless it is authorised,' he shouted at her.

'I have been to bed with him once,' she said.

'In the afternoon?' he bellowed. 'Five days before you flew to Tbilisi with Captain Asterharzy?'

'I do not see what this has to do with you, or the affairs of State,' she said, trembling.

Kazakov jumped to his feet and strode across the room, standing behind her with his back to the door so that she had to swivel round, moving the chair.

'Why have you emptied your apartment?'

Svetlana went pale. The bastards had been there. 'It is being redecorated.'

'So you remove everything. Where has it gone?'

'It is in store,' she said. 'The decorators . . .'

'Who are the decorators?'

Ivanovich and Nikolai were now at risk.

'I do not know their names.'

'You do not know?'

'It was black market enterprise. Weekend work. They promised to return the pictures when it was complete. I have business in Leningrad, so I let them have the place for a week.'

'They are not working there now.'

'Perhaps you have scared them off. The police.'

Kazakov did not like that.

'So you are going to Leningrad? On the same plane as the Englishman, Marriner?'

'I did not arrange that,' she said. 'Perhaps you did.'

His lips curled, as if to say don't fool. 'Why should we do that?'

'Because you seem so interested in our relationship.'

He was angry then, his dark eyes like hot coal. 'Listen. Relationships? You know that sexual relationships with foreigners are forbidden for Russians in senior positions, unless authorised. You were going to sleep with Marriner in Leningrad, just as you slept with Asterharzy in Tbilisi. You are a whore,' he shouted.

'I resent that. I resent your line of questioning. I have done nothing wrong.'

'Where is Asterharzy?'

'I don't know.'

'Don't lie to me.'

'I'm not lying.'

He sobered up, and looked at the electric wall clock. There was something very wrong here, but he could not pin it down: the disappearance of one lover, the arrangement to book a ticket to Leningrad that had been made in Tbilisi, the sudden clearance of the Arbat apartment, and yet he could not be sure. It needed more study, and he had already kept her there for three hours.

Svetlana tried to seem calm, as his eyes bored in.

'May I go now?' she asked.

'Go? Go?' He raised his upper lip again in the smile like a grating. 'Your flight to Leningrad is cancelled. Your flat is being redecorated. We will offer you a bed here. Then we can talk again.'

23

The next morning was still and bright, sparkling with frost, as Marriner prised open his eyes and realised he was still in Leningrad. He groped his way upright and forced himself towards the breakfast bar, only to find Brzezinski was reading a newspaper in the open-plan lounge half-way along the corridor.

The Pole waved and beckoned him across, under the eye of the matron on the room service desk. He was pretending to translate an article in *Pravda*, but under his breath he said, 'You were right. Delay on the London flights.'

Marriner's mind tightened again.

'They've just sent a message to Crashaw, apologising. Everybody fucking furious. Don't panic, they may be watching.' Brzezinski stretched and said lazily, 'Coming down with the trucks? Freight seems to be OK. It's only the passenger flights.'

He folded *Pravda* carefully, as if he was reselling it, and picked up

217

his coat. They strolled back to Marriner's room and then down in the lift. Crashaw was in the lobby looking angry, as if he might hit the hapless Intourist minders.

'Jesus Christ,' he said, eyeing Brzezinski. 'I've got a London engagement. We can't stay locked up here.' The company of players crowded round. 'Darlings, it will be all right. I'm going to have a word with that nice man, Mr Gorbachev.'

Brzezinski said something in Russian to the outlying circle of tourists and hangers-on. Suddenly Marriner saw little Borovik, slipping out through the swing doors, as Brzezinski said, 'Come on.' He realised that Crashaw as usual was hogging the attention; any moment now someone would present a bouquet to Susan Lawrence, who was dressed in chocolate-box furs.

The ETC trucks had driven round from the yard, and were standing with engines running, slow curls of diesel creeping over the concrete. The backs were unlocked and open as stage hands from the company loaded them with bags and cases. Brzezinski pushed Marriner through the crowd, elbowing past in the leather coat, and then they saw Borovik, just for a second, walking along with a girl carrying an armful of clothes, and disappear inside one of the trucks, as if he was helping her up. Simultaneously there was a bang as some clown let off a firework and all heads turned. When Marriner looked again Borovik was not around.

They were shutting the trucks up now, and Brzezinski clicked the padlocks, and thumped on the doors. Brzezinski climbed into the cab of the leading vehicle and Marriner squeezed in beside him. A police car appeared to escort them, looking a little flustered.

'OK. Let's roll,' Brzezinski called.

The convoy was moving again, the police escort in front, then the four Leyland trucks with their white and blue logo, and the playbills for *Othello* and *Hamlet* decorating their sides. They shunted round Nevsky Square and over the big bridge across the Neva, on to the ringroad heading south-west to the airport. The driver leaned across to Marriner, and grinned.

'Hello, mate. We met in Moscow. Remember?'

Brzezinski said, 'Save the memories until we are home and dry.'

'I'm keeping my fingers crossed,' the driver said.

'Don't do that, Jim, they might freeze.'

Marriner hoped against hope as they raced down the long flat highway, overtaking the suburban trams, past the ridge that the

Wehrmacht had held, out into the watery country which was being slowly warmed by the disc of the morning sun. Svetlana under questions, perhaps under pressure or even physical torture, somewhere in Moscow. God knew what would happen to her, or whether she would give them time, but inside these trucks he had the bulk of her pictures, and Borovik would be burrowed away. The least he could do was keep faith with her intentions, and hope that she got through somehow.

He shouted at Brzezinski: 'How do you know they won't stop us?'

'Anything goes,' the Pole said. 'They've just said the afternoon BA flight will be delayed. The bloody thing isn't in yet. Let's try and get this lot sorted out first.'

The road was thickening with traffic as they neared the airport and saw the long modern façade with five glass drums on the roof, the last stop on the way home. The police car was taking them round to a side gate for the freight bays. Brzezinski jumped down with papers and stood talking to the guards. For a moment Marriner thought they would search them but then they were waved through, across to a transit lounge.

Out there on the tarmac were two Douglas freighters in the livery of East-West Air, with a Union Jack on each tail.

Brzezinski was handing out cigarettes and exuding good humour as they stood by the trucks. Armed security police came over as he unlocked the containers again and presented his lists. Customs men with books of stickers, countersigning forms. Brzezinski had disappeared inside the second truck and came back with a crate of Bell's whisky which he handed around. Somebody shook his hand and he made a Russan joke, hopping up and down like one of the airfield crows while the truckers and Marriner looked on.

They were motioned to wait inside a prefabricated hut, while the checking continued. Brzezinski was busy explaining how to strap down the containers to the hooks in the trucks, taking the Customs and Security police through each one, opening the crates as required: properties, costumes, armour, stage furniture and lights. Be careful, he said, don't break them, and they all laughed, clutching their free gift. Marriner watched from the window as they jumped down one by one out of the back of each truck and finally nodded. Brzezinski had passed off the icons as stage props for their northern *Lear*, and showed them a photograph of Crashaw

219

as a Russian Tsar. Borovik must be squashed in somewhere, but Marriner did not know where.

The police car came back again, just as he began to relax, and a crisp young lieutenant leaped out. They could see him arguing with Brzezinski about some change in the plans, and the Pole shaking his head.

'No way,' Brzezinski said. 'These trucks are cleared for loading.'

The lieutenant began to get flustered. His orders were to unload them.

Brzezinski swore in fluent, obscene Russian.

'Whose fucking orders? Some obscure Colonel in Moscow?' He roared with laughter. Did he want a pair of tights from the wardrobe department? Or a picture for his wall? He clasped his hand on the lieutenant's shoulder and offered him a couple of bottles, a small black market fortune. The lieutenant shook his head.

'OK, forget it,' Brzezinski said, in front of the customs men. 'Who was it signed the order?'

The lieutenant showed a telex print.

'I'll have a word,' Brzezinski said.

'It's not allowed,' the lieutenant answered obstinately.

'I don't mean with him, you fool. I mean with London,' Brzezinski roared. 'Prime Minister. You understand? She will take it up with Moscow. If anything goes wrong with this trip. If you delay our return, after the chaos of our travelling arrangements, that God-awful cock-up in Kiev,' he glowered at the lieutenant, 'your Colonel's head will roll, and you,' he swore, 'will be a piece of fucking sawdust.'

The lieutenant began to back down.

The time on the telex message was only twenty minutes old. The lieutenant turned to the Aeroflot loaders, and the freighter captain from England. 'Are you ready to take off?' he enquired in two languages, forced to use Brzezinski as interpreter.

There seemed general agreement, apart from the awkward lieutenant, standing there in his greatcoat.

'Let's go inside,' he said, 'and sort this through.'

Marriner saw them troop in, Brzezinski, the Russians, the crew men, and heard an argument break out in the next room. Brzezinski was hammering the table and pointing to his watch. The Douglas freighters were slow, he pointed out, prop-jets which would take nearly twice the flight time of the British Airways

Boeing. The whole lot had to be in London for Crashaw's gala performance that evening . . . he paused for effect . . . and shouted, 'in front of the Queen.'

'The Queen, you Marxist sheep,' the Pole roared. 'Now let me phone 10 Downing Street, and explain what is stopping us, glasnost or no glasnost.' He managed to look very angry, a mottled colour of old meat and stormed towards the telephone.

The lieutenant saw them all watching: the customs men, the airport police, the freight crew and the English drivers, who had appeared in the doorway. The cards were stacked against him.

'Well . . . perhaps . . . ,' he said, backing off, reckoning he could report that they had already been cleared for take-off.

'Marvellous. I congratulate you,' Brzezinski beamed, 'on your good sense. Now please accept the bottles.'

The atmosphere slackened at once, as if a spring thaw had set in, and even the lieutenant smiled, as he stood with his booty, one bottle in each pocket of the blue greatcoat. The sun flamed across the airfield, the flight crews departed and somebody called to the drivers to get back into their cabs.

Even so it was a long, nerve-wracking wait, as the bureaucracy unwound, and fully another hour before the tailgates of the freighters came down, and the trucks slowly rolled forward, two into each of the whale-like holds.

Marriner sat in the freight hut, drinking a glass of tea while Brzezinski chattered on cheerfully as if it was all a big game. He wondered what would happen to Borovik, in the dark of the freight hold, but presumably Brzezinski had thought of that: it did not appear to be the first time that he was using this method. The real worry now was Svetlana, and why they were trying to stop her. Brzezinski had nobbled the lieutenant, who happened to be young and green, but somebody back there in Moscow apparently was on to something; Marriner did not doubt that it was the same bastards who had shadowed him in Svetlana's street and roughed him up under the bridge.

He wanted out.

At last the drivers came back, and said the trucks were stowed. Nobody travelled with them: Borovik was on his own. They all had a final tea and waited while Brzezinski telephoned through to the departure lounge. It was not twelve-fifteen p.m.

'Two hours' delay,' he said, 'on the British Airway flight, but you can see her arriving now.'

They walked round to the front of the terminal building, accompanied by the airport police: Marriner, Brzezinski, the drivers, and the young lieutenant, who had reappeared after losing the bottles. The blue and silver 737, inward-bound from London, was swooping in to land. Over the roar of its reverse thrust Marriner said, 'I hope it turns round as fast.'

Brzezinski looked at his watch. 'One hour late coming in,' he said. 'Keep praying.'

The question in Marriner's mind was whether the prayers would work.

'Why are we waiting, why – y – are – we – waiting?'

The sixty-strong English company were now draped over the brown seats of the airport lounge. Waiting, always waiting, trapped in the no-man's-land between Customs and the boarding gates. Aeroflot buses had brought them from central Leningrad and Marriner and the truck drivers had rejoined them in the passenger terminal. The company was hyped up: John Crashaw fuming over a glass of vodka in the corner, his elegant profile tipped back as in the cigarette ads; pretty little Susan Lawrence unbuttoned, playing cards; most of them drinking and talking in subfusc sweaters and jeans.

'I'm very sorry,' the BA girl said, 'they will not clear us to leave.'

'Why? Why?' Marriner asked.

Of course nobody knew. Technical fault. Confusion over bookings. The bland faces smiled and said that it would not be long, but as the early dark shut down their optimism turned to anger and finally burnt itself out. Even Crashaw gave up complaining, and stretched himself out to sleep.

Marriner found Brzezinski drinking Bloody Marys in the bar.

'What about calling London? That crap about the Queen.'

The squat Pole winked. 'Let's not push it,' he said. 'The important stuff is on its way.'

'All except us,' Marriner said. That was what now concerned him. Something had gone wrong for Svetlana, and they were left waiting for trouble. Three quick drinks did not alter it.

An Intourist girl came in. 'I'm sorry –'

'Don't tell us . . .' Brzezinski yawned.

'It will not be long now,' she said. 'The aircraft from Moscow is arrived.'

Marriner dragged himself to meet the threat that it posed. Brzezinski was different; the Pole he realised, was a professional, and looking at him now as he joked with the Russians it was hard to believe he chanced a rope round his neck. But Marriner himself was exhausted, an amateur preserving his sanity in the last stages of a cat-and-mouse game. His head hurt and his mouth was acid with the thought that Svetlana had shopped him, and that they were coming for him. The vodka on an empty stomach was eating the corners of his mind and the faces around him were whirring as the room moved about like a ship. He fought to control his nerves.

They were coming for him, he knew, as soon as two further policemen, in different dark blue uniforms, prised him out of the lounge, extracted him from the throng of ETC strolling players.

'David Marriner?'

He nodded as they singled him out, and felt the room go silent. He was the stranger there; not Brzezinski, but him.

'Don't worry, mate,' a voice said, and he saw it was the truck driver, Jim. Brzezinski might not have known him.

He followed their boots down the corridor. Endless corridors, endless peering, hard faces, into a smaller room. An office, a place with a desk and an interview chair, and men in civilian suits lining the walls. He half-expected to see Kirilov, or even Svetlana, but the man who had come was the Colonel from Moscow, the man who had once interviewed him in the basement with the round-headed windows. Kazakov, KGB.

'Sit down.' He indicated the single chair. Kazakov in an iron grey suit and a white shirt, a little like a medical specialist or a dispensing chemist with his sardonic face and buried eyes. He sat back and looked at the Englishman. For a time there was silence. Finally he asked, 'What have you really been doing in the Soviet Union?'

Marriner said, 'You asked me that once before, and I told you. Academic research. It is all in my papers.'

The Colonel sighed, and reached for his cigarettes. The three by the window sat down, and Marriner could now see beyond them to the smart British Airways livery of the waiting plane under the floodlights. He was two hundred yards from safety and it might have been a thousand miles.

'You have also slept with Dr Svetlana Malinkova, the Director of the Kremlin Armoury,' Kazakov said slowly, flicking at a dossier of notes taken from a leather briefcase.

'I told you that too, once.'

'Once, in the afternoon,' the Colonel growled, as if that was a particular crime.

'Why are you holding me?'

The Colonel shrugged and did not reply. Marriner went on to the attack.

'The London flight has been delayed for over three hours. There have been enough problems for the ETC party on this trip, through bureaucratic incompetence. They have already lost an important engagement in London tonight. We should have been home by now – all of us.' What about Borovik, he wondered. Had they discovered he was missing? He hoped to God the freight plane was unloading at Heathrow.

The Colonel let him finish, a slight smile on his narrow lips. His mouth was very thin, a letter-box. The cigarette burnt down and he lit another from the stub.

'Do you believe in God?' Kazakov asked.

'I need him in a place like this.'

The Colonel inhaled. 'A good answer, perhaps,' he said, in his correct English. 'Your friend Svetlana Malinkova does, do you not think?'

'That's her business. I don't know. I don't see what this has got to do –'

Kazakov's voice changed. 'She is praying now,' he said, 'in a police cell.'

Marriner's heart raced, as he read the menace in those words, and knew that they had tried to break her. If she had split on Borovik and Marriner's contact with him, it was the end of his road. He looked stonily ahead at the Colonel.

'I do not understand.'

Kazakov was enjoying himself as the little smile came and went.

'Svetlana had another lover. A Flight Captain Henrik Aster-harzy, of Aeroflot. Have you met him?' His eyes seemed to retract under the beetle brows, dark creatures deep in slit-trenches. 'Have you?'

'No.' Marriner was off-guard and puzzled. It was the second time he had been asked that question.

A fist came down on the desk.

'Don't lie to me. She had been pregnant by him. And she had an abortion in the summer.'

'Don't shout at me,' Marriner retorted, flushed and angry. 'If this questioning goes on I want to be represented by the British Embassy . . .'

'Shut up and listen, if you want to be sure of your skin,' Kazakov shouted back.

'Did you meet Asterharzy?'

Marriner remembered again the letter that Werndl had instigated, accusing him of the pregnancy. It did not seem so stupid now, or so crazy of her to send it, if she had. She must have been close to the edge of her sanity. No wonder she collected icons and lived with a gallery of saints.

'No. I've never seen him.'

The Colonel digested in silence. The floodlights round the waiting aircraft, seen through the window, suddenly switched off, as if it would never fly. The Colonel noticed and gave that same thin smile, like a movement in cold water.

'Asterharzy is dead,' he said. 'Shot in the back of the head.'

Marriner did not reply, but he felt he had to say something: silence was incriminating as he blundered deeper.

'Who by?' Surely not by Svetlana, he thought wildly. This was some terrible trap.

'We believe by Svetlana Malinkova,' Kazakov said. 'We have not yet found the weapon.'

Svetlana. The blood seemed to stop inside Marriner's body. Surely such a woman, enigmatic, beautiful Svetlana, had not murdered in a lover's quarrel?'

'I don't believe it. I don't understand,' he said blindly. 'And what has this to do with me?'

'Listen, my friend.' The Colonel's voice scraped like two plates of metal. 'Svetlana says you wanted her to flee the country. She has packed up her apartment, her valuable collection of icons, at your instruction.'

'That's not true,' Marriner shouted back. 'She wanted to do it herself.'

'Ah. I see.' The smoke rings curled in the air. 'Where are they now?'

'How the hell should I know?'

'We were told they were packed up and collected by an unmarked van. We have arrested two men who say they were decorating her apartment.'

'Is that a crime?' Marriner said angrily.

Again that insulting grin. 'No. But where are they now, those items, and why have they gone?'

'Why don't you ask them?' Marriner snapped, every fibre in his body shaking with the effort of control.

'We have,' Kazakov said thinly. 'They handed them, they say, to another van that cannot be traced.'

Brzezinski. Oh Christ, if they found the Brzezinski connection, the whole game was up, Marriner thought, but the Colonel was pressing on.

'Did you know that Svetlana Malinkova flew down to Tbilisi with this man Asterharzy, about a week ago?'

Marriner shook his head. 'Not with Asterharzy. But when she came back to Moscow she said she had been to Georgia.'

'Why? Why was that? You have said that you did not know him at all.'

'I've never met Asterharzy.' But he remembered how sheet-white she was when he had seen her in the Kremlin. Tired and ten years older. The stories began to fit. 'She told me she had been on a short holiday. She was in need of a rest.'

The windows shook as an Aeroflot jet took off, no doubt going back to Moscow, and he had a breathing space while the noise subsided.

Then Kazakov was accusing him. 'You have been part of a conspiracy to kill Captain Asterharzy, and help Svetlana Malinkova to leave Russia illegally. A lover's plot.'

'That's preposterous,' Marriner said. 'A pack of lies. I want to contact the British Embassy. Mr Wootten-Smythe.'

The Colonel was icily polite.

'That can be arranged.'

Fat lot of good that would do, Marriner reflected. Wootten-Smythe had told him that he was on his own if anything went wrong.

'The whole thing is a fabrication. Lies and innuendo. I want to be released.'

'In good time. We are checking the passenger list.'

'Checking the list?' Marriner said.

'Asterharzy ordered two tickets from Moscow to Leningrad, when he was in Tbilisi. He was seen with a woman corresponding to Svetlana Malinkova. One was in her own name, the other in the name of Borovik.'

Marriner stayed silent.

'Borovik flew to Leningrad with you, on the same plane. Where is he now?'

Borovik. Borovik. Marriner shook his head.

'Why should he want to fly here at the same time as you, unless he was leaving the country, as arranged by Malinkova?'

'I don't know,' he said woodenly. 'He did not tell me.'

The Colonel blew smoke in the air. 'We have to check who is on your aircraft. That is why it is delayed.'

'You can't hold me.'

'Why not?'

'You have no evidence.'

'Evidence is not always immediately available.'

'What does that mean?' Marriner retorted. 'I want to telephone, now.'

It might have gone on all night, they might never have given in, had not Crashaw appeared, with Brzezinski as interpreter, and the BA flight captain.

'Look,' the captain said, 'You are delaying my flight with over a hundred passengers on board.'

'On board?' Kazakov was clearly surprised. 'Who gave clearance to board?'

'I arranged it,' Crashaw said calmly.

Brzezinski winked. Never had John Crashaw seemed so imperious, Hamlet and Othello in one, with a dash of the King Lears. He roared, he raged, he cracked his cheeks and swore that they must take off. 'Have you checked your damned lists? Are we all under suspicion? What about human rights? Soviet justice? Come on, my Colonel. You must let him go. And let us all go, before the night falls. Otherwise there will be trouble, dead trouble for you, old son.' His sharp voice lanced the room and if they did not fully understand, the meaning and the poetry were fierce, as Crashaw recited gobbets of blank verse at them.

> 'Take but glasnost away, untune that string,
> 'And, hark, what discord follows.'

The inference was all too clear: unless the Colonel co-operated, future East-West relations and cultural tours lay in the balance. And the Colonel had no evidence.

He looked hungrily from Crashaw to Marriner and back, scarcely aware of Brzezinski, and shook his head.

Crashaw reached for the telephone in a gesture that was calling

God. The Colonel changed his mind. He spoke abruptly to his lieutenants and was told that the identities were checked. Marriner heard the name Borovik, and the reluctant 'Nyet.' Kazakov gathered up his papers and nodded briefly. 'The interview is over,' he said. 'And you may leave.'

As the Boeing taxied and took off into the night, Marriner was still shaking, in spite of the comforting reassurance of hot towels, gin and tonics and copies of the *Independent*, London, Monday.

Brzezinski sat beside him. 'You look pretty bushed,' he said.

Marriner could only marvel at the tough little Pole's robustness. 'You do this often?' he asked.

Brzezinski shrugged. 'Once in a while.'

'For Denis Orford?'

The Pole's face was blank. 'No names, no packdrill.'

But the names were exercising Marriner as the drinks settled his stomach and the plane droned steadily westwards out over the Baltic, out of Soviet airspace.

'Borovik,' he said. 'I hope the poor bastard doesn't die of suffocation, shut up in that box.'

'Vasily Vasilyvich Borovik wasn't inside a box,' Brzezinski told him. 'Have you ever tried to make a box with a false bottom, big enough for a man?'

Marriner admitted he hadn't. 'Where did you hide him then?'

Brzezinski rubbed his chin. 'Don't forget we were playing *Othello*. And dear old *Lear* in armour. Try looking inside the costumes. You can stuff a whole body inside a suit of chainmail.'

Marriner took another gin. 'But won't he freeze to death in the cargo hold?'

Again Brzezinski revealed that Orford's degree of planning was far higher than he had supposed. Orford had been using him, right from the first contacts.

'All that Comrade Borovik had to do was suffer a flight in the dark. There was a torch and food. And plenty to read. The hold was pressurised.'

Marriner looked out into the blackness over the North Sea. Coming home. Brzezinski settled down to sleep.

God help Svetlana now, he thought, for she would need him. Her road had ended, not his, but it might so easily have been the other way round. In his mind's eye he seemed to see her in a grey prison smock, the blonde hair shaved, a prisoner of the Gulag, her hopes, her career shattered. How had she come to kill this man Asterharzy, or was that another story, like the phantom pregnancy? What if the evidence was planted by the KGB, that chain-smoking Colonel? He shuddered, desperately sorry, left with a collection of icons which meant nothing to him. It was as if she had sold her soul, and perhaps in a way she had. She was beyond his help now, or Orford's or Brzezinski's or anyone's, but he could not forget her, the elfin head of hair, those eyes in the oval face, the long legs and thin body, making love in the afternoon.

It was over. It was done. He had a life to repair. A wife who had tried to divorce him, a child he was dearly attached to. Celia and Katie, waiting for him in England, and England was a different planet where the winter would be so much warmer. Celia, we've got to make it, he told himself, rehearsing what he would say, how he would rebuild the bridges, remembering Edmonson's letter which had said that she was coming round, as if from a mental illness. He recalled it again now. 'Rethinking her position . . . no further action on the second petition . . .'

The pilot came over on the intercom to say that they would be landing in twenty minutes. The sky had already cleared and he could see the lights of London, strung out below in spider's web. Christ it was good to be back.

24

It was the stars who got the welcome, John Crashaw and Susan Lawrence, as they came back in triumph to Heathrow; the ETC not Marriner to whom the honours went. He saw Denis Orford there in the mob at the arrivals barrier, unmistakable with his red thatch and the great turnip face, but Orford gave him the barest grin before snatching up the leaders of the touring company and bearing them off in triumph with an escort of helmeted motor cyclists like fighter pilots.

Brzezinski and Marriner, the truck drivers and the juniors, were left to make their own way. They shook hands at the taxi queue as if it had been a holiday, and departed to pick up their lives.

'Where are you going now?' Marriner asked him.

'Sheffield,' Brzezinski said, 'until they want me again. We're opening there next week.'

It did not sound much of a life, itinerant, plagued by logistics, but the Pole seemed to like it. And Marriner understood. Marriner, like Brzezinski, had never quite been inside the system, the peer group pik'n'mix which decided who got what, the top posts shared amongst cronies, like-thinking, right-thinking museum clones.

But as the cab took him home to High Barnet he saw his purpose very clearly. He came back to make a marriage work. The rain-washed streets swished by, full of parked cars and rubbish, modest semi-detacheds, keyhole residences standing behind front gardens like faintly disapproving aunts. He had to forget Svetlana, built his own satisfactions, play the cards he'd been dealt and not go after foreign adventures, erotic, unstable and bleak. Svetlana was behind him now. He had made his bed and must lie in it, coming home to Katie and Celia.

The house was there in the darkness of the suburban street, the pitched roof and the tall chimney silhouetted against the sky. He paid off the taxi and crunched over the gravel. The place even smelt of home, as he unlocked the door and stood in the hall, that dryness from central heating on polish and paper flowers. He put down his cases and called quietly up the stairs, but it was nearly midnight and they must have given up waiting.

He switched on the light in the kitchen and made himself a cup of tea for the sheer pleasure, the luxury, of being home. Whatever would happen now was only between equals, Celia and himself, not in some Soviet madhouse that seemed to consist of Svetlana and himself making love before icons, and ended up with a corpse. He must forget her. He must.

Wandering through the familiar rooms he found a difference that at first he could not place. The front lounge looked much the same with its cream settees, the decorations on the fireplace; and then he realised that the flowers were real, a vaseful of pink carnations, freshly cut. He was tired now, too tired to work it out, and he mounted the stairs quietly, so as not to disturb them. The door to Katie's room was ajar, and he peered into the darkness, but she was sleeping soundly, he could hear the regular breathing. He closed it and walked on, past Celia's bedroom, and softly opened the door to what had once been theirs.

A glimmer of moonlight through the drawn curtains showed him that she was lying there, sound asleep. She had moved back into his bed, unless she had changed rooms simply because he was away. Marriner could still not be sure, but he would not retract. Somewhere a long way off he heard the rattle of trains, but in the silent bedroom only the two of them existed.

He found she had laid out pyjamas on the chair by the bed, and undressed quickly. As he slipped in beside her he felt her body move, deep in the recesses of sleep. She murmured something that he could not catch, and then it seemed all over, as she held him.

She had gone before he awoke, leaving him a note. 'Darling. Welcome back,' he read, and then instructions for breakfast. Katie had scribbled kisses and Celia had taken her to school. He lay back in the bed in a freedom of new happiness, as if the hard times were over and he had won her respect. He was dog tired.

Soon after, Challenby rang, at ten o'clock. Marriner could easily picture him in that square room in Whitehall where they had once talked, looking down over the Thames.

'Glad you got back, old man,' Tom Challenby drawled in his public school voice. 'Denis said that he saw you at the airport last night. Bit of a problem in Leningrad, so I gather.'

'There was a problem,' Marriner agreed. 'Did Borovik get out unharmed?'

'Yup. Bloody marvellous. We are debriefing him now. A tremendous achievement,' Challenby said blandly. 'Now what about these crates?'

The crates. For a moment Marriner had almost forgotten that he had Svetlana's belongings, impounded in a customs warehouse at Heathrow.

'I'm on my way to inspect 'em,' Challenby said. 'Like you to come with me. Can I pick you up in an hour?'

'They belong to Svetlana Malinkova,' Marriner retorted angrily. 'Can't you leave them alone?'

'I'm afraid she won't be claiming 'em,' Challenby said.

It was a scalding statement, which Marriner found hard to accept, though it seemed so inevitable. He remembered their times together, working in the Armoury, visiting the Bolshoi, walking in the Moscow parks, making love in that strange apartment. He swallowed. All gone now, and it was men like Challenby, organised, backstairs generals who picked over the remains. Who were not hurt.

'Does it have to be now?' Marriner said. 'I'm waiting to talk to Celia.'

'Things going better?'

'I think so,' he replied. 'If we can give it a chance.'

'Great. But it has to be now. The expert advisers are coming to sift through.'

'Who?'

Challenby might have been dealing with a recalcitrant child. 'Valuers,' he said. 'Chaps from the BM and V&A who know about Russian stuff, and someone from Christie's.'

Marriner held the telephone at arm's length, not really caring what the M.o.D. man was saying. He stood there in his own house, too full of unease to be able to articulate clearly. Something about this abandonment of Svetlana, this failure to keep faith, cut into his bones, but Challenby was pressing him.

'I'll be there in an hour,' he said. 'In a black Rover.'

Marriner was almost dressed when Celia returned. He heard her footsteps running up the stairs and then she burst into the bedroom, and flung her arms round him.

'David, David.' There were tears in her eyes as they kissed like that for the first time in years; as if the dam had broken. 'I'm so glad,' she kept murmuring, before collapsing on the bed.

Something had happened to her, almost as if his trip had broken the spells on them both; or she was reacting to the threat posed by Svetlana? As he touched her he wondered if the mood would hold, and carry through into their lives, when she knew that the other woman could never come.

'Was it terrible?' Celia said, half to herself.

Marriner could not answer: it would have cost him too much. He needed time for perspectives on what had happened in Russia. Instead he kissed her forehead and said, 'Challenby's coming.'

At once she was on the alert. 'Where?'

'Here. In half an hour. He wants me to see the crates of stuff that we freighted back from Leningrad.'

'I don't trust him. I want you here,' she said. 'Stay with me here.'

'I know. I know. We got it wrong.'

'I'm sorry.'

'Forget it,' Marriner said. 'We've got Katie, and we can start again.'

Celia hesitated, as if just for a second the old doubts had resumed. 'I've burned the letter . . . from that woman.'

'It was a fabrication. Got up by that fool Werndl. She was pregnant before we met. And she had an abortion.'

Celia nodded, as if the past was over.

'Katie came to see you before she went to school, but you were still asleep.'

'It's been quite a trip,' he said. 'But I'm home now.'

'Don't go.' There was a note of alarm in her voice, as they heard Challenby's car roll over the gravel outside. She caught at him in alarm. 'David, don't go.'

But Challenby was ringing the bell and they had to answer it. 'Congratulations, old man. A great job,' he said. And then to Celia, 'He helped us to get our man out.'

'What man?' she asked sharply.

Challenby laughed. 'You shouldn't enquire about that. Just one more piece of business, my dear Celia, and then you can have him for good.'

'Don't go. Don't let them use you,' she said desperately, but David had already decided.

They came out of the house, and he wrapped himself in the raincoat that had served him in Russia. The leaves were still falling in England, brown and gold cut-outs against a pale sky. 'I won't be long,' he said.

He saw her waving goodbye.

As they drove round the North Circular, Challenby settled back on the cushions.

'Where is Borovik now?' Marriner asked. Challenby brushed a speck of fluff from his blue pinstripe. 'Safe house. Telling us all he knows. It will be a revelation in the SALT talks. They've got no one left like him.'

'Then why bother with Svetlana's things? Leave them in case she turns up.'

Challenby gazed from the window at the stream of traffic, and murmured. 'Not quite the point, old man. Fact is . . . how can I put this . . . your position is a bit, ah, embarrassing to HMG.'

'Embarrassing?'

'If the Russians get awkward. You understand?'

'No.'

'Well.' Challenby's hand grasped the strap that dangled in the car like a noose. 'If Svetlana talks, and tells 'em that you used her as a go-between, we shall have to deny it. We didn't send you there, is that clear?'

'What if I say you did?'

'Oh come on now, David, let's be reasonable. Why would we be involved with academic research?'

'Look,' Marriner said. 'I went there because you asked me. You and Orford. I'm not backing down on that.'

'Please. No one is suggesting . . . but if we get a request – if, I say – we get a request for help from the Soviets in tracking down a load of icons . . . we shall have to say you arranged it.'

'Arranged it?' Marriner's face flushed with anger. 'Your guy Brzezinski fixed the bloody thing up.'

'Don't say that, David. You know it's not true,' the silky voice admonished.

'Of course it's true. It was the price she wanted for helping with Borovik.'

'I said don't say that.' The car jerked and stopped in a queue, 'otherwise we shall have to disown you. Look, old man, it's like this. These crates are in your name –'

'My name?'

'Your name. So you are going to claim 'em. She wanted you to have them, to sell them for her.'

'Oh my Christ.'

'No swearing, David.'

'You bastard.'

'We think they may make a counterclaim to say that they're illegal exports. Don't want to upset them, David. Anyway if they focus on you, and your relations with Svetlana, it keeps them on the wrong scent. They won't know how Borovik got out, so we can use the same route again. You with me, old boy? You had an affair with Svetlana, maybe you had it off. I don't know. But that's the story we want, and it's the one we shall give 'em. You know, steamy affair between two museum buffs. Nothing so crude as sex. But that's how you got to help her and arrange for her stuff to come out.'

'Crap,' Marriner said. 'What makes you think they'll believe it?' But his blood chilled at the memory of his grilling by the Colonel in Leningrad, who told him she had shot her lover, Asterharzy, and had stripped her apartment. They knew too much already, too much they could throw at him. And he realised that the Colonel had already been in touch: the KGB and MI6 were brothers under the skin.

'They've telephoned you from Moscow?'

Challenby smiled. 'Right first time. Early this morning. While you were still asleep. Our Svetlana has talked. She says that you persuaded her to smuggle out the stuff, and to defect. Only it all went wrong when her boyfriend intervened.'

'Lies. All lies,' Marriner shouted at him. 'I've never even met him.'

Challenby considered the run-in to the freight sheds at Heathrow: PANAM, BA, Air France, TWA, Alitalia. 'Busy place this,' he muttered. He showed a pass at the wire mesh of the security gates. 'Lot of illegal stuff.'

'What are you trying to tell me?'

'That we may have to hand the pictures back. Interest of Anglo-Soviet relations. And . . .'

'And?'

Challenby sighed. 'It's the system, you follow? The need to show our good faith. Afraid that we may have to arrange your suspension for trafficking in stolen goods.'

For a moment Marriner did not understand, and then his anger flared, not just for his own future but the status that Celia saw in him. 'I'll have your guts,' he said.

Challenby waved his hand. 'Don't try anything silly. Remember we can always get you under the Official Secrets Act. Anyway, its only for show. Suspension or dismissal from the Tower Armoury. Helps our position with Moscow. In practice we'll see you all right. You'll just have to leave, that's all, under a bit of a cloud.'

Marriner hit the roof, his fists doubled as if he was going to attack, his face flushed and furious. 'You can't do it. You wouldn't dare,' he shouted.

Challenby smiled, as the car moved on.

'Wait and see,' he said.

Two police cars, and a half-a-dozen others, were parked by a big shuttered hangar, and as they pulled up a man in a Raglan overcoat introduced himself.

'Detective Chief Superintendent Fowler. Airport Squad.' He lead them inside through a small padlocked door.

'The others are in here, sir.'

Marriner saw nine people standing around two roped-off crates, marked 'ETC tour to USSR', under arc lights on poles. It was almost like a private view of some exclusive exhibition.

'Polgarth, Senior Customs Officer, Heathrow,' Fowler said,

pointing to a thickset man who might have walked off a tug. Ian Mulhose, British Museum, Anna Rostakova, V&A Mediaeval Department, three others Marriner knew, and John Sprague of Christie's. The remaining two were Customs officials. They seemed to circle the crates like spectators at a boxing match.

'Come on, let's get moving,' Challenby said, and the two Customs men began to undo the padlocks with Brzezinski's keys. The Pole was nowhere to be seen, but, as they waited, Marriner was conscious of another figure entering the hangar from a different door. An unmistakable silhouette with the build of a rugby forward and a rug of reddish hair.

'Hello,' Orford said, as if Marriner had not been away. 'Good trip?'

'You're all bastards,' Marriner muttered.

Orford smiled. 'What a welcome. Saw you at the airport last night. A splendid tour: very good for East-West relations. Musn't spoil the atmosphere, you know.'

'Bastards,' Marriner repeated, as the Customs officers knocked away the ends of the two wooden crates.

They ran the lights closer and peered inside. Somebody made an inventory. They were taking out one by one Svetlana's pictures, wrapped in old paper and rags, sealed up with masking tape.

The professionals elbowed each other, whistling with surprise.

'My God, what a beautiful thing,' Anna Rostakova chortled excitedly. 'It must be a Communion of the Apostles. I should think twelfth-century.' The picture glowed with old golds.

And then there were the heads. 'St Gregory. The prophet Elijah. Look at that beautiful face,' Mulhose said excitedly. 'We've nothing like that in the BM.'

They pulled out another head, a Christ with eyes like black plums, head bent in sorrow. 'Pure Byzantine,' Anna Rostakova burbled. 'And yet it must come from Russia, maybe thirteenth-century.'

Four more faces now. Heads that Marriner had seen gracing her great room in Moscow while the music thundered around them. The Virgin and Child, in rich brown and red and gold; an unknown saint; a painting on boards of St Luke against a gold and crimson sky; and an Annunciation. The man from Christie's was computing their value in millions.

It was the Annunciation that brought them to their senses, an icon of an angel in translucent blue robes, wings whirling like propellers, bringing the news of the Christchild to an amazed Mary with the face of a Botticelli maiden. A picture of softness and repose, with Mary seated under a scarlet canopy, and already ringed with a halo. In the background there stretched a landscape of trees in what appeared to be snow.

'That's from the Museum itself,' Anna Rostakova squeaked. 'I'm sure of it. It was hanging there when I saw it.'

There was a stamp on the back, identifying it as part of the Armoury collection.

'They would never have sold it,' Mulhose agreed.

'What about the others?' Challenby urged, as they pulled them out and digested them one by one, forty-seven pictures, a handful of silver ornaments, some painted ivory caskets and a set of golden goblets.

'Jesus. We could never sell most of this,' Sprague said. 'It's got no legitimate provenance.'

'A lot of it must come from the Kremlin,' Anna Rostakova argued. 'It's probably not even been catalogued. A secret store in the Armoury that she's been salting away. The woman must be mad.'

Mad, Marriner wondered; was it as simple as that? Or had she seen herself as able to give things more life, and perhaps one day to reveal them to the world outside.

'We've already had a call from the KGB,' Challenby said, 'warning us that they believe icons have been smuggled to England.'

'How do they know?' Sprague asked, seeing the prizes slip from his commercial grasp.

'They've arrested the Director of the Kremlin Museum, on a charge of manslaughter. I gather in self-defence she's told them about her lovers . . . and one of her friends . . . ah . . . is with us this morning.'

Marriner was to be the scapegoat. There was a long pause, and he wanted to run over and push his fist into Orford's great wall of a face. But he held his tongue.

'So, what are we doing to do?' Anna Rostakova enquired, rubbing the dust from her hands on to a twin-set and pearls.

'The Russians want 'em back,' Challenby said.

'Are you going to agree?'

It was Orford who spoke, almost for the first time, his voice booming from the shadows. 'Of course. Mustn't upset the Reds.

We're not answerable for private affairs. If these are stolen goods, then they must be returned.'

Challenby drew Marriner aside.

'Look, don't take it too hard, David. The point is we've got to cover ourselves. Happens like that some times. Svetlana was awfully useful, and so was your contact with her, in getting Borovik on-side. But we really couldn't hold the pictures, even if she had got out. Much too hot. You follow.'

'You mean that if she had come over, the icons would still be sent back?' Leaving him with Svetlana, unsupported.

Challenby walked him to the end of the hangar, out of earshot. 'Who knows? Most probably, old boy.'

'Don't patronise me.'

'Sorry. But you understand?'

'What are you planning now?' Marriner said bitterly.

'Well.' Challenby considered his shoes. 'We'll send this stuff back, with a note of apology, saying we found it consigned to your good self. Saying we believe it was arranged because of an infatuation, and that you paid the ETC, unknown to their management, to get it out in the transport. Deep regrets. Won't happen again. Measures to prevent recurrence. And to show that you're not on our payroll, a little bit in the papers about your resignation.'

'Resignation. For Christ's sake.'

'Oh, come now. I'll have a word with Vic Burgloss, the Master of the Tower. He'll understand. And of course you'll receive your pay. You won't be worse off at all. We'll try and fix you up elsewhere. But just for the sake of appearances, we need to make it clear that the Establishment doesn't approve of trying to get stuff out of the Kremlin. So that when they find out about the one who matters – Vasily Vasilyevich Borovik – they won't connect it with you; and they won't know how we arranged it.'

They took him back in the police car, for appearances as Challenby said. 'Don't worry, old boy, we won't hurt you. I've had a word with Victor Burgloss already this morning, caught him before he left home. Explained the situation. He understands.'

'Understands!' Marriner retorted.

'Sure. He's putting you on "gardening leave". Full pay, until we find a slot for you, when it all blows over. Of course we shall say officially that you're being relieved of your duties and the DPP is considering a prosecution –'

'Thanks –'

'But it will be all right. No problems for you or, ah, the family. You just keep out of the way.'

The two police cars used their sirens to blast a way up Victoria Street and he found himself by the revolving cheese cube of New Scotland Yard.

'Won't keep you a minute,' DCS Fowler said. 'Just for the record, a few particulars. Sometimes there's somebody photographing who goes in and out of here, from that bloody hotel opposite. Mind if we just pose on the steps?'

They stood underneath the hideous, stainless steel nameplate on its pole and Fowler waved his arms about as if he was explaining the neighbourhood. Challenby looked stern, glaring sideways at Marriner.

'OK, that will do,' Fowler said. 'Let's have a cup of coffee.'

In fact it was tea and biscuits, in someone's office as they went step by step through the procedures in Moscow and in Leningrad, a careful debriefing, as if he'd come back from a bomber run.

Challenby looked at his watch. 'Christ, David, I'm keeping you from your lunch.' There was no offer of the Athenaeum this time round.

Sod them, Marriner thought.

'Am I supposed to turn up at the Tower and hang around for the sack?'

'The bloody Tower? Nothing so crude, David. You're a kind of private hero; it's just a question of public style.'

'Tell that to my wife.' He feared that his new-found half-way harmony with Celia would be shattered by a public disgrace.

'I have,' Challenby said. 'While you were still in bed.'

'Jesus wept.'

'Oh come on now. It's in this country's best interests. We don't want a lot of publicity leading to an enquiry.'

Even in Moscow, Marriner had not felt so impotent, struggling against a system closing over him.

'No talking to the press.'

They had it all worked out: Challenby his one-time friend, the big chief Orford, the supporting cast of security men.

'Don't take it too hard. We'll not let you down.'

'I want to go home,' he said, and walked to the door without another word.

25

'Gardening leave' was something he had to take seriously. He found that the ranks had closed against his reappearance, but in spite of their efforts, the story of illegal imports of Russian icons broke on the following day, together with the Soviet request that they should be returned at once.

A spokesman for Christie's said that their value was priceless.

A spokesman for Sotheby's put it at £25 million. The telephone did not stop ringing as soon as he'd been identified as the go-between, the consignee in the UK, the lover of Svetlana Malinkova. The excitement blew across the front pages and consigned to oblivion the story of the ETC triumph; photographs of Crashaw in his white Cossack hat were replaced by smudged ones of Marriner, including one of him posing outside New Scotland Yard.

He tried to go back to the Armoury on Tower Hill, but he was hounded. Reporters were hovering there and when he did penetrate he found that his room had been cleared. Vic Burgloss, the Master, even came down to apologise, a gangling man with a beard who had once been an Engineer Commander, but had failed in his bid for the Maritime. The disappointment rankled, and left him permanently scarred. Marriner had the feeling that he garnered some strange satisfaction at being the focus of attention.

Marriner picked a few things from store: his notes on the firing range of the English musket, a copy of his published monograph, a few pictures and books, to be taken away in a van. Burgloss said they'd put him inside it as well, so that there would be no hassle when they drove out. In effect he was saying farewell to his second career.

Burgloss even shook hands. As the van drove into Great Tower Street he had one last glimpse through the window of the keep and battlements of scuffed white stone. It was not so very different from the Kremlin: the things one did for one's country.

There was no word of Borovik. He had gone quietly to ground as if he had never existed, but Challenby assured him that they had the information they wanted. The Soviets would not yet admit they had lost him because the truth was embarrassing to an administration harassed by perestroika and ethnic unrest. It would seem they were losing their grip; but the facts would be privately paraded, at the new talks in Geneva and Helsinki, the next round of arms control, and would alter the balance of power. The prospect of an agreement on chemical stockpile disposal was now immeasurably closer. In that sense Marriner had won.

He returned home to High Barnet to face the personal realities in terms of his relations with Celia, in terms of his peace of mind. And always the niggling uncertainty about what had happened in Moscow.

The media were relentless. For over a week they were hounded by knocks at the door, telephone calls in the evening, camera crews by the front gate. Katie was at first amused, and then completely terrified as the kids turned against her as if she were a pariah. They had to withdraw her from school, at the Headmistress's request. A television documentary about the ETC tour was turned into an enquiry about the theft of Kremlin icons. The *Sunday Times* colour supplement wrote up five thousand words about 'The Man in the Tower', this Romeo who had seduced the Director of the Kremlin Museum. His background was probed and distorted until he appeared a cross between Genghis Khan and Casanova.

Yet as Celia shut out the world behind drawn curtains, living off food in the freezer, they slowly edged closer together. She still had that air of unease about the Russian episode, but in one sense it had heightened his stature, given him a sense of drama in her eyes, on which she thrived. Even the press persecution was a mark of his importance. One day he would write a book, like *Spycatcher* she murmured, across the table in the kitchen.

'I wasn't a spy,' he said.

'I know. But you were the key. You got out the Borovik man, and provided the cover story.'

Marriner was rational and logical. This crazy world of mirrors upset him. Nobody would have invented it apart from people like Orford, and the KGB Colonel, who had rules in a private game, but it existed. It was an Olympic sport between the power blocs, basketball with chemical weapons.

And Celia was back in his bed. Not yet ready for love, but the bridges were being repaired, the ice had broken.

She lay there in the darkness with him. 'Tell me about the woman.'

'Svetlana?'

'Yes.'

He drifted uneasily across his memories.

'Did she really send you a letter?' he asked.

'Yes. I told you. I've destroyed it.'

'I believe you.' He touched her gently, but she was still resentful.

'Tell me what she was like.'

He considered. 'I suppose you would call her beautiful. A *femme fatale*. Good legs and a nice figure; sort of cropped blonde hair, almost like an animal's pelt, very fair, and fine.'

'That's horrible.'

'It wasn't. She could be very charming. Took me to the theatre, and to this wonderful flat where all the pictures were.'

'Pictures that she had stolen,' Celia said.

'I suppose so. Some of them. I didn't know.'

The telephone rang again and interrupted them. He could hear her talking in that antiseptic hall that somehow he had to change. to colour in, as a kind of symbol of their shifting relationship, becoming warmer, more understanding. When she returned, she said, 'Another one of those damned reporters. I hate the way they try and pursue us day and night. We've got to go away.'

It was the first time she had mentioned it, breaking away from the ties of their suburban existence. The lights were burning again. She faced him in her nightdress, and said slowly, 'I don't care what happened . . . with her. As long as we make good between us.'

The wheel had turned full circle.

'We could ask for the Jones's cottage,' he replied. 'They never go there at this time of year. We could stay there till Christmas.' Christmas with log fires in the open hearth, under a thatched roof: when he had suggested it, once before, years ago, she had turned her back in that unyielding way, but now she agreed.

'OK.'

Another ring downstairs – a telephone they did not answer.

He remembered the clear picture that he had had in the intense tiredness of that first night back, safe, driving home from the airport. He would rebuild his own satisfactions in the marriage.

'Let's go,' he said. 'Katie can stay with the Lanyards like she did before. I'm sure they'll be pleased to put her up with Janice. And we can get right away. There's no reason to stay bottled up here.'

Celia kissed him quickly, her features warm with new happiness, almost glowing.

'I'll phone them,' she said, 'and also Sonia Jones.' She smiled and relaxed. 'We can leave the Lanyards a key, and our address, and simply take off.'

'There's nothing to stop us,' he said, as they settled to sleep. 'Nothing.'

It took two weeks to arrange, and they were into mid-November before he could get away. In the meantime he had to see Orford at the latter's request, a message delivered by motorcycle courier.

'Please answer your bloody phone,' he read. 'I can't get through. Denis O.'

They met in Sydenham. Orford told him to drive there and they sat in an unmarked car, Orford's car, overlooking the Crystal Palace. It was a Friday afternoon, and the games fields and the terraces on which the glass palace had stood were empty and forlorn, apart from marauding dogs. Marriner took along his file of newspaper cuttings and waved them under Orford's nose as they sat in the front of his Volvo estate.

'The Kremlin Robbery.'

'The Man with £20 million Icons.'

'We want 'em back, say Reds.'

'For Christ's sake,' he told Orford. 'Think of my bloody career. Think of my wife. Even in *The Times*: "Tower of London Keeper Resigns".'

'How is Celia?'

'Celia's OK.' He slowed up his anger. 'For some reason it seems to have helped her. Notoriety.'

'Most people's lives are dull. They need the spark of adventure.' They watched two dogs try to copulate.

'Is that what you think you provide?'

Denis Orford laughed and picked his nose.

'I'm duty, David. OHMS. You know that. That's why we asked you.'

'You didn't tell me you would drop me in the shit.'

'Nobody's dropping you in anything, David. Mind if I smoke?' He pulled out a packet of cheroots and pressed the window button to let in some air. They could hear the shouts of small children sliding down the grass banks. The dead leaves along the railings had piled into decaying compost which an old man poked with his stick.

'Don't worry, David. The system will take care of you, and you get six months on full pay.'

243

'You do on sick leave. Without your name all over the papers.' Orford blew smoke.

'My advice is to get out of London. Leave the house. Until the interest dies down. It always does, you know, even with the Russians. They take longer to forget, because they're less quick on the ball – have you noticed that? – but they do. Sure you won't have a cigar?'

'No.' Marriner watched Orford blow his pockmarked nose. 'We've already decided to go: to get away.'

'Good.' A big puff of smoke reeled back inside the car. 'Where?'

'Suffolk. Friend of ours has a cottage near the coast that we can always borrow. Celia's never been keen before, but it seems different now.'

'Very sensible, David. Keep out of harm's way. You taking your little girl?'

Marriner shook his head. 'She's got school. But she can stay with friends.'

'Good.'

'What's happened to Borovik?'

'Borovik's OK. Don't you worry about him. Like you, he drops out of sight, in his case for a long time. We've got quite a little community of expatriates salted away. You'll see them come out of the woodwork as the politics change.'

Marriner wound his own window down too: Orford was one of those men who imposed a physical presence, almost like a smell.

'Why did you bring me out here?'

'To see Borovik.'

'Here?'

'Just over there.' He pointed to a row of tall Victorian houses, looking over the railings, opposite the park. 'Temporarily.'

They locked the car and walked across to Number 53. The door opened as they approached, and they found themselves in a hall monitored by a TV camera. A plainclothes man in a sweater was waiting there.

'He won't be here for long, but he wanted to say goodbye,' Orford muttered.

There was a room at the back, a lounge with some modern furniture and a reproduction of oasthouses in a Kentish lane above the empty fireplace. The room was warm and double-glazed, and Borovik was sitting facing them, upright, on a settee. As soon as he saw Marriner he jumped up and embraced him.

Marriner endured the hug from this brittle, scholarly man whose fading eyes danced with a sense of conviction or satisfaction, as if he had been relieved of a tremendous burden. He clung to Marriner with the defencelessness of a child who had suddenly met Father Christmas.

'Thank you. Thank you,' he said.

'I didn't do much. Brzezinski put you in the box.'

'That's enough,' Orford told them. 'Vasily Vasilyevich is not staying here. We are taking him to the country. You like the country, Vasily?'

Borovik smiled awkwardly, and Marriner began to wonder what hell would face him too, in time, when the excitement died. The emptiness of being alone, in a strange land, for the sake of his conscience; Borovik's future was bleaker than anything in front of Marriner.

He felt sorry for him.

'Good luck,' he said. 'Plenty of time for drawing now.'

'What do you mean?' Orford intervened.

'It doesn't matter,' Marriner replied as they turned to go.

They walked back to the Volvo without speaking until they were inside it.

The sight of Borovik had shaken him, perhaps not what Orford intended, and brought the other face to his mind.

'What is happening to Svetlana?'

Orford started the car and drove him back to the car-park where they had originally met. It began to rain.

'Not much news I'm afraid. We know that she's under arrest. Her flat is closed. Mail is being returned.'

So they had tried that already. 'Don't you have inside contacts?' Marriner asked.

'For Christ's sake, David. What do you think we are?' Orford huffed. 'A universal charity? It's cops and robbers, cowboys and Indians, them and us. We don't have a mole inside their prison system if that's what you mean.'

'But what will they do with her?' Marriner stood in the rain, between the two cars as Orford's big head looked out at him from the Volvo.

'Do? She's under wraps for manslaughter, possibly murder. Probably got her fingerprints on the gun, if they've found it. Asterharzy was a go-between, a good friend of ours, so we're lying bloody low.'

'But what did she do?' He remembered that bleak-faced Colonel in the jack boots, the one who had interviewed him, first in Moscow and then flown up to Leningrad, a man with a thin, clever face.

'That's what they'll try and find out.'

'Did she know about Asterharzy's double life?'

'I don't think so. Unless he talked in bed. Some buggers do.'

Marriner was getting wet, but he seemed unable to move, to drive away; Orford was anxious to go, and held out his hand.

'Wait a minute. I can't just abandon her. I could send them a letter, explaining my position. She asked me to help her, but I had no knowledge of another lover. There was no conspiracy to kill him. It might stop them pinning that charge. I owe her that.'

'Don't be so bloody ridiculous, David,' Orford chortled. 'Get back to your muskets. We don't know anything and we don't know nothing. That's the name of the game. I'm sorry, but it is. If they want to get her they will, and there's nothing that you or I can do about it. OK?'

Marriner stared at him. 'You mean that she could be charged with murder?'

''Fraid so, old man. Look. Leave her alone, will you? It's bloody well over. Nothing left in it for us. Concentrate on Celia, while you're some kind of private hero.'

Hero? It was a four-letter word in circumstances like this.

'I'll write,' he said obstinately.

'You're bloody cracked. You won't.'

It began to rain more heavily. 'Go away. Go away and forget her. And be careful. You may not be out of the wood yet. I don't trust those bastards in the KGB one inch. Old Gorbachev may be changing Russia but he hasn't sorted out the secret police. It's still a state within the state. So be warned, and watch it, David.'

Marriner's mind was a blank as he climbed back into his car, but Orford was shouting across to him.

'Wait a minute –'

'What?'

The big man squeezed out and lumbered across.

'You haven't given me your address. In Suffolk.'

'Does it matter? I'm on my own now. Through with you and all this subterfuge.'

'Yes, it does. We may need to make sure you're OK. I want an address,' he said.

It sounded so idyllic, so English, as Marriner wrote it out for him, that neither could quite believe it was to be so important.

'Orchard Cottage, Waverley, near Aldeburgh.' Orford read it back slowly, and gave a kind of salute. 'Enjoy yourselves.'

26

Katie resumed her school, and telephoned them daily, happy enough with the Lanyards so long as she was in touch, and knew that they were together. But it was hard for all of them before they could be sure the thing was truly over. It was Celia who wanted to stay, once they were settled in Suffolk down the lane where the clapboard houses had been smartened up as weekend homes. Thatch or slate, looking like upturned boats, the cottages were anchored in overgrown gardens and sheltered by a mudbank from the direct sea. In the weeks that they stayed there, it became to Celia almost a mystical place, as if the primeval sea-coast with its lonely mudflats and windswept grey-green horizons gave her a sense of peace. In the early mornings they would wake up together, and listen to the gulls, and scarcely believe their luck. Stolen weeks of compensation for what had happened between them, isolated in the borrowed cottage down the long, narrow lane between the hawthorn hedges that ended by the sea.

In mid-December it began to snow, not drifting but settled, cold, clawing in places along the wires of fences and half-blocking the roads. Celia almost welcomed it, confirming their isolation, their togetherness, as they made shopping expeditions into Aldeburgh or Woodbridge and battled back again.

'It's not as bad as Russia,' he said.

Celia smiled, neat in a belted overcoat and clumpy boots. 'I'm glad about that.' Gradually, as he talked to her, and she to him, each was beginning to recognise that they hadn't given the other a chance; his frustrated career, her worry that she had no fall-back. Katie came up to see them at the weekends, either by train to Woodbridge, or they would drive and collect her, but as the weather shut in they telephoned the Lanyards to suggest that she stayed in London.

'It's looking pretty bleak up here,' he heard Celia say.

'It's not much better down here. Katie and Janice are fine.'

But it was bitterly cold as they drove down the lane and settled in for the evening, on the Saturday. Greyness hung in the sky like a curtain and they were glad to be shut up indoors, with whisky and television. Once the fire was alight it was comfortable under the eaves and he remembered later sitting there looking at Celia, her face pink in the fireglow, after their meal together. The debris was still uncleared, their empty bottle of wine stood on the wooden table under the centre light.

'You've been a lot of trouble to me,' she said.

'I know. I'm sorry.'

'Me too.'

Then she thought she heard a noise, as if a car had braked suddenly, come down too far and reversed, skidding on the frozen pot-holes at the end of the track.

'What was that?' she asked, rousing.

He went to the kitchen for coffee, opened the door and listened. Could a car have come down and then reversed without calling? It was a moonless night and fresh snow was turning to sleet; he even went through to the outhouse and opened the door to listen. Ice was already forming on the inside of the windows.

'Nothing,' he said. 'No one there.'

Celia reached out an arm, and touched him gently. 'It's time we buried the past. If it's really going to work.'

He knew what it must have cost her to say that, and felt a surge of happiness. The cottage was built like a ship and the wooden stairs creaked as he followed her up to the bedroom, which was warmed by the brick chimney of the living room below. Celia pulled back the curtains, and stared for a moment over the snow-brushed fields between it and the North Sea.

'What's beyond there?' she asked.

'Beyond where?' Somewhere in the quiet a nocturnal creature – mouse or bird – was running about to keep warm.

'Beyond the sea, in that direction.'

'Holland, Germany, Poland, in that order,' he replied.

'And then Russia? Moscow?'

'Moscow's a long way east. That's why it's so cold there. What makes you think of that?'

'I don't know. It seems to haunt us. Turn out the light,' she said.

He watched her as she undressed, and moved towards him.

'We've been stupid,' she whispered. She was snuggling beside

248

him, goose-pimpled under the covers, pressing against him for warmth.

'Do you love me or your Russian?'

'You.' He was happy in the realisation.

'How much more?'

'Much, much more.'

'Are you sure?'

He levered himself on one elbow and stroked her face in the dark, her hair cascading against him. She felt his hand caressing her and responded lazily, confident at last that he now wanted her, as well as Katie.

'Yes.'

'We've got to make it work,' she whispered. Her hands touched his chin, and slipped slowly down his body.

'It will.'

'What was that?' She was coiled in the bed.

'What?'

The explorations had stopped, as if she had a sixth sense.

'That.'

He lifted his head and listened. 'I can't hear anything.'

She seemed to have stopped breathing, tense as a spring.

'Shut up . . . and listen.' She sat up in the bed, half-naked, her arms straining down on the bedclothes.

'Nothing there. It's an old house.'

'There. Listen. Again.'

'You're imagining things. Come on . . . please. Relax, darling. There's nobody out there, in that snow.'

For a second she seemed to believe him, and began to unwind, subsiding into the coverlet, but then she shot up again, quiet as a hare in a field.

'There it is again,' she urged.

He groped around in the dark to find the switch. It was cold outside the blankets and he could feel her shivering. 'Cover up and keep warm.'

'Don't put the light on,' she whispered.

'Why not?'

'It will alert him,' she said.

'Alert who?'

'Whoever it is. *Listen.*'

And then he did hear something, so it seemed. A small creak on the stairs, a board moving somewhere.

'All old houses make noises. It's nothing.'

'David. I'm frightened.' She put her arms around him. 'I've never felt like this before. There's something odd.'

'Odd? It's just an old cottage, that's all.' But he was whispering too, which was absurd..

'What was that?'

The noise of a window rattling, he suggested. No one trying to break in. They could see the snow falling outside on the empty field. But Celia was not convinced, sitting beside him and trembling, wanting physical reassurance.

Another possible creak, another noise in the dark.

'I'll put the lights on, and go downstairs. That will scare any ghosts off.'

'Don't leave me alone.'

He switched on the bedside lamp and lit up the room, from the old-fashioned mahogany washstand to the wardrobe and bed, making it seem more friendly.

'There you are –'

And then the lamp went out, plunging them into darkness more total for being so sudden.

'Sod it,' he said. 'The bulb must have gone.'

'Try the main switch,' she said.

He pulled on his trousers and moved across to the door, alert with excitement. The main light did not work. They were into total blackness and he pulled back the curtains to get the reflected glow from the powdered fields.

'This is ridiculous –'

'Listen!'

He heard it more distinctly this time, a tiny but definite noise. And then another. He could no longer deny it, and he pulled open the bedroom door.

The silence of the passage between the bedrooms wound its way down the stairwell, inky black, and through the house. He was conscious of Celia behind him, wrapped in her dressing-gown.

'You stay here. I'll go down.'

'No way.' Her teeth were chattering.

They both paused, straining to hear if there was any movement.

'Anybody there?' he called out.

And then three or four footfalls, somewhere below.

Marriner ran along the passage to the head of the stairs,

trying the other switches, but all of them were dead. Celia was screaming beside him. 'David. David, what is it? What is going on?'

The noises stopped as they stopped.

He pulled up panting, his heart pile-driving. Got to find a torch. And a weapon. Just in case. In the dark it was not so easy. There were matches downstairs, and a torch in the car, candles in one of the cupboards, but if there was somebody waiting he was at a disadvantage until he was fully prepared. He fumbled for the rope banister at the top of the stairwell and peered down.

'Anybody there?'

Not a sound now.

Slowly, carefully, he edged his way down, his feet cold on the wooden boards.

There was a door at the bottom, with a latch, that led into the big all-purpose room where they had been sitting in front of the dying fire. He eased it slowly open.

He knew it before he saw her, standing in the half-light at the other side of the room. Svetlana. Some instinct, or Celia's sixth sense, was ticking in his brain. She had waited until after midnight, and she was coming for him.

A small figure in the shadows of the room.

'Don't move,' she said. 'It's me.'

'I know.'

He realised she had a handgun. How, why, when, the questions crashed through his mind, but his first thought was for Celia, coming down the stairs behind him.

'Go back,' he shouted.

'No. Who is it?'

'Put that thing away.'

'My English lover.' Svetlana seemed to be speaking from some prepared position at the side of the room, behind the chair he had sat in a couple of hours before, but he could still not see her. For a moment it might have been an illusion, a dream sequence, but then a thin light snapped on, a torch beam behind which he glimpsed her figure and the matt black of the gun.

'Svetlana, in God's name –'

'Shut up,' she said, her voice as stretched as wires.

'Turn on the lights.'

'Shut up.'

251

Behind him Celia screamed and seemed to stumble on the bottom stair. For a moment she pushed him and the torch beam transfixed her, wrapped in the woollen dressing-gown, standing white-legged beside him.

'Svetlana,' he said again, not caring how she had got there, trying to prevent a carnage.

She cut him dead, pointing the light at Celia, her voice agitated. 'You betrayed me . . . for her.'

'Betrayed?' he heard himself say, attempting to find some cover, to move from the arc of fire.

'I wanted you. I loved you. And you betrayed me.'

'That's untrue, Svetlana.' He found that his fingers were resting on the edge of the table, close to things he could throw.

'Get away from there.'

The beam of light never left Celia's face, as the two women stared at each other.

'Svetlana. I tried to help. For God's sake listen.' The words tumbled out. 'It was your affair with Asterharzy that caused your arrest, not me.'

He could just see the shape of her head now, as his eyes adjusted, the room still smelling of woodsmoke and the remains of the meal. A silver glimmer of hair, the slim blur of a figure in a coat and trousers.

'Asterharzy was one of your men. They told me so. I know it now.'

Bastards, bastards, he thought in silent rage.

'I didn't know.' But it must have been why they let her go, after they had pumped and beaten her.

'Why have you come?' he heard Celia saying.

And then the reply. 'To kill you both.'

Love which had turned, or been turned, into hatred was the bitterest poison, and he heard it eat into her voice as the safety catch went back.

'Don't –' Celia screamed. Marriner pushed her and dived. 'Down. Under the table,' but the bullet was already aimed. On target they would have died but the room blew open in a frenzy of noise and broken glass as another gun fired through the window, into Svetlana's corner, blowing her aim to pieces. A shotgun, pump-action, firing from thirty feet into that shadowy body. At the same time he heard the word 'Police'.

The firing stopped, but the stench of it hung in the room. He found Celia on the floor, and pulled her to him. For a moment there was utter confusion.

'Are you hurt?'

She murmured, 'No,' from the depths of her fear.

'Thank God,' he said.

They were coming in through the door now, uniformed men with flashlights, a marksman carrying the shotgun.

He saw the figure of Svetlana slumped by the side of the chair, with two holes in her coat.

'Oh Jesus. Oh Jesus.'

'Don't go near, sir.'

The man in charge was in plain clothes, moving on oiled feet, a professional. He obscured Svetlana as he examined her.

'Christ. You didn't miss, George. She's a gonner.'

'I couldn't afford to,' the marksman said. 'She'd almost started firing. You left it too bloody late.'

'Where's the main switch?'

Marriner came to his senses, and showed them the fusebox in the passage. Svetlana had tripped the main switch.

Celia was semi-conscious as the lights came on and he saw the shambles. Svetlana lay crumpled near the big armchair, one hand sliding helplessly under her, the handgun fallen on the seat. She had been standing beside it, and the full blast of the shotgun had carved into her chest and shoulder. But her face was unmarked, and the eyes, those curious, wide blue eyes, were photographed by death in surprise. And staring.

'Take your missus upstairs,' the plainclothes man said. 'I'll get a doctor. We shall need an ambulance anyway.'

Marriner half-carried her, pulled back the bedclothes and tucked Celia up inside. She was crying softly.

'Darling,' he whispered. 'It's all over. It's done.'

There were four of them in the room when he returned: four marksmen in dark sweaters, one of them still carrying the shot-gun and a revolver, holstered across his body. He looked at Marriner, his own face shining with sweat. 'Sorry,' he said. 'But it had to be quick. I had no choice. Thought she was going to kill you.'

The plainclothes man introduced himself. 'Garrett, Special Branch.'

'Why didn't you warn her?' Marriner said bitterly. 'Or move in earlier. Why did you have to kill her?'

253

'We didn't think she was serious,' Garrett said. 'We've been shadowing her for three days.'

'Serious?'

'We didn't think she would fire: we wanted to find out who sent her, and why.'

'I can tell you who sent her,' he snapped. 'The KGB with help from someone. I could have told you.' But it was hindsight only.

They went outside to radio and he saw the lights come on in the police car sixty yards up the lane. Another, smaller car was nearer, the one that Celia had heard, illuminated in their headlights as they searched it. A hired blue Ford Fiesta.

Marriner stood by the cottage door, and watched. Svetlana's body, untouched, was covered by a white sheet on which there were spots of blood. He felt that he wanted to be sick, but when he retched nothing came.

'I'll make some tea, chum,' one of the constables said. 'We could all do with it.'

Garrett was examining the handgun.

'Ruger P.85,' he said. 'Looks brand new. Crafty buggers.'

'Russian gun?'

'No. American. Nice simple semi-automatic. Widely available in the States. Effective at close range. Fires NATO 9mm ammo. They buy this sort of gun for their agents: makes it look less obvious.'

'She wasn't an agent. She was . . .'

'Are you sure?' Garrett asked.

No, Marriner realised, he was sure of nothing now, only that she was dead, and had wanted to kill him. Somehow they had decided in the depths of the KGB that she could be reprogrammed, after they had pumped her dry, with God knew what drugs and tortures. They had sent her to get their own back.

'Cup of tea, sir?'

He accepted it without thinking.

Somebody else said, 'Better go up to your wife. The ambulance with a doctor will be here in five minutes.'

They had sent her to get their own back, he realised, and somebody else had known, somebody had had her shadowed, and let it run on to this bloody, mind-shaking confrontation.

He turned fiercely to Garrett. 'Who sent you? Who told you about her?'

And Garrett mumbled, 'It came through the system.'

Marriner's anger rose. He could have shaken him.

'Who told you we were here? That she might come here? Who gave you the address?'

But he knew already. He ran upstairs to kiss Celia, and tell her he had one more job.

'Hey. Where are you going?' they shouted, but they did not try to stop him as he grabbed an overcoat and walked outside to his car. He brushed the snow from the windscreen and the Audi started easily. 'I won't be long,' he yelled at Garrett. 'I'm going to see a friend,' as he squeezed past the police car in the lane.

The snow churned on the roadside like dirty sugar. He ran the car up the greasy hill, away from the sea and the cottage, forward to the main road, ribbed ice crackling under the tyres, changing from third to second as the wheels slipped on corners, seeming to go the wrong way.

He wasn't thinking about the road. The corners came at him suddenly in the headlights and he tore at the wheel with quick almost subliminal reflexes, as if in a driving film, and numbered off the considerations in his mind.

One. Svetlana had made the first approach, at that meeting in Brussels. But had it come out of the blue, as he assumed, or had it been engineered? By Asterharzy, who was already her lover, and might well have met Werndl? He had been sucked in to a process much larger than he imagined.

The car, on its way towards London, hit the main road at the Wickham Market roundabout, sweeping fresh snow into slush against the blanketed kerb. The countryside was white and ruffled like an unmade bed and flurries of cotton wool were blowing off the trees and drifting into the headlights. Open, empty country, and a rising wind which howled against the machinery. He slowed as street lights appeared, strung out along the road. A massive DAF truck ground past, coming from Ipswich. On the bypass his beams reflected the frozen stare of a cat, huddled under a cardboard box. Another poor bastard, he thought.

Two, then. Two of them inside the Kremlin. Borovik and Svetlana had both wanted to bale out. And Asterharzy would have passed on the message from Svetlana, on one of his overseas flights. That much was clear, he thought grimly. Both names had come to Orford, who had put them together, but he had needed a contact, someone to work on the girl. Orford had talked to Challenby, and Tom Challenby had known Marriner. Marriner recalled the new friendship from that great and good public servant with the regular features and battleship grey hair. A face from his past, which had given nothing away, a cardboard, Mandarin monk. He saw the connections now. The first meeting in Brussels, set up by Oscar Werndl, which persuaded him that Svetlana was interested, at the time when his own marriage was drifting on to the rocks.

The tyres hit rough ice again and he had to concentrate on pulling the car round. When he was through, the street, the corner, the kerb line had disappeared, and he skidded past the bodies of snowed-up vehicles. The landscape was looking Siberian. He tried the radio, but in the small hours the only stations were pop. The wind had blown the road clearer, revealing cats' eyes, and ruined, frozen hedges.

Three was Celia. His own wife had suggested, in the middle of a rocky marriage, that he should contact Challenby. She had remembered the name, and set him on this crazy path; and that must have meant that Challenby had put the idea in her head. Orford to Challenby to Marriner himself. He cursed himself for being a fool. It had been neatly set up, and part of it had worked; but when the Svetlana episode got out of hand they had been ready to drop him publicly in the shit. The bastards. Suspended and sent away, and then bloody near killed. Who did they think they were, he shouted into the slipstream, winding down the window to let in a draught of air.

More frozen homes, then he saw what he was looking for, on the other side of Colchester: a telephone kiosk in a slip road by a shopping arcade. Something else must have stopped there recently, for the snow had not yet settled over the parking space. He drove in and found himself shaking as he climbed from the car. The phone box was bitterly cold, with broken panes, and stank of urine and stale cigarettes, but it had what he wanted. Not a telephone but a directory for the Chelmsford area. Twenty miles further on Denis Orford was living, in one of those Essex villages redolent with commuters. Denis had told him so, and knowing Orford, with his high profile and public face, he probably wasn't even ex-directory.

Marriner tore through the phone book with frozen fingers, stamping his feet to keep warm. Orban, Orcady, Oregoni, Orford, D. There it was, at Hunter's Lodge, Great Fitchett, five miles this side of the town. Marriner considered phoning, and then decided to drive on. Snow was blowing under the door and where the glass in the box was missing he had white frosted squares on his coat. Denis Orford deserved being disturbed in the small hours of a Sunday morning.

Outside it had stopped snowing as he pulled back on to the road and covered the last few miles. A signpost, a side lane, difficult but not impassable, and then the ghostly houses of a village asleep in the night. A Tudor-style pub at the corner, the war memorial still with its Remembrance wreaths, the numb tower of the church. He prowled up the street slowly, trying to read the names and figures on the individual houses, no more than thirty in all, and at the end he stopped by a bus shelter and a frozen duck pond. The house on the corner was large, with a double iron gate, set behind a ragstone wall, and something drew him to it, by the way that its upper windows commanded an all-round view of the village and the iced-up fields. He walked across and rubbed the snow from the plate by the letter-box. He had arrived.

He pushed open the gate, tramped up the path to the door, and rang the bell.

27

'Svetlana's dead,' he said.

'Then don't stand around in the snow,' Orford replied, on the doorstep in pyjamas and midnight blue quilted dressing-gown, like a boxer. 'It's bloody cold out there.'

Marriner stepped into the hall, which was lined with faded stags' heads above the wainscoting. The grandfather clock said two-thirty-seven a.m. but Denis Orford seemed alert as a bird, almost relishing it. His carroty hair stuck up in spikes.

'What happened?' He led Marriner into an open-plan lounge connecting through an arch to a dining area beyond. The central heating seemed to be going full-blast against the cold. Whisky appeared, and glasses.

Marriner told him, and began to accuse him.

'You knew this was coming,' he said. 'You set the whole bloody thing up; and didn't bother to warn us.'

'I'll get dressed and come back with you,' Orford retorted.

'Listen to me, old boy. I work for Queen and country, and I can't afford to take chances. Have you got that?'

The whisky was burning their throats, and slowed Marriner up.

'Did you first suggest to Celia that I should report my meeting with Svetlana?'

The big man shook his head. 'Tom Challenby might have done, after you met him again at the reunion.' He refilled the glasses.

'Why did you send in armed police, tonight?'

Orford seemed rattled for the first time. 'That's a stupid question, David. We had her under observation. We didn't know she would go there, but I had an inkling that the KGB might pull a fast one after Asterharzy's death. Trading her life for yours. After all, what was in it for her, except disgrace and imprisonment, maybe even a rope? You with me, Dave?' He swallowed a second drink quickly, almost greedily. 'They would have worked on her, to try and find the connection. A woman in love.'

'Did they?'

Orford shrugged. 'I don't know. Time will tell. But the fact that they let her come showed they had no other use for her. She must have been wound right up like a clockwork doll, psychologically. Bursting with hatred, probably drug-induced. We'll check that now.'

'You could have warned me,' Marriner said bitterly.

Orford swore. 'We picked her up when she came through Immigration three days ago and have watched her ever since. How do you think I had coppers there? They saved your bacon.'

'I suppose you provided her with the address.'

'Oh, come Dave. Svetlana's a clever woman. She hired a car, she phoned your house and then she talked to the Lanyards. Katie was just back from school. That was when we started really getting interested.'

'Why didn't you stop her then?'

Orford jumped to his feet. 'Look. Time we were moving. I'll slip up and get dressed. Say cheerio to the wife, and you can drive me back. Before Celia starts missing you. Do they know where you've gone? Garrett and Co.?'

'No.'

'OK. I'll ring them now.'

He moved to the side of the room, and Marriner realised that he already knew the number of the cottage in Suffolk. Then he disappeared upstairs.

While he was waiting Marriner wondered how anyone could have been so gullible as himself; and yet it had happened gradually, taken in bit by bit, almost casually. It was not ability on Orford's part, but that extra edge of ruthlessness that let him take advantage of other people's situations, in Marriner's case the uncertainty of a marriage, and Svetlana's seductiveness. Maybe he had just been unlucky. Or lucky. He helped himself to another drink.

When Orford came down again in a couple of minutes, he was fully dressed in brogues, a tweed suit and a fisherman's hat like a country squire, but Marriner hadn't forgotten his unanswered question.

'Why didn't you stop her, before she could threaten us?'

Orford paused at the door, wrapping himself in a greatcoat. The wind blew in but there was no more snow and the stars were out, diamond-hard.

'I didn't think she would kill you. I thought she still loved you.'

They walked down the drive to where Marriner had left the car, before he remembered.

'The gun.'

'What gun?'

'She had an American semi-automatic pistol. Made by some firm called Ruger. Garrett said so. Where the hell would she get that?'

'Get in,' Orford said. 'Let's go and ask them.'

'But you must know. She came through airport security with it somewhere.'

Orford stuck his hands in his pockets and watched the village disappear into the darkness of the winter.

'Moscow, Sheremetyevo, with KGB marks on her luggage? You must be joking.'

The cottage was surrounded by police, and spotlights played over the walls. They had difficulty negotiating the narrow lane and had to abandon the Audi behind the last of the police cars. An ambulance had already arrived and was standing with its engine running.

Garrett was still inside, and the room was as he remembered it, with Svetlana's body covered by the bed sheet. Two policemen sat at the table, drinking tea, but the smell of the expended shotgun still hung in the air.

259

'Sorry about this,' Garrett said. 'She didn't leave us much choice. She started firing. Lucky they weren't hit.'

'Are you sure?' Orford asked.

'Oh yes. She fired first.'

How could they be certain of that, either he or Celia, Marriner thought to himself. It had all happened so quickly, simultaneously that it was impossible to tell. He had heard the guns, and the shouts from the police, in one split second of life and death. His life and Svetlana's death.

'Mrs Marriner is asking for you,' one of the constables said.

Marriner went up. He found her in the bed, her face buried in the pillow. Someone had plugged in an electric fire in order to warm up the room, and the orange glow showed her anguish as she turned her head towards him.

'It's over. It's ended,' he said.

And as Celia cried, he comforted her.

When he returned downstairs it was already dawn, a line of light through the trees, and the obsequies were concluded: the photographs had been taken and Svetlana's body, bundled on to a stretcher, was resting in the ambulance.

Inspector Garrett was washing his hands in the kitchen after they had cleared up the mess in the blood-spattered corner.

'You'll be OK now,' he said, 'but we'll keep a car outside, just in case. Don't want too many enquiries.'

'She still has a family in the Soviet Union,' Marriner said. 'A sister in Sverdlovsk. She told me.'

Orford appeared to inspect him, peering at his eyes. 'You need some shut-eye, old boy. Disturbed night.' He managed to give the impression that for him it was pretty routine, a big tough bastard.

'I admired her. I didn't want to see her die,' Marriner said slowly.

'Better not tell that to Celia, the way things are now,' Orford muttered.

In a sense he was right, Marriner decided, right to imply that Svetlana, who might have destroyed them in fact had drawn them together. He nodded slowly. There were some things he could never reveal and live with at the same time.

The policemen were departing, and Orford stood with him in the doorway, watching the lightening sky over the marshy fields towards the sea.

'What's over there?' Orford asked, pointing to the retaining banks of mud and grass.

'Nothing. Except water.'

'Ah.' Orford turned and his large blue eyes let down their guard for a moment as he rested one hand on the door before pulling it shut. 'I'm sorry it had to happen quite like this, David.'

'I'm sorry she's dead.'

'Sure. Nobody wants that, but sometimes the luck runs out. I mean, I'm sorry about what happened to you.'

'I wouldn't have volunteered.'

Orford laughed. 'But Celia pushed you into it.'

'And you engineered it.'

'Oh come on. You were looking for a role, and so was she. She wanted a hero, Dave, and now she's got one.'

'Not a very heroic one. Brzezinski took as many risks as I did.'

'Yes. But he's a Pole, and they are always half-mad.' Orford held out his hand.

'No hard feelings, about the way it worked out?'

'For Christ's sake, it wasn't a picnic, and it damned nearly went wrong, for me as much as for her.'

'That's life, David.'

Denis Orford shook his head and walked over to the waiting squad car.

'Sure you'll be all right here?' The old paternalism that had once so appealed made a brief reappearance.

'We'll stick it out for a day or so, while we catch up on things. What will happen . . . to Svetlana?'

Orford shrugged. 'We'll ask if they want her shipped back. They probably will, low profile. I'll let you know.'

It was then that Marriner realised the emotional tie had broken, finally broken. He did not care.

'The next time I go away,' he said, 'I'm not leaving my address.'

He took Celia to Brussels, the end of the exhibition, in the week before Christmas as he had promised. Belgium, bloody Belgium, and the rain coming down on the fine shops, the drab streets around the Berlaymont and the Musée des Beaux Arts, but she wanted to see it, and he realised it was important. Important to Celia to begin to understand this world of arms and armour, and Euro-exhibitions, that he inhabited: 'The Guns of Yesteryear'. Important to him simply that she was there.

261

'Will you go back to it?' she asked, as Ritterman met them, as much a dandy as ever, and showed them round the cases.

Marriner made a face. Ritterman looked as cheerful as an open grave.

'Doubt it,' Marriner said, 'I'd rather sell ice-creams.'

'That would be a pity.' Celia was beginning to enjoy his success. Perhaps he would go back to it, in another place, another time. At least the jobs were around, it was an expanding profession, but for the present he had had enough of pikes and muskets.

It was the final week of the exhibition which had opened at the end of July.

'A tremendous success,' Ritterman said. 'A quarter of a million visitors in five months. And yours was the most popular part.'

They were walking between the cases in the main hall, the place where Marriner had first seen Svetlana. He remembered the glass doors opening as she suddenly appeared, six months before, a blonde with straw-coloured hair (different elsewhere he'd discovered), the wide oval face and good legs, and that indefinable air of Slavonic intrigue. 'Good morning,' she had said, and Ritterman had introduced them, just as he was wittering on now about some new exhibition that wanted to borrow British guns.

'I've left the Tower,' Marriner said abruptly.

'I'm sorry?' Ritterman stopped, puzzled; clearly he had not heard.

'I'm not going back there,' Marriner said. 'There's been a spot of bother.'

'Ah . . .' He saw the understanding come into Ritterman's eyes. 'David . . . you were not connected . . . that terrible accident to Svetlana?'

Marriner shook his head. 'I know. Appalling. Found shot in a hotel room in London. Self-inflicted. The verdict was misadventure.'

Ritterman said, 'How terrible. Why should she be there?'

'They said she was coming to visit me.' It was extraordinary how easy it was to fall in with a pattern of half-truths.

Ritterman hesitated. 'That business about the Kremlin icons?'

David Marriner held his wife's arm and saw in her eyes no concern, if anything a moment of pride.

'I know. We sent them back of course when we knew what they were. National treasures.'

'But to think that Svetlana . . .'

They walked on along the cases of cold steel that had shaped the destiny of Europe: row on row of flintlocks, pistols with snaphance locks, Spanish locks, English locks, Brown Besses, *armes de luxe* for the gentry in control of the slaughter, Imperial arms and ciphers, guns that had determined nations, checked, mounted, inscribed, displayed with his own professionalism.

'Svetlana was mad,' he said. 'Beautiful but slightly mad.'

Ritterman chewed that over. 'But to me she did not seem so.'

It was nearly six o'clock. They were switching off the lights at the end of the hall.

'Tomorrow,' Ritterman sighed, 'is our last day.' He stood with Marriner and Celia at the end of the long tunnel of cases and display stands, by the sign saying 'Waterloo'. After that the exhibition changed theme, into the nineteenth century, and ended up with the Schumann Plan, Jean Monet and the founding fathers of the EEC, and cabinets of tinned food, signifying prosperity. He seemed to be searching for something at the back of his mind.

'Why did she come to see you? Svetlana? If the pictures were already returned to Moscow?'

'They were on their way,' Marriner said. 'Maybe she wanted to thank me. We shall never know.'

'The Russians did not give her a big funeral.'

'No. Because she had sent the stuff out.'

'I suppose so. Do you know this man Aldanov who has got the Directorship?'

'A little,' Marriner said.

'But perhaps you will visit him there?'

'Probably not,' Marriner said.

'OK.'

They had reached the exit, and Ritterman was shaking hands.

'It is so good to see you, Mrs Marriner. And to find you are so interested.'

Celia smiled. Perhaps happiness could last, Marriner thought, looking at her. He certainly hoped so. A satisfactory pedestrian happiness was the only solution; dancing naked in front of icons was for once in a lifetime.

And then Ritterman remembered.

'Wait a minute. There is something that I should show you.' He darted through the door marked *'Privé'* and led the way to his office, a large room looking out on dripping trees. 'Please, sit down, I have it here in the safe. Extraordinary, I almost forgot.'

263

He fiddled with the combination lock on a small wall-safe, and took out a paper parcel about the size of a large book. It was addressed to Marriner, typewritten labels and a Russian seal, and it had come through the post to the Beaux Arts.

Marriner turned it over in his hands, and knew that it was from her.

'When did this come?'

'About a week ago. But I think the postmark is October. It was registered post, and was a long time delayed.'

October. Marriner peered at the date stamp and the Customs declaration. He could not read the Russian but it said 'picture' in English. Value twenty roubles. Something she had bought in the street market in Arbat. The date was the twenty-fourth, three days before he had left. She had posted it to him in Brussels in case something went wrong.

Ritterman said, 'Please, it's yours. I'll get some coffee.' He was left there in the room with Celia, and Svetlana's parcel.

'Go on,' she said. 'Open it.'

Something made him draw back, as if it was a secret between them that he did not want to reveal.

'Go on.'

He found a pair of scissors and cut the string, then carefully slit the masking tape around the binding. Inside was some plastic padding, and a thin picture on board.

A single piece of board, an icon in brown and silver, and dull gold. St George slaying the dragon, his red and white banner unfolded against a surreal sky. He recognised it at once as the picture that he had seen hanging close to the chair in the alcove where they had sat together, that afternoon when they had loved.

Ritterman came back and gasped. 'It is beautiful. Not exactly twenty roubles.'

'The price was a life,' Marriner said.

St George for England. She had chosen deliberately. Celia said, 'It's amazing. What will you do with it?'

'Send it back,' he said, as if it was a jinx to be refunded.

At first he had thought that there was no message, but then he saw two envelopes had fallen out with the wrapping. He opened the larger one first, and read the typewritten letter, addressed in English from the Kremlin Armoury.

'Dear David,' she said. 'You asked me to confirm that our meetings have been purely professional. As you know, that is so.

There has never been any question of personal relations. Yours sincerely, Svetlana Malinkova. Director.'

He turned to the second, smaller, envelope which had been attached to the picture, and slit it with a fingernail. Inside was Svetlana's card, embossed with the same address.

'With love,' was all she had written.

He tore both the card and the letter into pieces and threw them into Ritterman's wastepaper basket.